I felt two ir⸺ ⸺
around my u⸺

"It was foolish of you to venture this far from the fire in the dark," a man's voice said, so close I felt his breath hot against my cheek. "You should never be out alone in a wild place like this. Anything can happen . . ."

The arms tightened about me, and his muscles brushed against my breasts. I felt Doran's breath on my cheek. My heart was pounding so fiercely that I thought surely he would feel it throbbing against the steel cords of his arms.

And then, guided by some instinct I hardly understood, I shifted slightly in Doran's arms, my body relaxing against his.

At this, his arms tightened even more and then moved across my waist, turning me so that I was facing him.

And then, slowly, Doran traced a gentle line along my cheek to my lips. His touch lingered there a moment, and then moved along the outline of my mouth, where his eyes dropped hungrily.

An immediate response stirred deep inside ⸺e—hot and pulsing, starting in my loins and ⸺oving swiftly upward.

⸺nd then I felt his broad palms press against ⸺ back, pulling me against the hard length of his ⸺dy. His mouth came down on mine.

TWILIGHT'S KEY

TWILIGHT'S KEY

CHRISTINE ROBB

PAGEANT BOOKS

𝄢

PAGEANT BOOKS
225 Park Avenue South
New York, New York 10003

PAGEANT and colophon are trademarks of the publisher

Cover artwork by Charles Moll

Printed in the U.S.A.

First Pageant Books printing: February, 1989

10 9 8 7 6 5 4 3 2 1

*To Gary, for his support through the rough
    times;
to my many siblings, for their love;
to my parents, who made everything possible.*

I knew at once that I had come upon the city of some extinct civilization, hidden away in this inaccessible mesa for centuries, preserved in the dry air and almost perpetual sunlight like a fly in amber, guarded by the cliffs and river and the desert.

—Willa Cather
The Professor's House

Chapter One

◆◆◆◆◆

IT WAS IMPOSSIBLE. I simply could not believe what I was seeing. After a moment, I reached out my hand, then quickly drew it back.

It could not be, I told myself again. But there it was—strange and yet so terribly familiar—nearly lost among the jumble of old, cracked, somewhat dull and dirty artifacts on the table.

I had come, on that seemingly unexceptional day in July, to view an exhibition of ancient Indian relics on display in Denver for the first time. They had been discovered the year before, in 1890, by a handful of men who had stumbled upon an obscure group of cliff dwellings in the Southwest. Always fascinated by such antiquities, I had convinced my editor, Mr. McNeeley, to let me cover the exhibition for his newspaper. I had hoped to convey a sense of my own excitement to my readers. But I had no inkling, when I walked into the exhibition hall, what I would find there and how it would change my life.

For now, as I stared down at the object on the table, it was as if everything fell away before me—as if I were no longer there, in that cavernous building made hot and stifling by Denver's unpredictable summer weather, but back in St. Louis on another sultry July night when I was very young. Suddenly, my memory of that night came back surprisingly vividly: I could almost smell the thick, sweet scent of lilacs that had hung heavy on the air, and feel the cool earth beneath me as I sat hidden by the leafy green barricade their hedge made along the lawn.

And yet, something was wrong. Even as the memory of that night flashed across my mind, parts of it remained elusive, hazy, and indistinct. Why was I hiding? And the scent of lilacs . . . that couldn't be right. By July, the lilac blooms were long since gone. Perhaps it was just the ghost of their fragrance I felt that night. It had been twilight, that odd, in-between time when the senses are muddled and easily confused. And it had been about to storm, the air charged with restlessness, I remembered, and the near-palpable sense that something was about to happen.

The whispering, furtive voices nearby were part of it all, and the man—the man who had come that night and changed all our lives—he was part of it, too. He had been talking to someone I could not see, and when he saw me edging from my hiding place, he called me to him. In the shadows of the yard, he looked very large to me and oddly familiar, although I was sure I hadn't seen him before. I shrank from him at first, but then he took my hand and drew me aside and, still whispering, pressed into my palm the object I have never understood but have carried with me ever since.

Now, as I stared down at the table of relics, my hand went deep into my skirt pocket, searching among its folds for what I still carried there with me, every day. I did not need to extract it to see that it was identical to the object that lay on the table: a set of six tubular bones, polished on both ends and bound together by a thin strip of hide. Some kind of charm, I guessed, although I had never been able to identify it before. An Indian trinket, perhaps.

It was obvious that both the object in my pocket and the one on the table had come from roughly the same time and place. But what were they? What did they mean? And how could it be that one had lain hidden for hundreds of years and the other was given to me on that July night so long ago?

"It's an amulet," came a male voice, suddenly beside me. "The Indians wore them to ward off danger."

Caught off guard, I jumped a little, and my hand instinctively slid deeper into my pocket. The man stood so close I could smell the faint scent of wood smoke on his twill jacket as its sleeve brushed my arm.

I glanced up at him, and an odd thing happened. As he looked down at me, his eyes (green, or were they gray?) met and held mine a moment too long, and it seemed a flash of recognition sparked between us before it flickered out again, just as quickly.

Startled, I searched my mind for where I had

seen the man or how I might know him. Those
sculpted features; the fine high cheekbones; the
jaw, strong but not square; the ears, tucked
closely against his head, which along with the
cheekbones gave his face a subtle upward slant,
almost elfin . . . No, I would not have forgotten a
face like that. But where had I seen him? I came
across so many people in my interviews for the
Crier. This man could have been any one of them.

He had moved away slightly, resting his weight
lightly against the table and standing beside a
small, grizzled mummy that was propped on an
adjacent chair. Next to the grotesque form of the
shrunken woman, this man loomed tall and sup-
ple and most definitely alive. There was a grace-
fulness in the way he stood, an agility in his
movements that gave him a quality I can describe
only as very fine.

"You seemed so fascinated by that particular
amulet," the man went on, resuming the conversation quite naturally. "I couldn't help coming
over to tell you a little about it. Actually, you
seemed quite . . . transfixed. Does the amulet
have some particular meaning for you?"

I looked at him sharply. "Why no," I said. "Not
at all. It's just that . . ." Trying to regain my poise,
I tugged on the hem of my jacket and started
over. "What I mean is no, the amulet does not
have any special meaning for me, but yes, I was
quite fascinated by it. I . . . I have always been
interested in these kinds of things, relics and artifacts. Evidence of past lives."

"Indeed?" The man's brows lifted subtly, and I
saw that his eyes were indeed a muted green.

Certainly not easy to read. His face was tanned, suggesting months spent in the sun.

"Delving around in the past seems an odd interest for a woman," he went on. There it was again, that impish quality that somehow lifted his features from their controlled, almost aristocratic lines. "Most ladies of my acquaintance are more interested in the here and now—what gown they plan to wear tonight or what party they're invited to attend tomorrow—than in what happened centuries ago. You are obviously a woman with education and breeding, quite attractive really. And young—twenty or twenty-one, perhaps?" He paused, musing. "Well, as I said, it seems an odd interest."

I stared at him, not sure whether I was being insulted or complimented. Did he mean to insinuate that I didn't care about my appearance or that I had nothing better to do with my time? I knew that my tan serge suit was not very fine. But it had not rained for weeks, and the streets were hot and dusty. I'd had to make several stops before walking eight blocks to this building for the exhibition. I couldn't go about wearing my best silks in the daytime, especially in a city like Denver.

And my hair . . . well, my hair was never the way I wanted it: too coppery in color and too thick, and always falling out of its pins despite the small bonnets I wore to anchor it, so that it curled haphazardly about my face when I was hot or uncomfortable—as I was now.

"I've come to the exhibition to write a newspaper story," I said stiffly. "I write for the *Denver Crier*."

"Ah," he said, considering me a moment. "I think I've seen a few issues. But your byline—would I recognize it?"

I colored slightly. "It's Loring," I answered shortly. "Heather Loring. You probably haven't seen many of the stories I've written. I'm not a regular reporter."

"Oh?"

"I'm a . . . kind of correspondent. I submit stories when I find them or when they interest me."

"You are allowed to come and go as you please, then? You have no specific beat?"

"No, I only cover stories, as I said, that interest me." I shifted a bit uncomfortably under the man's questioning.

"Ah, how wonderful, that freedom. It must be quite an education. I imagine your work takes you into all kinds of neighborhoods and introduces you to subjects and people you might not otherwise have the opportunity to know."

"Why yes," I said, somewhat surprised. The man had voiced what I myself had often thought.

"This must be the first time you've written for a newspaper."

"Oh, no. I have always worked on a newspaper."

At the man's surprised, slightly disbelieving look, I quickly amended my statement. "My Uncle Charles was the editor of a weekly in St. Louis," I explained, "where I was raised."

"Surely your uncle did not allow you to write stories for *his* paper. Didn't you go to school?"

"Of course." I bristled at the man's question and increasing presumptuousness. "But after school hours I spent much of my time with Uncle

Charles at the paper. I set type and ran errands at first, learning the business. Uncle Charles insisted on it. Then I wrote a few columns on my own before I showed any to my uncle, and he required me to write several more under his direction before he published them. I did mostly society things, at first. Then Uncle Charles began to teach me how to find stories—or how to see the unusual in the usual, as he called it. Mr. McNeeley helped me as well. He worked for Uncle Charles before coming here."

"I see," the man said, nodding knowingly. "You had connections."

"Well, it was not as if I had no experience." I bristled again.

"You say you were raised by your uncle, but you don't mention your parents at all. Did you lose them as a child?"

All at once, I saw what the man was doing. He was using a technique—quite an effective one—I myself knew how to use when interviewing people. Taking care to show obvious initial interest, I would ask carefully phrased and placed questions, then spend most of the interview just listening to draw my subjects out. That was what this man had done to me. And yet he continued to regard me with that rather calculating expression, as if he were not at all surprised by anything I had told him.

"Pardon me," I said, pulling myself up straighter. "I can see I've taken up too much of your time. I really must be going. If you'll excuse me . . ."

"You're not leaving so soon? But you came to get a story about the exhibition, didn't you? Surely you'll need more information."

He reached out a hand to detain me, and as his fingers wrapped around my forearm, the heat from them penetrated my jacket and the thin fabric of my blouse to my skin. He was so close. How old was he? Twenty-five? Thirty? It was difficult to tell, for he seemed curiously mature and young at the same time. Just below his eyes, in the hollow between his cheekbones and the lower fringe of his lashes, I could see that his skin was soft, not as tanned as the rest of his face, and somehow more vulnerable. I felt my stomach twist curiously.

I tried to shake my arm free. "Really, I *must* be going."

Still gripping my arm firmly, the man ignored my protests and steered me back around the table of exhibits. "You can't leave yet. You haven't even examined most of these relics. Look at this mummy, for instance, the one everyone came to see." He motioned toward the shrunken form. "I call her Rose," he said, a glint in his eye. "After the flower. Appropriate, don't you think? Actually, this mummy is one of our most perfect specimens. Can you imagine—she has been frozen in time for hundreds of years now by nothing but sun and wind and a hidden cave. And this pottery. It was all made by hand by a primitive people, and yet it is almost perfect in symmetry and form."

As he warmed to his subject, the man's voice lost its jesting overtones, and I saw clearly that this was something about which he cared deeply.

"We know so little about these people," he went on seriously. "Obviously, they were quite an advanced civilization for their time and place, but they just disappeared centuries ago, before white men ever entered the Southwest. We found some of their remains, the items exhibited here, in a place called Twilight Mesa. There are ruins there, tucked high in caves cut out of sheer cliff walls, that were left as if their inhabitants had simply walked out and might be coming back momentarily—pots and bowls left on tables, food and grain stored in baskets. There is so little to tell us who and what they might have been."

He gestured toward the relics, then turned to me again. "You might call it evidence," he said, a look of challenge on his dark face. "Evidence of past lives."

I turned my eyes away for a moment. Something about what he said, about the image of past lives left suspended, frozen in time, mysteriously lost . . . The idea inexplicably disturbed me. And yet at the same time, the image triggered something deep in my mind, drawing and attracting me in a way I did not understand.

Next to a gracefully contoured jar were several bone tools, and next to them lay the Indian amulet identical to the one in my pocket.

I looked up to see if the man was watching me, but he had turned and was hailing a tall, squarishly built man who had just entered the exhibit hall.

"Will! Will!" he called. "Come over here! I have someone I'd like you to meet."

Will approached before I could say anything. He was older, in his midthirties perhaps, and his face, too, was tanned, but his smile was open and friendly, and I relaxed a bit.

"Will, this is Miss Heather Loring," said the man beside me. "She's doing a big write-up on our exhibition for the *Denver Crier*, and she needs more information. Don't you think we should invite her down to the ranch and give her the grand tour of the cliff dwellings?"

"But I—"

"That's a great idea!" cried Will, grinning at me broadly. "We could really use some exposure in the papers to fund our excavations. We just do it ourselves, you know—me and my brothers. The Kendall boys, they call us." He glanced over at the man beside me and grinned again. "That's a great idea, Doran!"

Doran. So at least now I knew his name. Strange—for brothers, he and Will did not look at all alike.

Will took my hands and clasped them in his two large callused ones. "Would you come, Miss Loring? We'd be honored to have you as our guest. Lots of people have been visiting since we found the ruins. The ranch isn't much, but there's plenty of room, and—"

"Of course she'll come," said Doran. "We'll make her welcome, won't we, Will?"

They both stood looking at me, Will with his easy grin and Doran with a slight twist tugging at the corners of his mouth, as if he were trying to contain—what? Amusement? Interest? Knowledge?

"Excuse me," came a lilting voice to my right. "Did I hear one of you say he was Will Kendall?"

We all turned and met with our first sight of Julia Hastings: slight, dark, her thick black hair swept up beneath a plumed hat, ice-blue eyes reflecting the hue of her gown and matching silk cape. The cape was flounced at the shoulders and edged with lace and black braid, and her umbrella was black as well, with an ivory handle and blue tassels.

I felt rather than saw Doran stiffen beside me, his stance taking on a kind of alertness. When I glanced at him, I saw that his features had tightened and his eyes narrowed.

Even Will, it seemed, was momentarily thunderstruck by the woman. "That's right, ma'am," he burst out. "I'm him . . . I mean, I'm Will Kendall." He stepped forward awkwardly to take her hand.

She let her white-gloved fingers stay only a fraction of a second in Will's hand, looking immediately past him to Doran. Only after a rather brazen appraisal did she return her eyes to Will.

"Mr. Kendall," she said, her words taking on the soft accents of a southern drawl. "It's such a pleasure to meet you. I was told I'd find you here. My name is Julia Hastings, and my fiancé—"

"Miss Hastings! Of course! I've been expecting you. Mr. Webb told me you'd be coming. He said I was to make sure you got on the right train for your trip down to the ranch. I can go get your tickets right now, if you want."

"Will," Doran said slowly. "You didn't tell me about Miss Hastings. Did you say she'll be staying at the ranch?"

"Haven't told you?" sputtered Will. "Course I did—didn't I? Miss Hastings here is engaged to be married to Mr. Prescott Webb—you know, the government surveyor who's been staying in that cabin west of the mesa. She's come all the way out from Virginia, and she's going to stay with us at the ranch until she and Mr. Webb go back and get married in Virginia in the fall."

"And I'm *so* excited to be here," Julia gushed, emphasizing her drawl as she looked out from under black lashes at Doran. "I just think that Prescott's—Mr. Webb's—work is so fascinating. I couldn't wait to come down and see what all you've been doing. And I even hear there might be buried treasure down there where you all are digging. Do you think we'll be lucky and find some?"

Doran didn't reply.

"Buried treasure? Ha!" Will said. "Pardon me, ma'am, but there ain't nothing but rocks and old pots and lots of sagebrush where we're going." He laughed, but then remembered himself. "But what about your bags, Miss Hastings? Did you leave them at the train station? And do you have a place to stay tonight? There's a run down to Durango that leaves early tomorrow morning that we could put you on. I'll see that you get to the station all right."

"Thank you, but I have already purchased my train tickets. I will be staying in Denver a few more days," Julia said, glancing at Doran again. "I have some . . . business to attend to here."

"Perhaps when Miss Hastings does come down, she can ride with Miss Loring," said Doran, his tone even.

At Doran's words, Julia looked over at me sharply. "Loring? Did you say Loring?" she asked, as if seeing me for the first time. She stared at me a moment, then looked at Doran. "I don't believe I've had the pleasure."

"This is Heather Loring," Doran explained. "A newspaper writer for the *Denver Crier*. She's coming down to the ranch to prepare a story on the Indian cliff dwellings."

"I'm not—"

"Why, Miss Loring—Heather—it's so nice to meet you!" Julia said, grasping my hand with sudden friendliness. "Of course we'll ride down on the train together. When are you leaving? Oh, I *must* change my tickets to match yours! It will be such fun. You can tell me all about your writing, and I'll tell you all about Prescott."

What on earth was happening?

"I'm sorry, but I really cannot . . ." I shook my head. It seemed that events had gotten suddenly away from me. Why was this Julia Hastings treating me like some kind of girlhood chum? And why were Doran and Will Kendall acting so forward and familiar as well? Did they really expect me to come and stay at their ranch? The situation might even be humorous, I thought, if it were not so confusing.

And all the while, Doran continued to regard me with that watchful, calculating expression, as if I were some kind of experiment whose outcome he was interested to discover.

Julia continued to gush on, and I took a step back, reaching behind me for the table's edge. As I did, I felt my hand knock against something. I turned and saw it was a small framed photograph that had been propped against a large bowl. I hadn't noticed it before. Glad for the distraction, I picked it up to set it right again and, in doing so, looked at it more closely. I felt the blood drain from my face.

For the second time that day, time seemed to have stopped. I could not believe what I was seeing.

Pictured in the photograph were several men, all dressed in dirty clothing and battered hats, standing against the background of a streaked rock face in what appeared to be one of the cliff dwellings Doran had told me about. Two familiar faces in the photograph leapt out at me immediately—Doran and Will Kendall. But it was the man on the far left, standing apart from the group with his head turned from the camera and his image slightly blurred, who caught my attention. It couldn't be, and yet it was. Or was it?

The memory of that night in St. Louis flashed again, lightning quick, across my mind. First the amulet and now the face in the photograph . . . Why had it all come back now, here, in this place?

I looked at the photo again, and suddenly it was as though something lost in a hidden corner of my mind leapt forth for just an instant—some deeper, buried memory that I couldn't quite grasp. Fruitlessly I strained after it. And then, with a sick dread, I felt one of my spells coming on. I had had only one such spell since coming to Denver, and it had been so short I thought I had conquered the problem completely. But here it was, back again and worse than ever.

I felt the nausea first, rising in sick waves, then the dull ache climbing my legs, my arms, my shoulders. The rushing in my ears began, and I knew that soon it would grow, increasing in intensity until it overpowered everything else, blocking all further thought and memory from my mind.

"Miss Loring, are you all right?"

I was not sure who spoke. I only knew that I had to get out, to get air. Blindly I turned and started toward the door, stumbling past the table and ignoring the muted voices behind me. I felt a hand touch my arm, but I shook it off. My only thought was to escape from the exhibit hall into the fresh air outside.

Just as I reached the door, I felt someone come up beside me and grip my arm, steering me outside. It was Doran, his presence suddenly large and strong beside me. For just an instant, I allowed myself to lean into his support.

"What is it?" he asked, drawing me back alongside the brick wall of the building. "What's wrong?"

"It's nothing. I . . . I'm just . . ."

"Was it something you saw in the photograph? Or someone? Tell me. What was it that disturbed you so?"

I felt the rushing sensation grow in my ears, in my mind. With every ounce of control I could muster, I straightened and stood apart from Doran, removed my hand from his arm, and forced myself to answer him calmly.

"I saw nothing in the photograph that disturbed me," I said, my voice sounding wooden even to me. I took a breath and went on. "It's just . . . I get these . . . spells sometimes. They are the result of an illness I suffered as a child." I paused a moment. "Now, if you will excuse me . . ."

"But you should sit down and rest," Doran

said, trying to take my arm again. "There's a bench over here. Let me help you."

"No. I must insist. I do not need to sit down. I really must be going."

"But—"

"No." Picking up my skirts, I nodded to the man rather curtly and then turned, hesitating slightly, and started down the street. My mind and senses were still confused, but I knew that I had to get away from him and all that had happened as quickly as possible.

"You will come to the ranch and Twilight Mesa, won't you?" I heard the man call after me.

I did not turn or answer. But just before I rounded the corner of the block, I glanced back over my shoulder. The man was still there, watching me. I nodded again, then turned the corner swiftly, hoping to leave him and what had happened behind.

I walked toward a small park only a few blocks away where children were playing happily, mothers or nurses in tow, and I somehow found it reassuring, as if this were indeed a calm, ordinary day, just like any other.

Finding a bench in the shade of a tree, I sank down, not realizing until then just how warm I had become as I walked. The sun beat down with a steady heat, and I was stifling in my tan serge. At least the leaves on the tree overhead were green and full and provided some respite. I leaned back against the wooden slats of the bench, trying to get my bearings. My heart was beginning to slow, the symptoms of my spell had abated somewhat, and my mind felt as if it had finally stopped whirling.

Perhaps now I could think, I told myself.

It was as if my life had taken a complete, irre-vocable turn. Only this morning, I thought, I had felt reasonably content with my new life here in Denver. I had my work, which occupied my time and interest; I had a home, temporary as it was, with Mrs. Gresham, Aunt Natalie's childhood friend; I had Father's money and all the freedom it provided, which had enabled me to come to Denver, alone, eight months ago. I was just be-ginning to feel comfortable here, to consider the city a home of sorts.

But today had shattered all that—as an unex-pected blow will shatter a too-fragile pane of glass. I could not ignore the incident at the exhi-bition. I could not block it from my mind as I had other, earlier memories.

Although the sense of panic I'd fought in the exhibition hall had since receded, it was now re-placed with that odd, residual feeling that would often follow spells like these—the same feeling, I realized suddenly, that I'd experienced when I looked at the photograph. It was as if, in my mind, I could just barely glimpse something at the edge of my consciousness; as if, had I turned quickly enough, I would see whatever it was that had just flickered past the corner of my eye.

Even now I instinctively turned on the bench, trying to move fast enough to catch it. But, as always, nothing was there after all—only a soli-tary squirrel, which scampered across the grass and up a tree.

As I turned, unaccountably disappointed, I spotted a familiar figure rounding the corner and striding toward me, along the edge of the park. It was Mr. McNeeley, out on a late post-luncheon walk. A large, stout man, Mr. McNeeley was rarely able to resist the richer offerings of his mid-day meal out and always tried to compensate with what he called his "daily constitutional"—huffing and puffing his way up and down the blocks near the *Crier* office. And once he saw me, he strode off across the park in my direction.

I watched him approach with some chagrin, remembering the conversation I'd had with him that morning where I tried to convince him to let me cover the exhibition.

"A bunch of old pots and stuff?" Mr. McNeeley had said with a loud guffaw when I told him about the Indian relics. "Bring in something *live*, girl. Something folks want to read about. Nobody cares what some dead Indians in some dry, dusty cave did God knows how many years ago. This is 1891, girl. I have a paper to get out, you know."

Only when I mentioned the mummy and the interest it was beginning to stir within certain Denver social circles did Mr. McNeeley relent.

"Weeell, I guess you could try it," he finally said, pulling out a cigar with one hand while dismissing me with a wave of the other. "But mummy or no mummy, don't expect me to print the story unless it's good!"

Now I watched him come closer, wondering what I would say.

"Heather, my girl!" he cried. "What are you doing here? Why aren't you at that confounded exhibition you were so fired up about this morn-ing?" He stopped in front of me, breathing heavily, and took a large cotton handkerchief out of a pocket inside his coat to wipe his face. "Sitting down on the job, eh? We can't have that! It's no way to get ahead in this business, you know."

I smiled, glad for Mr. McNeeley's ruddy face and good-natured scolding, for something routine on this increasingly confusing day.

"Well, you can't expect me to behave like one of those two underpaid slaves you call your reporters, can you?" I returned. "Even Uncle Charles let me take a break now and then." I paused. "Actually, I've already been to the exhibition, Mr. McNeeley. I had planned to come back to the office and write it up immediately but, something rather odd occurred to me there, and . . ."

"Come, come, girl, I haven't got all day. I'm on my constitutional, you know. Here. Why don't you just come along with me, and we'll discuss this on the way back to the office? He pulled me up beside him and placed my hand on his arm. "But you'll have to keep up with me, mind you. I don't do this every day just for fun."

Before I had a chance to speak, Mr. McNeeley was off, and I was forced to match my stride with his, which was indeed surprisingly vigorous.

As we crossed the park together and headed toward the *Crier* office, I tried to gather my thoughts. I did not want to tell Mr. McNeeley everything, certainly not about the amulet and the photograph or the way they had both affected me. But I felt I had to talk about the exhibition somehow, to help straighten it all out in my mind.

"Well? What is it, girl?" Mr. McNeeley bent slightly to look into my face. "I must admit you've got me quite intrigued now."

Deleting certain details, I told Mr. McNeeley

about the relics and the tribe of Indians who had inhabited the cliff dwellings of the Southwest. I mused as I finished, "It's curious how these people's lives are a mystery now, as if a great chunk of the past has just dropped out of human history and memory. I do believe it's an important story, especially for anyone with ties to the historical society."

"So what's the problem then? I'm sure we could find room for the story somewhere."

"Well, while I was at the exhibition, I received a rather curious invitation," I said, still unwilling to go into certain specifics. "Two brothers in the Kendall family—the family that found the relics—asked me to visit their ranch down in the southwestern part of the state. They think I need to tour the cliff dwellings to complete my story."

Mr. McNeeley was silent a moment as we continued to walk along. "Well, why not?" he finally burst out. "Why not take them up on it? It might be just the thing to infuse some life into this story. No one's done much in terms of actually going inside those ruins, as far as I know, and you could get some excellent first-person accounts. It could be quite exciting, really, quite revealing. Yes. Yes indeed. When would you leave?"

"Why I haven't even . . . I couldn't . . ." I was surprised and a little shocked at Mr. McNeeley's reaction. "Mr. McNeeley, I really hadn't considered this invitation seriously. I couldn't just . . . pick up and go down there. What would Mrs. Gresham do? And Uncle Charles and Aunt Natalie—what would they think?"

Mr. McNeeley frowned. "That doesn't sound like the girl I know, the one who foisted herself on her poor uncle and me and the newspaper business in St. Louis, then just picked up and came out here alone. You know what your aunt and uncle would think, girl. You know how they raised you— to do what you wanted to do, what you felt you had to. To use that pretty head of yours, not let it sit idle on your shoulders."

"But I don't even know this family."

"Good God, girl! It's not as if you'd be going into a den of wolves down there. Kendall family, did you say? Hmmmm. Yes, I've heard of them. Friend of mine in Durango knows them. Good solid ranching stock, I hear. A little plain, maybe, a little homespun. But respectable enough."

I thought of Doran. Plain and homespun he certainly was not, although I had to admit Will Kendall certainly fit Mr. McNeeley's description.

"The mother of the Kendall family, I'm told, is a real matriarch," he went on. "She keeps her boys in line, if that's what you're worried about."

I tried to avert my face before Mr. McNeeley could see the flush creeping up my neck, but I wasn't quick enough.

"What's the matter, girl?" he said, stopping abruptly in the road and turning me to face him. "Is that infernal Mrs. Gresham beginning to rub off on you? If so, it *is* time you left Denver. Beginning to get a little stuffy here, if you ask me. My God, if I were younger . . . Why, I'd jump at a chance like this. What an adventure it could be."

He paused with a faraway look in his eyes, and as I stood beside him, I felt my heart begin to beat queerly. What Mr. McNeeley had said was true.

Traveling to the cliff dwellings *would* be exciting and new, an opportunity to discover what few men had seen.

And it would also be an opportunity to visit the place where the amulet had been found and the photograph taken, I thought. Knowing that, how could I *not* go?

"Well, come along, girl, let's get back to the office," Mr. McNeeley said suddenly, taking my arm again. "Only a block to go. No time to fool around."

Starting off again as abruptly as he had stopped, Mr. McNeeley strode down the street, leaving me to stumble along beside him. Before I had time to think, we had reached the *Crier* office—the bottom portion of a nondescript, rather shabby, two-story brick building flanked by a laundry and small drugstore on either side.

"Ah, here we are," said Mr. McNeeley. "Home sweet home. Are you coming in?"

Without giving me a chance to answer, he twisted the unpolished brass knob and opened the door. I was immediately hit with the strong, mingled odors of ink, cooked onions, sauerkraut, and bratwurst rising from the cluttered desks of Mr. McNeeley's two fledgling reporters. They did not lift their heads or acknowledge me but continued to mumble and swear and scratch their pens to paper between bites of the makeshift luncheon they had just bought from old Pete's roving pushcart.

I smiled, relaxing for the first time that afternoon. Here, at least, things were always the same—chaotic on the surface but underneath straightforward and routine. Despite the mess of papers and pens and books and plates and mugs of coffee piled high on each desk; despite Mr. McNeeley's grumbling and shouting and his reporters' pained looks; despite the perpetual, permeating odor of ink coupled with the hot steam and medicinal smells from the neighboring laundry and drugstore, this was a newspaper. Facts had to be gathered, deadlines met, stories written. Out of the clutter, I knew, would eventually come clear, concise print, something tangible and complete, week in and week out.

"Well, girl, are you just going to stand around mooning all day? If you don't have anything better to do, I could use some help on a couple of stories for this week's issue. Why don't you grab a pen and some paper and come into my office."

Perhaps that was just what I needed to help clear my mind, but just as I reached his door, a sudden thought flashed through my mind.

"Oh dear, I'm sorry, Mr. McNeeley," I said, entering his office. "I completely forgot. I have to get home right away—I have a dinner party to attend tonight. Mrs. Gresham is still on her shopping trip in New York, and I promised her I would go in her stead. It's supposed to be one of those important dinner parties, you know." I grimaced. "Mrs. Gresham said it would be a good chance to mingle with 'Denver's Cream,' as she calls it. I would think she might have given up on me by now. She knows how I hate these things."

"Your Mrs. Gresham again, eh?" Mr. McNeeley growled. "Infernal woman. Ah, well, you do what you have to, my girl." Then, as was his way, he abruptly shifted moods and looked at me sharply. "But don't forget what we discussed earlier. I want that story. Have you thought any more about it?"

I didn't answer, and Mr. McNeeley must have seen something in my face—confusion, panic, fear—for after considering me a moment, he rose from his desk, came over to my side, and, in a very uncharacteristic gesture, put his arm about my shoulders.

"Listen to me, girl," he went on in a gentler tone. "I don't want to get you upset—you know I'm just playing devil's advocate here. The story itself isn't that important. What bothers me is your reaction to it. This just isn't like you, girl, to balk at a story. Obviously something at that exhibition troubled you, and you aren't going to tell me about it. No, I don't want to hear. What I want is for *you* to decide what you want to do. Mind you, I don't want you backing away from anything, but it's up to you, my girl."

It's up to you. Mr. McNeeley's words echoed in my mind. With a lump in my throat, I nodded, gave him a brief embrace, and then quickly left.

Mr. McNeeley had been right, of course. Uncle Charles and Aunt Natalie would approve of such a trip, and I had the money and freedom and incentive to go, as well as a story to write that might mean something important. This was, truly, an opportunity I should not miss.

So what was holding me back? I was afraid—of something I thought I had seen for just an instant at the exhibition. It was as if a door in my mind, firmly closed and locked long ago, had opened just a crack, and now I could see a faint glimmer of light behind it. Whatever was behind that door beckoned me at the same time it frightened me.

I stood outside the office a moment, so engrossed in my thoughts that at first I did not notice the figure across the busy road. Vaguely I recognized him, realized that I'd seen him standing there before, just a few days ago. A tall, tanned, lithe figure, he was leaning casually against a brick wall.

With a flash I realized fully that the man *had* stood there two days ago. At the time, he had seemed to just be waiting for me to come out.

Now he smiled at me, and his green eyes met mine. They were not muted now, but clear and blazing. Even across the heavy traffic of carriages and buggies and wagons, I could see the expression in those eyes. It was not amusement this time, or suppressed knowledge. It was challenge—pure and unbridled, directed straight at me. The same challenge I'd seen in his eyes at the exhibition, when he had shown me the relics.

Doran stared at me just a moment, then, lifting his hand to his head in a kind of farewell salute, turned and disappeared around the corner.

But I knew, watching him go, that this would not be the last I would see of the man. Indeed, it seemed only a beginning.

Chapter Two

✦✦✦✦✦

THE LOUD CLANGING of the bell on an approaching cable car broke abruptly into my thoughts. Disoriented, I glanced up and realized that the sun was beginning to sink below the jagged blue line of mountains to the west. Much as I dreaded going, I knew that if I did not get back to Mrs. Gresham's quickly, I would be too late for the dinner party I had promised to attend.

The cable car stopped at the corner, and I hurried toward it, jumping lightly onto the running board before pulling myself inside. Within moments I was gratefully lulled by the motion of the car, the passing sights, and the sense that I was moving forward, going somewhere instead of standing trapped in my own thoughts.

The cable-car bell clanged, and I saw we were approaching a familiar cross street. To my right lay one of Denver's wealthiest residential districts. The city's empire builders, men who had made their fortunes in gold, silver, real estate, railroading, banking, and mercantile investments, had built their homes there—great stone or stucco or brick mansions, many of them patterned after palaces or castles, replete with gardens and stables and stone-columned porches, massive beamed ceilings, tapestry-covered walls, and windows of Tiffany stained glass.

Because of invitations strategically wangled by Mrs. Gresham, I had been inside a few of these mansions. I had walked through their wrought-iron gates, up their broad stone steps, into their Italian-marble reception halls. I had seen their plated gold doors, their crystal chandeliers, their solid silver lamps, their carpets from Belgium and furniture from France, their grand, winding, hand-carved mahogany staircases. One such mansion housed a skating rink, one an art gallery, one a bowling alley. They were fabulous, almost beyond description. And yet it seemed to me that in some, at least, much of the energy and optimism, the dreams and hopes and promises that had erected these mansions had been spent in the building—leaving them glorious monuments outside, but empty shells within, devoid of the life that had initially built them.

Mr. McNeeley had described it most accurately, I realized suddenly. Denver was indeed becoming too stuffy, he said. His offhand words had articulated a feeling that had been growing inside me, for I had discovered only gradually that many of the people I encountered in Mrs. Gresham's social milieu wanted to put their pasts behind them. They did not want to remember that they were once poor farmers or clerks or bookkeepers back East, children of immigrants, failing as breadwinners themselves. They wanted to forget that they had come to Denver with little or no money and had struggled in rugged, sometimes harsh conditions to make their fortunes and establish their positions. They were now Denver's leading citizens—responsible, staid, decorous— and that's how they wanted things to stay.

I came back to myself as the bell rang again, and we jolted past the wealthy district into a less opulent, although thoroughly respectable, neighborhood of two-story red brick and brownstone homes. This was where Mrs. Gresham lived. Weaving a bit with the motion of the car, I stood and made my way toward the front, still trying to shake off the sensations the day had wrought within me. The gripman smiled at me and stopped the car, tipping his flatcap as I got off.

Mrs. Gresham's house was two blocks down the street. As I started down the sidewalk, I saw that the drapes had already been drawn in the houses I passed and the lamps lit, infusing each front parlor window with a soft yellow glow. The sun had gone down, and there was a slight chill in the air although it was July. It was very quiet in the street. Twilight dropped down about me and familiar objects—trees, shrubs, porch steps—took on a blurred, amorphous appearance.

I immediately thought of Doran. What if he were somewhere near, watching, waiting? I stopped abruptly and glanced around, instantly alert, my heart beginning to pound. But I saw no one. Watching and listening another moment or two, I hesitated and then started off again, quickly. I could not shake from my mind the fact that the man had followed me, waited for me, before, and I had been quite unaware of it.

With relief I soon reached Mrs. Gresham's narrow brownstone. No one met me at the door, and I remembered that Kathleen, the housemaid, had the evening off and that I had told Mrs. Hansen, the cook, that she could leave early for the day as I was dining out.

Despite Mrs. Gresham's pretentions of great

wealth and social standing, she could only afford these two house servants, explaining to her friends and guests that she really hadn't the strength to handle a full household staff. Only Kathleen lived in, sleeping in a tiny set of quarters on the top floor. Mrs. Gresham also had Robert, of course, her brother's old gardener who drove her carriage and acted as a footman on formal occasions. But he had quarters over the carriage house and was no doubt up there now enjoying a surreptitious smoke on his pipe, which Mrs. Gresham forbade him the eleven months out of the year she was home.

The house was quite empty. Kathleen had left a light burning in the hall, and as I stepped inside and shut the door, I was immediately struck with the oppressiveness of the interior's dark mahogany and cherry wood, and the stale mustiness that, along with the faint, lingering fragrance of the lavender soap Mrs. Gresham always used, permeated every room of the house no matter what the season.

Mrs. Gresham did not care greatly for sunshine and fresh air. Staying inside during the day, she left the house only to pay calls and went off to her dinner parties only after dark. When she made the supreme sacrifice and traveled to New York on her annual shopping trip, she left strict instructions that the house remain tightly shut up in her absence. It was as if she believed that by staying behind closed doors, she could keep herself and all the personal possessions she had brought with her from St. Louis in a perfect state of preservation.

Suddenly feeling tired, I took off my hat and set

it along with my gloves and bag on the hallway table, where a small gold bowl held a disheveled stack of white, engraved calling cards. Indeed, Mrs. Gresham had been most gracious to offer me a place in her home when Aunt Natalie wrote and told her I had decided to come to Denver, but she had frustrated me often over the intervening months. A widow for over twenty years, Mrs. Gresham still wore black and was extremely old-fashioned in matters of propriety. She seemed much older than Aunt Natalie, although they had grown up together. She stayed in St. Louis for ten years after her husband died before coming to Denver to look after an older, ailing brother. When he, too, died, she inherited this house and dedicated herself to what she considered the only worthwhile project left to her: establishing an unshakable place in Denver's society.

I had to smile a little, remembering Mrs. Gresham's reaction when I had returned from my first day at the *Crier* office.

"Newspaper stories?" she had cried, scandalized. "A young lady from a good family like yours, traipsing around Denver alone, writing for a . . . newspaper? I can't allow it. No, it will never do. I can't allow it."

But I did what I had planned, firmly and unobtrusively. Many young women my age were out working in Denver and all over the West, and I had the blessing of Uncle Charles and Aunt Natalie. Besides, I had not come out to Denver to be bound by the limitations and conventions that had hampered me in St. Louis. I had traveled west, as many had before me, to try my wings, to see a bit of the world, to experience the vitality of a place not yet completely dulled and dampened by an established protocol.

And so, while Mrs. Gresham spent her days supervising Kathleen or meeting with her dressmaker or going out to pay calls (taking care as she left to make obvious her disapproval that I did not accompany her), I slipped outside into the cool, fresh air to interview the curator of a new museum or a woman who was touring the Rockies on horseback, perhaps, or an old miner who had made and lost his fortune and now loved to spin tales of the old Denver.

In the evenings, however, I could not escape so easily. Mrs. Gresham frequently had some social occasion she wanted me to attend, gatherings I invariably found as dull and stifling as her house. If I made an excuse, I could see in Mrs. Gresham's eyes that she felt she had somehow failed, despite her best efforts, to launch the niece of a dear friend into respectable Denver society. It was a duty I could see she felt keenly, and so I went out with her for another evening, and yet another . . .

Now I gave an inward groan, thinking about what lay ahead. So much had happened already. I was so tired; I hadn't the least appetite. I only wanted to go up to my room, change into my dressing gown, lie on the bed, and sort out my twisted thoughts.

But I had promised to attend the dinner party, and I knew with a dull, heavy feeling that I would have to keep my word. And, if I were to be on time, I would have to change and prepare myself immediately. With a hopeless sigh of resignation, I slowly started up the stairs to my room.

My room, at least, had always been a bright

spot in the house. It had a big bay window, and I
kept the inside shutters folded back all day to let
in the bright summer sunshine. The huge, black
walnut bed in the center of the room was Mrs.
Gresham's, but I had thrown over it a colorful
patchwork quilt made by my maternal grand-
mother and given to me by Aunt Natalie when I
left St. Louis. I also had Aunt Natalie's big china
water pitcher and washbowl—with its cheerful,
painted morning glories—on the bedside table
and several pictures from home hanging on the
wall: a portrait of Aunt Natalie and Uncle Charles,
one of my mother and father taken the day they
were married, and three landscapes. The room
also had a black walnut bureau with a large mirror
and marble top, and a tall oak wardrobe.

Trying to marshal my spirits, I chose a subdued
jade green silk dress from the wardrobe that I
knew would complement my coloring and bring
out the highlights in my hazel eyes. It had fitted
sleeves that ended in a lace appliqué about my
wrists, and a high collar trimmed with the same
appliquéd lace and a row of crystal beads. The
skirt was full, falling from an ivory silk belt at the
waist in a wide sweep to the floor. Aunt Natalie
had it made for me before I came to Denver, and
although fairly simple, it was one of my best.

I would wear my hair up, I decided, in a chignon at the crown of my head, and I'd wear the
small opal earrings my aunt and uncle had given
me for my eighteenth birthday. Taking off my
skirt and blouse and laying them carefully over a
chair for Kathleen to pick up and launder in the
morning, I walked over to the bureau in my chemise and petticoats (I had forsaken corsets long

ago) and drew from the bureau's third drawer a magenta leather jewel case. Inside lay the jewelry I had accumulated over the years: several pairs of earrings, a few thin bracelets and bangles, a strand of seed pearls, three gold necklaces, a cameo brooch, and a blue enamel locket. I picked out the earrings and a few bangles. With the lacy trim of my dress, I would need little additional jewelry.

I shut the jewel case and put it back in its drawer. And then, hesitating slightly, I pulled open the drawer beneath, the lowest one in the bureau. Beneath a stack of folded handkerchiefs lay a single object, which I placed on the marble bureau top. It was another jewel case, this one covered in a soft gold velvet that brushed my palm as, hesitating again, I opened its lid.

Inside, nestled against the satin lining, were the items Aunt Natalie had given me years ago—items that belonged to my parents. There was my mother's heavy gold watch and chain, her onyx breast pin, the diamond ring my father had given her on their first anniversary. Next to Mother's things were Father's billfold and ivory-handled penknife, and his medals from the war. Father was much older than my mother, Aunt Natalie told me. He was already a well-to-do bachelor when she came along.

I looked down at the contents of the jewel case for a long moment. Although I had always kept it nearby, with my other things, it had been a very long time since I had opened it. I was quite young when my parents died, and then became ill for long afterward. When Aunt Natalie first gave me the jewel case, I devoured the items within, going to them several times a day, looking at them, touching them, trying to keep the memory of my parents alive. But over the years, as life inevitably went on, I took out the jewel case less and less often, until I opened it only every year on the anniversary of their death, and then, over the last few years, not at all. Perhaps I was afraid that the wound caused by their death had not healed as completely as I thought, and that in opening the case I would reopen the wound as well.

But something about this day, the old memories revived at the exhibition and the accompanying odd feelings, had drawn me to the jewel case and prompted me to open it. Now, mercifully, I felt not pain, as I had feared, but only a kind of sad longing and then a strange comfort. Seeing my parents' things for the first time as an adult, I felt they were passing on to me some sense of continuity.

I glanced up again at the portrait of them on the wall, faded slightly over the years, and then at myself in the mirror. Aunt Natalie had always remarked, fondly and with a tinge of pride in her voice, how much I resembled my mother. Now even I could see it. We had the same shape of face, the same bone structure, the same smile. But my hair and eyes were different, unlike the dark brown shades of hers. Father was very fair, and I had never been able to account for my features at all in his looks.

"Those eyes and that hair are all your own, my dear," Aunt Natalie used to say. "Your very own."

Setting down the jewel case, I crossed over to

my skirt lying on the chair. I reached into its
pocket for the amulet, the loosely bound bones
still cool to the touch. How many times had I held
it, wondered what it was, what it meant! And
now, today, I had at last found a clue . . .

Quickly I placed the amulet alongside my mother's gold watch and shut the lid of the case firmly,
replacing it in the bottom bureau drawer. For a
few hours, at least, I wanted to forget what had
happened today. For once I would leave the amulet here. I would go out tonight and then come
home and sleep, and tomorrow morning I would
be able to see things in a new perspective and
decide what to do.

With no further thought, I washed quickly
and changed into a fresh chemise and clean petticoats, donned a pair of black silk stockings,
and stepped into a pair of black kid evening
slippers. The silk dress fairly glided on. I attended to my hair, allowing a few unruly wisps
to curl about my face and sweeping the rest into
a chignon. I added two small ivory combs, collected my wrap and a small silk purse from the
wardrobe, and was ready to go.

I started to leave the room, but at the door I
paused and turned back. In an impulsive act I
still do not understand, I went back over to the
bureau, and in one movement threw open the
bottom drawer, removed the gold jewel case,
took out the amulet, and slipped it quickly into
my bag. I had never been without it in all these
years, and something made me feel I needed it
still, especially now.

A thought nagged at my brain as I hurried

down the stairs: Had I somehow known all along that my object was indeed some kind of charm, some kind of protective talisman?

I hurried down the front steps and into the waiting carriage, and before long, Robert pulled up in front of a large, two-story brick home belonging to Mrs. Alice Compton, an influential matron who worked on various committees for social improvement with Mrs. Gresham. Tonight she was giving the week's most important dinner party. Mrs. Compton's home was much larger and grander than Mrs. Gresham's, though not as fine as some of the city's most elaborate mansions. I knew it had been a real coup for Mrs. Gresham to receive an invitation to this party, and I also knew, though Mrs. Gresham would never admit it, that she had begun her hospital charity work on Mrs. Compton's committee expressly for this purpose.

Squaring my shoulders and trying to draw forth enthusiasm I did not feel, I stepped out of the carriage, gave Robert instructions to return for me in a few hours, and slowly climbed up the long flight of stone steps. The house was brightly lit, and I could hear laughter and the steady hum of voices from within as a humorless, black-coated butler met me at the door. He led me into a spacious reception hall where Mrs. Compton herself came bustling over to greet me, resplendent in a voluminous green taffeta gown with quite large puffed sleeves, a beribboned and bow-trimmed collar, a frilly, lace front, and a full, flounced skirt trailed by gold lace streamers.

"Heather, my dear!" she cried, taking my arm and leading me toward a large drawing room,

where I could see small knots of people conversing and drinking before-dinner sherry. "I'm so
glad you could attend tonight in place of your
dear Mrs. Gresham. You're just the young, fresh
face we need. I'm afraid to say that most of the
other ladies here are settled old matrons, you
know—although I daresay most of them aren't
much older than you. The girls of really good
families are marrying so young these days." She
made a mock grimace and looked at me pointedly. "Are you, ah, still writing those . . . newspaper stories, my dear?"

"Yes, I am," I answered. "I—"

"Oh, it's such a *shame* your Mrs. Gresham
couldn't be here," she cried again, and chattered
on as she led me into the drawing room. Here I
was given a glass of sherry, and, surprisingly, left
quite alone as Mrs. Compton bustled off to greet
another arriving guest. I saw that there were indeed several young married couples present, mingled with the few young single guests. The
women and men laughed and gossiped among
themselves, while most of the older matrons sat
in their brocades and velvets along the wall, lips
pursed in disapproval, and their husbands—the
real movers and shakers of the city—were scattered in small groups, talking about their new
investments and the state of the economy.

I stood near the doorway, unsure just where I
belonged. The most fascinating conversational-
ists, I had discovered when seated next to them at
other dinner parties, were usually the older men.
They loved to regale a young, interested listener
with their stories of the early West—and what
lives they'd had! They were the ones who dug the

gold and silver from mountain mines, tamed horses on cattle ranches, laid the first rails for the trains, drove oxen across the prairies with the first wagonloads of merchandise for Denver's fledgling stores. Although these men had settled down now, grown older and heavier and more complacent, content to live off their fortunes and invest their money in a growing city, I found they still had a spark about them, a sense of lives well-lived.

Their wives, who had shared many of their husbands' experiences on first coming West, now seemed reluctant to discuss these experiences on social occasions—or any time at all—I had found. They preferred instead to concentrate on proper etiquette or how many calling cards they might receive in a day. Their daughters were worse, it seemed to me, without the essential backbone and determination their mothers had shown in pioneering days.

And the sons, the younger men . . . I found them most disappointing of all. Many of them were quite successful, attractive, and intelligent, really, but they seemed to lack the fire that had once driven their elders. The West had already been tamed by their predecessors, and they seemed content to ride on their fathers' coattails. I knew that they never would have the character-building experiences of the older generation. They would inherit the investments, the businesses, the mansions—not build them. And so, although I had spoken to many and a few had called on me, I found that none of these younger men held my interest for long.

I had just begun to approach a group of young,

married women when Mrs. Compton bustled up to me again with a tall, attractive man in tow.

"Heather! Now don't run away!" she cried. "I have someone I'd like you to meet. This is Frederick Mankins, a nephew of Edward Thompson, the banker. Mr. Mankins has just moved to Denver to help his uncle out in the banking business."

I looked up at the man. He was attractive enough—fair haired, blue eyed, smooth and debonair in his pearl gray waistcoat and dark trousers, his wide tie impeccably knotted beneath a stiff white collar. He looked intelligent and quite pleasant, and as he smiled and took my hand warmly, my heart lifted slightly. Perhaps this man would be different, I thought. Perhaps this time . . .

"Mrs. Compton tells me you write for a newspaper," he said, leading me to a set of wing chairs in the corner. "I wrote for my college newspaper back East, a few small items on sporting events and the like. Do you like writing?"

"Why yes, I do. I find it quite interesting, especially getting out about the city and—"

"I found it quite interesting myself. But now I see that to be involved in the *real* stuff of life is the important, the vital thing, not just writing about it. Take banking for instance. It's quite a fascinating business. Why, just yesterday . . ."

As Mr. Mankins launched into lengthy detail about his experiences thus far as a junior banker in Denver, giving me no further opportunity to speak, I felt my heart sink again. He was no different from the others, showing no interest in my work. Although Uncle Charles and Aunt Natalie had always encouraged my writing and taken it

as seriously as I myself took it, I had found that
very few others did, men in particular.

"And then, when Uncle Edward took me into
the vault and actually *showed* me . . ." Mr.
Mankins went on as the butler announced dinner
and the guests began to file into the dining room
in small groups. Taking the arm Mr. Mankins
offered me, I stretched my mouth into a smile that
I hoped did not appear too artificial and tried to
look interested as we were seated at the long
table, which glittered with Mrs. Compton's best
china and silver.

My heart sank further as I realized that, in a
sorely misguided attempt at matchmaking, Mrs.
Compton had seated me next to Mr. Mankins,
and I sighed inwardly, remembering the conversations at Uncle Charles and Aunt Natalie's dinner table.

Uncle Charles, of course, always came home
each night full of news and was eager to draw us
into discussions about the current political senti-
ment and what could be done to change the city,
the state, the nation. Often we had guests to dinner, although we entertained much more infor-
mally than Mrs. Compton. With no children of
their own, Uncle Charles and Aunt Natalie pursued full lives and had many interests and
friends. Aunt Natalie had always been active in
woman's suffrage, and Uncle Charles met a wide
variety of people as a newspaperman. Guests
with all kinds of ideas and views graced our table
in St. Louis, and dinner conversations were never
stilted or dull.

I soon realized this dinner party would not provide the distraction I'd hoped for. Even as Mr.

Mankins droned on, scenes of the day played themselves out again and again in my mind, and I felt anew the odd, displaced sensations I'd experienced upon seeing the amulet on the table for the first time.

I felt the bulky outline of my own amulet through the thin silk of the bag in my lap. What was I going to do? If only this day had not happened.

"My dear guests," called Mrs. Compton, standing at the head of the table and rapping her glass lightly with her fork to get our attention. "If the ladies will retire to the drawing room and the men to the library, coffee shall be served."

Vaguely, I found that my thoughts had taken me entirely through the six courses. I blinked and looked at Mr. Mankins, and saw a distinct line across his brow. Although he took my hand again and smiled politely as we parted, I knew that at some point in the dinner he must have finally seen through my surface interest.

Nevertheless, I sighed with relief as I rustled with the other ladies into the drawing room. The evening was almost over. I chose a small armless chair beside a rosewood side table and next to a large window thickly draped in plum velvet. Here I was a little off by myself, so that I could listen to the other conversations but not have to actively participate in them. I glanced at the ormolu clock on Mrs. Compton's mantel. Robert would return for me soon. If I could only get through this next hour. . . .

After a short interval, the men came into the drawing room and seated themselves among the ladies, fulfilling their obligation to mingle

for the last part of the evening. I had just gathered
my skirts and started to stand, preparing a polite
thank-you and the excuse of a slight headache for
my early departure, when I glanced toward the
drawing room door. There, standing alone and
looking about, was the man I had already seen
too many times that day. Doran.

For a moment my heart stopped. Just stopped,
in a way it never has, before or since. I sat back
down on the brocaded chair, although I did not
feel myself do it. My body went suddenly cold, as
if all the blood had drained from it.

A moment later, as I watched the man walk in
and stride gracefully toward Mrs. Compton in an
opposite corner of the room, I felt the warmth
return to my body in one great rush. It was as if
the room had suddenly become brighter, louder,
much more close and clear and in focus than before. With his entrance, Doran seemed to have
infused a sense of life into the gathering that was
lacking before.

He did not see me. Shakily I sat back, still
watching him, astonished at the grace with which
he took Mrs. Compton's hand and kissed it. Fault-
lessly dressed in an expensive, finely cut waistcoat in a shade of dark smoky blue I had never
seen before, I could hardly believe this was the
same blunt, rather ill-mannered man who had
accosted me at the exhibition. This man was obviously quite cultured and refined, and much
more experienced socially than I would ever have
guessed. He must have known Mrs. Compton
well to have arrived at her party so late, and he
seemed to know many of the other guests, too.

Several groups had greeted him when he walked into the room.

As I watched him accept a snifter of brandy from a footman and approach a group of ladies, who, tittering like a flock of cockatoos, opened their circle to admit him, I felt something twist within me. Anger perhaps? Or betrayal? Yes, betrayal and shock.

But why? Why would Doran's mere presence here cause me to feel such intense emotions? Because the man was obviously not all he seemed? Because after causing me such distress and upheaval today, after questioning me and probing into my personal affairs and following me about the city, he now proceeded to casually charm this bevy of women as if this were a day like any other?

Watching him, I did not know what to do. He still had not seen me. I did not want to call attention to myself by getting up to leave, and yet I was afraid that if I remained where I was, he would eventually notice me. And that prospect, for some reason, terrified me. Just seeing him had caused my emotions enough turmoil. Being forced to socialize with him . . . What would I say? What would I do?

And so I sat riveted in my spot, trying to withdraw into the shadow of the draperies, watching Doran make his rounds. He was obviously quite comfortable with everyone present. Again I noted with some astonishment how polished his manners were, how well-bred he was.

And yet there was something else about the man that made him stand out from the others.

Despite his refinement, in the group of younger men he seemed somehow more elemental— perhaps because of his tanned, somewhat roughened skin and dark suit—and also more alive in a way I found hard to define. It was as if, beneath his rather sleek exterior, there was an energy, an animation, that hovered just below the surface, controlled but ready to spring forth. I saw this energy express itself in the restless way he tossed his head and glanced about, and in the quick, light step he used to move from one group to the next.

It was only when Doran approached a group of older men that I realized just what set him apart from his contemporaries at the party. These pioneers, the empire builders, immediately brightened in Doran's company, became more animated as well. He seemed to suddenly bring them back to their younger, more energetic selves. And in that instant I saw that Doran possessed the same spark I had noticed in them, the same sense of drive and adventure and energy that had initially brought them out West. And in Doran that spark was still alive, burning, ready to ignite whatever he chose to set it to.

In the moment I realized this, staring at him across the room, Doran suddenly turned and looked directly at me. It was as if he had known I was there all along, as if he knew what I had discovered about him. In his eyes was the same clear challenge I had seen earlier, fueled by the spark within.

With a few graceful movements, he excused himself from the group of men and began striding toward me. Panicked, I stood again, clutching up my skirts and bag and glancing about for some form of escape.

"Leaving so soon?" he said, reaching my side and taking my arm as he had at the exhibition. "How rude. Where are your manners, Miss Loring? We have not yet had an opportunity to talk."

He led me smoothly over to a small plush loveseat on the other side of the window. I noted in a disconnected way that my heart had begun thudding curiously, and that my hands had grown clammy. The situation seemed so unreal—this man, here in the upper-class home of Mrs. Alice Compton, expertly replaying our encounter at the exhibition. I felt as if I were watching the scene from somewhere outside myself.

And then, as Doran sat down beside me on the loveseat, his hand left my arm and his warm fingers touched mine.

"Your hands are like ice," he said. "Is something wrong?"

It was as if his touch had a life of its own, transferring his suppressed energy into the empty shell my body had become. Instantaneously, I felt a flash of heat course through me, blazing into a sudden anger.

"Of course something is wrong!" I cried, withdrawing my hand from his touch. "Who are you? What do you want? Why are you here?" Seeing several heads turn in our direction, I lowered my voice and tried to regain some control. I took a long breath. "I do not understand what you seem to want of me, sir. I do not know you. We have never been introduced. And yet you act so very forward. What right do you seem to feel you have,

to intrude so on myself and my personal affairs?
You are the rude one—questioning me about very
personal matters, extending me an invitation to
your ranch, following me about the city. And
now, in respectable company, you confront me
again as if we had some reason to speak with one
another. I must ask you again sir—what is it that
you want of me?"

At my words, something changed deep within
Doran's eyes. His mouth twisted in an odd way,
and he seemed about to say something when his
eyes dropped to the purse I held in my hand, on
the loveseat between us.

It was only then that I noticed my bag had
fallen open and the amulet had slid partially out.

Doran looked at it and then up at me. "I think
the question should be, Miss Loring," he said in
a low, penetrating voice, "what is it that you
want of yourself?" He looked at me probingly,
and in such close proximity I found his eyes
almost overpowering. They seemed to contain a
depth of knowledge and experience I could not
begin to measure.

"You could come down, you know," he said,
still fixing me with his green eyes. "You could
come down to the ranch and stay with us. You
could see the ruins for yourself, and the other
relics." He paused a moment. "And you could
face there whatever it is that has caused the
photograph—and the amulet—to disturb you
so."

He reached down and very lightly slid my amulet back into the silk purse. As he handed it to
me, our fingers touched again, and the shock was
even greater this time, seeming to affect even

Doran. Rigid on the loveseat, I saw emotion flicker in his eyes. Then, regaining his composure, he reached inside his waistcoat and from a pocket drew out a long white envelope.

"I had planned to leave this with Will, at the exhibition," he said. "I knew you would come back eventually. But now, because of our meeting this evening . . . Here. Take it. I think you'll be needing it."

He handed me the envelope, and when I did not open it, he looked at me curiously.

"Well, do as you please, Miss Loring," he said, rising to his feet and straightening his waistcoat. "But think about what I said. It may be an opportunity you'll regret missing."

With that, he nodded slightly, looking down at me a moment, then turned and walked away. I watched him say a short good-bye and thank-you to Mrs. Compton and then, speaking to a few other guests on his way out, finally leave the room.

I don't quite know how I managed to make the motions to get through the rest of that evening. The sense of unreality had dropped over me again, as if all this were happening to someone else. It was only when I was back at Mrs. Gresham's, sitting on the big black walnut bed, surrounded by my beloved possessions, that I felt some sense of reality come back. The envelope Doran had given me was cool and feather light in my hand. Slipping my thumb under the seal, very slowly I opened it.

Inside lay a single train ticket for the trip from Denver to Durango, the departure time designated for three days hence at four o'clock.

At that moment I knew. I knew that my future

was somehow determined, out of my control, as this entire day had been. I had never believed in fate, but at that moment, holding the train ticket, I felt as if forces outside myself were shaping a part of my destiny even as I sat warm and safe in Mrs. Gresham's house. I had known this somewhere inside myself all day, resisting the truth as if it might go away like a passing toothache or a bad dream at night. But it had swept me up finally, and I could no more stop it now than push away a ten-ton weight bearing down upon me. I was part of it, irrevocably.

For, you see, I had the key.

Slipping off the bed, I went over to the bureau. No longer hesitating, I withdrew the gold velvet jewel case and opened its lid. Deliberately, I removed all the objects within, and when the jewel case was empty, I slid my fingernail down one side, releasing its false bottom. As this too sprung open, I reached in and removed the object that lay hidden there. I had not touched it for fifteen years.

I picked it up and stared down at it, its cold, inert weight heavy in my palm. It was a single, worn Spanish doubloon, made of pure gold and inscribed with the date 1632.

"Take this and keep it," the man had said as he pressed the doubloon, along with the amulet, into my hand on that hot night in July so many years ago. "Keep it safe. When the time comes, you'll know what to do with it."

Now that the time had come, I did not know what to do, not really. I took the amulet from my silk bag and placed it alongside the doubloon on the bureau's marble top.

I had to go. How could I *not?* How could I ignore the signs?

In a way, it was almost ironic. I had made no permanent place for myself here in Denver. I was a correspondent for Mr. McNeeley, not a hired reporter; I was living with a woman whose home was not really mine; I had made several acquaintances but no real attachments; I had begun to grow weary of the very city that had lured me west in the first place.

Maybe I had known all along that Denver was to be only a temporary stopping place in some larger journey. Had I been drawn here by some vague memory that had lain hidden for too long? For seeing the amulet and the photograph, meeting Doran and removing the doubloon again had opened the door of my memory just enough so that I had gotten a glimpse of what it was I was seeking.

Tomorrow I would start packing. And by the end of the week, whether I used Doran's train ticket or not, I would begin the trip I knew was inevitable.

Chapter Three

✦✦✦✦✦

LEAVING WAS MUCH easier than I had expected. Once I made the decision to go, it seemed, all the things to be done for my trip fell into place quite easily; nothing could stand in my way or prevent me from leaving Denver.

The morning following Mrs. Compton's dinner party, I went immediately to the *Crier* office and told Mr. McNeeley what I had decided to do.

"You're sure about this, girl?" he asked, his eyes fixed piercingly on me. "This is what you really want to do?"

When I nodded, he leaned back in his chair, relaxing a little, and lighted a fresh cigar. "Well good, I'm glad you decided to go after all—although I must admit I'm going to miss your face around here. God knows, I get tired of the two out there." He waved vaguely toward the outer office. "Groan and moan, that's all they ever do. They don't know the value of a little hard work." His eyes fell on me musingly. "At least you had the gumption to get out and find your own story ideas, crazy as some of them were. The way you'd badger me about them!"

For a moment, Mr. McNeeley's blue eyes appeared to cloud a bit, but then he turned his head and let out a great puff of smoke, and when he turned back to me his eyes were clear again.

"So, remember girl—I'm counting on you to come back with a good story for my paper. None of this dusty old pot stuff! Something live. I have a newspaper to run, you know."

Pulling his bushy eyebrows together and down, he frowned at me. And then, just as suddenly, his expression softened.

"If you need anything, Heather, my dear, anything at all . . . ," he said, lowering his voice and unexpectedly pressing his beefy hand just an instant over mine. "If you find that you're still troubled by whatever it is that has prompted you to go . . . you know where to find me. You know I'll be glad to help, my girl, if you need it."

Mr. McNeeley applied the slightest of pressures to my hand, then released it abruptly and ushered me into the outer office.

I left the office with a smile and a strangely nostalgic feeling. Although I had only been a small part of its daily chaos, the *Crier* had become a home of sorts, and as I walked away I felt as if I were bidding good-bye to a rather eccentric friend I was not sure I would see again soon.

Boarding a cable car, I went next to Denver's Union Station to check train schedules. Upon awakening that morning, I had considered using the ticket Doran had given me for quite a long time and finally decided that it would be best to purchase my own ticket, for a train other than the one Doran was expecting me to take. I thought it most probable that Doran had a reason for giving me a ticket on that particular train—that he might be on the train himself or have another surprise planned for me. Although I knew that in making the trip itself I would be entangling myself in his plans somehow, I felt that the actual decision to go had been mine alone, and I wanted to determine at least the first portion of my journey.

And so, walking up to the ticket seller in his

booth behind his iron grill, I requested a ticket for a day earlier than the one Doran had given me.

After that, there was not much left to do but pack—a far from difficult task, as I had not brought a great deal with me to Denver in the first place. It was crucial, of course, that I leave Denver before Mrs. Gresham returned from New York. I could only imagine what she would say and do when I told her I was leaving the protection of her home to travel, unchaperoned, to a relatively un-tamed corner of the state. No, it would be easiest all the way around to depart before she returned, and so I planned to leave a long note for her and make arrangements for Mrs. Hansen, the cook, to stay in the house in my absence. I expected that Mrs. Gresham would hardly approve of this last measure, but I could not in good conscience leave the care of her home to Kathleen, barely eighteen, or to Robert, who could be quite forgetful at times.

I wrote a brief letter to Uncle Charles and Aunt Natalie about my plans, not going into great de-tail but promising them I would send a new ad-dress when I had settled myself in Durango. I had decided that I couldn't stay at the Kendalls' ranch, of course, no matter what Mr. McNeeley had said. I planned to stay in Durango and visit the ruins from there, engaging Will Kendall to act as my guide.

It was for this purpose that I returned to the exhibition hall the day before I was to leave Den-ver. It was the last of the arrangements I had to make, and I had put it off as long as I could, afraid I might see Doran again. Our encounter at Mrs. Compton's had produced too disturbing an effect on me, and I was not ready to throw my emotions into that kind of turmoil again so soon.

But when I walked into the exhibition hall, only Will stood behind the long wooden table, looking rather large and forlorn. Seeing him standing there, it struck me for the first time to wonder why he had not come with Doran to Mrs. Compton's party. And yet the thought of Will at that party was completely incongruous.

His face brightened when he saw me.

"Miss Loring!" he cried. "You came back! What happened the other day? We were worried. Doran went after you, but when he didn't come back . . . Was everything all right?"

"Quite all right," I answered. "I just felt a little faint and needed some air. In fact, I've come today to tell you that I've decided to take you up on your offer to come down to Durango, at least in part, and—"

"You are? That's great! Just think—a big newspaper story. When are you coming down? Have you got your train ticket yet? I'm not leaving here for two more days, but Doran is supposed to be back in Durango before me. Maybe he could meet you there and bring you out to the ranch. It's a long, bumpy ride, but you'll be glad once you get there, Miss Loring. It's the best place in the world, you'll see."

"You said Doran is returning to Durango soon?" I interrupted. "He—is he here now?"

"No, ma'am. I don't know where he is. For all I know, he's already headed back down to Durango. Might be there already. Hard to tell with him. I think by now he would have finished the business he said he had to do up here. He's had almost two weeks to do it, whatever it was."

"Business?" I echoed. "Didn't you two come up to Denver together?"

"Oh, no, ma'am. Doran came up ten days before me. It was that business he had, like I told you. Something special, I guess, although he never did say exactly what it was. He travels around sometimes like that, when he's not working with us at the mesa. I'm not sure what he does."

"But . . . pardon me, Mr. Kendall, I don't quite understand. Wasn't Doran here, with you, the other day?"

"Sure, that's right. And I was mighty glad to see him, I'll tell you. I hadn't eaten since breakfast. He gave me a nice break for lunch."

At my blank silence, Will looked puzzled, and then a slow grin of comprehension spread over his broad face. "Oh, I get it!" he cried. "You thought we came up together." I could almost see the wheels turning in Will's head as he gave a little chuckle. "Oh, I can just see it. You walking in here and seeing him there behind the table. I'll bet it looked like he was running the show. He must have had you all fooled. Ha! Doran likes to do that sometimes. He's a pretty slick character when he wants to be. I found that out quick enough after I met him."

"Met him?"

"Yes, ma'am. Met him last summer. Just showed up at the ranch one day. Said he heard about our excavations in the cliff dwellings and wanted to help. He was a city slicker from back East somewhere, and I wasn't too sure about him, but he pitched right in the first day out and he's been working with us at the mesa ever since. Ain't never seen nobody like that work so hard or catch on so quick. And he ain't never done that kind of work before, though he says he's done lots of odd jobs and such all over the West since he was nineteen. I guess that's when he left home, but he don't talk about that much."

"But, I thought . . ." I swallowed, my mouth suddenly dry. "I thought Doran was your . . . brother."

"Brother?" Will's grin broke into a belly laugh. "Brother? Miss Loring, I got three, but Doran Hunt ain't anywhere near like any one of them. Did you think we looked alike or something?"

I flushed. "Well, no, but you were together, and I was under the impression . . ."

"Brother? That's a good one!" Will laughed again. "Excuse me, Miss Loring, but if you could see my brothers . . . Well, it's just night and day. Owen's got this red, kinda bristly hair, and Ben is big boned and square, like me, and Charlie is stocky . . . Well, we'll all have a good laugh when you come down, won't we?"

I smiled rather tightly. Doran Hunt. So that was his real name. "Coming down is exactly what I came to talk to you about, Mr. Kendall," I said. "I truly appreciate your offer to let me stay at your ranch, but I'm afraid it's out of the question. I plan to stay in Durango for my visit, and perhaps, if you have time, engage you as a guide to the cliff dwellings from there."

"Now I won't take no for an answer!" Will cried. "And don't you go calling me any Mr. Kendall. Name's Will, pure and simple. You're coming to stay with us at the ranch, Miss Loring, and

that's that. We *like* company. Summer's the only
time we get to have visitors. Gets lonely the rest
of the year. What you worried about? If you think
Ma will mind, just forget about that. She loves
company, especially ladies like you. She gets tired
of all us menfolk; always wanted a daughter, she
says. And you won't be the only gal there, remember. There's Miss Hastings coming to stay
with us this summer, too, don't forget."

I *had* forgotten about Julia Hastings. Remembering her rather suspect, sudden friendliness at
the exhibition, I decided that she was one more
reason I should not stay with the Kendalls.

As I listened to Will carry on, however, I decided it best to agree with him for the time being
and somehow gracefully decline staying at his
ranch once I got there.

"So just sit tight once you get to Durango," he
said, finally summing up his thoughts, "and we'll
have somebody come out to meet you. I'll take
care of it somehow."

I thanked Will, and when he took my hand and
smiled at me warmly, I was oddly touched. It
occurred to me then that I might be in need of
such simple concern once I arrived. I had no idea
what else I might be met with there.

As a new visitor entered the exhibition hall, I
bid Will good-bye and started for the door. But
when I reached it, I turned back impulsively and
looked at the table of exhibits. The amulet and the
framed photograph were gone. I was not really
surprised, but nevertheless a slight chill went
through me. Doran had obviously taken them.
But why?

I returned to Mrs. Gresham's with no answer to

that question. And I spent a long, restless night before I was ready to leave for Union Station the next day. I arrived there at promptly three o'clock—ready to begin the trip that might provide the answers I sought.

Alighting from Mrs. Gresham's carriage and instructing Robert to take my luggage to the baggage department, I straightened my back and entered the station's doors with both nervousness and excitement fighting for space in my tight stomach. The station was huge and bustling. All about me, people were rushing, rushing to meet a train that would take them somewhere different, somewhere away from Denver. I was a part of this activity and movement, and suddenly I felt excitement coursing through my veins, quickening my step, brightening my eyes as, clutching my small valise, I started across the station.

"Oh, Heather! Miss Loring!" I stopped abruptly, hearing myself so unexpectedly hailed. "Miss Loring, over here! Oh, *do* come and help me please!"

I turned and saw, amidst a huge pile of Saratoga trunks, hatboxes, various bags, boxes, and valises, the diminutive form of Julia Hastings, waving a white linen handkerchief in my direction as if it were a limp flag of surrender. She was wearing a suit of turquoise blue in the smooth princess style that was just coming into fashion. It was trimmed in black velvet about the neck, wrists, and hem, and on her head was a small-velvet toque trimmed with black fur and aigrettes.

As I approached, she smiled weakly and, with a small but quite audible sigh of relief, sank down onto a trunk.

"Oh, I'm *so* glad to see you," she said. "The porter who helped me into the station simply abandoned me, and I hardly knew where to turn. Oh dear, I'm so helpless when left on my own like this!"

She turned her small white-gloved palms upward, indicating her pile of luggage, and heaved another heartfelt sigh. But then, spotting an approaching porter, Julia quickly straightened, and over the next few moments I watched in astonishment and then admiration as Julia, with a wave of her handkerchief, a flutter of her black eyelashes, and a few honeyed words, dispatched her baggage with seemingly no effort at all.

"Mama just *insisted* I bring a servant along for this trip," she said, turning back to me as her luggage trundled off on a dolly in front of the porter. "But I said, 'Why Mama, people don't do things like that in the West. If Prescott has chosen that place as his home for the time being, I will abide by their customs while I am there. I want to experience the West as it was *meant* to be experienced.' And so I left Lacey, who's been my own personal maid since I was a little girl, at home. But as you can see, I don't quite know what to do without her."

I had to pretend to adjust a tuck in my skirt to hide my smile. It was quite obvious after her encounter with the porter that this woman was neither helpless nor silly. Indeed, she seemed quite skilled in the means of getting what she wanted or required, however passively she managed to do it.

It was clear that Julia Hastings was not quite the innocent southern belle she professed to be, but I could not begin to guess her full background. On closer inspection I realized that Julia was much older than I had previously thought. I had guessed her age to be near mine, but now I saw that the delicate lines of a face several years older were skillfully hidden by carefully applied powders, and a certain brittle hardness seemed to lie just beneath her soft demeanor, hinting at a worldly experience well beyond my own.

Julia now glanced in excitement about the station, and then, with the same concentrated focus I had noticed at the exhibition after she had learned my name, her eyes, bright and snapping, came at last to rest on me.

"Well," she said appraisingly. "So you decided to come down to the ranch after all. I am *so* delighted, but I must say that I wondered a little when you ran out of the exhibition hall like that." She glanced at my simple camel suit, trimmed in braid, and then questioningly at the one small valise at my side.

"My other bags are already on the train," I explained, wondering at the sudden defensiveness I felt. "I leave in fifteen minutes."

"Why, so do I! We must be on the same train! Isn't that funny how it worked out that way?" Her focus seemed to sharpen even more. "Now we can have our little talk just as we planned."

She started to say something more, but then, seeing a bearded, distinguished-looking conductor in his frock coat and heavy gold watch chain making his way across the station, she hailed him and, in her highly effective yet passive way, quickly acquired his assistance in leading us to our train. But after he helped us up a set of narrow metal stairs into a rather small sleeper car, he turned to leave. Julia stopped abruptly, looking sharply around. She hailed the departing conductor.

"Please sir! Could you come back and check our tickets once more? I believe there's been some kind of mistake. We are first-class passengers. Surely this isn't our car?"

I saw that the sleeper in which we stood was a standard Pullman, equipped on either side of a carpeted aisle with its familiar multiple sets of plush seats, which formed individual sections that would eventually be made into separate lower berths. Above each set of seats hung the decoratively carved, enclosed upper berth, folded up against the ceiling and secured by a lock by day but swung down on its stout brass hinges by night and made up as a bed to accompany the one below it.

Dutifully, the bearded conductor returned to Julia's side and inspected the ticket she waved at him.

"No, ma'am. There's been no mistake, ma'am. This is your car. These are our first-class accommodations overnight to Alamosa. From there, tomorrow morning, you'll transfer to a narrow-gauge train to Durango."

"But surely . . . ," Julia stumbled. "Surely you offer some kind of private staterooms on this train, don't you? I have always traveled in private staterooms, some of them quite spacious. I have certainly never slept in this kind of open berth! And I see only two small washrooms at either end of this car. . . ."

As the conductor sadly shook his head and Julia

continued to argue with him, I took a seat and examined our car once more. Although it was not furnished as lavishly as some, it was not quite as rustic as a tourist car, and it still displayed the excellent craftsmanship and taste of a Pullman, with its fine marquetry on the upper berths, the silver Pintsch lighting fixtures hanging in an orderly row along the center of the ceiling, and tasseled shades at the windows. Despite Julia's disgruntlement, I felt quite sure that our trip in this car would be more than comfortable.

"Well," said Julia with a sigh, sinking into the seat across from me, "I suppose if one is to travel in the West, one must learn to make do." She glanced up dubiously at the fastened berth above us and then around at the mix of other passengers rapidly filling the car. "But I hardly know how I will sleep in such a thing as *that*," she said in a lowered voice, leaning toward me and lifting her eyes upward. "And in the public company of so many strangers! Why, we'll only have a flimsy little curtain to shield us from their scrutiny."

I began to reply, but at that moment the train's engine gave a sharp blast of its whistle and the conductor bellowed, "All aboard." After a series of great jolts and jerks, the train began to move beneath us. I felt a sudden rush of exhilaration. The train's halting forward movement seemed to pass on to me some of its power and strength. It was venturing out on a new journey and taking me with it.

As the train began to gather momentum and move south out of Denver, toward Colorado Springs, I peered out the window. On my right was the long blue line of mountains that formed

an indomitable barrier to the west; on my left
stretched out the seemingly limitless plains to the
east. I had heard that much of the scenery on this
trip was quite stunning, and I hoped to enjoy as
much of it as I could before the day's last light
faded.

But this, I soon learned, was not meant to be.

"So tell me," Julia said, leaning toward me intimately, "do you really write newspaper stories?
I should think that it's quite a *shocking* kind of
occupation for a lady."

I turned from the window with reluctance and
looked at her. "No, not really," I answered non-
comittally. "Many educated women are engaged
in such work all across the country. It's become
quite acceptable over the last several years."

"But your mama and your papa—surely *they*
don't approve."

I paused, looking down to wipe a speck of lint
off the seat beside me. "My mother and father are
. . . no longer living," I said after a moment.
"They died when I was very young."

"Oh, how tragic!" Julia's face was drawn in
consternation. She touched my sleeve with her
long, delicate fingers. "How old were you? How
did it happen?"

"I was five years old. My parents died in an
accident. A . . . fire."

"Oh, no! How terrible for you! My goodness,
how did it happen?"

"I don't really know. No one does. It happened
in our home, in St. Louis. Somehow the fire
started and my parents were trapped inside. I
was inside as well, I am told, but was pulled to
safety. I was injured, however, and ill for months

afterward, and I lost much of my memory as a result."

I did not tell Julia that the doctor who attended me told me that I might never regain all of my lost memory, and that my injury was the source of the spells that had begun to plague me months later. Their symptoms could recur any time, the doctor had said, perhaps throughout the rest of my life; evidently the consequences of head injuries were difficult to predict. What it had done deep inside no one knew; what might recur, he could not say.

"How terrible!" Julia cried again. "Don't you remember anything?"

"Very little."

"Oh dear! Were you left an orphan then?"

"My mother's older brother—my Uncle Charles—took me in. He and Aunt Natalie lived in St. Louis, too, and they raised me there. They were unable to have children of their own, and they treated me as if I were their own."

"How very kind." Julia paused. "You were an only child then?"

I swallowed and looked out the window, feeling the train beneath me straining against the incline we were beginning to ascend. "I had a brother," I finally answered. "He was seven or eight years older. He disappeared after the fire. His . . . body was never found, so it was assumed he somehow escaped and ran away."

"Oh, my goodness, I wonder why! Do you remember him?"

"I remember him only in a very dim way," I answered, allowing myself to reminisce for just a moment. I remembered my brother, I suppose, the way any adoring five-year-old girl would remember a much older sibling: I remembered following him around the yard and the house and into town, pestering him to include me in his games. I'm sure I must have loved him a great deal.

"I didn't remember him at all for months after the fire," I told Julia. "No one spoke of him, I suppose to avoid upsetting me further. But eventually I asked about him, and my aunt and uncle finally told me that he had disappeared. We never heard from him again."

"Oh, how tragic," Julia repeated. "What was his name?"

I glanced out at the line of mountains to the west again. "His name was Peter."

Julia was quiet a moment, and then she said, "So you have come out here to look for him?"

I turned sharply from the window and stared at Julia, startled. The blurred image in the photograph at the exhibition flashed suddenly across my mind, and I shifted uncomfortably in my seat.

"Why, no," I answered, trying to keep my voice calm. "I have long since given up hope of seeing him again. I'm sure that if he were able he would have contacted me. Something must have happened to him long ago. That's the only explanation." When Julia did not reply, I went on. "I came out to Denver simply to travel, to see something of the West before it disappears entirely. That is why I was interested in seeing the cliff dwellings, where we are going. They are relatively unexplored. I want to write about them, experience them firsthand."

"And your aunt and uncle approve of this?"

"Certainly. They have always been most supportive of me. Uncle Charles was perceptive enough to notice my interest in his newspaper quite early, and after I completed my basic schooling, he invited me to join his staff. And when I explained to him and to Aunt Natalie that I intended to pursue my writing rather than become a teacher or get married, as many of my friends were doing, they seemed surprised but they understood. They themselves have chosen rather unconventional lives. When I turned twenty-one, they gave me the money my father had left me, and I then had the means and freedom to do as I wished."

"How very . . . unique," said Julia with a mixture of puzzlement and slight distaste. "Now, *my* Mama would never hear of such a thing. And I . . ." She paused a moment, musing. "But I suppose I'm just used to the way things are done in Virginia."

Stirring myself from my reverie, I realized that, however unwilling initially to participate in this conversation, I had become quite caught up in it and done most of the talking.

"Do tell me about Mr. Webb," I said, turning the conversation to other matters. "You are engaged to be married?"

Julia immediately brightened. "Oh yes, and Prescott is a wonderful man! He is such a striking figure, so handsome and very aristocratic by nature. You'll see when you meet him. And he's very influential, especially in Washington. I'm sure that some day we will be quite rich and powerful." She paused a moment, her eyes shining. "It just did my Mama's heart wonders when Prescott and I announced our engagement this spring.

She has never quite recovered from Papa's death after the war, and it weakened her considerably when we had to sell our land in the country and our house in Richmond. . . . Mama has prided herself greatly on our match, although it was I, of course, who made it. I wanted to be married right away, and Mama planned a big, wonderful wedding for us in Richmond. It just about broke her heart when Prescott said we would have to postpone the ceremony until he was finished with his work out here. It's very important work you know, for the government. He just can't leave it now. And since I do love Prescott so"—here Julia let her gaze fall speculatively on a passing gentleman in the aisle—"I have come out to be with him and help him until we can return to Virginia to be married."

She gave a last lingering glance to the gentleman as he left the car and then returned her gaze to me, sharpening it with that odd focus I had noticed before.

"I do believe it's a woman's duty to bend to the wishes of the man she chooses, don't you?" she said, raising her perfectly shaped eyebrows and adjusting the velvet trim at her neck. "It's really an investment in her own future. That's why I plan to do all I can to help Prescott while I am here—for our future together." She looked at me thoughtfully a moment, and then impulsively leaned forward again. "But," she added in a confiding tone, "I have made up my mind that after Prescott's work is finished and we are married, we will stay in Virginia. I'm sure that after this summer we will have adequate finances to restore some of Mama's—and my own—former comfortable style of living."

She settled back against her seat with a satisfied smile and, seeming to have expended herself, said nothing further. I settled back as well, glad for the conversation's rather abrupt end. Talking about my past—my parents and the accident—was always difficult. I had known since I first saw Julia at the station that I would have to tell her about my background sooner or later. I did not know why she was so interested in me, and at first thought it had something to do with Doran Hunt. Indeed, he was not on this train, but *she* was. Was it only a coincidence? As we talked, however, I began to think that her interest was simply that of one woman in another. She seemed to need a woman friend.

In any case, I was glad our conversation, for the time being, was over, and we each sat musing until we'd passed Colorado Springs and Pueblo, and the conductor came into our car to announce that dinner was being served in the dining car.

Swaying with the movement of the car, Julia and I stood and made our way to the dining car, where we were seated by white-gloved and -coated porters at tables draped with damask and set with fine silver and china. I found the menu quite extensive, with a selection of prairie chicken, quail, venison, and fresh mountain trout, as well as an excellent wine list. But Julia found fault with nearly every course that was served and hampered my enjoyment of the meal further as she began to talk yet again about Prescott, her wedding plans and wardrobe, her mother and the maid she had left behind in Virginia.

Only one point in our dinner conversation really interested me.

"Do you remember that man at the exhibition, the one standing with Will Kendall who introduced you to me?" asked Julia, taking a delicate sip of the champagne we had just been served. "His name was Doran, I believe. I did not ever learn his surname. Prescott didn't tell me about him, only about Will Kendall, and I don't know why this Doran was there at the exhibition. In any case, he struck me at the time as quite familiar, and later I remembered I had seen him at a function in Richmond last year, before I met Prescott. The man—oh, I *do* hate to use only given names when I haven't been properly introduced—anyway, this *Doran* was visiting from New York, I believe. He was a friend of the hostess. I don't know what he was doing so far from New York. I do detest the way standards have simply fallen in Richmond, the way just anyone is invited to all the good parties nowadays. Out here, of course, we all mingle, and rightly so. But in the South there is still a certain decorum. . . ." Julia picked at her food delicately. "In any case, I am sure I saw the man at this social function, and he was quite dashing, as I remember. I was never introduced, however, so I did not learn who his family was, only that they are very wealthy and from New York. So when I saw him at the exhibition there in Denver, it struck me as so strange and somehow . . . intriguing. He looked so . . . well, rather rugged, you know. I almost did not recognize him. But I am sure he

recognized *me*, although he refused to acknowledge it. I have no idea why, but I was willing
to play along with his little game, at least for
the time being. I do wonder though—do you suppose we will see more of him at the Kendall
ranch?''

Julia's words echoed in my mind as we finished
our meal and started back to the sleeping car. We
would indeed see more of Doran Hunt. Of that I
had no doubt. From Julia's words, though, it did
not seem as if she and Doran were connected, as
I had thought earlier. Nevertheless, his own interest in me remained. I almost expected to see
him emerge from another car as we made our way
back to our own.

He did not, however, and when we returned to
our seats, a porter had already made up our
berths. As he started to work on the seats across
the aisle from us, I turned my attention to him,
watching the process that had always fascinated
me. Julia looked on as well, although on her face
was an expression of distinct distaste.

The occupants of the berth the porter had just
made up, a tired-looking woman and her young
son, had just returned from washing up—the boy
in striped bedclothes and robe, the woman in a
long dressing gown, her hair brushed out and
rebraided for the night. Neither appeared to feel
the least bit conspicuous or uncomfortable;
throughout the car, other occupants of all shapes
and sizes were also preparing for bed. But something about the sight of the mother and son—the
way she smoothed the blankets over him as he
climbed into the lower berth and lay down, the
way she placed her hand against his forehead for

just a moment as she sat with him there—twisted something deep inside me. It had come, I knew, from talking to Julia earlier about the fire, my parents, my brother. But there was a strangeness in the feeling, an inexplicable intensity to it that I could not quite account for. For the first time, I wondered seriously if I should, indeed, have left Denver and made this trip. And I continued to wonder until, my gold jewel case by my side, I fell into a restless, tossing sleep—the dreams of which I do not remember.

In the morning, we reached Alamosa, boarded the narrow-gauge train's coach and settled ourselves on modest but comfortable brocaded seats. There was room enough so that we could each sit by a window, and as Julia stared moodily out the window ahead of me, lost in thought, I leaned back in my own seat with a sigh of relief. Perhaps this time, I thought to myself, I would be able to enjoy the trip.

My heart quickened as I looked out my own window. As the train began its steady course south and then westward, I could already tell that we were venturing into a type of country I had only seen in illustrations. The doubt I had felt the night before was replaced, for the time being, with the pure excitement of travel and the morning's promise.

We traveled through a long green valley and then entered a rolling, arid region covered with odd lava outcroppings and fragments; later we were to see strange stone monoliths standing like phantoms along the track. On our ascent up over the Continental Divide, I felt a thrill of fear as I peered out my window and saw how tenaciously the train rounded its sharp curves and clung to the edge of abrupt chasms that dropped dizzily down along their jagged granite sides to the threadlike rivers and streams that had cut the canyons thousands and thousands of years ago. On our descent down the other side, we saw far into New Mexico and passed over a high trestle that set up a great clattering in the train and prompted Julia to move over toward the aisle.

When the train at last entered the rolling sage-brush-covered country below, passing through pastures of sheep and acres of Indian reservations, I felt as if I had experienced over the last few hours more new sights and sensations than I had in all my life before.

Straining forward to look out the window, I saw that Durango was a rather rustic but bustling town closely surrounded by a ring of pine-clad mountains and ridges, and situated in a lovely valley formed by the river that wended its way through the town. The conductor told us the river was called the Rio de las Animas, or "river of lost souls," the name the Spanish initially gave it. Back behind the depot and across the river, Durango's coal smelter belched its gray masses of smoke against a large, hulking hill that rose to the south of town. Opening my window, I could smell its acrid odor as the train came to a long, shuddering halt beside the depot. Peering out, I looked past the smelter, along the river and toward the cleft of hills to the west of town. Somewhere beyond them, I knew, lay the Kendalls' ranch and Twilight Mesa.

"I don't see anyone here to meet us," said Julia fretfully, peering out her own window at the eclectic mixture of people milling about on the wooden platform alongside the train. Rather shaggy-looking men in rough work clothing mingled with businessmen in their frock coats and derbies, while women and children in all manner of dress, dogs, and even a few blue-coated army officers paced up and down, waiting for the train to unload its cargo.

"Prescott *promised* he would send someone," Julia went on. "I'm sure it's too late to go to the ranch today. Where am I to stay tonight? I can't be expected to walk about in a town like this and find my own accommodations."

Hardly wishing to sit and listen to Julia's complaints, I hurried down the train's metal stairs, remembering Will's words at the exhibition hall. I scanned the crowd warily for the face of Doran Hunt. It was entirely possible that he would be the one sent to meet us.

To my relief, however, I did not see him. But to the south of the depot I noticed a group of buggies and carriages jockeying for position behind a long white line chalked on the boardwalk. They had evidently been sent from different hotels, and each had a driver who, waving his buggy whip, called out the various amenities his establishment provided and offered to take embarking passengers there in the comfort of a private vehicle.

"Here is our answer, I think," I said as Julia joined me, and before I could say another word, a liveried driver from the largest, fanciest conveyance represented—an enclosed tallyho, rosette bedecked and pulled by a team of dapple-gray

horses—jumped off his perch at the reins and
hurried over to us. He was a young boy, only
fifteen or sixteen, I guessed, with a red, raw face
and a long neck and wrists that stuck out from a
uniform decidedly too small. After ascertaining
our names, the boy swept off his cap and bowed
awkwardly before us, announcing that he was
there to drive us both two blocks south to the
Strater Hotel—which was, according to him, "the
finest, best, and only first-class hotel around."

"Ah," said Julia, relaxing a little. "I *knew* Prescott had made provisions." Then she turned and
looked at me curiously. "Why didn't you tell me
you had reservations at this hotel?"

Before I could answer, she set about instructing
the boy just how to secure her pile of luggage,
now unloaded from the train, onto the coach.
Before long we reached the hotel, and I saw that
it was indeed a first-class establishment. Four stories of sturdy, pink brick rose in well-constructed
elegance above me; looking up, I could see the
projecting curves of the white-trimmed window
cornices above, as well as the stone-railed banis-
ter that circled the pointed rooftop cupola. Bay
windows on the second and third floors projected
out between decoratively carved and white-
painted fretwork, with small-railed balconies
above.

The boy held the heavy front door open for us
and we entered the lobby. It was a spacious room,
with velvet draperies and comfortable furniture
scattered about, and a polished, tiled floor. At the
far end was a large mahogany desk, behind which
stood a smooth-shaven, eager-looking clerk.

"May I help you ladies?" he asked brightly as

we approached. "A room for the evening? Or two perhaps?" Although appearing to be in his late thirties, the man had a fresh, innocent quality about him, from his dapper bow tie down to his immaculately polished black shoes. He looked to me as if he had been plucked straight from a barbershop chair in some midwestern city and dropped in Durango without transition.

"Yes," I answered, smiling. "We do need rooms for tonight. I believe my companion, Miss Julia Hastings, already has a reservation and I would like to make one also. My name is Loring, Heather Loring."

"Let me see. Hmmm." The man slipped on a wire-rimmed pair of eyeglasses and bent to consult a large, leather-bound book. "Ah yes. Yes, indeed. Here we are. Miss Hastings is in room 314, and . . ." Looking up in surprise, the clerk peered at me over the top of his glasses. "You are in room 312, right next door, Miss Loring. I already have a reservation here."

Guessing that either Will Kendall or Doran Hunt had made the reservation, I commented casually, "How nice. I was not aware of that. Could you tell me, perhaps, who made the reservation?"

The man looked surprised at my question and somewhat disconcerted. "Why, I don't know ma'am. I didn't take the reservation myself. I must have been, ah, lunching at the time. I could call for the boy who replaces me then—"

"Oh, no, no. Don't bother," I said, waving my hand in the air. "It's not that important. Perhaps, if the porter could manage our bags, we could see our rooms now?"

"Oh. Yes, of course." The clerk rang a small

bell on the counter of the desk, summoning a uniformed, colored porter, who took us up to the rooms. The window of mine looked out over the railroad tracks toward the cleft of hills I had seen earlier from the train, and was furnished quite nicely with a large high-backed bed, an oak armoire, a walnut washstand with a marble top and a china pitcher, a wicker chair, and a small bureau with a looking glass on the wall above it. Julia's room was quite similar. Both rooms had hardwood floors with small rugs scattered about.

"At last," Julia said, sinking down on the edge of the bed in her room after the porter left. "This is surely not the *best* hotel I have ever seen, although there is a certain rugged elegance to it. I suppose it's the best we'll find here. I am thankful, at least, that we did not have to stay in some wretched boarding house. I am *so* fatigued."

Crossing over to Julia's window, I lifted the draperies back and looked out. Her view faced the street, toward Main Avenue, and as I opened the window slightly, I could hear shouts and the wheels of passing carriages and wagons crunching on the busy street below.

"Oh, do let's go for a walk," I said, turning back to Julia. "The sky is so clear and such a lovely blue, and it's not at all hot out. My legs are still stiff from the trip, and I would love to get out and stretch in the fresh air."

"A walk?" Julia looked at me blankly, as if I had uttered something unthinkable. "In this town? Unchaperoned? Did you see some of the buildings we passed? And the people? Heavens no! I plan to stay in my room and rest until dinner. I do hope they serve a proper meal in the dining room tonight. They do have a dining room here, don't they?"

Removing her hat and starting to take the pins from her hair, Julia sighed. Then glancing up and seeing the look on my face, her own expression changed.

"Oh, but *you* go, Heather," she said. "Don't let silly old *me* stop you. I'm just not much for walking, but I'm sure it would do you good, as you say. Yes, why don't you do just that? I'll stay here and rest and you go out for your walk. I'll meet you in the lobby in an hour or so."

"All right then," I said, surprised by her change in manner. "Are you sure you don't want to come with me?"

"No, no. You run along. Perhaps I'll read that magazine of yours I started on the train."

"Yes, I'll drop it by on my way out." Closing Julia's door behind me, I went into my own room and unpacked, placing my two jewel cases far back in the bottom bureau drawer, behind some linens that were there. Then, washing up a bit and twisting my hair into a loose chignon, I fastened on a bonnet and stepped out into the hallway, locking the door behind me.

I went back down to the lobby and stopped to talk a few moments to the desk clerk, who told me a little about the town before I started out the front door. I was halfway down the front steps when I realized that I hadn't stopped by Julia's room on my way out with the magazine.

I hesitated, then decided that most likely Julia was asleep anyway, and that if she wanted to read the magazine, she could always ask the desk clerk to let her into my room.

Once I stepped outside, I was immediately glad I had decided on a walk. The temperature was indeed perfect, and the prevailing breeze had blown the smelter's smoke away from town. As I walked down the street, it struck me just how far from St. Louis—and even Denver—I had come. As I had felt this morning, last night's doubts and worries seemed to disappear as the excitement of a day of discovery swept over me.

A block north, I passed a hardware store, a grocery, a carriage works, a steam laundry, and a dry goods store. The desk clerk had told me that Durango's main street had been destroyed by a disastrous fire two years earlier. Now the street, lined with sturdy brick buildings, looked quite solid and substantial. Up a few blocks from Main Avenue, I spied several church towers and fairly nice residences. The streets were busy with daytime activity, and the town seemed to give off an air of prosperity and permanence even while retaining a kind of frontier quality in its mountainous setting.

I walked another block or two, glad for the sidewalk despite the boards that had sprung loose here and there. Then, seeing what appeared to be a long line of saloons ahead of me, I stopped. I noticed that the other women on the sidewalk had crossed over to the other side of the street very pointedly, and I hesitated before turning down a side street, intending to circle around and continue walking. But I quickly found that conditions became even worse. The board sidewalk ended abruptly and the bare street was uneven and rutted. I had to pick up my skirts and choose my steps carefully as I made my way down the street, and it was only when I crossed the railroad tracks that I realized I had unwittingly moved into a rather rough section of town. I was just beginning to wonder if I should turn back when I heard two male voices raised sharply ahead of me.

Glancing up, I was hit with the sudden strong odor of a livery stable a few yards away. Standing along its long wooden side were two figures: an old, stooped man in worn work clothes and mucked up boots, gesturing rather appealingly and explaining something to a much younger, taller man dressed in dark denim trousers and a blue work shirt, his sleeves rolled up to his elbows.

The younger man had his back to me, but I recognized him immediately. I would have known him anywhere.

"Got loose, she did sir," the old man was saying. The plaintive, almost fearful look on his face was clear to me even given the distance that separated us. "She was a wild one, that horse. You were right. She didn't like being cooped up while you were gone to Denver, sir. Kept butting herself against the gate of her stall, almost breaking it twice. And then when you came back this morning to check on her and left again, not saying when you'd be back for sure . . . well, she just went wild. She knew you were about somewhere, she did, and she wasn't about to sit around and wait for you again. It was that rainstorm at noon that finally done it. Lightning crashing all around. Scared all the horses bad, but yours—she was the worst. She bucked and thrashed and finally tried to jump clean out of her stall. That's when she broke her leg. You know how it is when they break their legs, sir. We had to shoot her. We would have waited until you came back, but she was in bad shape and we didn't have no idea when you'd be back. For all we knew, you might be gone another night or two. We couldn't leave her like that. We thought it best, sir, what you would have done if you were here. We only did it less than an hour ago, then moved her out here."

The old man stepped back slightly, and it was only then that I saw what lay beyond him, back behind the livery stable: the prone, still body of a large horse. I'd had little experience with horses, but even I could see it was a splendid animal. Doran stood motionless, looking down at it.

For a moment, it seemed the air around me ceased to move. The seconds ticked by as Doran stared, the old man mute beside him, his hands hanging uselessly at his sides. I stood frozen, knowing that I was intruding on something private. Holding my breath, my skirts still clutched in my hands, I made a move to leave, hoping to retreat as unnoticed from the scene as I had approached it.

But even a small noise rang loud in that awful silence. As I turned, my skirts rustling slightly and my boot crunching on the small pebbles of the road, Doran heard and looked up at me sharply.

For a moment, as our eyes first met, it seemed Doran did not even recognize me. Indeed, he seemed hardly to see me at all. He had glanced up without thinking, and the raw emotion he must have felt at seeing his horse had not time to be mitigated or erased. Now, on his face, I saw it—a look of naked, unguarded pain and vulnerability.

I tried to turn my head, but the expression in Doran's eyes deepened as he realized who I was. For just an instant, something in those eyes, still unguarded and wounded, seemed to leap out and reach toward me, bridging the distance between us with an intimacy, an understanding that took my breath away. Although neither of us took a step toward the other, I felt as if we had touched with some kind of searing impact, as if I had been affected by a connection or current that was more powerful than anything I had ever felt.

It was over in an instant. Doran regained his composure quickly, and I saw, like an iron veil, the familiar control drop swiftly over his eyes, his face, his entire being. Letting out a barely perceptible breath, he straightened and then, tossing back his head slightly, approached me.

"So you came down," he said, his voice even and betraying none of the emotion I had just witnessed. "Did you use the ticket I gave you?"

"Yes." I answered him dully, feeling suddenly limp and empty as our connection, like a fine thread between us, was abruptly severed.

"And your trip? Was it comfortable?"

"Quite." I almost laughed at the absurdity of it all. The two of us speaking like polite, distant strangers, while I was still reeling with the force of our meeting. "Julia Hastings was on my train," I added sharply, watching his face. "But perhaps you already knew that."

"No, I didn't." I could not tell if Doran's surprise was truly genuine. He paused a moment, and then asked, "Are you both staying in town tonight?"

"Yes. I believe Miss Hastings will be traveling to the Kendalls' ranch tomorrow." I paused. "That *is* where you live as well, isn't it—the Kendalls' ranch?"

He gave me a curious look. "Of course. I'll be returning there tomorrow. Perhaps I could accompany you and Miss Hastings there. We could rent a buggy. What time will you be leaving in the morning?"

"I beg your pardon. I said Miss Hastings will be traveling to the ranch. I plan to stay in Durango until Will Kendall returns. Then I will hire him as a guide and visit the cliff dwellings from here."

Doran looked at me a moment, and in his silence I was very aware of the dark, curled hairs on his arm below his rolled-up sleeves and the rough texture of his denim trousers, so different from the attire I had seen him in that night at Mrs. Compton's.

"As you wish," he finally said. He seemed about to say something more, but then ended with, "Perhaps I will see you and Miss Hastings tomorrow, however. Where did you say you are staying?"

"I didn't say." Hesitating for a reason I could not quite discern, I finally answered, "We're staying at the Strater."

"Ah." Doran looked at me again. "Well then . . ."

He made a movement to leave, and as his back, strong yet somehow pliant beneath his work shirt, turned away, something inside me seemed to loosen and flow outward to him. Impulsively I reached out a hand and laid it on his arm.

"I'm sorry," I said, looking over at the stiff body on the ground. "About your . . . your horse."

Doran looked at me, and I saw in his green eyes just a glimmer of the emotion that had been there earlier, before it was quickly snuffed out.

"These things happen," he answered brusquely. He glanced down at my hand on his arm, and then let his arm drop to his side, knocking my hand away. Turning away without a backward look, he walked over toward the old man, who had been watching us with a rather fearful, avid interest. Together they entered the livery stable.

I stood a moment after they had gone, feeling the heat rising in my neck and breaking over my face. Everything around me seemed blurred as I found my way back to the hotel, and I needed more than anything to go up to my room and shut the world out for a time. But when I entered the lobby, I found Julia waiting for me, looking quite rested and fresh in a burgundy gown and short cape.

"Oh, I'm so glad you're back," she cried, taking my arm and drawing me toward the dining room behind the lobby. "I was just about to go after you. I feel as if I am about to *die* from hunger, which is a confession you must take to your grave, for it is something no true southern lady would ever admit to." Her laughter made a soft tinkling sound in the air, and her eyes were bright—a complete change, I thought, from the way I had left her earlier.

"You seem quite rested," I commented dryly.

"Oh, yes. I had a nice rest up in my room. I washed and changed, and now I feel like a new person. I have come to realize the true *excitement* of our situation here. The possibilities! I can hardly wait to see Prescott and tell him everything. I know he will be quite proud of me . . ." Suddenly she stopped and turned to me, her face and voice at once serious. "Oh Heather—I may call you Heather, mayn't I?—I do want to tell you how truly *grateful* I am for your company on this trip. Why, without you, I don't know what I would have done. All we have talked about . . . I do feel we have become very dear friends. Now—why Heather! You look quite pale. Is anything the matter?"

"No, nothing, but now I am a little tired, and I'd like to go up to my room and rest a bit before dinner. . . ."

"You'll do nothing of the kind! Any fool can see that what you need is some proper nourishment. My Mama always said there is nothing better for a weak constitution than a good, clear bowl of homemade broth, and the desk clerk informed me that they are serving the most excellent consommé in the dining room tonight. Now come along."

As she spoke, Julia led me to the dining room, and before I could summon the energy or the words to protest, we had been promptly seated and served by a young waitress in a white apron and cap. The meal, I'm sure, was excellent and did provide some nourishment, but I hardly remember tasting it as Julia jabbered on and on.

It was over an hour later when Julia finally took a last bite of her lemon torte and seemed satisfied enough to leave. She lingered a moment at the table next to us to speak with a couple she had met earlier in the lobby, and I escaped the dining room with relief, craving some solitude and privacy.

When I entered the lobby, though, I thought I saw, out the corner of my eye, a familiar form leaving the hotel. I stared after him. Had it really been Doran Hunt?

I stared at the door another moment, and then went up to the front desk, where the eager clerk stood waiting.

"That man . . ." I began.

"Your cousin?" he replied brightly. "Oh, yes, I'm so sorry you missed him! I told him you were dining just in the other room, but evidently something came up, for he had to leave quite suddenly, as you could see."

At my blank look, the man smiled and rushed on to explain. "Your cousin came in earlier, after you and Miss Hastings had gone in to dine, and he introduced himself. He has quite fine manners; I'm sure you are very fond of him. He explained how mortified he had been when he was unable to meet your train at the station and accompany you here as planned, and so he came here to make sure you had indeed received the best accommodations available. It seems he made the reservation for you, as a kind of surprise. He seemed so deeply concerned. You are very fortunate. I have cousins myself, but . . . well, in any case, he told me how he was staying here tonight also and asked for a room near yours, and so I gave him one right down the hall. I took him up myself and pointed out where you would be staying. He wanted to see your room, to make sure it was proper enough, but when I assured him that all the rooms were quite nice and that the amenities in his own room were identical to yours, he seemed satisfied. Again, I was quite impressed with his solicitude.''

The man beamed, and then, drawing his brows together in a puzzled frown, leaned closer toward me. "It was rather strange, though, the way he left. Perhaps you understand it, knowing the nature of his business. I left him alone in his room, as he said he wanted to rest a bit before joining you and Miss Hastings in the dining room. But after about a quarter of an hour, he came back down and said he'd changed his mind and didn't want the room after all, that something quite important had come up as to his business and he had to leave immediately. But no one had been up to see him or sent up a message, and we had no calls for him here at the desk. Perhaps he saw someone on the street, out his window? In any case, he didn't leave a message for you, but I assumed you'd understand. Oh dear, I do hope I haven't upset you. I'm sure that whatever came up, your cousin will be back soon. Unless, of course, it was some kind of emergency that took him away and . . . oh dear, I can see quite clearly that I *have* upset you. Would you like me to leave some kind of message should your cousin return?''

Gathering up my skirts, I was halfway up the staircase as the clerk called after me, my heart pounding in my ears. I knew I had to get to my room immediately—that something had happened there while I was gone. Even as I rushed toward it, however, part of me shrunk away in dread. I was hardly startled when I reached the door and found it already open.

Nothing seemed outwardly changed or disturbed. The room was clean and tidy, as I'd left it. But there were little signs. The catch on the armoire was not fastened properly. A few bottles on the bureau had been moved slightly. And my valise was not quite in the same position as I had left it; it had been opened and not closed tightly.

And the bottom drawer of the bureau—it was open just a crack.

My breathing stopped as I slid open the last drawer. Inside, the pile of linens was folded as before, but the stack seemed slightly askew. I grabbed the magenta jewel case first and scanned its contents quickly, discovering with relief that everything was accounted for. None of my jewelry was worth very much, but each piece held sentimental value for me.

It was the gold velvet jewel case, however, for which I had the most concern. Opening its lid, I saw that Mother's ring and breast pin and watch were still there, as well as Father's medals and other items. And the amulet lay there among them, nestled on the satin lining.

But when I removed all the items, carefully, I saw with a catch in my throat that the false bottom was not quite locked securely in place. Sliding my thumbnail alongside it, I released it and stared.

My gold doubloon was gone.

Chapter Four
✦✦✦✦

AT FIRST I could find no breath at all, and then it all returned to my lungs in one great rush. Only gradually did commonplace, everyday sounds begin to penetrate: shouts and wagon wheels on the road outside; laughter and muted voices in the hallway; a few short, truncated blasts of a train whistle as one of the depot's engines was readied for its night's rest. Glancing down, I saw a stack of carefully folded extra bedding set out on the bed's neat cover—most likely the work of a chambermaid, I realized, carried in while Julia and I were eating downstairs.

Somewhat shakily, I lowered myself into the wicker chair. Surely the chambermaid had not taken my gold doubloon. I stared down at the empty jewel case, then lifted my head and glanced about the room. It would have been quite simple for her to do so, of course, safe in the knowledge that I was dining downstairs. But the possibility seemed highly unlikely. Although Julia had proclaimed the hotel rustic by her standards, it was obviously a superior establishment, furnished with care and run quite conscientiously.

He wanted to see your room. The desk clerk's words echoed in my mind. *I took him up myself and pointed out where you would be staying. Then I left him alone . . .*

Had Doran taken the doubloon? He *had* seen my amulet at Mrs. Compton's, I remembered suddenly, my heart beginning to pound. Had he come looking for it for some reason and then, searching further, found the doubloon?

Or perhaps he had been looking for the doubloon all along. Could he have known, somehow, that I was carrying it?

But how would he have gotten in to search my room? I was certain I had locked it. Had the chambermaid left it ajar after bringing the bedding? And then Doran could have come in to search . . . through my armoire, my valise, my bureau . . .

The thought chilled me. I glanced again about the room almost furtively. Doran Hunt, here in my room, going through my things, invading my privacy, my life. . . . I felt the same sense of unsettledness wash over me that I'd experienced when I had discovered that Doran Hunt had been following me around Denver.

But what possible reason could this man have for following me, watching me, and now, searching my room? And, if he had found the doubloon, why had he taken it?

I started at a sudden noise behind me. Julia, her dark full skirts rustling about her kid boots, entered the room.

"Why Heather, when I came into the lobby and saw you bolting up the staircase like that, I couldn't imagine *what* had happened. Is everything all right? Did—'' Julia stopped abruptly, staring at the object in my hand. "Why, what a lovely jewel case! Heather, you sly fox. You never let on you were carrying valuables on this trip.'' Her blue eyes gave a swift, cursory glance at the few items on the bureau, and then with a swish of her skirts, she crossed the floor to my side.

Did I imagine it, or was Julia's surprise just a touch too genuine, her drawl just a little overpronounced? It struck me then that Julia could have been in my room earlier as easily as Doran or the maid. She had wanted to read my magazine, and I had not dropped it by her room as promised. Hadn't I even told myself as I left the hotel that Julia could quite easily ask to be let into my room if necessary?

"And, oh my! Is that a secret compartment at the bottom of the case? How exciting! But why is it empty?'' She indicated my parents' belongings with a brief nod. "Oh Heather, do let me see.''

With a quick movement, Julia reached across me for the case. Her ruffled sleeve brushed my hand, and I caught the faint, elusive scent of her cologne.

Lilacs. The memory came back again in a rush. Lilacs and the storm and the man who had held the amulet and the gold doubloon . . .

I snapped the lid of the jewel case shut before Julia could reach it. "It really is of no interest,'' I said, turning away from her to place it in the bureau. "I rarely use the compartment itself, and I certainly store no valuables within it. You have seen for yourself what it holds. They are just some things left to me by my parents.'' I paused, fingering them. "I rushed up here so quickly because I remembered that I had left the case out of the bureau, and I was afraid that perhaps the maid might look through it. It's a . . . very private and precious thing to me."

"Oh, of course, Heather. I understand." Julia's tone was still as thick as honey. "Please forgive me. I am so impulsive! Mama has always said it would get the best of me one day. I just do and say whatever pops into my little old head." Turning suddenly, she crossed over to the window with another swish and rustle of her skirts. Lifting a delicate hand, she drew back the lace curtain to peer outside just as a clamor of raucous laughter rose up from the street below.

"My but this is a *wild* little town!" Julia's narrow shoulders rippled in a shiver. "You were so brave to venture out into it alone this afternoon, Heather dear. Did you meet anyone interesting?"

Julia turned to me as suddenly as she had flounced away, her blue eyes clear and piercing. For a moment it seemed as if they could see into my mind.

"Why no," I said, shifting my eyes from hers to look out the window. "Just men and women in the street, some children playing—townspeople, you know."

Julia considered me a moment, her head tilted, then turned to gaze out the window. "Oh, dear. I had hoped you might have seen that man, that Doran person somewhere about town."

"Hunt," I supplied. "His last name is Hunt."

"Oh, yes, Mr. Hunt. Anyway, I don't know *how* we shall travel all the way to the Kendalls' ranch alone tomorrow. Both Prescott and Will

Kendall did assure me that someone would be here to accompany us. But if you didn't see Mr. Hunt . . . oh, Heather, whatever shall we do tomorrow?" Julia's voice trailed off as she continued to look out the window.

It was time, I decided, that Julia Hastings knew my plans. "Julia," I began, clearing my throat, "I am not going with you to the Kendalls' ranch tomorrow. I am staying here in Durango for the duration of the summer. I plan to hire Will Kendall as a guide when he returns from Denver and then travel to Twilight Mesa from here, rather than from the ranch. It will be much simpler that way, and much more comfortable for me."

Julia turned to me, her fine dark eyebrows raised in what I recognized, this time, as a genuine expression of surprise. "Why, that is . . . simply ridiculous!" For once, Julia appeared at a loss for words. She must have seen something in my expression waver, however, for her own expression changed quickly. When she went on, her voice was once again strong and sure. "That is impossible! You must come! You can't stay here. You simply must meet Prescott."

"I am certain I will—in a few days when I visit the ranch on my way into Twilight Mesa. It is not my intention to stay away entirely."

As Julia stared at me, her eyes narrowed and her brows drew together into a frown. "Now Heather, stop this. I cannot possibly travel to the Kendalls' ranch by myself. Why, even if Mr. Hunt or someone else were to accompany me, I certainly could not travel there alone with a man, *unchaperoned.*" ·

The thought that Julia was reluctant to travel alone with a man brought a quick smile to my lips. Julia immediately seized her opportunity.

"Oh, Heather, you *do* understand! What a dear! I knew you would, if I explained the situation. It is settled then. You *will* come with me tomorrow." She paused, but only an instant. "And you *will* stay at the Kendalls' ranch with me for the rest of the summer, as well. You'll see, once you get there—it will be wonderful. That plan of yours was simply absurd."

Dropping the curtain, Julia strode back over to my side and took my hands in hers. "Dear, dear Heather," she said as she briefly pressed her cool lips to my cheek. "You are such a friend. Already I feel as if we are sisters." Then she pulled away and regarded me with a fond smile before raising the palm of her hand delicately to stifle a yawn.

"Dear me, how unladylike!" she said. "I have quite forgotten my manners this evening. You *must* forgive me, Heather. It is just that I am so fatigued. I do believe I shall retire now."

Holding her skirts, she swept over to the doorway. "Goodnight, Heather," she said, pausing there a moment. "And sweet dreams."

Giving me one last smile, Julia turned and was gone. As I heard the soft click of her adjacent door, I could still smell the elusive scent of her lilac cologne wrapping about me, mingled with the sharper scent of piñon logs burning in a bonfire somewhere outside.

Woodsmoke and lilacs . . .

Another clamor rose up from the street outside. Crossing to the window, I pulled back the curtain and saw a group of rough-looking men staggering down the train tracks below. One had fallen and was sprawled facedown across the rails in a drunken stupor. I heard coarse laughter and then saw the filthy boot of one of the other men suddenly whip out to send the prone figure rolling over onto his back.

I flinched and drew back slightly. Then, farther down the tracks, I glimpsed another figure standing alongside the far corner of the hotel, almost lost in the shadows. Something about the figure—the man's stance, his height, perhaps simply the way he waited there, so still, so selfpossessed—made my heart quicken queerly in my breast again. I strained forward, staring, and for a moment it seemed as if the man straightened slightly as well, then turned his head as if to listen, or to look at something below my window. I saw the profile only barely—fine, sculpted, alert—and for another prolonged moment it seemed as if the face might turn up toward me, drawn by the force of my stare.

Reflexively, I pulled back from the window even further, the lacy cloth of the curtain bunched roughly in my hand.

But the man in the shadows did not look up. Suddenly distracted, he jerked his head toward the opposite side of the hotel. Then, before I could move, he disappeared around the corner, as silent and sure as a tomcat on the prowl.

Although the room was warm, I felt the cold, clammy chill of a draft snake about my ankles and legs as I stared down at the empty place where the man had been. Or had it, indeed, been a man?

All I had seen were shadows, elusive and suggestive. Had I imagined the rest—the profile, the grace, the sculpted features?

I looked out the window for another moment, then finally let the curtain drop and crossed the room to extinguish the lamp on the table by the bed. I undressed quickly in the dark room, shivering only slightly as I dropped my cotton nightgown over my head and climbed into bed. I snuggled under the covers and pulled the bed's white linens to my chin. I would have no answers tonight, I knew, to the confused, crowding questions that had begun whirling again about my mind. Yet sleep soon claimed me so completely that I still cannot recall laying my head down on the pillow.

The sharp, shrill blast of a train whistle woke me the next morning. For an instant I did not know where I was and lay in bed for several moments trying to gather my wits. The room was already bright with sunshine, and the curtain at the window—which, I realized, I must have left open slightly the night before—billowed inward from a breeze wafting into the room. My nose wrinkled suddenly at the acrid odor of coal smoke; outside a locomotive's great engine hissed and clanked.

Throwing off my covers, I crossed the room to stand at the open window. I shivered slightly, in my cotton nightgown, but the sight that met me was quickly warming.

Rising steadily, the sun cast its sharp morning

rays onto the mountains like some kind of spectacular, dramatic light show. The furthest, highest peaks west of Durango were illuminated first, their rocky, regal outlines pristine against a brightening blue sky. Then the sun's rays continued downward, successively brightening each layer of hills nearer to town—from the hulking peak with its summit like a ship in profile, to the range of flatter ridges with their shrub- and evergreen-covered slopes—until I watched its light play on the cleft of hills leading to the Kendalls' ranch and Twilight Mesa, touching a far rocky cornice in tantalizing display.

My heart caught in my throat for a moment. Below me the tracks were bustling with workers in blue overalls. The hasty activity there, combined with the widening scope of the rising sun, conveyed to me an undeniable sense of promise.

I turned. My jewel case was still open on the bureau top, and I did not know who had taken my gold doubloon or why, but in the fresh morning light its theft did not seem as frightening or as sinister as it had the night before. I no longer harbored suspicions that anyone employed by the hotel had taken it; indeed, some instinct told me that whoever had taken my doubloon—Julia, or Doran Hunt, or someone else I did not yet know—was somehow involved in what had brought me down here. And the same instinct told me that if I remained quiet about it, I would eventually learn who had taken the doubloon—and why.

I quickly dressed and replaced my parents' things in the jewel case before tucking it away in the bureau drawer, taking no pains to hide it. After all, I thought with a twist of irony, had not its most valuable object already been taken? Impulsively, I reached for the object I had left out on the bureau—my amulet—and slipped it into a side pocket of my skirt.

As I reached the lobby, the ever-dapper front desk clerk beamed at me, then turned a concerned expression on a portly middle-aged gentleman in a bulging waistcoat who was waving a gold pocket watch indignantly in the air. The aroma of freshly baked biscuits and frying bacon emerging from the dining room was nearly irresistible; as I crossed the lobby, I saw a sleepy-eyed porter, who was pulling on his red-and-gold uniform jacket, stretch his mouth into an enormous yawn and stuff what appeared to be a buttered biscuit in one pocket. He grinned at me sheepishly as I passed him to open the great front door of the hotel and step outside.

The sun was now strong and high in a sky that curved overhead in a deep blue arc. Its rays warmed the hotel's chiseled stone steps and the brass rail under my hand and gave the rough brick on the front of the building a rosy glow.

For a moment I paused on the top step, raising my face to the sun's heat and soaking in its warmth like the lazy gray cat that lay curled on the walk below. The street before me bustled and clattered with wagons and buggies, and the hotel's coach, already full with passengers and luggage; the town's cable car clacked by, and down the road I saw merchants in their long white aprons and striped shirts opening the front doors of their shops to put out their wares and sweep off their portion of the wooden sidewalk.

The scene was much more rustic and homely than any in Denver, and yet I felt almost as if I were standing in front of the *Crier* office on a busy Monday morning. There was the same sense of industry, of purpose, of business ready to be transacted.

And there was something else. Pausing there, the hotel's brass rail still warm under my palm, I felt pass over me one of those uncanny sensations that most everyone experiences in life at one time or another—the curious, familiar feeling that what is happening right then has already happened exactly the same way sometime before.

I felt the hairs at the back of my neck prickle. I *had* experienced this moment before. Not long ago I had stood like this in front of a building, watching passing wagons in the road and growing aware, only gradually, of someone standing on the opposite side, very still, watching and waiting. A tall, lithe figure with a deeply tanned face.

I was grateful for the quick feeling of anger that swept through me then, for it gave me a quick, responsive energy—energy that impelled me down the last few steps to the sidewalk, out among the snorting horses and rattling conveyances of traffic and across the road to the opposite wooden walk.

My face was flushed when I reached the man. He stood with his hands plunged deep into the pockets of his denim trousers, lounging against the side of a one-story wooden building. As I dropped my skirts and faced him, I felt my chin jut ridiculously forward.

But as the man slowly straightened and turned the full force of his green gaze on me, I found I could not speak. He stood so very near; I could see the curled wisps of hair on the side of his neck where his collar bowed out. My heart began to beat irregularly.

"Good morning, Miss Loring," he said. "Were you about to say something?"

When I had first seen the man standing here across the street, waiting and watching me so blatantly, I had felt my temper flare. My intention had been to confront the man as openly as he had stared at me, to demand some kind of explanation from him once and for all. It was obvious that he was interested in me for some reason, and I wanted to know why.

But now, standing only feet away from Doran Hunt, I found that I could hardly utter a word.

"I was just going to say . . . that it seems I have seen you like . . . like this before," I finally said.

"Oh? And how is that?" Doran's voice was deep, and tinged with a kind of amused curiosity, his face lifted in that characteristic elfin expression I had seen at the exhibition. He shifted from one foot to the other and I caught the faint smell of woodsmoke again, as well as a more elusive, spicy scent I could not identify. His face seemed very close; I saw fine lines splayed out in the tanned skin at the corners of his eyes. I remembered the day before, when he had looked at me after learning about his horse, and for an instant I thought I saw a glimmer of the same emotion I had seen then, far, far back in those green eyes. My mouth went dry.

"Across a busy road, I mean," I replied. I wet my lips. Something changed in Doran's face, and then his brows raised in question. "Watching me."

Doran's brows arched further, and his lips curved at the corners as he regarded me in silence. I felt the damning heat of a blush burn my cheeks, and then suddenly, blessedly, I was angry again.

"Oh come now! You surely know what I mean. I saw you. I saw you many times. Watching me, following me in Denver. And now you are here, watching me again." I paused, forcing myself to face his probing glance. "What is it you want, Mr. Hunt? You have never answered that question to my satisfaction. I do not understand why you were so determined that I travel down here, and I have resigned myself to the fact that, for reasons I cannot fathom, you are interested in me. But I will not allow you to interfere in my life further, Mr. Hunt. My privacy is very important to me. What did you want last night when—" Just in time, I bit off my words.

"Last night?" Straightening to his full height, Doran narrowed his eyes slightly. Then his expression changed and deepened even more, and I felt something tighten in my chest. I noticed that his hand went deeper into the pocket of his trousers.

"Last night," he repeated. "I hope you had a most restful sleep." Doran's voice was pitched lower than before, his eyes more intent. I saw him hesitate, and then, as if drawn against his will, he pulled his right hand from his pocket and reached forth suddenly to brush a tendril of hair off my cheek. I drew in my breath. Doran's fingers were blunt and his touch abrupt and awkward, but the gesture was so gentle, so unlike the man I'd seen so far, that I stiffened and glanced at him in surprise.

And then it was there, in his eyes—the look, the vulnerability I had seen the day before—but only for an instant. When Doran saw my reaction, he let his hand drop as abruptly as it had reached out, and I felt only a faint, hot tingling along the skin of my cheek where his fingers had brushed.

"Yes, I hope that you had a good sleep last night because today you have a long, arduous trip ahead of you." Doran's voice was impassive as he went on, and he dug both his hands back into his pockets and turned away from me slightly to stare across the road at the hotel. "As soon as you and Miss Hastings are ready, I will take you to the Kendalls' ranch. I have hired out a buggy large enough for the three of us."

"You obviously listen very poorly, Mr. Hunt," I said, a quick anger beginning to stir again. "I recall telling you just yesterday that my plans are to remain here in Durango for the next several weeks, not at the ranch. In a few days, when I am more settled and Will Kendall returns from Denver, I will hire my own buggy, and—"

"That's impossible." Doran's voice was direct as he turned to look at me again. "It is a long and fairly difficult trip to the ranch. You couldn't possibly manage it on your own." He paused. "And, if you were raised with any manners at all, you would know that you can't refuse the Kendalls' invitation. I am sure that Will has already sent word down that you will be coming. To refuse his family's hospitality now would be more than rude and offensive—it would be an affront to their pride. The Kendalls don't make such invitations lightly. Surely you can see that." He paused again, his brows raised slightly. "Or are you one to let your own pride prevent you from considering the feelings of others?"

Doran's words found their mark. I thought of Will Kendall, excited and eager that I stay with his family. Had I indeed, in my own determination and self-minded objectives, neglected my manners and common consideration of the Kendalls? Yet before I could speak, a voice rang out.

"Heather! Oh, Heather! And Mr. Hunt! You *are* here. How wonderful! Have you come to rescue two poor damsels in distress?"

Doran and I both turned to see Julia standing on the hotel's front steps, waving one of her white, lace-trimmed handkerchiefs in our direction. Dressed in a rose-colored morning dress and magenta mantle trimmed with taffeta, she looked like a rare, hothouse flower in the wilderness.

"Oh *do* come over here!" she cried. "I most sorely need some assistance. These porters are mere *boys!* They have no notion of the proper way to handle my bags. I—oh!"

Julia emitted what could only be described as a squeal as the young porter I had seen earlier, emerging from the hotel with her luggage, fumbled the collection of bags clutched precariously in his arms. He made a desperate but ineffective grab at a tumbling hatbox, and Julia's squeal turned into a shriek as it bounced down the steps, onto the wooden sidewalk, and into the dirt road below, where it was narrowly missed by a passing cart's heavy wheel.

Moving with surprising swiftness, Doran darted from my side and across the road in seconds. In one graceful swoop, he rescued Julia's hatbox and returned it to the pile of bags the sweating porter had deposited on the sidewalk. He was already addressing Julia by the time I could maneuver through traffic to reach them.

"Why, whatever were you doing over there, Mr. Hunt?" Julia was saying to Doran as I joined them. She had one white-gloved hand set prettily on one hip and her head tilted to the side so that the pleated taffeta fans on her straw hat slanted as coquettishly as her speculative blue eyes. "I would think that surely a man of your caliber, Mr. Hunt—a man of the true West—would act more aggressively. I would think that a man like you, sir, would have come into the hotel to find us."

"Why, Miss Hastings!" Doran's dark brows were raised in a surprisingly boyish expression. "Do you think me so unrefined? Surely you realize that a gentleman—whatever his background—would never dare come into a hotel like the Strater searching for a lady."

As Doran returned Julia's smile and sparring words, I could fairly feel the sparks that leapt between them. But the next instant, with a sweep of his gaze, Doran included me in their exchange. "I am sure Miss Loring understands that. Certainly *you* don't believe a gentleman like me would come searching in a hotel for Miss Hastings—or for you."

His eyes fairly glittered with challenge, and the corners of his mouth twisted again in . . . what? Amusement? Derision?

I met his eyes squarely. "Perhaps not, Mr. Hunt. That is, if one is, indeed, a true gentleman. I hardly know in your case as we've only just met." I paused. "However, I do know that my *cousin* was so kind as to come into the Strater asking after my accommodations last night. It was unfortunate, but he had to depart rather hurriedly soon after. As my cousin ascertained, however, my room was quite comfortable. I daresay *he* was quite the gentleman. But then I know him—he is my cousin, you understand."

"Ah, yes. Your cousin." The expression in Doran's eyes did not change, but his mouth curved into a smile that quite opened up his face and made it appear boyishly young again. He regarded me with a kind of approbation that I had not seen on his face before.

"Cousin?" Sharp-eyed, Julia took in the exchange between Doran and me. "Why Heather, you didn't mention a cousin in town."

"It's of no matter." Smoothly, Doran bent to pick up one of Julia's portmanteaus. "I'm here to look after you two now, am I not? But I'm afraid we will not be able to take all your luggage over in the buggy, Miss Hastings. I'll load only this and another of your bags for now, as well as one or two of Miss Loring's, and then leave word for Will to bring the rest when he arrives."

"But . . . but . . ." Julia began.

"I am afraid you really have no choice. Now you ladies wait here. I'll load this on and then bring the buggy around for the rest of your bags—and for you."

Doran suddenly grinned at us, then turned and sprinted across the road, still carrying Julia's portmanteau. It was a display of masculine grace and prowess lost on neither of us. But for whose benefit was the display, I wondered—mine or Julia's?

It took Doran only a few moments to load Julia's bag and maneuver the buggy, pulled by two large horses, alongside the curb before us. But when Doran swung down and I saw the luggage he began loading into the rear, I let out a short cry.

"Wait! Those bags are mine. I do not know how they became mixed up with Julia's, but I cannot allow you to—"

"There has been no mistake." Julia turned to me, her blue eyes cool and steady. "I told you last evening I could not bear you staying here in Durango all alone. I ordered the porter to bring your bags down with mine." Her voice at once honeyed and intimate, Julia leaned closer to curve a placating hand on my arms. "We are dear, dear friends now, Heather. You simply *must* come with me to the ranch. We have so much to share this summer."

"Don't worry, she's coming." Throwing the last of the luggage onto the buggy's rear platform with a thud, Doran turned to us. Perspiration gleamed on the skin of his chest, exposed by his open collar, and on the creases of his neck where his hair curled slightly in back. "That is, if she has decided she has any manners at all."

Doran was smiling at me again, as if daring me to rise to his bait.

"All right," I said, my voice cool. "But I do not plan to stay long, perhaps not even overnight. It will be my decision how long I plan to remain."

As Doran helped me onto the buggy's leather seat, I took great care arranging my skirts and settling myself. But I could not miss Doran's knowing look and Julia's triumphant, smug smile. I did not care. By then, I had decided that perhaps it was best if I did accompany them, if only to discover just why they both seemed so adamant that I go—and, perhaps, to discover if either of them had taken my gold doubloon.

Doran helped Julia up next to me, secured the harnesses, then came around on the other side of the buggy. But then, glancing at me, his brows drew together in a quick frown and he went around back again to our bags. Startled, I saw him open my valise and begin to rummage quite unceremoniously through it.

"What are you doing? That's my bag!"

"I know." Clapping my valise shut, Doran came around the side of the buggy again, and I saw that he carried my fur cape. With a quick motion, he draped it across my shoulders, and for a moment, I felt the weight of his long, muscular arm across my back.

"You would never have been warm enough in that light suit," he said, picking up the buggy's reins. "It may be July, but we'll be climbing to an even higher elevation before we drop down into Jackson Valley later in the day."

I adjusted the fur cape on my shoulders, sur-

prised by the thoughtfulness of Doran's gesture.
I had no more time to ponder it, however, for at
that moment Doran lifted his arms and flicked
the reins, sending the horses trotting forward.
At the sudden movement I reached down to
grasp the edge of the seat and felt the warmth
and hard strength of Doran's torso, hip, and leg
press against me. It was a tight fit, bunched together on the buggy seat; at the same time that
I felt Doran's leg muscle flexing as he propped
his boot in the front to brace himself, Julia's
light lilac fragrance wound about me.

Then we were off and jouncing down Main
Avenue, and it was all I could do to maintain
my place on the seat. Soon we swept around a
bend, crossed a narrow bridge above the River
of Lost Souls and entered the cleft of hills I had
seen from my hotel window. Green and shaggy,
the slopes climbed steeply around us as the
buggy was swallowed up in the new terrain.
The road was fairly narrow and of a rough
grade; the only sounds in the still morning air
were the pop and snap of the horses' harnesses,
the thud-thud of their hooves on the dirt road,
and the creaks and clinks of the buggy beneath
us. We were all silent as we rode along, as if
caught up in a spell woven by the magnificent
setting and the clear, crisp morning.

"This is Wildcat Canyon," Doran said as he
swung the team left a few miles beyond town.
"We climb through it before dropping down into
the more arid country where the Kendalls live."

As Doran spoke, we entered the canyon and
the sun disappeared behind the steep, pine-clad
slopes that rose sharply around us. I shivered and

pulled my fur cape more tightly about my shoulders, glad for Doran's foresight. I still felt the hard length of him beside me, shifting slightly as he guided the team, and a tingling, responsive warmth down that side of my body. The smooth bones of the amulet pressed against my thigh.

Could Doran feel the amulet as well? I wondered, sitting so close beside me? Although Julia was well padded with her heavy mantle and layers of skirts, she provided little warmth herself. She sat motionless and aloof, her lilac perfume mingling with Doran's indefinable male aroma and the numerous scents of the expansive wilderness around us—evergreen, wildflowers, sage, and fresh clean air. Birds joined in, warbling and twittering all around us, waking to the new day.

"This was all Indian land once," Doran commented. "There were no trains, no roads, no buggies like this. Just wilderness." He gestured toward the aspens lining the slope to our right, their white trunks slender and graceful, their leaves like green raindrops rustling and shimmering in the breeze.

"Indians? Do you mean there are Indians around here?" It seemed that all at once Julia sprung to life, sitting up with sudden alertness as she peered rather fearfully about.

Doran laughed. "No, I'm afraid all the Indians are living on reservations now." He paused. "Actually, the Indians in this area—the Utes—weren't that hostile until their way of life was threatened. The Spaniards came first—missionaries looking for converts and explorers looking for gold. Then it was the prospectors, scrounging for gold and silver, and other explorers who wanted to photograph or survey or just pass through. It wasn't long after that that the ranchers and settlers came to farm and cultivate whatever land they could find."

As Doran spoke, we came out of the canyon suddenly and over a steep hill into a lush, grassy area lit by the sun. It was thickly bordered by dark green pines and patched here and there with small farms.

"I have nothing against farmers and settlers, of course," Doran went on. "The Kendalls themselves are among the best in the area. They are an excellent, honest, hardworking family. It's just that . . ."

Tilting his chin and turning slightly in the seat, Doran scanned the horizon of piñon- and juniper-covered hills in the distance. He let the reins go slack in his hands a moment, and when he continued his voice sounded far away. "There are places in this region that are still untouched, un-explored, just the way they were centuries ago—the way the land has always been. You find them sometimes. You . . . stumble on them by accident."

Doran lapsed into silence for a moment, and then, appearing to come back to the present, gave a quick flip of his wrist and snapped the reins again.

To my left, the sky was a deep blue, but as I turned slightly in my seat to look back over my shoulder, the sky dimmed to a near ivory along the ranges of mountains falling away behind us. My heart gave a little jump. Back there, nestled in the midst of those mountains, was Durango—hardly as familiar to me as Denver but nevertheless more known than the place into which I was now journeying. As fast as the straining horses could carry me, I was entering into a part of the country for which, I realized, I had no measure. It seemed that with every step they took, I left Denver—and St. Louis—further and further behind.

As we reached the crest of the hill, I felt Julia stir restlessly beside me.

"Those prospectors you mentioned," she said, leaning forward slightly to peer around me at Doran. "Did they find any of that gold they were looking for around here?"

I stiffened. Julia was interested in gold? Had she indeed taken the doubloon? But if she had, why would she now be speaking so openly on the subject?

Doran laughed at her question. "Hardly. Most of the area's valuable ore has been found in the San Juan Mountains north of Durango. Some in New Mexico, too, and in other parts of the state." He gestured vaguely behind us. "We leave the mountains behind here. The area we're going into is another world entirely."

Within a few miles, his words proved true. The high terrain begin to melt into gently rolling hills covered with low green growth for as far as the eye could see. The land before us was much more dry and decidedly less dramatic than the mountain scenery near Durango, but as we continued on in silence, I felt its expansiveness was almost a relief. It seemed the land itself went on forever in muted grays and greens and browns; scanning the vistas, I felt a great sense of freedom—and at the same time an odd loneliness. Perhaps I sensed even then what a profound price that terrain's wildness might exact.

"I must say this part of the trip is hardly attractive." Julia sniffed and shifted again restlessly beside me. "I do hope where we are going is more beautiful."

After a brief glance at Julia, Doran was silent a moment. "It depends, I suppose, on how you define beauty," he finally said, an odd tone to his voice. "You will see that the land around Twilight Mesa is not outwardly pretty. But it has its own kind of beauty, and one must learn to cultivate a taste for its brand of attractiveness. So much of what this land has to offer is subtle, hidden below the surface."

"And, as a man, you do abhor superficiality." Julia's tone, although most likely meant to be light, was unexpectedly sharp, and the look her blue eyes shot Doran was shrewdly challenging.

For an instant Doran looked surprised, then his eyes narrowed. "No, I don't abhor superficiality, as you so generalize, Miss Hastings." Still holding fast the reins, he looked past me at Julia. Again, I felt that strange, exclusive tension between them. "I simply find it boring. Beauty that has no substance does not earn my respect."

"Ah." Her eyes still sharp, Julia tilted her head so that her dark curls bobbed against her cheek. "You *are* a true man of the West then. A man who likes challenge. A man who wants to conquer the wilderness." Julia regarded Doran appraisingly another moment and then, in a tone poisonously direct but coated with syrupy sweetness, she added, "That goal is shared by so *many* men from the East, is it not? Charming, of course, but rather trite, in a way, I should think."

I felt rather than saw Doran's muscles stiffen beside me. When I glanced at him, his jaw was set and his features hard.

"Oh, don't misunderstand me," Julia went on in the same honeyed tones. "I do so admire a man who likes a challenge. Once such a man conquers the land, however, he must then turn his many talents to other things that interest him. Such as . . . well, *women*, for example." Julia paused for effect, then tilted her head again and looked sweetly at Doran. "Tell me, Mr. Hunt, do you prefer your women with many layers as well?"

Julia's words, cloaked as they were in innuendo, shocked me, and the look that passed between her and Doran was so charged I could feel its intensity crackling in the air. Trapped between them, I wished with all my heart that I were not.

And then something happened that mortifies me to this day. Within my empty stomach, I felt a low, deep rumbling begin, growing in intensity until it resounded forth into the charged silence of the buggy.

"What was that?" Startled, Doran's eyes snapped toward me. Immediately the tension between Doran and Julia broke, dissolving in such an absurd way that I felt a dark red flush spread rapidly up my neck and across my cheeks.

"Are you hungry?" Doran asked, still looking startled.

"No, of course not. It's just . . ." As if to belie my words, my stomach rumbled again. "I just

. . . I neglected to eat breakfast this morning, and then last night I—"

"Here." Reaching into a side pocket of the heavy jacket he had bunched behind him in the buggy seat, Doran withdrew a paper-wrapped bundle. Inside was a large slab of white cheese and a hunk of rye bread, which he handed to me. His features were perfectly even and serious, but in his eyes I detected the beginnings of a gleam. Miserably, I reached for his bundle of food, not daring to glance toward Julia, whose smirk I could fairly feel fixed on my turned head.

As I took the bread and cheese from Doran's hand, our fingers touched. It was just as it had been at Mrs. Compton's dinner party—I felt an immediate spark, a transference of his warmth to my body. Glancing up, I saw Doran's eyes darken; for an instant he leaned closer to me and I felt the brush of his body against mine, smelled his elusive scent, and saw the line of his lips open ever so slightly. He looked at me again, and then, abruptly, sat back on the leather seat and jerked on the reins, sending the horses into a trot.

"Go ahead, eat it." Doran's words were blunt, but not hard. "We still have at least ten miles to go before we reach the ranch. I expect Sarah Kendall will give you one of her huge meals there, but you'll not see any more food until then." He hesitated a moment, glancing at me briefly. "I apologize for not thinking of lunch," he added. "I rarely eat on the road myself. That food is leftover from yesterday, I'm afraid. I hope the bread is not too stale."

I shook my head, mortified at how quickly I had begun to nibble at the food but too hungry to stop. I was grateful that Doran said no more and that he did not offer any of the food to Julia; at least I was spared the scalding refusal she would no doubt have offered, aimed insultingly at my own "unladylike" behavior.

We rode on in silence. The tension between Julia and Doran may have lessened temporarily, but I still felt it hovering in the air. We passed through more open country covered with rolling hills, and at last started up a long steady incline that, Doran said, would lead into the valley in which the Kendalls had built their ranch.

After we reached the crest of the hill and began descending toward a broad, cultivated valley dotted with farms, ranches, and a small settlement, I noticed mountains and low hills bordering the valley to the north and east. To the southwest, however, rising like a great fortress, was a steep, massive plateau, its sides thickly covered with brush and its abrupt, flat-topped surface crowned with a jutting sandstone cornice.

"That's it," Doran said. "That's Twilight Mesa."

The breath stilled in my chest. I had expected to feel chilled by my first sight of the mesa—filled with the trepidation I had experienced ever since Denver. But what I felt now was entirely different and quite unexpected.

I felt, looking at Twilight Mesa for the first time, an odd sense of familiarity, as if somewhere deep inside I had always carried a sense of it with me, an image. But how could that be?

I shifted on the seat and saw that Doran was watching me. "That is only the north end of the mesa, actually," he said. "Behind that abutment and the cliff that runs alongside it is an enormous tableland. It is rather difficult to describe. You see, Twilight Mesa is not simply one, flat-topped plateau but a series of high tablelands and intersecting canyons. It spreads out like a great hand—the mesa tops are like outstretched fingers and the canyons form the large gaps in between. That north rim rises over fifteen hundred feet up from the valley and runs about fifteen miles along it. The mesa itself is about ten miles by fifty miles and within it . . . Well, you'll just have to see it yourself. There are no adequate words to describe the kind of country that makes up Twilight Mesa."

Doran stared at the cliffs as if he, too, were seeing Twilight Mesa for the first time. When he went on, his voice was low. "The Indians are afraid of the mesa, you know. They believe it is a sacred place of the dead, disturbed only at a great—and dangerous—price." Doran was silent a moment. "And it is sacred, in a way," he said, as if speaking no longer to Julia and me, but almost to himself. "It's another world, there among those cliffs. There is something very special hidden there, preserved in time, never disturbed. It's full of secrets, things no one has ever known or seen before. Myths and superstitions about Twilight Mesa have persisted for centuries."

Now I did feel a chill, curling snakelike down my spine, and a quick sense of fear that set my heart thudding in my breast.

What *did* lie within that land of desolate canyons and impervious cliffs Doran had just described? My hand went instinctively to the amulet in my pocket. Had it really come from somewhere beyond those massive rocks? And what of the gold doubloon? The stranger who arrived that hot summer night sixteen years ago had carried both objects with him to St. Louis. But where had he gotten them? Who else knew about them? And why—*why*—had he given them to me?

I stared at the massive, silent mesa, knowing that something had begun there many years ago, setting into motion the inexorable chain of events that had finally culminated in this moment, here, now, as I sat viewing it for the first time. I was so close now, even from this distance, so close to the answers it seemed I had been seeking all my life.

"Let's be off then," Doran said, picking up the reins in his hand and sending the horses off down the road. "The Kendalls will be expecting us."

As the buggy jerked forward and I gripped the seat for balance, a sudden thought flashed through my mind.

Doran had told us of the legendary danger of even setting foot on the mesa. Had the stranger given me the amulet, then, to lead me to Twilight Mesa—or to protect me once I arrived?

Chapter Five

✦✦✦✦✦

"THIS IS JACKSON." Doran slowed the horses to a walk as we started down the dusty main street of the settlement we had seen from the crest of the hill. It was made up of a smattering of one- and two-story frame buildings, a few squat houses, and a small church, its spire rising up as if to pierce the brilliant blue sky overhead. A few townspeople stared at us curiously as the buggy passed by. A beefy merchant in shirtsleeves and apron lounged outside his general store, soaking up the afternoon sun, while several barefoot children played in the street nearby; a few dusty-looking cowboys in battered hats and bandannas tied about their necks sat outside one of the town's seedier looking drinking establishments with their boots propped upon a wooden rail.

"We won't stop here," said Doran. His smile widened as we progressed down the street. Obviously, he enjoyed escorting two attractive women through this sleepy town. "The ranch is just three miles beyond town. We'll go on there now."

Before long, we noticed a small cluster of buildings about half a mile away, situated on a small rise above the nearest bend in the river. As we drew closer, I saw there were three or four barns and sheds and a few other outbuildings I could not identify—all circling a long, low rambling ranch house set in a shady grove of cottonwoods. To the west, toward Twilight Mesa, there were several corrals—bordered by neat, white fences—where horses and livestock moved about, pawing and snuffling at the ground.

"The Kendalls were one of the first families to settle in this valley," Doran said. "Old Nate and Sarah Kendall come from Quaker stock, and with four strapping sons, it didn't take long for them to turn their ranch into one of the finest in the area."

In the yard beyond the ranch house I could see chickens clucking and pecking at the ground. A rather thickset dark man with a colored band about his head was chopping firewood nearby. He wore a light blue denim shirt and some kind of silver bracelet on his wrist; as his arms rose and fell with each stroke, the shiny metal of his bracelet caught and reflected the rays of the afternoon sun.

A few moments later, we drove into the yard, sending the flock of chickens scattering in a squawking mass of dust. The man chopping firewood looked up—for an instant I saw his dark face, his broad, blunt nose, and sharp cheekbones—and then set down his ax and disappeared around one of the nearby barns.

"Well, here we are." Pulling up on the reins, Doran brought the buggy to a halt and jumped out.

I sat there on the seat for a moment. After riding such a distance, the sudden stop set my ears to ringing and left me curiously disjointed. Although the buggy itself was still, I had the sensation that part of me was still moving. The sun slanted through the shimmering mass of green cottonwood branches, and I raised a hand to shield my eyes as Doran reached up to help me down.

I felt his hands at my waist first, spanning it

with ease as he lifted me from the buggy's
wooden platform. And his hands remained about
my waist even when my feet had touched the
ground and I stood at his side, looking up at him.
I did not know whether the sudden weakness I
felt then in my knees was due to six cramped
hours in the buggy or the warm, firm sensation of
Doran Hunt's fingers through the thin fabric of
my suit.

"Well! You're here!"

At the abrupt bang of a wooden door behind
us, Doran and I turned toward the ranch house,
and Doran dropped his hands to his side. I caught
a glimpse of Julia still sitting in the buggy, her
blue eyes sharp and shrewd, and knew right away
she had watched everything that had passed between Doran and me in that brief moment.

My attention was soon taken up by the robust,
rather imposing figure starting down the wooden
plank walkway from the ranch house toward us.
Her graying hair was wrapped in thick braids
about her head, and she wore a white apron tied
about her stout form.

She was wiping large, flour-coated hands on
the apron as she reached us. "Thank you,
Doran," she said, smiling broadly. "I was hoping
you might bring the girls with you! I would've
sent one of the boys, but they've all gone off on
another of their trips to the mesa. I was just thinking I might have to take the wagon to Durango
myself tomorrow, but it looks like you beat me to
it and saved me a trip."

The woman's keen gray eyes swept over us,
narrowed slightly, and finally seemed to soften

somewhat. She pursed her lips and nodded once, as if satisfied.

"I'm here to tell you, it'll be darned good to have some female company around here! Well, come on, Doran. Get those bags out of the back. We can't have these ladies out in the sun all day, now can we? You girls must be sick and tired of that buggy. Come on inside. I'll show you to your rooms. Dinner isn't for another few hours. You can rest all you want until then. Just follow me."

Without waiting for a reply, the woman turned briskly and started back to the house, her shoulders staunch and square under a faded calico blouse, her long work skirt brushing the wooden walk.

"I'm Mrs. Kendall, by the way," she called back over her shoulder. "But you girls can call me Sarah."

Julia and I exchanged a glance, and I saw Doran smile. Then, as if compelled by the force of the woman's personality—or perhaps the maternal authority she so naturally seemed to assume—we wasted little time obeying her directions.

The ranch house itself was simple and unimposing. The far eastern wing seemed to be an old log cabin—the first building on the homestead, I learned later, built by Nate Kendall and his sons years ago. The rest of the house had obviously been built more recently, erected with smooth wooden boards and fronted by a long wooden porch which was shaded by a shingled overhang. The overall feeling of the house, I thought, was one of efficient, well-planned space.

"Here now," said Mrs. Kendall, waiting for us

just inside the wooden front door. "You girls come on in and get out of that sun. I don't know what Doran was thinking of, letting you both sit and bake in that open buggy all day. Well, it has that top, of course, but even so. . . . Might have helped to have an umbrella or parasol or something of that sort. Don't use one myself, but then my tough old skin is used to this dry weather and sun. We have to break city skin like yours in more easy." Mrs. Kendall smiled, and as if to prove her words, a sun-roughened network of lines crinkled at the corners of her clear gray eyes.

"Come on, now. Follow me. I'll take you to your rooms. Might be a squeeze, but I think we can manage to give you each one of your own. It's lucky we don't have any other visitors right now. A month or two ago, we had so many the boys had to sleep out in the barn."

"Oh, dear," I said. "Mrs. Kendall, please. I had initially planned on staying in Durango, and if that would be simpler . . . I certainly do not want to inconvenience you in any way. . . ."

At my words Mrs. Kendall stopped abruptly and fixed her gaze on me. "Now I won't hear any of that kind of talk in this house! Inconvenience indeed! Why, we've been looking forward to your visit ever since Will sent us word. I got everything all set up. Just don't you mind what I say when I jabber like that. I can go on and on sometimes, just ask one of the boys. Doesn't mean a thing. You have to get used to me. When I let everything spout out like that, I don't think about how it will land on somebody else's ear. I didn't mean that we *minded* having visitors, Miss Loring. That week the boys slept in the barn was one of the best times they ever had!"

With that, Mrs. Kendall sallied forth into the main part of the house with all the stolid dignity and bulk of a battleship. Glancing at Julia, I saw that her mouth was crimped in a derisive smile.

The first room we passed, fairly large and surprisingly dim for the time of day, was obviously a parlor, with its conventional clutter of knickknacks and heavy furniture; the second was smaller and furnished only sparsely with handmade pieces. Both, however, had been decorated with the simple, homey touches of rather rustic-looking needlework and bunches of wildflowers set here and there in thick clay pitchers. Past the front rooms and to the left was a narrow hallway lined with closed doors. Mrs. Kendall stopped before the first two.

"The accommodations here may not be what you'd find in a hotel, but they're the best we got." Reaching forward, Mrs. Kendall swung both doors open simultaneously with a flourish.

The rooms were nearly identical—small and furnished simply with low, narrow beds, handmade wooden dressers and chairs, wardrobes, and a square table bearing a large blue-and-white-painted pitcher and bowl for washing. There was also a large fireplace in each room and a bright scarlet blanket folded carefully across the bottom of each bed.

The most striking feature in each room, however, was the carpeting laid across the wooden floor. It was of the most extraordinary thing I had ever seen—strips of blue denim fabric sewn carefully together and stretched over some kind of padding. As I crossed the threshhold of the first room and stepped inside, the denim was thick and springy beneath my boots.

"That's straw there under the carpeting," Mrs. Kendall explained as she and Julia followed me into the room. "Gives the room some warmth in the cold months. One visitor we had last spring said it felt just like walking on a mossy river-bank."

Julia made a sound beside me, and I saw that her smile had turned into an open smirk. This time Mrs. Kendall saw it as well.

"Like I told you, nothing fancy here," she said, bending to smooth the folded, unwrinkled blanket at the end of the bed. "When you live on a ranch like this one, you make do with what you have, and you stick with what works. Them's corn-husk mattresses on the beds—I made 'em myself. I got spare Indian blankets, too. Throw them on the beds at night if you get cold or on the floor in the morning. Helps to take the chill off your bare feet until you get into your clothes. Course, summertime is pretty warm around here, but the nights and mornings still have some chill to them. I hope you girls brought nighties nice and warm. Now my boys used to sleep in their long underwear all the time, it seemed like, so I didn't have to worry about them none—"

At the expression of distaste on Julia's face, Mrs. Kendall bit off her next words.

"Well," she continued, her lips pursed, "there's water fresh poured for washing in those pitchers. I'll just leave you girls alone for a bit. Supper's at

six, so you both get a good rest and we'll all have
us a talk later and get better acquainted. Most of
the boys will be here, but I believe, Miss Hastings,
that your Mr. Webb said he wouldn't be ridin' in
until tomorrow. Don't know about Doran—never
can tell what his plans will be." Mrs. Kendall
paused. "And of course, Mr. Kendall will sup
with us."

This final remark was spoken with such a sense
of affection, respect and pride for her husband
that I smiled at Mrs. Kendall, warmed inside. But
I felt a quick stab of anger at the look I saw on
Julia's face and moved slightly so that Mrs. Kendall would not see it. I was both embarrassed and
appalled at the manners of this companion I
would never have chosen myself.

"Well, I got bread dough rising in the kitchen.
It's probably all over my tabletop by now. You get
a good rest before supper, you hear? I'll just have
Doran Hunt bring—"

As she spoke, Mrs. Kendall stepped out the
door of my room and stumbled into a row of bags
lined up neatly in the hall.

"Why, that rascal! Quiet as a cat, that one, and
just as sly. Didn't I tell you? Must have slipped in
here while we were talking. Never heard a
sound." She chuckled. "Can't keep my finger on
that one."

Shaking her head, Mrs. Kendall peered sharply
down the hall. Then, with a strength that surprised me, she bent and hefted Julia's two largest
bags. "Now, where do these go?" she asked. Julia
gestured toward the adjacent room, and Mrs.
Kendall deposited them within without cere-

mony, then returned to the hall to gather up and carry the remaining bags into our respective rooms.

At our rather startled looks, Mrs. Kendall straightened from her task and stood in the hall with large hands planted on the ample width of her hips.

"I didn't raise four boys for nothing!" she said with another of her broad smiles. Then her voice softened. "But, like I said before, it'll be nice having some female talk around here for a change. Work me like a slave, those boys do, with hardly a word of thanks or a how-do-you-do before they're off in the morning doing chores. They just don't respect me, that's what it is. . . ."

Starting back toward the kitchen, Mrs. Kendall waved her hand over her shoulder at us with an abstracted air, her words trailing off as she went. When she had disappeared around the corner, Julia turned to me with a pained look.

"These rooms! Prescott never warned me, never even intimated to me that this place would be so, so . . . crude. I *never*, simply never, would put up with all of this if not for the sake of my dear Prescott. I daren't tell Mama about any of what I have had to endure on my journey."

Julia's expression grew distant, her fine eyebrows drawing together in a frown, and then a gleam came into her eye. "But after Prescott and I are married and the summer is over and we have all we have worked for—" she broke off and looked at me as if suddenly realizing I was still beside her. She tilted her head and smiled sweetly at me.

Thinking of Prescott and their future together

seemed to have given her renewed energy, for the color came back to her cheeks and her eyes shone brightly. But she went on in an apologetic, wilting tone.

"I am *so* exhausted, Heather. Aren't you? I think I shall retire for that little rest Mrs. Kendall insisted on. If Prescott is riding over tomorrow, I must be prepared. It has been over three months since I've seen him. He has been working so hard, the poor dear, and I miss him so."

She stopped herself and looked at me, then clapped a hand to one cheek. "But, my heavens, here I go on and on about Prescott, and you, poor dear, aren't even engaged! How insensitive of me. I do forget how boring it must be when those of us who are in love go on and on about it to those who *aren't*."

Waving her hand in a gesture of farewell—or dismissal—Julia stepped out of my room and in seconds I heard the click of her door and the muffled rustlings of her movements in the next room.

Smiling ruefully, I closed my own door firmly and crossed the room to sit on the quilt-covered mattress. It rattled slightly with my weight, and I smiled, then frowned, thinking of Mrs. Kendall's expectant hospitality and Julia's unconcealed rudeness. It seemed, unfortunately, that Julia and I were destined to be thrown together at every turn that summer. But I certainly did not have to like or accept it. The accommodations Mrs. Kendall had provided seemed hospitable and generous to me—the clean cotton sheets and scarlet Indian blanket on the bed, the carefully swept carpeting, the water ready in its pitcher, and even the small glass jar of yellow primroses on the dresser.

Sighing, I reached my arms over my head in a long stretch, looking at my bags on the floor. The bed was comfortable and tempting, and for a moment I considered taking that well-advised rest. But my muscles were still stiff and my back sore from the long ride, and I knew I needed to move about to loosen the tautness in my body.

And so I set about unpacking once again. Oddly, I did not find it a nuisance. Instead, I felt an unexpected surge of energy as I opened my valise and other bags. And, as I had traveled fairly light, packing only the essentials, I had with me most everything I would need for the next few days. After shaking out my few rumpled suits, I looked at the items remaining in my bag. At the bottom of my valise, wrapped in a long sheet of muslin I had borrowed from Mrs. Gresham, was an item I had not unpacked at the hotel in Durango. I unwrapped it now and held it up before me.

My parents' wedding portrait. There was Mother, looking rather sober but quite lovely in her formal gown, and Father, distinguished in a frock coat and tie. They were not smiling, but in their eyes I saw the warmth I had often felt as a child, safe and secure in the home they had made for me. Gripping its frame, I peered at the portrait more closely, as if this preserved image of my parents could speak, could tell me what to do next, now that I was so near to Twilight Mesa.

But what could they tell me? Indeed, had my parents ever really been a part of the forces that had brought me here? I wondered. Where had they been, that night I'd met the strange man? It had always seemed, in my memory, that the stranger and I had been alone for those few moments in the yard, alone in our own private, concentrated, and intense little world. My parents were not with me there. They must have been in the house. Did they even know, then, that the stranger had arrived? Or . . . had he been leaving?

I tried yet again to recall the details of that night. Yes, it seemed the stranger *had* been leaving then, for my brother, Peter, followed him out into the yard, and I slipped out after them. . . .

My heart seemed to stop for one long moment. Peter had been there too. With the stranger. It was Peter's voice I had heard whispering to that man.

Never before had I remembered that. For years the image in my mind had only been of myself, hiding in the shelter of the lilac bushes, and then the stranger seeing me there, and pulling me aside. But I had also always remembered the stranger whispering to someone in a hazy, vague way. Why had I never conjectured about who that person might have been?

Because I had always known. Known it was Peter.

And before I could even ask myself why, I knew the answer. The memory was too painful. My mind had suppressed it along with everything else that might harm me. It had simply hurt too much to remember that the next day, after the fire, he had been lost to me. . . .

I did not want to start thinking of him again, hoping as I had all those years that he might come back. Peter, the older brother I had adored: tall, gangly, all angles and bones, with that lean, narrow face scowling in adolescent sullenness. How I had wished that he would turn that face in my direction with an expression that included me, invited me into his world! What had happened to him—that brother I had hardly known?

Looking down, I saw that my knuckles had gone white from gripping the frame on my parents' portrait. Their faces looked up at me, unsmiling and sober as ever, and for a moment it seemed as if the warmth had gone out of their eyes. They stared up at me unseeingly, without connection, without answers.

Perhaps they *were* involved in all of this, I thought suddenly. If Peter had been . . .

The sound of horses in the yard outside diverted my attention. As I bent to open my window, I plainly heard the squeak of saddle leather, the heavy thud of boots and packs dropped to the ground, and the loud exchange of good-natured male voices. Then I saw two figures emerge from around the side of the nearest barn.

They were cowboys—stubble faced and dressed in rough clothing coated with grime and dirt from the trail. Their hats were stained and battered, and they removed them as they approached the house, beating the wide, dusty brims against their leather leggings. One of the cowboys was rather stocky and the other much taller, square and big-boned.

I began to smile as I watched them cross the yard. They had Will's characteristic lope and a distinct family likeness.

Of course. The Kendall boys. The two brothers

disappeared into a far wing of the ranch house, and after a moment I saw three tired-looking horses amble into the ranch's far corral and head immediately for a large stack of hay. Then one more cowboy—his hair coarse and an unmistakable shade of angry red—emerged from around the barn and started toward the house as well.

Halfway there, however, he stopped and turned his head toward a nearby outbuilding. He paused a moment, head cocked as if listening to someone who had hailed him, and then he smiled broadly. It was, I noticed, nearly an exact replica of Will's expansive, easy grin. Then he shouted something, and his voice carried to me on the breeze.

"Yep! Five days in Twilight this time. Just got back. You missed a good trip. Found lots for the collection." He paused, as if listening again, then nodded his head. "Yep, we found a few bones in the trash heap of one dwelling. Two whole skeletons. One of the skulls wasn't in such good shape though. It was crushed. Don't know what got to it. It was pretty small too, like maybe it belonged to a little kid."

I jerked back from the window, my stomach constricting in sudden revulsion. Were these the kinds of secrets to which Doran had been alluding, secrets hidden in Twilight Mesa?

"What? Yeah, sure. All right. See you at supper." After pausing to listen one last time, the cowboy in the yard gave another big grin and touched the rim of his battered hat in a departing salute. Within a moment he, too, had disappeared, and as I glanced quickly back in his direction, I thought I saw a flash of faded blue. Had it been Doran Hunt, in the denim shirt he had worn that day?

Perhaps. But then perhaps it had just been my imagination.

Yet, if it had been Doran, could he have seen me watching at the window?

Drawing back, I dropped the curtain and scanned the room. Although my cramped legs craved a walk, I knew I would feel too uncomfortable setting off about the grounds of the ranch so soon. I could at least look about the house, though. Perhaps, I thought, I could even find Mrs. Kendall and help her in the kitchen.

As I closed the door behind me, no sound emerged from behind Julia's adjacent door. I imagined that by now she had become quite accustomed to the luxurious southern tradition of afternoon naps.

Indeed, the entire house was quiet and still. I wondered vaguely where the three clamorous brothers had gone; all the doors along the cool hallway were still closed shut.

Then I saw I had been mistaken. The very last door, at the end of the hallway, had been left slightly ajar. A narrow shaft of light angled out from its threshold into the dim hallway.

I stood very still a moment, my palms suddenly damp. I felt as I had earlier in Durango, when I had sensed Doran across the busy road, watching me. This moment, too, had happened before. There was something oddly familiar about the scene—the door at the end of the hallway open just a crack, the shaft of light beckoning with its hint of what lay beyond, waiting to be approached and discovered, and I drawn irresistibly toward it. . . .

"Well, don't just stand there gawkin', girl. Come on in."

The voice, old but hardly querulous, shot forth from the room like the crack of a bullet. I jumped as if struck, and then instinctively obeyed the force of the command.

"Glad you could make it, girl. It's been too dang quiet around here this afternoon. I was ailing for some company."

It took my eyes a few moments to adjust to the brightness of the warm, inviting room. A cheerful fire crackled in the huge stone fireplace, and several narrow bunks covered with the same colorful Indian blankets I had found in my room lined the adjacent wall. A few other items of handmade furniture were scattered about the room, as well as several shadowy paintings and photographs on the otherwise bare walls. It was warm in the room but surprisingly not hot from the fire although it was July, and I realized the walls were quite thick. I also realized the occupant of this room was sitting in a wicker rocking chair to the right of the hearth. His white hair, its outline almost luminous as it caught the fire's glow, was full and downy and contrasted with his lean face—the skin of which was tough and leathery but stretched tautly over the underlying, sharply jutting bones.

"Well, don't just stand there. Didn't I ask you to come in? What's the matter girl? Are you *afraid* of me?"

In the firelight, the old man's topaz eyes gleamed like gemstones. "Well, pull up a chair.

You must be that reporter Mrs. Kendall told me about. Come sit down here beside me. I have plenty I can tell you, if you're willing to listen."

The old man's laugh was not quite a cackle but something close to it, and I have to admit I shivered a bit as he gestured me forward. But as I drew closer to him and took a seat, I saw that beneath the speculative gleam in his eyes was a surprisingly warm expression of welcome and interest. I realized then that age itself had sharpened the man's features, making him appear much more intimidating and irascible than he really was. Indeed, as the leathery skin of his cheeks creased in a wide smile, I glimpsed the ghost of the Kendall boys' own open, good-looking features.

"I'm Old Mr. Kendall, if you haven't already guessed," he said, his gnarled hands gripping the edges of the Indian blanket on his lap as he leaned toward me. "Nathaniel's my given name, but I hear what they call me when they think I'm out of earshot. Don't mind, really. I put in the years all right. Now it's only fitting that I get some of the credit." Leaning back against the flowered cushion tied to the rocker, Mr. Kendall pursed his mouth to study me.

"You're awful young to be one of them reporters, ain't ye? And pretty, too. I always have been kinda partial to that color of hair. But listen now—don't you go telling Mrs. Kendall I said that! She'd be after me with the blunt end of her broom—she was blond once, you know." He paused, still studying me. "A reporter, eh? Sure you're not after one of my boys? No. I guess not. I can see already that you're a might too fine for one in my rough-and-tumble bunch. And too skinny. You'd need a lot more meat on those bones to make a good ranch wife like my Sarah. She rules this roost with a fist of iron, let me tell you. Not much gets past her." It seemed that Mr. Kendall's eyes nearly disappeared in the mass of wrinkles his face become when he grinned, and for a moment I saw on his face the same expression of affection mingled with respect I had seen on Mrs. Kendall's earlier.

Then he went on. "No, I 'spect you're here for some other reason. Came to see the ruins, did you? Lots of folks have since my boys found 'em. But nobody's written about them much, 'cept those scientist types who come through here now and then and make up a lot of fancy terms for what my boys find. Ark-e-ol-o-gists, or so they say. Some newfangled title they give themselves for the excuse to be boys again and dig around in the dirt like young colts!" This time Mr. Kendall's laugh really was a cackle.

"Is that what Doran Hunt says he is?" I asked. "An archaeologist?"

The old man's eyes sharpened on me immediately. "Doran Hunt, eh?" he said, as if to himself. "Now I hadn't thought about him. But he brought you all the way over here, didn't he? And you met him up in Denver, too, from what Will wrote us." Mr. Kendall paused, seeming to consider something. "Nope, not one of my boys," he finally said. "But mebbe Hunt. Yep, that could work, all right. You'd suit each other fine, to my mind. But what's this, girl? Fire too hot for you, or you gettin' red cuz of my rambling on? Don't worry—you'll get used to it. Everybody does."

Mr. Kendall blew out a breath, then turned to look toward the hearth. Against the light of the fire, his profile was as sharp and lean as a skull. I shivered; the image of the Kendall brothers' latest find in Twilight Mesa mingled with the sight of the restless flames in the hearth, and I shifted uncomfortably.

"No, Hunt don't call himself one of them whatchamacallits," Mr. Kendall went on. "But he's as good as any I've seen with their fancy schooling and so-called commissions from the government—just pitches in and does what needs to be done, digging in the dust and working as hard as my boys. He don't take much credit, neither. Seems to like it, though. Been here for about a year now. Rode up in the yard one day last summer and said he heard about the ruins and wanted to see them. Been here ever since. We don't pay him no money, though he insists on helping out with chores and such, specially during our busy times. He gets his money from somewhere else and seems to have plenty of it. Disappears regularly 'bout every two months— traveling on some kind of business, the boys say. I don't ask no questions. I know a man's got to do what he's got to do, and there's lots of ways to make money out here. But I watch and listen. I'm a crafty old man, if you haven't already guessed. I know what's going on in this house and hereabouts." With a sly grin, the old man tilted his head and tapped a gnarled finger to his temple.

"Have you been to Twilight Mesa?" I asked. "Have you seen the cliff dwellings yourself?"

"Good God, no, child! You think these creaky

old bones would make it through a trip like that? Takes two days just to get there. No, I leave the exploring to my boys now. I had plenty of that in my youth, yes ma'am. I was an Indian agent on the Great Plains at one time. Bet you didn't know that, did you? Well, now you do. Did my share of prospecting and exploring, too, before we came here to settle down and start the ranch. I was always too restless to set in one place before . . . then I got my aches and pains, damned fool nuisances that they are."

I saw a shadow cross Mr. Kendall's features. He looked away with a bitter twist to his mouth and his eyes dulled. For a moment he looked shriveled and wizened, a mere shell of the man he had once been.

But when he looked back at me, his expression was suddenly defiant, and his eyes again like hard little jewels. "I can tell you one thing about Twilight Mesa though, girl. I'd be careful if I was you. It's a mighty hard trip. Just because I haven't been there myself don't mean that I don't know. It's hard getting there in the first place and even harder getting into the canyons and up to those cliff dwellings. The Indians didn't build them up there for nothin', you know. Them ruins hang up there right in the cliff like birds' nests, the boys tell me. One false step and it's a long, hard drop to the canyon below. Have to climb down to 'em by hand and toeholds carved right in the rock or else use ropes. And ropes break. Happened to Owen last fall. Dangling in the air one minute and the next he's sprawled over his own broken leg on the slope below. Lucky for him he landed in some scrub oak. The boys had to carry him back on a donkey like he was a big pack himself. Leg took all winter to mend. And Charlie darn near got his head chopped off when a big slab of loose rock come shootin' down from the roof of one of those caves while he was digging. That's what happens, I guess, when you go rootin' around in places you have no cause to be.''

Mr. Kendall's white eyebrows drew together like wings on his face, and he peered at me from beneath them. He was silent a moment, looking at me, as if testing me somehow. But despite the slight shock and unease I felt at his words— reactions I am sure he had quite intentionally tried to cause—I met his eyes steadily.

''The Indians say that if you go there, to Twilight Mesa, you'll die.'' Mr. Kendall tipped his head slightly, and his eyes narrowed, still fixed on me. ''That's what one of 'em who lives hereabouts told me—Kianeech, his name is. He lives in one of the closer canyons, before you really get into the mesa. His nephew does odd jobs around the place for us, but the old man, he's kind of a hermit. Anyway, when he saw my boys ridin' off into Twilight Mesa for the first time a few years back, looking for cattle and set to explore a bit, Kianeech made a special trip in to see me himself. I couldn't have been more surprised if you'd dropped a barrel full of molasses over my head. Mrs. Kendall brought him in here, right to this very room. He sat in that chair where you are now and he looked at me and said in that dead serious tone they have, he said to me, 'Your sons—they should not go into that place. It is a forbidden place. It is a place of the dead. And when you intrude on the spirits of the dead, you die too.' "

In the sudden silence of the room, a log in the fire popped, sending forth a spray of orange sparks that hissed along with the thud as the log fell to the grate. I thought of Doran's words in the buggy. He had said almost exactly the same thing.

"A man—or woman—could wander for months in Twilight Mesa and never find the right way out." Mr. Kendall's voice had taken on an almost eerie tone. "God knows how many have gone in there and never come out. Look at them ancient Indians—nobody knows what happened to them. They just disappeared. Mebbe nobody will ever know. Lots of secrets hidden in those canyons and cliffs—things that shouldn't be poked into in the first place, that mebbe people like you shouldn't even try to dig up—"

"Nathaniel! Shame on you! Look at that poor girl—she's scared to death! Haven't I told you to stop frightening folks with your awful tales?"

In one instant, the loud, reproving voice of Mrs. Kendall broke the spell that her husband had so effectively woven about me. I blinked, turning to her stolid figure planted in the doorway, elbows jutting out from her hips and a disapproving frown on her broad face.

"Honestly! Can't leave you alone for a minute! You're just like a crafty old spider here, sittin' in your nest waiting for the next poor soul to come along so's you can trap 'em with your talk and spin your old web around them."

Mrs. Kendall's frown grew more stormy, and glancing at Mr. Kendall, I saw him try to hide a sheepish smile. He looked for all the world like a schoolboy caught in the act of putting a toad in the teacher's desk.

"I come down the hall, looking for Miss Loring here, all set to ask her if she's had a nice rest and's ready to wash up for supper. And what do I find? She's been lured in here and scared to death by her own host!"

"It's all right, really." I stood up quickly. "I came in to see Mr. Kendall on my own. I couldn't sleep, and this room was so . . . beckoning. Really, we've had quite a nice talk. Mr. Kendall wasn't frightening me. I need to get as much information as possible for my series of articles, and what he's told me will make wonderful background material."

"Humph. Well." Mrs. Kendall looked at me doubtfully before frowning at Mr. Kendall. "Just remember to take everything this old geezer tells you with a grain of salt. The way he talks, you never know what's truth and what's been stretched by half a mile."

Mrs. Kendall cast an exasperated look at Mr. Kendall, but I could see that it was now mixed with fondness and even a kind of pride. Mr. Kendall saw this too and smiled, his thin lips curving smugly.

"Well, come along dearie." Mrs. Kendall gestured me forward. "Supper's almost on the table. You go on along to the dining room, down the side hall here and to your left. If you'll excuse me, I'll stay here just a minute. Mr. Kendall *insists* on accompanying me to the supper table every night. As if I didn't know the way!"

Clucking and shaking her head, Mrs. Kendall

made the pretense of waiting impatiently as Mr. Kendall began the slow, painful process of rising from his chair. He stood with the assistance of a cane, and Mrs. Kendall slipped her arm through his, as if planning to let him lead her from the room. But I saw the expert way in which Mrs. Kendall provided most of the support for him even while appearing to lean into her husband in need of support herself.

I glanced down the hallway and saw that Julia's door was now open. Mrs. Kendall must have already woken her, I guessed.

Looking the other way, I saw a short side hallway that I hadn't noticed before, opposite and on the other side of Mr. Kendall's door. I assumed this was the way to the dining room, but just as I reached it, I caught a glimpse of something blue disappearing around its far corner—a snatch of fabric, as of a skirt, or a shirt. I could not tell if the person wearing it had been a man or a woman.

Had it been Doran Hunt again? Julia? The Indian I had seen in the yard when we arrived?

Whoever it was, I was quite certain that he or she had been standing there quite close to Mr. Kendall's room, perhaps for some time.

Listening to us, I thought. Listening to everything we had said.

Chapter Six

✦ ✦ ✦ ✦

THE THREE COWBOYS were already seated at the long dining room table, chattering away, large cotton napkins tucked into the collars of their clean buttoned-up shirts, when I entered the room. Their conversation stopped abruptly; then, as if made all of one piece, they bolted up from the table in unison, flipping up the cotton tablecloth and nearly sending Mrs. Kendall's tableware and thick crockery plates careening to the floor.

"Evenin' ma'am," said the one nearest me. "Welcome to our home." Washed, shaved, and dressed in what was obviously his best shirt and pair of trousers, the man was nearly unrecognizable as the dirt-caked cowboy I had seen shouting across the yard. His red, bristly hair must have been freshly washed, for it no longer lay matted to his head but shot off in all directions despite what I am sure had been vigorous attempts to tame it.

"You must be Owen," I said, smiling. "And you two—let me see. You're Ben, right? And you're Charlie?"

The three dropped their jaws in unison, looking so surprised it was hard to keep from smiling. "Will told me about you," I explained, "in Denver."

At that, the Kendall brothers grinned, and Owen awkwardly pulled out a straight-backed wooden chair for me. Its hard seat was covered with an odd-shaped chintz-covered cushion, and I realized that the chair offered to me must have been the one reserved for the family's guests of honor.

"You're Miss Loring, the reporter." Charlie, sitting directly across the table, stared at me with open interest as I sat down. His tone was respectful. "You gonna write us all up in the Denver paper?"

"Well, I certainly hope so. I—"

"Well, of course she is, with all you fine, handsome gentlemen to tell her all your excitin' stories!"

With her usual flourish and perfect timing, Julia Hastings swept into the room. She was wearing a fitted, blue silk gown, its full sleeves ruffled at the shoulder and wrists and trimmed with lace and ribbons, its flared skirt pleated and gathered at the waist with a dark sash. Her heavy mass of dark hair was pulled up and fastened to the back of her head with a pair of tortoiseshell combs and a spray of blue wildflowers.

Was it Julia I'd seen disappearing down the hall? I glanced at her blue silk gown again, and then rather ruefully down at my own rumpled suit. In my earlier restlessness to be off and about, I had not changed out of it, and once in Mr. Kendall's room, time had just seemed to slip away unnoticed.

But if it had been Julia in the hallway, I wondered where she had been since I had entered the dining room. She would have had ample time to arrive here before I did.

Mrs. Kendall's carefully set table survived another near upset when all three of the Kendall brothers bolted upright again, and after another brief round of introductions, Ben pulled out a chair, also adorned with its homemade flowered cushion, for Julia.

"You westerners are such gentlemen!" she cried as Ben seated her rather clumsily. The brothers responded with sheepish grins, a suspiciously red coloration creeping up their ruddy necks. As usual, Julia Hastings' charm was having its desired affect.

Before Julia could say anything more, however, Mrs. Kendall entered the room on the arm of her husband.

"Well, I see we are all here," she said, beaming. "Supper's a little late tonight, but it's still good and hot. Mr. Kendall, you may take your place now. I'll get the food."

As Mr. Kendall propped his cane against the far end of the table and lowered himself painfully into the wooden chair pulled out for him there, Mrs. Kendall disappeared through the opposite doorway and returned moments later with a huge platter of fried chicken. A steaming bowl of boiled potatoes and carrots followed, and successive trips to the kitchen brought bowls of gravy, pots of butter and honey, and three loaves of freshly baked bread ready to be sliced on a wooden cutting board.

Finally, evidently satisfied that not another platter or bowl could be wedged onto the brimming table, Mrs. Kendall settled herself at the end of the table opposite her husband and motioned for him to begin grace. The table immediately became quiet. Mrs. Kendall squeezed her eyes shut, bowed her head, and clasped her roughened hands, and her sons followed suit as Mr. Kendall intoned his simple prayer. When he had finished, Mrs. Kendall looked up with a big smile.

"Well, dig in, dig in. What do you think all this food is for—lookin' at?" She leaned toward Julia with an apologetic air, "I usually have some help for serving up the food," she explained in a confidential tone. "But the girl I hired the beginning of this summer just ran off with a young fella from Jackson. Last we heard they were heading for Nevada." Mrs. Kendall glanced around the table at her sons, then lowered her voice even further and leaned closer to Julia and me. "Just between you and me, I think that girl was in a family way from the start. The way she used to serve up them fried eggs in the morning, like she couldn't bear to look at them much less think of eatin' 'em herself. . . . And, well, there were other signs. I just hope those two make it legal before they get where they're going. Anyway, I just wanted you to know, Miss Hastings, that's why dinner is so informal and all."

Mrs. Kendall did not see the expression on Julia's face, but I would have liked to have captured it at that moment—shocked, aggrieved, slightly aghast, as if Mrs. Kendall's gossip had done irreparable damage to her delicate sensibilities.

The platter of fried chicken came my way then, however, and all my attention was consumed by the wonderful flavors and aromas of that memorable meal. Until I took my first bite of the crusty chicken, I did not realize how famished I was, or remember how hungry I had been earlier in the buggy. Now, each bite tasted to me like a gift straight from heaven, and as I feasted, I saw Mrs. Kendall's smile widen.

I believe I was on my second helping of chicken when Julia spoke up.

"Oh, Mr. Kendall, do tell me," she began, her drawl more honeyed than ever as she turned her ice-blue eyes to the man at the end of the table. "I have heard such exciting tales about hidden treasure out here in the Southwest! I am sure you know what I mean—all those lost mines and wonderful jewels stolen by murdered outlaws. And gold, buried Spanish gold! People do love to talk about such things. Are the stories true? Have you and your sons found any secret treasure nearby? Or hidden here on your very own property, perhaps?"

Across from us, Charlie let out a guffaw. "Nothin' round here but rocks and sagebrush," he said, digging into a mound of potatoes he had mashed with a fork on his plate. "Heck, anybody could tell you that."

"Your elder brother William did just that in Denver, as a matter of fact," Julia replied sweetly. "But come now, surely you've heard the stories. Why, I myself was acquainted with a gentleman from New York whose friend discovered an old map among some papers in an attic. It was a treasure map, leading to this very area. Or . . . perhaps somewhere near it." Julia waved her slim white hand vaguely in the air. "In any case, the two immediately packed their belongings and arranged for transportation to Colorado." Julia paused a moment. "Or was it New Mexico?"

"Have you heard from these fellows since?" Knife poised in the air, Owen looked at Julia curiously, the red hair on his head sticking up just as quizzically as his bristly eyebrows.

"Well, you must understand that I was only barely acquainted with this gentleman. We were told of his departure and then . . . well, it's perfectly understandable, really, given the nature of their wilderness expedition, that we never did hear—"

Owen laughed. "Not meanin' any disrespect, Miss Hastings, but we've seen folks like your friends coming round here before, more'n once. They get off the train in Durango as green as the grass in our pasture, lookin' hopeful, asking questions, carrying their brand-new store-bought shovels and picks. Usually they head for the mountains, but now and then they come around here, thinking the Spanish left something somewhere, like the gold you were talking about. It's funny, usually they got just one little clue to go on—an old map maybe, or a set of mixed-up directions an old miner gave them on his deathbed, or just an old story they heard somewhere. They disappear into the mountains and a few weeks later they come back, flat broke and dirty as all get out. That's all it takes for most, just a few weeks digging around in the dirt, looking for something that's not even there, sweating all day in the hot sun and sleeping on the cold, hard ground at night."

"Some of 'em come back, though," observed Ben who, with his reserved nature, had been silent until then. "Some get a whiff of that treasure and the fever grips them and never lets go. They keep comin' back, lookin', year after year, spending their money till it runs out in the hope that maybe this very next time they'll find it if they just look in the right place. . . ."

"Just a pack of fools, all of 'em." Mashing his carrots in carefully with his potatoes, Charlie raised a forkful of both to his mouth and was thoughtful for a moment. "Lookin' all their lives for gold and a trunkful of God-knows-what, when all the time, the treasure's right under their nose. Heck, we know where it is, don't we, boys?"

Julia sat up sharply, suddenly alert. "What? Why, I thought you said you had found no treasure here on your property."

"We didn't say that exactly." With an exaggerated slowness I am sure he did not even notice, Ben carefully buttered a huge slab of his mother's bread. "If all them treasure seekers had any sense, they'd see it, right here, all around us. The land, that's what it is. This whole dang land is buried treasure to folks who have a little stick-to-itiveness and aren't afraid of hard work. For folks who want to mine the land instead of some darn mountain slope, there's all kinds of treasure to be had—a good living, plenty of time and freedom, the feel of the sun on your back and a good horse to ride, days you can call your own. . . ."

Visibly disappointed, Julia sagged back in her seat as Ben placidly went on. But then a calm voice spoke up, and Ben stopped talking. The rest of the table stilled immediately, too.

"Miss Hastings is right," Mr. Kendall said. "There is buried treasure here in the Southwest, and not just the kind Ben was talking about. It's around all right, but it's hidden, and not too many have had much luck finding it." Mr. Kendall paused, and when he saw all eyes were turned to him, he went on, looking at Julia.

"You were right about that gold, Miss Hastings, and all the rest, too—them lost mines and outlaws' caches. I've heard all the stories, and they had to start somewhere. The Spanish believed in 'em, too, when they first started lookin' around up here near on two, three hundred years ago. Heck, they were positive that this whole area was chock-full of gold and valuables; they were sure that they would find a shining, bright treasure in the New World that was going to make them all rich. Ha! They even believed that there were seven cities up here paved with gold and studded with turquoise. They named them the Seven Cities of Cibola." Mr. Kendall chuckled, a dry sound deep in his throat.

"Well, those seven cities turned out to be some pretty measly Indian pueblos, and when the Spanish came up here to the New World, they found nothin' but a bunch of hoppin' mad Injuns! The explorers cleared out pretty quick, but the missionaries stayed, and what they left behind is important."

Mr. Kendall leaned forward, propping his bony elbows on the table and fixing his eyes on Julia. "You see, Miss Hastings, them Injuns didn't like those missionaries comin' up here and tryin' to get 'em to go to church and change their lives and such. So, lots of times, the Injuns would just up and turn on 'em, killin' and lootin' and runnin' them Spanish priests clean away. But them priests also had lots of valuables—gold and other things like their church chalices and such. Those were all made of gold and silver and would be worth quite a bundle today. Well, sometimes the priests had time to hide or bury those things, and sometimes they even had time to scribble directions to their hidin' places on an old piece of parchment or something and tuck that away.

"I've heard of mines, too—mines that were found, worked, then lost again right back to the elements. And as for those murdered outlaws— well, I did hear tell a few stories about them. Crafty fellas, those. Ruthless renegades." Mr. Kendall chuckled again. "They were the ones who would lay in wait for pack trains of missionaries in the early days, looting and killing and taking off with those valuables I was tellin' you about. Later, they'd hold up stagecoaches and freight wagons too, and stash their loot in the hills. Some of those caches are still there. An old man in Jackson told me about an outlaw, all shot up in a gunfight, who dragged himself to a little homestead in New Mexico and whispered the location of his secret stash to the woman who nursed him before he died. There's all kinds of tales like that. I like the one about the gypsy who drove six white horses. He had a map to a Spanish treasure too, see, but he hired other folks to dig for it. Then, while they was sleepin', he'd steal off with what they'd found, never to be seen again! And there's other tales like—"

"Yes, tales! And that's all they are!" With her resounding, no-nonsense voice, Mrs. Kendall broke the riveting spell her husband had woven about the rest of us in the room. She turned an exasperated look on the old man, then looked at

Julia apologetically. "I don't know why I put up with all this foolishness. You have to understand, Miss Hastings, that out here folks spend a lot of time on the range or around a campfire, spinnin' yarns like Mr. Kendall here has been feeding you."

"Oh, but the stories are so exciting! Even if they do get a little puffed up now and then—surely what they are based on must be true." Julia's eyes glinted.

"There's one thing I didn't mention though." At the sound of Mr. Kendall's voice, all eyes turned toward his end of the table again. "To find one of those treasures I was talking about, you got to be the right person."

"The right person?" Julia's brows pulled together in a puzzled frown.

"Yep, the right person. See, there's an old Spanish belief that buried treasure is meant for one person, and one person only, to find. Has to be your *fate* to find it. If it isn't, and if you meddle where you shouldn't, you're just lookin' for trouble. There's a whole string of things that's happened to folks lookin' for the kind of treasure I was talking about." Mr. Kendall paused. "You know, accidents and such. Like gettin' sick or injured, losin' all your money, dying. Even gettin' murdered. Especially that. Tempers get hot and flare up pretty bad when a whole fortune is at stake. Some say there's even a curse on certain treasures. Strange things have happened. Bad things."

I felt gooseflesh rise on my arms at Mr. Kendall's words. Mrs. Kendall shook her head again and began stacking plates. Julia, her eyes still gleaming, addressed Mr. Kendall, apparently undeterred by his words.

"I am sure all that is true, Mr. Kendall," she said, leaning toward him eagerly. "But tell me—you seem to know so very much. Have you heard any tales of treasure being hidden in Twilight Mesa? It seems like such a good place to me—all those winding canyons and cliff dwellings. Surely somewhere in there, someone could have hidden—"

"Now Julia, my dear. Don't you think you've questioned poor Mr. Kendall quite enough? He must be growing weary of your interrogation."

The words—strong and resonantly male— made us all turn in surprise toward the doorway. There, blocking all light from the hallway, stood one of the most charismatic men I had ever seen.

I am not sure what about him gave me this impression. I have puzzled about it many times since. The man was not really handsome in any conventional way, or particularly tall or large. But the way he stood there—feet planted apart, jet black hair smooth against his head, clipped black mustache twitching above an amused smile—gave off an almost tangible aura of success and virility. Perhaps it was the slight touch of gray at his temples that gave him such a distinctive air, adding a dignified touch to his rather crooked features. Or perhaps it was simply the way he stood in the Kendalls' doorway—as if he belonged there and anyplace he chose to stand, seeming to take up more room than he really did because of some kind of repressed energy that radiated outward from his presence.

"Prescott!"

With a cry of delight, Julia jumped to her feet and rushed over to him. The man closed his hands on hers and then drew Julia to him so that their intertwined fingers rested on the checked yoke of his Norfolk jacket. I could not see Julia's face, but I could see her fiancé's; the expression in his eyes as he looked down at her and the slight inclination of his body toward hers, only inches apart, were gestures so intimate and charged that I had to turn my eyes away.

There was an uncomfortable murmur and shifting around the table as the others also averted their eyes, and then Prescott released one of Julia's hands and led her over to the group.

"Please excuse my untimely arrival," he said, stopping beside Mrs. Kendall's chair and bending forward in a graceful bow. His voice was low and deep, but its accent was definitely not southern. I could not place its origin.

"I know I sent word that I would be arriving tomorrow," Prescott went on, "but I was able to get away from my work unexpectedly early and found I could not wait any longer to see Miss Hastings." His black eyes grew even darker as he looked at Julia.

"Oh, Mr. Webb, you know you are always welcome here." Mrs. Kendall's cheeks were flushed and her gray eyes bright with Prescott Webb's gallant attention. She smiled up at him like a young schoolgirl. "Now you just pull up a chair and sit down a spell. Most of the chicken and other vittles is gone, thanks to my growing boys here, but I was just about to serve up rhubarb cobbler and some of my coffee. You could probably use some after your trip. Did you ride all the way over from the mesa? Don't look like you've been on the trail for two days."

She ran her eyes down Prescott's near immaculate suit as he seated Julia and as if on cue, both Ben and Charlie sprang up at once, followed by Owen, all mumbling greetings to Prescott, then excuses of chores to do about the ranch. They excused themselves again before grabbing their hats off hooks near the door, bumbling noisily from the room and banging out the rear of the house from the porch off the kitchen.

Gracefully taking a seat across from Julia, Prescott said, "I would be most delighted to accept your invitation and stay, Mrs. Kendall. I well know how famed your cooking is in this valley. People talk about it for miles around." As he spoke, Prescott's eyes flickered over me briefly, politely, then moved back to Mrs. Kendall. "To answer your question, Mrs. Kendall, you are right, I did not ride over from the mesa. I had some business to attend to further north, beyond the valley. I've been absent from the mesa for over a week now."

"But you have that young fella to take care of things for you there, don't you?" Mr. Kendall said. His narrowed topaz eyes had obviously taken in everything. Prescott turned to him.

"My assistant. Yes. He stays in the cabin and watches over things when business takes me away."

"Government business, you mean?" Mr. Kendall's question was quick and rather sharp.

Prescott answered with a wry smile. "Yes. And I am afraid that when one commits to work for our fine men in Washington, one loses a certain amount of freedom. I must go where they bid, when they bid."

Mr. Kendall did not reply, but continued to look at Prescott keenly, and in the silence I, too, looked at Prescott Webb more closely.

He was older than I'd first thought—in his forties, rather than his thirties, judging from the two deep creases around his mouth. His skin was tanned from the sun, like most of the men I had seen in the area, but on his face it did not result in swarthiness, but rather seemed a complement to what I perceived as a kind of inherent refinement.

And yet, as Prescott smiled at Julia, I saw that his teeth were yellowed and chipped in places. It was in such direct contrast with his otherwise polished appearance that for a moment I could not help staring. A series of splayed lines radiated from his dark eyes as well, and all at once I was struck with the same feeling I'd had after closely inspecting Julia Hastings for the first time. Beneath the surface appearance of both, it seemed, lay a kind of hardness, a reserve of tempered strength built up through years of experience.

Prescott's expression deepened as he looked at Julia, and as his eyes met and held hers, I felt something more vital, more powerful than I had ever witnessed pass between two people. It was much more than mere understanding or mutual attraction. What leapt between them in that instant was more of a restless energy, a compulsion, a sense of excitement about all that had happened, was happening and could happen between them.

Mrs. Kendall must have sensed this, too, for she rose from the table. "Well, Mr. Kendall, shall we take our cobbler and coffee into the parlor?"

"What's that?" Mr. Kendall started, jumping slightly in his chair. He had been watching Julia and Prescott, too. "Now why would you want to do a fool thing like that? We never—"

"Mr. Kendall." Sarah Kendall raised her eyebrows and looked pointedly at her husband. "I think these young folks might like some time to themselves, don't you? After all, you remember how it was when *we* was courting. Now why don't you just escort me to the parlor, and I'll get our places all settled, and then I'll come back with the dessert."

As the Kendalls left the room, Prescott and Julia smiled at each other again in their charged, intimate way, and I raised my napkin to my mouth rather uncertainly, wondering whether I should stay or go. I was just about to retire to my own room without either coffee or cobbler when Julia turned and fixed her blue eyes on me.

"Why Heather! In all the pleasure and surprise of Mr. Webb's unexpected arrival, I have completely neglected to introduce you. How awful of me!"

Prescott's black eyes flickered over me again with a mild curiosity.

Julia curved her fingers about my arm in a rather possessive gesture. "Prescott, my darling, it is my extreme pleasure to introduce a dear, dear friend I have made over the last several days. We traveled all the way down here together from Denver, and have become so very close." Julia paused, still looking at Prescott, an odd, almost vibrating timbre to her voice. "This is Miss Loring, Prescott. Miss Heather Loring."

At that moment, Mrs. Kendall bustled back into the dining room. "Oh, my heavens! Look at all these dirty dishes! I plum forgot about 'em!" Scooping up a great mound of plates and tableware in her sturdy arms, Mrs. Kendall started toward the kitchen, calling back over her shoulder, "Now don't you worry. I'll be right back with your coffee!"

Prescott had glanced up as she entered, his attention diverted. But I had seen the look of sharp, startled surprise he'd focused on me the instant before, at Julia's words.

"Here you go!" With a flourish, Mrs. Kendall set three steaming bowls of ruby-colored cobbler on the table before us. The servings were heaped high in crockery bowls and swimming in fresh heavy cream. Then Mrs. Kendall vanished into the kitchen again and returned with three thick mugs of hot coffee.

"That should do you," she said, nodding her head in satisfaction. "Now I'll just get Mr. Kendall's and mine, and leave you young folks alone. You stay up just as long as you want. 'Spect you're too old for chaperonin', and I never did hold much with that custom anyway."

Once she had gone, Prescott Webb fixed his eyes on me. "Miss Loring," he said slowly, tilting his head slightly as he studied my face. "It's a pleasure to meet you. How nice that you and Julia have become friends for the summer. Where did you say you met?"

"Heather is a *reporter*, Prescott," Julia interjected. "I met her at the Kendalls' exhibition in Denver. She was planning to write a story on the relics and the cliff dwellings and all, and Will Kendall invited her down here so she could visit Twilight Mesa herself. Can you imagine that? I mean, what a coincidence! Why, with me traveling down here too, at the same time. And then Heather and I ended up on the same train! We had *such* a cozy chat on the way down, and we learned so much about each other. Now we are like sisters, aren't we, Heather dear?"

Julia squeezed my arm and smiled at me, her blue eyes fairly leaping with sudden intimacy.

"How very nice. And what is to be the angle of your story, Miss Loring?" Prescott asked.

"Angle?" Uncomfortable again, I shifted on the chair's flowered cushion.

"Yes. Are you writing about the historical angle—by that I mean focusing primarily on the tribe of Indians that once lived in Twilight Mesa and the artifacts thus found and what we know of them; or the more modern angle of the excavation work currently being carried out in Twilight Mesa and what the Kendalls, and others, have found there?"

"I . . . I had really planned to blend the two angles, I suppose." Prescott's low, almost intimate tone confused me. It almost seemed that he was testing me somehow, probing for something beyond my simple answer. "Actually, there is so much material to cover within the scope of Twilight Mesa that I had planned to write a series of articles, each with its own angle and focus," I went on. "I know little of the cliff dwellings themselves. I am sure I will have to carry out several preliminary interviews with the Kendalls, and then perhaps do some investigating and exploring on my own."

"In Twilight Mesa?" Prescott's tone sharpened suddenly.

"Yes—there, and also here at the ranch. I understand there is quite a storehouse of artifacts, and that is where I can start, at least, to learn something about the cliff dwellers. The Anasazi, they are called, are they not? The Ancient Ones?"

"Yes," Prescott said, although he seemed more intent on posing his own questions than answering any of mine. "But you say you might journey to Twilight Mesa itself," he went on, watching me closely. "Are you aware, Miss Loring, just how difficult a prospect that is? It is a rugged—four days all told—trip into extremely harsh country. Visitors often think they can make the full journey, only to turn back in defeat after a day on the trail."

"Yes, I have been made aware of the conditions. But Will Kendall has agreed to be my guide to the mesa, and I'm sure that with him—"

"Oh, but Prescott darling, *we* shall take her!" Julia cried. Her eyes had been darting avidly between Prescott and I as we spoke. "We are going to the mesa together, are we not? If I go, surely Heather can accompany us. And if we are in your capable hands, dearest"—here Julia paused, looking quite effectively out from under her thick black lashes at Prescott—"how can any harm possibly come to us?"

Prescott's eyes rested on Julia a moment, smoldering with some repressed emotion I could not quite identify. "Ah, Julia," he finally said, reaching across the table to place a large, well-manicured hand over hers. "As you have probably already discovered for yourself, Miss Loring, my fiancée is not all that she appears. Beneath Julia's rather fragile appearance is a reserve of stamina that still surprises me. If she were at all otherwise, I would not even consider taking her with me into Twilight Mesa. She is quite strong." Prescott looked back at Julia. "Or perhaps *head*strong would be a more apt description," he added.

Some kind of unspoken communication again passed between Prescott and Julia as their eyes met, and I could almost feel, quivering in the air, the tension and energy I had sensed between them earlier.

"Oh, my darling Prescott, you know how *dearly* I have wanted to be with you over these last months, to help you with your work!" Julia cried. "You know I would do *anything* to contribute to our future together. Why, ever since you wrote me that letter and asked me to come—"

"Yes, Julia." Prescott's words were clipped. "I quite understand."

"But I am afraid you *don't* understand! I don't think you realize how much I want to be a part of your work. How I have dreamed of the rewards we will reap this summer—"

The expression on Prescott's face stilled Julia's next words abruptly and their eyes locked again, seeming to be in some kind of combat. I felt the tension between them build to a point much too uncomfortable to bear.

"Your work," I interjected rather hastily, addressing Prescott. "Julia tells me you work for the government, Mr. Webb. May I ask, in what capacity?"

Rather reluctantly I thought, Prescott shifted his attention from Julia to me. "Ah, carrying out your duties as a journalist already, Miss Loring?" His smile barely curved the thin line of his lips and did not touch the expression in his eyes. "I am not involved in any kind of surveying, Miss Loring. Nor in an organized ethnological program. I am . . . somewhat of an independent agent, exploring the canyons and dwellings of Twilight Mesa on my own."

"But Mr. Kendall mentioned an assistant, didn't he?"

Prescott's gaze once again sharpened on me. "Yes. He helps me with manual labor when I require it. He has been with me for several months now. He came to me and asked for the job when he was passing through the area last summer."

"I didn't know you employed transients, Webb."

Spoken right behind me, the words made me jump. But I recognized the voice. Indeed, in a way it did not even surprise me, interrupting without introduction or preamble as it had done often enough before. I should have expected that its source—the man who spoke the words—would be somewhere near, waiting and watching as seemed to be his frequent wont. I should only have wondered, indeed, why he had not appeared sooner.

My skin suddenly flushed with heat as I felt Doran approach lightly behind me. He stopped directly in back of my chair, and as he rested his hand on its curved wooden back and I felt his knuckles graze my shoulder blade through the soft fabric of my suit, I gave an involuntary shiver.

"Ah, Hunt. I didn't realize you had returned from Denver already. I had assumed you would remain up there until Will returned." Although cordial and correct, Prescott's tone was guarded, and, it seemed to me, laced with an odd undertone.

"I finished my business up there," Doran answered shortly. "There was no reason to stay." His hand shifted on the chair behind me, and its heat seemed to burn like an iron on my skin. I sat frozen there, my shoulders and back rigid.

"Oh, do you two *know* each other?" Julia said, looking from Doran to Prescott. "What a fortunate coincidence! I met Mr. Hunt at the exhibition in Denver, Prescott. If he and Will Kendall hadn't persuaded Heather to come down—"

"Persuaded her? Did you have a hand in that, Hunt?" Prescott's features were drawn in a frown as he looked at Doran.

"Miss Loring hardly needed persuading," Doran answered.

Easily, as if it were the most natural gesture in the world, Doran placed his hand on my shoulder. "She was extremely fascinated by the exhibition—in fact, by several items in particular. There was an amulet, isn't that right? And a photograph?"

The pressure of Doran's hand on my shoulder increased, and it seemed his touch enveloped me, wrapping about my very nerves and causing an odd, tingling sensation to stir in my breasts.

"Actually, it was only a matter of time before Miss Loring came down here on her own, Webb." Casually, Doran lifted his hand from my shoulder and I heard him shift behind me. The spot where his hand had rested was cold and prickly, making my body feel suddenly light. "She's a reporter, after all, and knows a good story when she sees one. I believe I heard her asking you a few questions. Perhaps *you* will become the subject of one of her articles." Doran paused. "Considering the nature of your work—and mine—in Twilight Mesa, it should be quite interesting having Miss Loring here this summer."

"Quite." Still seated, Prescott's black eyes narrowed as they regarded Doran. He seemed about to say more but then tossed his crumpled napkin on the table and stood up. "Well, I must say it's been a pleasure to see you again, Hunt. But now, if you and Miss Loring will excuse us, I think perhaps Julia and I will take a turn about the grounds before I leave."

"Oh, but you've only just arrived!" Julia's disappointment, visible and keen, turned into a petulant pout.

"Now Julia, you know the nature of my work. I will return again very soon." Prescott paused a moment, looking at me as if considering something. "In fact, I think your earlier suggestion that we take Miss Loring with us on our first trek to the mesa, is an excellent idea. Shall we plan it for early next week, after Will returns? He could guide you there, and I could meet you once you get to the mesa and show you what I have been doing there."

"That should be interesting," Doran commented dryly. At Prescott's look he went on. "I refer to the reaction of these two ladies, of course, when they get their first taste of Twilight Mesa." Doran paused, as if considering something himself. "As a matter of fact, I think that perhaps I'd like to come along, too. I need to get back to the mesa myself, and Will will need some help on the trip, especially with these two on his hands." I heard Doran's short laugh, but I still could not see his face.

Prescott rounded the table to help Julia from her chair. "Having you along on the trip might be interesting in itself, Mr. Hunt," he said, not looking at Doran directly. "And now, again, if you'll excuse us . . ."

Rising, Julia gathered up her skirts and took Prescott's arm. As I turned slightly in my chair, I saw her slant a shrewd look at Doran, and then down at me. Then she looked up at Prescott with a brilliant smile, and with brief nods in our direction, they left the room on the rustling of Julia's skirts and the light tinkling sound of her laugh.

"Well?" Doran said. His voice was low and very near. Still behind me, he bent slightly and I felt his breath touch my cheek. "What did you think of Prescott Webb? Are you looking forward to your trip to Twilight Mesa?"

I turned my head slightly and saw his green eyes, the upward, elfin slant of his features. He was smiling, laughing at me.

"I don't know that it's of any concern to you, Mr. Hunt," I said stiffly.

"Oh, isn't it?" With easy grace, Doran dropped in Mr. Kendall's chair at the end of the table. He was wearing a clean denim shirt, I noticed, and carried a heavy canvas jacket in his hand. "I am going with you and Julia to the mesa, you know. Therefore I am extremely interested to learn what you think of the situation and what you hope to find there."

"Indeed? And what makes you think I am interested in revealing my private thoughts to you?"

Doran looked at me in silence, his eyes widening in the way I had seen before, and for an instant my stomach knotted.

"I have learned to trust my hunches," he said. He stared at me another long moment, and I saw the muscles in his jaw jump slightly. Then he stood abruptly.

"Excuse me. It's time that I get back to work." Doran began to pull on the jacket he had been carrying. "Perhaps I will see you tomorrow." He paused, as if debating something in his mind, and then all at once, he grinned. "I think I could be available for one of your preliminary interviews some time after lunch. Say, two o'clock or thereabouts?"

Still smiling in his surprisingly boyish way, he shrugged his jacket over his shoulders. With the movement, I caught a quick glimpse of something long and white—like a folded sheet of paper, or an envelope—half-concealed in an inner pocket.

"Until tomorrow afternoon, Heather." Touching his hand lightly to his hatless brow, he smiled and was gone, out across the back porch. I heard the wooden door slap shut and the crunch of his boots on the rocks outside.

I stared at the table rather stupidly for several moments before I realized that Doran had used my Christian name. Heather. The memory of my name uttered in that intimate tone caused a quick heat to flare within me.

I finally rose from the table when I heard Mrs. Kendall in the kitchen, washing the dishes.

I looked down rather ruefully at the untouched bowls of cobbler. I hesitated, wondering if I should take them to Mrs. Kendall and perhaps offer her my assistance. But some instinct told me that it would be an insult. I was her guest, after all, and she was without her hired girl.

A woman's work is never done, I thought, slipping silently out and down the hall. It was then I remembered the other words Doran had spoken—*It's time that I get back to work.*

It was past nine o'clock at night. What work could Doran possibly have to carry out now?

All the doors along the hallway were shut except for Julia's, which was slightly ajar. As I passed it, I saw that her room was dark and empty. Mrs. Kendall must truly not have believed in the custom of chaperoning, for Julia was obviously still out with Prescott at this late hour, alone.

Whatever—it was not my concern. What Julia Hastings did with her time was entirely her own business.

The moon was just starting to rise, and its feeble light shimmered through the parted curtains at my bedroom window. In the distance, the northern point of Twilight Mesa loomed dark and massive like a great beast, an impenetrable buttress, protecting its centuries of secrets within.

Over the next few weeks, I suddenly realized, I would pay a price for my freedom here in the shadow of Twilight Mesa—an exacting and perhaps a frightening price. There was nothing and no one, I knew, to shield and protect me from what I might find within those canyon walls.

I heard the call of a coyote, lonely and piercing, in the distance, and a dog barking in answer somewhere on the ranch. My window was still open and the smells of hay and sage drifted in on the breeze, mingled with all the other, indefinable scents of the vast, open country. Above, clouds skimmed lightly across the sky, playing a game of cat and mouse with the rising moon; its light showed in shadowed forms and dappled patterns in the yard, visible one moment only to be hidden from view the next.

I was just about to prepare for bed when I saw two black silhouettes detach themselves from a shadow at the other end of the house. One was quite tall and solid; the other petite and feminine. The moon escaped and shone briefly on their faces. Julia's was turned up toward Prescott's and his was bent to hers. As I watched, he wrapped an arm about her waist and pulled her tight against him, and she twined her arms about his neck. Their lips touched, merged, melded together in an embrace that was too prolonged for me to watch. Inexplicably disturbed, I turned my eyes away, and when I looked again, the two forms had parted. Within moments I heard the rustle of Julia's skirts and the soft tapping of her boots on the uncarpeted wooden hallway outside, and then the creaking of her door and her muffled movements in the adjacent room.

I remained at the window, standing back so that I was half-hidden by the softly billowing curtains. I saw Prescott's dark form move over to one of the barns and pause there a moment, looking out toward the corrals. From my vantage point I could see another quick, lithe form slip along the side of the barn toward Prescott's turned back. In a moment, it joined him. Prescott started, caught off guard, then the two bent their heads in swift, furtive conversation. I could hear their whispers, carried to me brokenly on the breeze, but I could make out no words.

Then the moon slipped out again from the clouds and illuminated Doran Hunt's shadowed, unsmiling face as he reached into the pocket of his coat. I saw a flash of white pass between him and Prescott Webb. Prescott slipped the object into his jacket and turned to leave, but Doran placed a hand on his arm. Prescott paused and Doran pressed something else into his hand. Then Doran said a few words and turned quickly away, slipping back alongside the barn and disappearing from my view. Prescott stood where he was, watching him go. After a moment, he slipped his hand into his pocket again, turned and then quickly strode toward a waiting horse and buggy tethered in the yard.

When he reached the buggy, however, Prescott stopped and reached into his jacket, extracting something. It was not the sheath of white paper, as I had expected, but a small round object which he held up to the light still burning on the Kendall's front porch. It did not flash, as it might have in sunlight, but glinted dully for the instant he held it aloft. It could have been made of gold or silver or even bone; I could not distinguish which. Prescott's movement was too swift, and appearing fearful that someone might be watching, he quickly replaced the object in his pocket. Then, climbing into the buggy, he grasped the reins and urged the horse forward, passing by the house and down to the road toward Jackson.

The breeze wafting in was cool. I reached up to close the window. All was quiet and still outside. The only sound was another distant call of a coyote.

And there was Twilight Mesa, black and enormous across the valley.

I heard a movement in the room next door and realized that Julia had just shut her own window and climbed into bed. Had she also been watching the two men? Surely she would have wanted to see Prescott leave. But had she seen anything else?

I felt suddenly exhausted. Too much had happened over the last few days, too suddenly. What did it all mean? And what part did I play in this strange, unfolding drama? I knew without a doubt, as I slid under Mrs. Kendall's cool cotton sheets, that I was involved in some basic, inevitable way.

When I finally closed my eyes, I remember feeling grateful that I was sinking into a fast, deep sleep. But I should have known what kind of nightmare images my subconscious mind would create that night.

So much of it was jumbled at first. I dreamed of

outlaws and miners and Spanish missionaries, of gold coins and silver chalices and gleaming treasure packed away in huge trunks, buried, unearthed, and then stolen away by a great giant of a gypsy pounding by on a team of white horses.

Then I was on a great white horse myself, galloping alone toward Twilight Mesa, clutching the stallion's tangled mane in my fingers. But as fast as I spurred the horse on and the more distance we covered, farther and farther away the mesa grew, seeming to retreat from us as we approached. And then it disappeared entirely, and I was running, breathless, down a long, twisting hallway, my white nightgown billowing about me like curtains at a window, my long hair loose and flying about my face as I struggled toward the open door I could see at the end, a ray of light angling out from beneath it. The closer I came, the more the door opened until at last I could see inside.

There was old Mr. Kendall in his chair, his face turned toward a blazing fire in the hearth, his hunched form huddled beneath one of Mrs. Kendall's scarlet Indian blankets. But when he turned to me, in place of the expected welcoming smile was a terrible, twisted expression of horror and warning. He reached a bony hand to me and called out, but his voice sounded very distant, as if it were coming from the end of a long tunnel.

"No!" he cried, his voice echoing, his face still twisted. "Don't go! Remember, when you intrude on the spirits of the dead, then you die, too. . . ."

As Mr. Kendall's words faded away, the fire in the hearth seemed to blaze brighter, harder, its flames leaping up and forward as if to engulf the room. As I stared in horror, the skin on Mr. Kendall's face seemed to melt and fall away, leaving only a bleached white skull leering at me with its gaping grin. His frail body shrank away too until only a skeleton sat in the chair. Then all at once it rose and began to come for me, its bones clanking loosely and illuminated by the raging flames behind it, its mouth still gaping, taunting me. . . .

Terrified, I tried to turn and flee back down the hallway, but my feet felt as though they were mired in some vast, sticky substance I could not see. I could not move and the door opened wider until the room itself seemed to reach out and swallow me up.

I opened my mouth to scream. . . . Then, suddenly, I felt a pair of strong, firm arms about my waist, pulling me back, away from the raging room. I tried to turn, to see who had rescued me, but the arms were too strong. I sank back against their solidity and warmth, but in doing so I suddenly dropped the amulet that, I realized suddenly, I had been grasping tight in one fist.

As the amulet clattered to the floor, I felt the arms tighten around me more fiercely, hurting me, cutting off my breath, seeming to squeeze the very life out of my body. The air grew dark about me, and I heard a laugh echoing down the hallway as my captor began pushing me forward into the room I had just escaped. With a last, wrenching effort, I turned my head and saw the green, gleaming eyes of the man who held me. Then, with one great shove, he pushed me into the blazing inferno, and I heard the grating sound of a key turning in the lock behind me. After that I felt a great crushing blow to my shoulders and head, and then there was only darkness.

Chapter Seven

✦✦✦✦✦

I AWOKE IN a sweat, the worn cotton sheet twisted sideways around me and the blanket in a heap on the floor beside the bed. The room was lit dimly by the first gray light of dawn, and as I lay there, my heart still thudding from my nightmare, sounds from outside the window drifted into the room: the cluck of chickens scattering in the yard; heavy boots clomping toward the barn; the jangle of harnesses; horses snuffling and whinnying; good-natured male voices; and then in a rush the brisk sounds of saddles being tightened, harnesses secured, horses mounted, and at last several riders departing the yard with another flurry and squawking from the chickens.

I sat up. The room was growing lighter, and I smelled hot coffee and frying bacon. It took me several moments to realize that it was morning, that I was at the Kendalls' ranch, and it was the beginning of a new day—a normal, ordinary day, full of the routine chores and homey details of rural life. As the light grew and expanded in the room, illuminating its simple dimensions, the night's vivid terrors began to fade, loosening their fierce grip on my consciousness. Gradually, my heart resumed a somewhat regular rhythm again.

So I had been dreaming. And, indeed, the more I thought about it, I could almost trace each aspect of my prolonged nightmare back to something that had been said or done only just recently. Mr. Kendall's tales about Twilight Mesa, Owen's talk of skeletons and skulls and the conversation at supper about buried treasure—all had played a large part in my dreams, I now saw, as had my own rekindled memories of the fire in which my parents had died.

Thinking of my parents, I remembered how strongly I had been affected on the train by the simple sight of a mother and son preparing for bed. Then, as now, I wondered if I were indeed ready for what I had undertaken in journeying here to Twilight Mesa. Could my mind, which for years had been protecting itself from something I could not remember, contend with all these new sensations and provocations?

I did not know. I only knew what instinct had told me in Denver—whether I liked it or not, I was obviously part of something much larger than myself, something that went beyond the puzzle of my own past and the intricacies of my mind.

Whatever it was involved Twilight Mesa, as well as Doran Hunt, Julia Hastings, Prescott Webb, and perhaps others I did not yet know. For some reason I was very important to all of them. Again, I could only trace their interest in me to the fact that I had a key of some sort—a key to something they wanted or were looking for. Judging from Julia's repeated, eager questions about buried treasure, I could guess that the secret had something to do with my gold doubloon. But what?

I did not know. But at least the night was gone, and with it the fear and helplessness. I was not trapped in a nightmare any longer, a passive victim of terror. I was here, now, and there were things I should do.

As I began to dress, I tried to decide what to do for the day. First, of course, I had interviews and research to carry out, notes to write, plans to arrange for my trip to Twilight Mesa. If I were to return to Denver with the articles I had promised Mr. McNeeley, I would have to begin on the groundwork immediately. That was an important and fairly formidable task in itself. And, while working on my research, I could also begin the more subtle task of uncovering the answers to deeper, personal questions I had hoped to find by journeying here.

I finished dressing quickly and heard Mrs. Kendall clanking pots and bustling about the kitchen before I even reached the dining room doorway.

"You're up!" she cried when she saw me. Cheeks crimson and the hair about her face curled into tight wisps from the heat of her wood stove, Mrs. Kendall stood in the doorway holding a blue and white speckled coffeepot in one hand and a platter piled high with golden, steaming biscuits in the other.

"I was hopin' you would be up and around. I just made this batch of biscuits fresh, and the boys are already off doing their chores. I didn't want to have to eat them myself! Come on, now. Sit here at the table. I got a special place laid for you. I put fresh butter and honey in the crocks there, and I was just fixin' to fry up some eggs, too. How many do you want?''

"Oh, thank you, Mrs. Kendall, but I really think I'll just have coffee and biscuits this morning. They look wonderful.''

"You'll do nothing of the kind! We need to get some meat on those bones, girl. You're too durn skinny. If you're plannin' to go all the way to Twilight Mesa in a few days, you'll need to get something solid in you. Now you start in on those biscuits and I'll go make you some nice eggs. They're from my own chickens, you know. Nothin' like fresh eggs on a summer morning.''

It did not take long for the hot coffee and food to work their magic. As a responsive warmth spread throughout my body, my mind seemed to revive with fresh clarity and alertness.

Oh, yes, I had much to do today. And I would begin immediately after breakfast, seeking out the Kendalls' storehouse of relics and learning what I could. After all, Mr. McNeeley had said he wanted a *good* story for his paper, something interesting, alive, like a mystery. Perhaps, I thought as I buttered my third biscuit, there was something else I could discover—or uncover.

Thinking about Mr. McNeeley, I felt a sudden twinge. In many ways, he took the place of my family when I came to Denver, serving as a kind of surrogate—albeit irascible—uncle. But now Mr. McNeeley was hundreds of miles away. I heard the ticking of the Kendalls' old clock on the mantel above the hearth, its beats slow and measured in the silence of the room. I had only myself to count on now, I realized. I was truly alone.

"Now you eat all these up and no excuses!" Mrs. Kendall's stout form loomed suddenly large beside me, snapping me out of my thoughts. After she slid three huge fried eggs onto my plate, she watched me sternly until I lifted a fork and began to eat. Then, seemingly satisfied, she disappeared back into the kitchen.

I couldn't help smiling again. I may have been far away from family, I thought, and from people who really knew me. But with maternal Mrs. Kendall around, I supposed I could hardly call myself alone.

I was especially grateful to Mrs. Kendall for insisting that I eat, for I finished everything she'd cooked before I was satisfied. Then, I gathered up my plate and mug and the other few items remaining on the table and took them into the kitchen.

"Now, now, I'll have none of that!" she cried when she saw my loaded arms. Clucking like one of her chickens, Mrs. Kendall took the dirty dishes from me with a disapproving frown. It was just as I had guessed the night before. "You're one of our guests, Miss Loring, not the hired help. I'll not have you totin' about your own plates!"

Stacking the dishes on the wooden counter, Mrs. Kendall turned and eyed me appraisingly. "Get enough to eat? I hope so—lunch won't be until late today. The boys took their noon meal with 'em when they left this morning. Went off to round up some cattle and check things on the north end of the ranch. They'll be out all day."

Still considering me with her keen gray eyes, Mrs. Kendall finally nodded. "Charlie didn't go with the rest of the boys, though," she added. "I told him to stick around so's he can show you some of them relics. He'll tell you all about 'em. Mr. Kendall's restin' in his room this morning, but after lunch you can go there and talk to him, too, if you want to. 'Spect you've probably guessed that's where you'll get most of your information. You already know how he can talk your ear off! Heaven knows it won't do no good to ask me about those things. I never have figured out why folks get so excited about those dirty old pots and things. Just clutterin' up a perfectly good barn, I say, and takin' my boys away from chores that need to be done. . . ."

I hesitated at Mrs. Kendall's words, again wondering if I were interfering with her daily routine. If she really needed Charlie's help about the ranch, I certainly did not want to take him away from his work simply to answer my questions.

But as Mrs. Kendall went on, pouring heated water into a huge tub and setting the load of dirty dishes in it with a clatter, I realized what I had suspected the day before: her grumbling was quite good-natured. Indeed, she seemed to enjoy griping about her lot as much as she obviously enjoyed her position in the household.

"Well, then," I said, "thank you for the wonderful breakfast, Mrs. Kendall. I truly think I have never had one finer. I certainly haven't eaten so much in a very long time. I think I will go out and find Charlie now. I'm glad you asked him to stay because I do have a great amount of work to do, and I will need his help."

Mrs. Kendall's flush of pleasure told me I had said the right thing, and as I thanked her again and left the kitchen, I heard her start up a new

round of loud humming as she plunged her beefy
forearms into the dishwater. I could not place the
melody, but it sounded suspiciously to me like a
marching song.

As I stepped outside, I was immediately
warmed by a patch of sunlight so golden it
seemed to have melted like butter onto the worn
wooden boards of the porch. The sky above was
brilliantly blue, untouched by a single cloud. To
the east and north lay low hills and distant mountains; to the southwest rose the great blue bulk of
Twilight Mesa.

This morning, however, the sight of the mesa
did not startle and make me wary. It was just as
massive and imposing, but in the fresh light of a
new day it seemed more of an impressive landmark than a place of terrors and danger. It rose,
dramatic and dignified, as if it had earned its
place by sheer durability and strength, its thickly
forested sides bushy and its rocky tip touched
with slanting rays of sun that softened its sandstone peak to a warm rosy hue.

Across the yard I saw Charlie chopping wood
by the barn, the sleeves of his cotton shirt rolled
up to the elbows and the muscles of his arms
bulging as he swung the ax over his head and let
it fall with a muffled thunk into a huge round
piñon stump. I could smell the distinctive, sharp
scent of the wood's sap as I crossed the yard.

"Mornin', Miss Loring," Charlie said with a
grin. He straightened, then pulled a large, red-
checked handkerchief from his back pocket and
paused to wipe his face, already ruddy and
beaded with perspiration. Of all her sons, this
one reminded me the most of Mrs. Kendall.

"Gonna be a hot one today. Did you sleep okay last night?"

"Oh, yes. And you? I hope Miss Hastings and I didn't inconvenience you and your brothers too much."

"Heck, no! We like to bed down outside come summer anyway, so's we can get up and off early. House is too darn confining for us. 'Sides, Ma likes to keep it nice for folks who visit. Her house is her pride and joy, too good for the likes of her own sons!" Charlie pointed toward the largest barn nearby. "That's where we all sleep—the hay barn. We just take our bedrolls and some straw, and we have a fine time. It's kinda like campin'. The alfalfa in there smells so good, you know, so sweet and fresh."

"Does . . . Mr. Hunt board there in the summer as well?" I asked.

"Oh, yes, ma'am. Doran sleeps with the rest of us. Works with the rest of us, too. He didn't go off with Owen and Ben this mornin' though. Said he had some work to do around here. He's probably in the other barn right now, with those relics. Never seen a fella so particular about a bunch of bones and such. Will's crazy about them, too, but the rest of us . . . well, we like the exploring all right—it's kinda like a treasure hunt, you know?—but to dust off all them pots and so on, pack 'em all up and organize 'em in the barn, now that's *work*. And we already got plenty to do around here as it is. But Hunt, he really likes that kind of stuff. He's got them pots and things all lined up neat and tidy . . . well, come on, I'll show you."

Taking my arm, Charlie led me toward a smaller

barn not far from the large one he had pointed out. I had a moment to wonder where Doran Hunt might be—inside, waiting for us, or somewhere else nearby, watching and listening?—before we went in the barn's great open double doors.

Immediately, I felt as though we'd stepped into another world. The sudden transition from the bright sunshine outside to the near-twilight gloom of the barn's rather musty interior made spots dance before my eyes for a moment, and I felt suddenly hemmed-in, confined in that large, enclosed place. As my vision adjusted, I saw dust motes drifting in and out of a weak ray of sunlight that slanted from somewhere above, angling across the wide, hay-strewn floor before us. My nostrils twitched as if tickled.

"See here?" Charlie said. "This is where Doran's got all the relics set up."

He pointed to several narrow tables set up on the dusty floor in the middle of the barn. As I moved closer, I saw that they were covered with rows and rows of Anasazi artifacts, carefully laid out and neatly arranged by category. One table held only bowls and pots, another was devoted to bone tools set alongside stone weapons, and on still another were what appeared to be miscellaneous bits of tattered clothing and some kind of woven rope or cord made into small mats and shoes.

It was exactly like the exhibition in Denver, only much larger and more comprehensive. As I reached out to run my fingers along the perfectly rounded curve of a squat bowl painted in symmetrical black-and-white lines, I felt that same tingling thrill I had experienced for the first time in Denver; I sensed that something still *alive* pulsated from these artifacts, communicating another life, and that by actually reaching out and touching this simple household vessel made hundreds of years ago, I was somehow touching the life lived then, too.

"Got them bowls in a ruin we named Kendall House," Charlie said with a grin. "Heck, we figured if we do the work, we should get some of the credit! It was a nasty job, too, gettin' into that ruin. There's nothin' worse than diggin' through God knows how many hundreds of years of dirt and dust in them ruins—chokes ya, blinds ya, makes your head hurt somethin' fierce! It's hard, dirty work, all right. But once you find somethin' good . . . well, then it all seems worth it."

"Did all four of you Kendall brothers excavate that ruin?" I asked.

"Heck, no! We can't all be spared from the ranch at the same time, leastways not in the summer. And, to tell the truth, I think I like the ranch work better anyway. No, we just go two at a time to Twilight Mesa, sometimes three if we can slip by Ma. And if it's a real big job, like in Kendall House, sometimes we hire out a day laborer or two to take with us."

"A day laborer?" I remembered the assistant Prescott Webb had mentioned the night before. I had not given much thought to the subject then, but now it seemed to make a vague connection with something else in my mind.

"Yes, ma'am. Somebody from Jackson, maybe, or a drifter just passin' through, lookin' for a quick way to make a buck." Charlie threw back his head and laughed. "Poor fools! Don't know what they're gettin' into with us! Ranch work is easy compared with breakin' your back diggin' in them ruins day after day. Most of the workers we hire only stick around a day or two, then move on, and we never see them again."

"There was a photograph at the exhibition in Denver," I began, the hazy connection in my mind sharpening with sudden clarity. "It was taken in a cliff dwelling like Kendall House, and there were several men pictured—Will, Doran Hunt, and perhaps even you and one of your other brothers. . . . And there was one other man standing away from the group. His face was rather blurred, but I thought I . . . thought I recognized him. Do you think he might have been one of those day laborers you were talking about?"

"Might have been." Charlie answered slowly. "Kinda hard to tell. You know when that photograph was taken? Will and Doran went out diggin' lots this summer and last, too. You know where the picture is now?"

I turned my palms up in a gesture of helplessness. "I don't know. It was part of the exhibition, but . . ."

"Recognized the fella, eh?" Charlie rubbed the stubble on his chin thoughtfully. "Ain't that funny! Course it really ain't so strange—like I said, those fellas come and go. You might've seen him before easy enough. But I don't recall none of them staying for long, and for sure none of 'em are still around from last summer, leastways not around the ranch. Course, it could've been a mistake, just somebody you *thought* you knew."

Charlie's expression was so serious, his broad forehead creased with a frown and the features of his ruddy face screwed up into such an expression of puzzled concern that I almost smiled. Obviously, he could not help me.

"Thank you for showing me these relics, Charlie. I think I'll look them over now and take some notes."

Charlie appeared relieved. "Well, all right, Miss Loring, if you're sure . . ." He began to back rather awkwardly from the barn, as if anxious to get on with his chores. "But if you have any more questions now, you be sure and come get me. Okay?" He grinned at me again before finally disappearing into the beckoning sunshine of the yard.

It beckoned me, too, with its bright rays falling on the clumps of grass and wildflowers beyond the barn, illuminating the lazy flies and the bees that darted busily to and fro. But something even stronger held me in the barn. The filtered shafts of grainy light falling softly across the tables of relics, the shadows in the corners, the sounds muffled by piles of hay . . . It *was* like another world—just as isolated and protected, it seemed to me, as the place high in the sheltered cliffs of Twilight Mesa where all these artifacts had first been found.

My hand, resting on the table beside me, brushed against what appeared to be a sandal, made of some sort of thick, coarse leaf, plaited into the shape of a rather broad human foot. As I picked it up, I saw that a ragged circle had been worn through in the upper surface of its heel, and suddenly I was reminded of all the shoes I myself had worn through and discarded over the years—shoes I certainly would not have wanted put on display. For a moment I felt as if I were trespassing on someone's personal life.

On the next table were stone tools and weapons which, I thought, a warrior might have used. The arrowheads alone attested to great skill in the making. For a moment I could almost imagine a man, a very old one, kneeling on the edge of a rock cavern set back high in a canyon wall, teaching a young boy the precise moves with which to strike the perfect arrowhead from a slab of rock. . . .

The image flashed strong and true through my mind, surprising me with its intensity. It was as if, for just an instant, they were there in the barn with me—that man and that boy. As if, through these everyday items, left to be discovered, a vivid part of their lives had leapt forth to affect my own story. And something about those lives touched something in my past, too. It was the same feeling I'd had earlier, only stronger and more defined.

Just the idea that these lives, once full and vibrant, had been cut off so suddenly and mysteriously, lost to time for hundreds of years, triggered something far back in my mind and disturbed me as inexplicably as it had in Denver.

"So, here you are again."

The words, softly spoken, came from a shadowy corner of the barn. I froze, but not in surprise. I had known that he would appear sooner or later. I just had not known when.

Turning, I saw him slowly advance toward me, the slanting light outlining his sculpted features and throwing his denim-clad body into shadow.

"Tell me, Heather," he said as he stopped beside me. "What is it exactly that you expect to find here?"

I could see the lean, tanned muscles of his forearms beyond his rolled-up sleeves as he stood beside me, and smell the scent of hay mingled with sweat and Doran's own, indefinable essence. I could feel him smiling down at me, but I could not look up into those green eyes—not yet.

"A story," I answered, finally looking at him. I gripped the rough wood edge of the table and felt splinters against my palm. "I expect to find a good story for Mr. McNeeley."

"Oh, but I don't think that's all you're looking for."

I couldn't speak for a moment. Something caught in my throat as Doran's eyes met and held mine. The expression in them was much different than I had expected, full of so much and yet containing so little I could understand. Probing mine with a kind of smouldering intensity, Doran's eyes seemed to be searching for some kind of response from me.

In the silence I heard a field mouse scuttling through the straw in a corner of the barn. Then Doran spoke, his voice was tinged with an odd, piercing quality I had not heard before.

"Tell me, Heather. Please. What is it? What did you come down here to find?"

For a moment it seemed as if Doran's eyes and voice penetrated through me, into me, deeper into my mind than I myself had ever dared to explore. And it frightened me.

"What did *you* come down here to find, Mr. Hunt?" I asked, moving away from him. I could only fling my own challenge to counter his. "It seems to me that you are also interested in the past—inordinately so. Could it be that you are looking for some kind of . . . buried treasure of your own?"

For a moment it appeared as if my words had hit their mark. Doran looked startled, and my heart quickened. Had he taken my gold doubloon and passed it on to Prescott Webb? But no, if Doran and Prescott were involved in something together, I thought, why had I felt such tension between them the night before?

Then Doran's face darkened and something hard dropped over his eyes, making them more distant and unreadable than ever.

"I came to Twilight Mesa for one thing and one thing only," he said. "To preserve an advanced, dignified way of life that might otherwise be lost to us, a way of life we can all learn from."

Only the controlled, tight tone of Doran's voice and the skin showing white across his knuckles as he gripped the table's edge gave any visible indication of the anger I felt radiating from him.

"I don't think you realize, Miss Loring, just what the Anasazi Indians accomplished in their lifetime, or what kind of miracle it is that we are even able to imagine how they once must have lived. They lived in caves, in cliffs, for God's sake! Can you imagine how that must have been—cramped and precarious, living with a huge slab of sandstone curving over your head and a sheer drop to sure death in the canyon below? Why do you think they built their homes there? They must have been protecting themselves from enemies—enemies so fierce that the

Anasazi were forced to flee and live in such conditions. Life couldn't have been easy then, for anyone. And yet the Anasazi not only survived, they flourished."

Waving his hand, Doran indicated the table of pottery. "The Anasazi used the skill of their own hands—there were no potter's wheels—to shape their pottery into vessels sturdy enough to carry water from the canyon floors and made them beautiful as well. Look at these jars. They are perfectly symmetrical and their finish would rival the work of any craftsman today. And yet the people who made them were primitives—some would call them savages. And look at the paintings we have found on some of the pottery, these patterns and designs. The Anasazi weren't just craftsmen, they were artists. They were an extremely advanced tribe."

Doran paused, staring at me. "Put *that* in your articles, Miss Loring. I have been struggling to unravel their civilization for over a year, and I have only scratched the surface in understanding them as a people. You will understand when you go to Twilight Mesa yourself and see their homes. As architects they were every bit as meticulous and fine as they were as potters."

Doran had raised his hands and begun gesturing as fiercely as he spoke. Feeling the intensity with which he was trying to communicate, I felt something move inside me.

"I do understand the value of these Anasazi relics, Mr. Hunt," I said quietly, "which is why I convinced Mr. McNeeley to publish my articles. But you are right, I have not yet grasped the magnitude of who the Anasazi were and what they did. I have you to thank for giving me a glimpse of that and for, I hope, instructing me further during the weeks to come."

Doran's eyes held a curious expression. For an instant I felt that same odd connection I felt that day in Durango near the livery stable—intense and strong, it was a kind of understanding that went almost deeper than feeling itself, seeming a part of the past and the future and everything around us, joining us in a kind of bond I had never experienced with any other person before.

"You are a curious woman, Heather Loring," Doran finally said. "I know hardly anything about you and yet . . . you told me in Denver that you were raised by your aunt and uncle, but you never answered my question about your parents. Did they die when you were young?"

The abruptness of his question and the direct intensity of Doran's eyes caught me off guard. "Yes," I answered. "They died when I was five years old. In a fire. In St. Louis."

"What happened? How did it start?"

I hesitated. "No one is really certain," I said. "It was July. The fire spread rapidly and my parents . . . were both trapped inside."

"And you, where were you, Heather?" Doran stood very still, watching me.

"I don't remember." I paused. "I was told afterward that I ran inside after the fire started and was badly injured by falling debris before I was pulled outside to safety. Everyone has always said that I was very fortunate to have . . . survived."

"Ah," Doran said. "No wonder you are so interested in the past. And that spell you had in Denver, was it caused by this injury?"

"Yes. I was ill for some time."

"And this affected your memory?"

"Yes. The doctor who attended me told me I might never regain all of it. I remember some of what happened the day before the fire, but very little of the day itself and nothing of the weeks immediately afterward."

"And what of the rest of your family?" Doran's eyes sharpened on me again. "You have never mentioned any sisters or brothers."

Doran's nearness was like a magnet, pulling on me, pulling *from* me.

"I had one brother. He was there the day of the fire but . . . no body was ever found so he must have escaped somehow. He disappeared after that; no one knows what happened to him. I have always felt, always believed that . . ." I stopped, looking away.

"Yes? You always believed what?"

"I've always believed . . . that Peter is still alive. I don't know why. It's just a . . . a feeling."

"And it was his face you saw in the photograph?" Doran's voice was very low. He moved close to me and looked down into my eyes.

"Yes. No. I . . . I am not certain. It has been over sixteen years since I last saw him, and my memory at best is . . ."

Doran's eyes did not leave my face. "What happened the day of the fire, Heather?" he asked again. "Where was your brother? Why did you go inside the house? What happened to your mother, your father?"

Under the force of Doran's eyes and the power of his voice, I felt my knees go weak beneath me and my body begin to sway forward. There was a rushing in my ears, and my eyes began to blur. Then all at once, Doran's arms shot out to steady me, his hands clenched as strong and hard about my forearms as an iron brace.

I looked up, and in Doran's eyes I saw such raw, direct emotion that for a moment I could not move. By sheer force of will, Doran seemed to be trying to wrench something from me, to seize something hidden deep inside and bring it forth where we could both see it. The intensity in his eyes went beyond mere curiosity—he *needed* to know my answer.

And in a flash I saw that it was vitally important to Doran that *I* know the answer as well. That was truly what he was trying to force from me.

Perhaps that is why I had allowed our conversation to reach the point it had—because of the sheer, compelling force of Doran Hunt's personality.

Drawing a shaky breath, I pulled away. "All that is in the past, Mr. Hunt," I said. "It happened a long, long time ago. It is finished now, over. I cannot . . . I do not wish to discuss it any further."

"As you wish," Doran said evenly. If not for my quick glimpse at his hands, which had clenched tightly into fists, I would not have known that my words affected him at all. He glanced away, and when he looked at me again, his expression was impassive.

"I believe we've looked at these relics long enough for now, don't you, Miss Loring? If you're planning to travel to Twilight Mesa in a few days, don't you think you had better learn how to ride?" He cocked his head and looked at me. "Come.

I've saddled Lady. She's waiting right outside in the corral for you."

When I glimpsed the saddled mare outside, I felt my stomach knot in a sudden spasm. Doran took my arm but I pulled away from him.

"Come, Heather. Don't tell me you're afraid of horses." I could tell by his amused smile that Doran knew exactly what I was thinking. It was odd, then, that it did not occur to me until later to wonder how Doran Hunt had known how frightened I felt around horses.

He crossed over to the corral and unlatched the rough, wooden gate. Inside stood a large, reddish-brown horse, its huge head bent to the ground, cropping a bit of grass in the far corner.

Doran turned and gestured me forward. "Come along now, Heather. Lady is hardly intimidating. She earned her name with her disposition, you know. She's as gentle as can be."

I took a deep breath. I had little experience with horses, and although I knew that to get to Twilight Mesa I would have to ride a horse, I had not been looking forward to the prospect.

Now, however, with what I hoped appeared to be confidence, I strode across the yard to the corral and joined Doran beside Lady. Less than a foot away, the mare appeared even more enormous, her sorrel coat glistening and shiny in the sun, her powerful front leg pawing at the ground. Sensing my approach, she turned still chewing, to look at me. I swallowed.

"There's nothing to be afraid of." Doran's voice was surprisingly gentle. "Riding is the easiest thing in the world."

Doran seemed much more at ease than he had

in the musty confines of the barn. His face was open now, free of its earlier shadows and boyish again. His hair was tousled and glinted as richly as Lady's coat in the bright sunshine.

"Let me help you up. Stand right here and face me . . . that's right. Now turn a little and try to reach the saddle. . . . Good. Now bend your left leg a little."

Taking firm hold of my shoulders, Doran positioned me beside Lady. I did as he said, and I had just half turned and felt my hand slide along the smooth warm leather of Lady's saddle when Doran grasped my left calf just below the knee in his two strong hands and heaved upward. Before I knew what had happened, I was boosted high into the air, my hand clutching at the saddle and my right leg somehow swinging over it instinctively until I was sitting high astride Lady, my skirts bunched up around me on the saddle and my legs dangling down in a quite open display of petticoats, stockings, and high-buttoned shoes.

Seeing Doran's smile, I gathered my wits about me and quickly rearranged my skirts so they covered as much as they should. "I am hardly dressed for riding," I said a little stiffly. I clutched the saddle horn and looked down at Doran.

"That doesn't matter." Grabbing Lady's reins, Doran tossed them up to me. "Here. I'll go sit on the fence and tell you what to do."

"But . . . no! Wait!" As Doran started to walk away, I felt a band of panic tighten across my chest and my mouth go suddenly dry. "I can't just—"

Doran turned back to me. "It's the only way you'll ever learn. Just do as I say."

Obviously bored with the whole procedure, Lady bent her head again to crop off a clump of grass, and as I felt her body shift beneath me, I slid slightly sideways in the saddle. I caught myself and pulled hard on the reins, and Lady lifted her head to look at me, as if insulted.

"Now cluck to her," Doran called from the fence. "Click your tongue a few times to make her go."

I stared at him a moment, then clutched the reins and the saddle horn more firmly before leaning toward Lady's head slightly and clicking my tongue.

Nothing happened. I clicked again, louder, and this time Lady took one step forward and then stopped, turning her head toward Doran on the fence, as if looking to him for assistance.

"You have to give her a squeeze, too," Doran called. "Squeeze her with your legs so she knows you want to go."

I swallowed, then tried to do as Doran said, my knees and legs meeting the formidable resistance of Lady's warm, firm side. Lady stirred slightly, but did not move. I shot Doran a helpless look.

"No, no. You have to do it at the same time."

I turned back to Lady, took a long deep breath, and then, clicking my tongue, pressed my legs with as much effort as I could muster into her great sides.

As if finally alerted to her task, Lady suddenly took off in a quick trot. I was jerked backward, then forward on the saddle, so that I felt a quick

snap of my neck. Then I was holding on for dear
life, clutching the saddle horn as I bounced
against the hard, unyielding leather, trying desperately to regain my balance.

"Ease up!" Doran called from the fence.
"Relax!"

I felt prickles of pain in my rigid back and along
the insides of my legs and tried to do as Doran
said, but I could barely manage to stay astride
Lady. It took several moments to gain enough
presence of mind to pull back on her reins again.
She responded immediately, slowing to a walk,
and as my breathing and heart slowed, I did begin
to relax, although I was still clutching the saddle
horn so tightly it had become slippery from the
perspiration of my hand.

After one more circle around the corral at a
walk, I had relaxed enough to look around. It was
then I realized, with breathless exhilaration, just
how high up I actually was. Beyond the corral,
the Kendalls' land stretched out acre after acre,
down to the river, its winding way lined with a
full green border of cottonwoods. Beyond it, rising as blue and formidable as ever, was Twilight
Mesa.

"Had enough for now?" Suddenly Doran was
beside me, and I realized Lady had stopped. "You
don't want to stay on too long the first day out.
You'll see what I mean when you get down and
walk around a little. You'll have to swing off the
saddle yourself, but I'll help steady you on the
way down."

Trying to be as graceful as humanly possible, I
swung my leg back over the saddle and hung for
an instant alongside Lady's satiny side before

Doran caught me about the waist and my feet touched the ground. His hands did not leave my waist immediately and I was glad, for my legs were so wobbly I am afraid I might have fallen had he not been there.

"Whoa now, careful." Still close behind me, Doran bent his head and his voice was a whisper in my ear, a stirring of breath on my cheek. I felt his hands, strong and firm, spanning my waist, and for a moment it seemed they tightened just a bit, then slid around as I turned to face him.

"You did just fine, Heather Loring," he said. His eyes deepened to an almost emerald color as he looked at me. "I'm sure you will have no trouble in Twilight Mesa at all."

My breath caught in my throat at his nearness, and I saw his eyes drop to my lips as I quickly moistened them.

Then he gave me a kind of half smile before he dropped his hands from my waist and disappeared into the barn.

I stood, watching him go before I headed for the house, my legs already stiff and aching, especially where they had rubbed against the hard saddle. I had the sudden, intense urge for a hot bath.

You did just fine, Heather Loring. I'm sure you will have no trouble in Twilight Mesa at all.

I certainly hoped not. But I was not at all sure time would prove Doran Hunt right.

Chapter Eight

✦✦✦✦✦

"I THINK WE'D better stop here for the night."

Reining in his horse, Doran leaned back in the saddle to look at Julia and me, astride our own horses on the trail behind. As we approached, I saw that Doran's cotton shirt clung to his shoulder blades, and that sweat glistened on his neck above his knotted red kerchief. I had to push back the tendrils of hair curling damply at my own neck and wipe away the perspiration that steadily trickled down the sides of my face as well.

I peered up at the sun, still blazing unmercifully in the azure sky. Although it was late afternoon and the sun's rays slanted toward us rather than burning directly from above as they had earlier, I felt no lessening of their searing force. My dress—a simple, homespun affair made of cotton mattress ticking and given to me that morning by Mrs. Kendall—clung to my skin in uncomfortable, wet patches. I suppose the large, floppy-brimmed hat Mrs. Kendall also insisted I wear helped shield the sun, but its strap chafed about my chin and I couldn't help comparing it to Julia's small, smart bonnet, pinned at a jaunty angle over her upswept black hair and trimmed with a slight sweep of veil.

Now she reined up cool and unruffled beside me, looking regal in her light gray riding habit. It had a short fitted jacket edged in silk braid and ornamented with an embroidered monogram, and a brooch was fastened about the neck of her high-collared blouse. If the suit and the black patent leather boots she wore appeared slightly out of place in the piñon-and-cedar-covered wilderness, Julia made up for it with her erect posture and obvious ease in the saddle. She rode a spirited gelding and handled it with an expertise that made me feel inept and clumsy on gentle, steadfast Lady.

"Let's go ahead and make camp. I doubt that Will found anything much better further on." Swinging down, Doran unstrapped his bedroll and then moved toward the packhorse behind, loaded heavily with the rest of our supplies for the trip.

We had left the Kendalls' ranch early that morning, rising well before dawn and moving away from its tidy, comforting grounds before the sun had begun to rise. It had been cool then, and our ride was pleasant as Will, Doran, Julia, and I crossed the broad Jackson Valley and headed west, toward the northern buttress of Twilight Mesa. For the first part of the morning, we followed a rutted wagon road through miles of sage- and rabbitbrush before reaching an old Indian trail where we began our steep, zigzagging ascent up and around the front of the mesa. This part of the trip was more difficult; the trail was extremely narrow and the hillside blanketed with a thick growth of piñon, cedar, and chaparral that constantly snagged on our clothing and packs as we passed through.

When we reached the top, however, we paused to look back toward the mountains, now glowing bright and jagged in the morning sunlight, and at the farms, laid out like a huge, colorful quilt in the valley below. Then Will led us up over what he called the gap, and we dropped down into a small, narrow canyon. Our horses had to pick their way slowly past the scattered boulders and along the sandy loam of the trail, itself a dry streambed; the canyon floor around us was dotted with gray-green sagebrush, spiky yucca, cactus, and scattered clusters of delicate blue lupine and soft red Indian paintbrush. As we followed this harsh, winding way, I lagged behind, my legs feeling rubbed raw on the insides and my lower back aching from the long journey on the hard leather saddle.

I was certainly having some misgivings about the trip by then, but the others did not seem to notice my discomfort and I was glad, for I was determined to keep my doubts to myself.

It was here, as we truly began to penetrate the harsh terrain of Twilight Mesa, down into another much more enclosed and steep canyon, that my misgivings began to deepen and grow more serious. With every plodding step, Lady was taking me further and further into a land quite callous and unforgiving. Everything that grew around me—the tough, thorned cactus; the stunted piñon; the age-old, rock-hard cedar—seemed to survive by virtue of sheer tenacity. By contrast, I felt neither tenacious nor hardy; barely holding my own on the back of Lady, a hot, steady pain shot up my legs and through my torso, and I asked myself for the dozenth time that day what I was doing in Twilight Mesa.

Over the previous few days at the Kendalls'
ranch, I had spent much time in the barn, studying the relics, learning about the Anasazi. And I
had learned of Twilight Mesa itself, especially
about any previous visitors to this rugged place,
from Mr. Kendall, whose room I visited every day
after lunch.

"I can't say that my boys were the very first to
go in there and find things," Mr. Kendall told me
carefully, "although they were the ones who
really made a job of it, and they're doing it damn
well, too. But there were others—miners, freight-
ers, ranchers—who wintered their stock in some
of the closer canyons, just like we did. Some of
'em might've ridden into the mesa a ways and
found something—a few pots, maybe, when they
were easy to come by. Nobody wanted to work
hard to dig those things out 'cept my boys. There
were always pothunters, I guess. Good pots will
fetch a pretty fair price these days."

"You mentioned miners," I said. "Were there
many who went into the mesa prospecting, looking for gold or silver?"

"Might've been, if they was damn fools! Hell, if
there was gold to be found in the mesa, we
would've been in there lookin' long ago. I told
you I dabbled a bit in that at one time. I know
about these things."

"Could there have been anything else those
prospectors were looking for besides pots and
gold? Some other kind of . . . valuables?"

Mr. Kendall's eyes gleamed in the firelight.
"You thinkin' about some of that buried treasure your friend Miss Hastings was askin' after?

There are tales, you know, like the kind I told you about." He paused, looking into the fire. "Why not? Makes as much sense as any of those other treasure tales. Twilight Mesa would be a great place to hide a treasure. If I had one to hide, that's where I'd go."

He turned his eyes suddenly back to me. "But the question is, if somebody did hide a treasure somewhere in them canyons . . . did they ever come back out? The mesa's a nasty place. It's been known to swallow people up—folks see 'em go in, but never see 'em come back out again. Old Kianeech, that Indian I told you about, he knows all about that. Bet he could answer your question about who's been in the mesa over the last twenty years. He sees everything, living alone there as he does. You'll probably run into him—why not ask him a few questions?" Mr. Kendall grinned at me, his face shadowed in the dim light of the room.

Then, suddenly, he leaned forward. "But I'll tell you something, miss. I can guarantee that more have died in Twilight Mesa than them Anasazi. Someday somebody's gonna run across bones a lot newer than those old Indian bones."

At my shudder, Mr. Kendall laughed. "Oh, you don't fool me a bit, girl! You like all these stories I tell you. I've got you all figured out. You're curious, all right—a real listener. Course you'd have to be, but you're different in a funny way. It's like you're listenin' so much 'cause you're waitin' to hear somethin' you've been wonderin' about for a long time, like there's somethin' missing inside of you and you want to fill it up somehow."

And it appeared that Mr. Kendall had been right. For why would I be here now, in this hot, barren land, if I had not needed so desperately to come?

"Bring your horses over here to dismount," Doran's words shook me out of my reverie. "We'll hobble their forelegs for now so they can drink and eat, and make camp in this grove of pines."

He led two horses over to a small spring nearby. I turned and saw that Julia had already dismounted in one easy, graceful motion. Shifting, I tried to do the same.

But as I swung my leg over the saddle, I found it would not obey. First it felt as stiff as a board and then it went as wobbly and limp as the thick white noodles Mrs. Gresham's cook had insisted on serving at least twice a week while I lived in Denver.

My dismount was undoubtedly extremely clumsy, and I am sure I would have fallen had Doran not caught me. I do not know how he moved to my side so quickly, but as I dropped from the saddle, I felt his large hands span my waist and steady me, setting me as firmly on my feet as the rocky ground would allow. Then, gripping my forearm with one hand, he took Lady's reins in the other.

"Had enough for one day?" he asked. His green eyes scrutinized mine and his face was so close I could have reached out and touched the dark points of stubble that roughened his lean cheeks and jawline.

"It has been a good day's ride." Releasing my arm from Doran's grasp, I tried not to let him see how stiffly I moved away from Lady.

He smiled. "Yes. And now we have more work to do, setting up camp. I'll tend to the horses, but someone needs to fetch wood for the fire and stretch out the sailcloth. Of course, there's dinner to be gotten as well—that's always a good job for a woman."

I ignored the glint in his eye. "I'll fetch the wood," I answered shortly, trying to wipe some of the trail's dirt and grime from my hands onto the skirt of Mrs. Kendall's old dress. I had to clamp my lips to keep from crying out from the pain in my legs as I began to lead Lady toward the spring.

"Fetch the wood?" Julia cried. She was already at the spring, bending gracefully to dip a snowy white handkerchief into its sparkling water. "I don't know why he didn't employ some kind of *servants* to come along on this trip," she said, wringing out the handkerchief to dab delicately about her face. "You can hardly expect us to do all the work ourselves! Oh, I do wish Prescott was here. I'm sure he would have thought to provide more conveniences."

Doran did not bother to hide his smile and swiftly went over to tend to the horses. I moved to the water immediately with my rather tattered handkerchief so that I could wash away the dirt and perspiration from my own face.

Alone with Julia, I noticed that despite her languid pose and the wistful way she gazed off down the canyon, there was actually a kind of tenseness in the way she held her body, a sense of contained excitement or anticipation. When she turned to me, I saw two high, bright spots of color in her cheeks and a glitter in her blue eyes.

"I would be careful around Mr. Hunt, if I were you," she said suddenly, her voice low. "I have noticed how interested in you he seems, and how he insisted on accompanying us here. What do you suppose he wants? It does seem that he wants something from *you* Heather, although I cannot imagine what. As for myself, I don't trust him at all. I am sure I have met him before, and yet he will not acknowledge it at all. He is very evasive." She paused a moment, thinking. "And so very possessive of all those filthy relics. I do believe he thinks this whole mesa is his as well, that it belongs just to him! Perhaps he thinks we are intruding by coming here, and that is why he came along on this trip. To watch us."

Julia leaned closer. "You know, Heather, if Doran does not like the idea of us being here, I think it might be wise for us to watch him as well, to be wary of the things he says and does. And since he seems so very interested in *you* . . . well, it would only make sense to be careful, Heather. You know how accidents can happen."

As Julia walked away, I glanced up at the opposite canyon wall in time to see the rim of the sun dip down below, its last rays lighting the jutting mesa top in a splendid display of crimson and gold. A mere moment later it had disappeared entirely, leaving the canyon in shadow. I shivered at this sudden absence of light and warmth—and at the realization, again, that here in Twilight Mesa we were all at the mercy of the wilderness.

When I arrived back in camp with an armload of fallen piñon branches, I saw that both Doran and Will had returned as well. A great pile of saddles, saddle blankets, bridles, and packs lay in a heap under one of the stunted green pines, and in a clearing, Will had started a small fire with pine needles and small twigs. When he saw me, he jumped up.

"Why, you didn't need to do that, Miss Loring," he cried, rushing over to take the load from my arms. "Don't forget you're our guest! And a lady guest at that. You just let Doran or me handle the heavy work. Now you get on over there and set next to Miss Hastings and get warm by this fire. I'm just fixin' to get it good and hot so's we can cook some dinner on it. Doran's getting that ready."

"Thank you, Will." My tone was warm as I smiled at him, but I deliberately spoke loud enough for it to carry to Doran, who was squatting with his back toward us, mixing something from a flour sack in an old, blackened frying pan near the pile of packs. "What is Mr. Hunt preparing?" I asked as I took a rather precarious seat next to Julia on a large, flat rock Will had dragged up to the campsite.

Doran stood up and faced us. "You might be disappointed, I'm afraid, if you're expecting something fancy—or something good as Will's mother makes back at the ranch."

Doran tipped the frying pan toward us so we could see the white, floury mass of dough he stirred with a flat wooden spoon. The dough was so stiff that it stuck on the bottom of the skillet even when Doran carried the frying pan over and set it handle-up next to the fire. Then, returning to the packs, he cut several thick white slices of bacon off a rectangular slab, lined them up in another blackened pan, and filled a speckled coffee pot with coffee grounds and water poured from his canteen. He walked back over and placed both pan and pot directly on the fire. He finally stood up to face us again, wiping his hands on his heavy denim trousers.

"Hot bread, bacon, and coffee. That's what you get for supper on trail rides like these," he said. "And, if you're lucky, for breakfast, too. On longer trips we take a Dutch oven and cook meat and beans overnight. Now, that's a real treat for the morning meal!"

As the bacon and coffee began to send their irresistible coils of aroma wafting into the cool night air, I felt my stomach rumble in response. Although Mrs. Kendall had sent us off with one of her enormous breakfasts that morning, we had shared only dried fruit on the trail since, and I found my mouth watering at the thought of the upcoming meal.

Doran must have seen my expression, for he grinned at me across the fire, his features looking more boyish than ever in the shadows thrown by the leaping flames.

"So hungry you'll eat even my cooking, eh?" he asked.

"Your menu sounds delicious." My reply was a bit stiff. "I certainly would not expect anything more elaborate."

"Not from me, anyway." Doran laughed, and his face suddenly softened in a way I had seen only a few times before.

Indeed, he seemed young, sitting there hunched by the fire, his hair tousled, his rough clothes carelessly dirty, his gestures eager as he poked at the crackling piñon logs and turned the sizzling bacon slabs with a long, pointed stick. It occurred to me then that while the trip to Twilight Mesa was quite an arduous enterprise for me and even a somewhat difficult trip for Julia, it was really more of a lark for both Doran and Will—an opportunity to leave life's heavier responsibilities behind at the ranch and indulge in a diverting adventure. Despite the careful and efficient way they both had set up camp and gone about preparing supper, I noticed that Will seemed to share some of Doran's youthful eagerness, and that they both had a rather carefree, jaunty manner. I smiled to myself. No wonder the Kendall boys were so eager to take visitors to see the ruins, I thought.

"Better eat up while it's hot." Doran dished the bacon out on tin plates, then passed them over to Will to add the bread.

"Now remember," he said as he handed me my plate and silverware, "the camp rule is that if you don't like the food, you have to cook the next day."

He looked at me, still smiling, as I stuck my fork into the mass of bread and half-cooked pork on my plate. The strips of bacon were burned to a crisp in the middle, raw and fatty on the ends; the bread was dry, mealy, dirty and blackened on the outside and nearly raw dough in the middle, and the coffee was black and bitter.

I cannot remember anything ever tasting so good to me in my life.

"It appears Miss Loring won't be our next cook," Doran commented as I quickly cleaned my plate. I glanced up and saw that all three were watching me. Doran and Will had cleaned their plates as thoroughly as I had, but Julia had taken only her few customary bites before setting the plate delicately on the ground.

"That's all you get until morning," Doran warned. He rose and gathered up the plates to plunge into a pan of spring water he had heating on the fire.

"That's perfectly fine with me," Julia sniffed. "It was all very *delicious*, of course, but I really don't require much food."

Doran grinned at her ploy, and I rather sheepishly handed him my plate. The fire had nearly died down to embers. Removing the pot of water, Doran added more piñon logs until the flames leaped and danced before us.

I shivered again, surprised at how chill the canyon air had become once the sun disappeared. It was dusk, deepening into twilight, and in the silence I could hear the gurgle of the spring, the horses pawing and snuffling at the ground further down the trail, and the far cry of a coyote, followed by another and another.

Mrs. Kendall had also insisted I bring an old, oversized jacket made of heavy canvas that I now went to retrieve from one of the packs. Beyond our campsite, the canyon stretched out lonely and bleak, its odd-shaped boulders shadowed and obscure in the gathering darkness, the slopes above it rising in forbidding steepness. The others had all drawn near the fire, now blazing with the logs I had gathered. They

hissed and spit with sap, and I wrinkled my
nose at the sharp, pungent scent they released
into the cooling night air. In the darkness the
fire was like a beacon, I thought. An age-old
symbol of light and warmth and protection in
the wilderness. As I sat down again next to Julia
and stared into the flames, they seemed to draw
me in, toward the fire's very center—powerful,
magnetic, cryptic; ever changing and eternally
fascinating.

It had taken me years to overcome my terror of
fire after my parents were killed—years to stop
waking up screaming in the night, and even more
years to force myself to sit in front of a fire as I was
doing now.

For fires did not mean comfort or warmth to
me. They meant danger; danger, terror, and
death. Flames were living, dancing symbols of
unbearable pain and loss, everything I did not
want to think about and dared not face.

And yet even as a fire's greedy, leaping flames
frightened me, taunted me with their potency,
they fascinated and drew me with equal force. For
I knew that within them lay the answers to my
own fear, and that those answers, if discovered,
would make me whole.

I heard a noise and looked up to see Doran
prodding the burning logs with a long, charred
stick. In the firelight, his profile was so well out-
lined that I could see tiny fine hairs tinged with
a golden glow across his high cheekbones, dropping down to the curved line of his cheek. He
was not looking at me but into the flames, and
his eyes glowed clear and green against the
shadows on his face.

I felt a sudden flutter in my breast. I was just as afraid of Doran Hunt, I realized, as I was of the fire. I did not trust him; I did not know him; and I was not sure who he was or what he might do.

And yet at the same time I was drawn to him irresistibly. Did I sense that he, too, held some of the answers I was seeking? Or was our attraction more elemental than that—part of the land and sky and fire and air around us?

Doran raised his eyes and met mine, intent on his face, across the fire. I could fairly feel the energy that passed between us then, part of everything and nothing, as old as the ages and as new as the very instant in which it passed. We did not touch. And yet it was as if we had—in the most intimate way imaginable.

"The ancients gathered like this once, around a fire like this one," Doran said, still looking at me but addressing us all. "Perhaps they lived down here in the canyons first, then up in the cliffs. Up there, fire must have been the central force of their lives. Did you know the roofs of the caves where they lived are still streaked with black soot from their fires, fires they lit hundreds of years ago? You can reach up and chip it off with your fingernail."

"Are there many of the . . . dwellings near here?" Julia's voice was hushed, as if she, too, had been affected by the quiet mood around the fire and Doran's words, or perhaps the darkness of the night itself.

"Not in this canyon," Doran replied. "We're only on the outermost edges of Twilight Mesa. Further in, there is an intersecting maze of canyons, a labyrinth you could quickly lose yourself in if you didn't know your way. Most of the canyons are not as hospitable as this; some have no water at all, and very little for the horses to eat. The Anasazi knew which ones to build in. Tomorrow we'll take you to see the largest ruin—Twilight City—in a canyon not far from here. But there are numerous smaller dwellings, many of them still undiscovered, scattered throughout the mesa."

Julia did not answer, but I saw her lift her hands and rub them together toward the fire in a quick, excited gesture.

"It's a sight you'll never forget," Will said, gazing at the fire as well. "That first look at Twilight City. I still remember the first time I saw it. We were across the mesa, just ridin' along, and there it was, all quiet and still, just settin' up there in the cliff all by itself. A whole city. It was like a . . . dream. Like somebody had put a sleepin' spell on it, and it had been there forever and would stay there forever, just the way it was."

In the silence that followed, the fire sizzled and a log fell, sending an orange spray of sparks shooting up into the black night sky.

"Ain't seen nothin' like it before in my life," Will finished in a quiet voice. "Not before nor since."

There was another silence, and then Doran stood up. "Well, they'll see it all for themselves tomorrow, won't they, Will? We wouldn't want to spoil it for them." He crossed over to the packs. "For now, I think we should all get some sleep. It's not an easy ride, and we'll have to leave early."

"Right." Will stood up, too, stretching out to his full height with a groan, then scrounged around in the packs until he found a broad length of sailcloth. With Doran's help, he soon had it hung between two squat pines and the bedrolls laid out underneath.

"Don't look like rain, but you never know," he said with a grin. "We'll all have to sleep here kinda crunched together. 'Sides, it's warmer that way. Miss Hastings and Miss Loring, you'll sleep in the middle. Me and Doran'll take the ends, to protect against snakes and critters and such."

At Julia's alarmed expression, Will rushed on. "Oh, don't worry. We're not likely to see many. Most we might run into—or that might run into *us*—is a skunk or two. But if we're real quiet and leave them alone, they'll leave us alone, too. They'd probably be lookin' for our bacon anyway."

Julia still hesitated by the fire, and Will grinned again. "Now don't you worry, Miss Hastings. We'll take good care of you and deliver you safe and sound to Mr. Webb tomorrow. Like he said, he'll meet us right there across from Twilight City, a bit past noon. In the meantime, we won't let nothin' hurt you."

"Do you mean to say that we will *all* be sleeping together, the men with the ladies?" Julia asked.

"Oh, sure, that's how we always do it. But we'll be perfect gentlemen, won't we, Doran?"

"Oh, yes," Doran said. "Perfect."

He had been standing to the side of the makeshift tent, watching us. His face was in shadow, but as he answered Will, his voice sounded so odd that I looked up at him quickly. Immediately, I sucked in my breath.

I could still see his eyes, and in them was all the attraction, all the dynamic energy I had felt between us before over the fire, now leaping blatantly outward at me, inviting me, riveting me, so that for a moment it seemed that Doran Hunt and I were the only two people in the world. My skin tingled with the impact.

"And where, may I ask, do the ladies change and prepare themselves for sleep?"

Julia's voice came as the sharp intrusion I am sure she meant it to be. I shook myself slightly and saw her narrowed gaze move from Doran to me and then back again.

"Change?" Will scratched his head. "Into what? Out here on the trail, we just sleep in the clothes we got on. Easier that way."

"What a barbaric custom." Julia stood. Although I was still sitting motionless by the fire, the intense sense of connection I had felt with Doran was now quite effectively broken.

"Well, then," she went on, "I do hope you men will have the decency to leave for a time and give us ladies a chance to prepare for bed in some privacy. If we can't have the comforts of civilization, we can at least expect the common courtesies, can we not?"

"Oh, sure. Me and Doran, we'll just go see to the horses, make sure they're all right." Will sounded embarrassed. "Come on Doran, let's go."

I could no longer see Doran's eyes. He did not

answer Will, but I saw him turn and then both of them walked away.

"Well, I certainly am not going to sleep in this riding outfit," Julia said, rummaging in the pack. "My Mama would simply faint dead away if she were here right now, watching me prepare to sleep with two strange men in nothing but my underclothes. Now where did I put that . . . ah, here it is."

Triumphantly, Julia extracted a long flannel nightgown from the pack. Then she turned to me. "Oh, dear . . . Heather! I completely neglected to tell you. Before we left, I slipped one of your nightgowns into the pack for me. Mine are silk, you know, and entirely inappropriate for a trip like this. I do hope you don't mind. But, my goodness gracious, I do hope you have another one for yourself."

"That's all right. I'll sleep in my clothes, as Will suggested. I'm sure I'll be more comfortable that way."

Brushing past Julia, I reached for a cotton handkerchief among the now-scattered contents of the pack. I wanted to be alone. "I am going down to the spring to wash up. That will give you some privacy."

Before Julia could reply, I snatched up the handkerchief and turned away from her, starting across the uneven ground toward the spring. After what I had experienced with Doran a moment before, I needed time to gather my thoughts and emotions together again.

As I reached the spring, I heard Doran and Will's low voices further up the trail, and the snuffling and snorting of the horses. A small animal skittered away through the low brush at my feet. I looked up, feeling the night air cool and fresh against my cheeks. The sky above was so black and spangled with stars it looked like diamond-studded black velvet.

Behind me the fire had burned down to a pile of glowing red embers that cast a dim light about the campsite, closing it in and confining it in its small, defined circle. But out here in the open there was nothing but wilderness. The earth was soft and yielding beneath my feet, and the canyon yawned like a deep black hole in both directions, its bordering slopes rising like great guardian monoliths.

All was quiet and still. Timeless. The way it had always been, for centuries. No wonder the Anasazi had chosen to retreat further into the cliffs and protection of Twilight Mesa, I thought. Here on the floor of the canyon they would have been utterly defenseless. Who knew how many enemies might lie in wait behind the boulders at the base of the slopes, in the thick forest rising above, or even on the mesa tops, watching their every move? A coyote called, sending a cold finger of awareness down my spine.

Utterly defenseless . . . Dipping the handkerchief quickly into the spring, I wrung it out and stood, ready to return to the campsite.

All at once I felt two iron-hard arms twine about my waist from behind, and a warm torso press up against my back, imprisoning me. I gave a stifled gasp.

"It was foolish of you to venture this far from the fire in the dark," a man's voice said, so close

I felt his breath hot against my cheek. "You should never be out alone in a wild place like this. Anything can happen. One moment you are safe, and the next . . ."

The arms tightened about me, and his muscles brushed against my breasts. I felt Doran's breath on my cheek. My heart was pounding so fiercely in my ears I thought surely he would hear it—or feel it throbbing against the steel cords of his arms.

And then, guided by some instinct I hardly understood, I shifted slightly in Doran's arms, my body relaxing against his.

I felt his sharp intake of breath, and could almost hear the quick beating of his heart. He seemed to hesitate a moment. His rough whiskers brushed my cheek, and I turned my face partially toward his.

At this, his arm tightened even more and then moved across my waist, turning me so that I was facing him. His face was dark as night as he looked at me, his eyes in shadow and his jawline hard.

And then, slowly, Doran raised his hand and I felt the callused skin of his thumb as it traced a gentle line along my cheek to my lips. His touch lingered there a moment, and then moved along the outline of my mouth, where his eyes dropped hungrily. Something changed in his face and he shifted, pulling me closer against him with one hand while his other dropped from my lips to my throat, parting the fabric of my open collar.

An immediate response stirred deep inside me—hot and pulsing, starting in my loins and moving swiftly upward. Doran's touch lingered on my throat, teased the skin above the top button of my bodice. Then his palm dropped down to the swell of my breasts.

I drew in my breath. As I looked up at Doran, I saw a question in his eyes. He hesitated again, and then I felt his broad palms press against my back, pulling me against the hard length of his body. His mouth came down on mine.

It was not a tentative kiss, like the ones I'd received from beaux in St. Louis. It was hungry and insistent. At first I pulled back, but Doran's arms only held me tighter, and as his lips moved inexorably over mine, possessing them, I felt the hotness sweep through me again, making my legs and body go weak. I finally gave into the sensations that coursed through me as Doran's tongue parted my lips and tentatively explored inside. Then his lips dropped to my throat.

Doran's hands moved up to my breasts, molding themselves against my soft curves, circling sensuously, and I found myself straining shamelessly toward the pressure of his touch. His lips moved lower down my throat, further parting the fabric of my bodice, and I was sure he could feel the throbbing of my heart as his mouth blazed a trail back upward to claim my mouth again.

My lips gave into his, my body into his, in a burning sweetness I had never experienced before. . . .

And then all at once Doran stiffened. He pulled away from me slightly and lifted his head, as if listening to something on the trail. He loosened his grip and released me. I could not see his face, but in a moment I saw the sudden flash of his smile.

"Anything could happen," he said, taking a step back. "You see?"

I could not determine from the tone of his voice if he was taunting me somehow, or apologizing, or just stating a simple fact. But even now I still felt the strength of his arms about me, the searing impact of his mouth on my lips and throat, the feel of his body pressed against mine.

"You need to get back now," he said, taking the wet cloth from my hand and grasping my arm as he led me back toward the campsite. "Will sent me to fetch you. He was worried about you out here alone."

As if in confirmation of Doran's words, I saw Will's large, raw-boned face peering out in concern before we had even gone halfway along the trail. Will smiled and his worried expression cleared immediately when he saw us.

"Found her out there, did you? Didn't like the idea of her goin' off by herself. I was just comin' to check on you both myself. Come on now, Miss Loring. Doran and me are done with the horses, but we'll find something to do while you get ready for bed. You need to get warm inside that bedroll. Fire's nearly out. Let's see to the food, Doran. Think we could string it up over here from a branch to keep it away from the critters tonight?"

Releasing my arm, Doran nodded and turned, following Will back into the grove of pines. I was left alone with Julia. She sat on the ground under the sailcloth, already in her bedroll. Her blue eyes regarded me sharply.

"So, Mr. Hunt . . . found you?" she said, her dark brows raised in two fine arcs. When I did not answer, she went on in an admonishing tone. "I hope you heeded my earlier warning, Heather. You must be careful of him. That man is not all he seems."

That, I thought, was one of the most blatant understatements I had ever heard.

Had it all been some kind of prank then? Had Doran come to the spring simply to sport with me for his own amusement? I remembered again his sudden smile flashing in the darkness. Was he even now laughing at me, at the way I had turned in his arms, responding so readily, so foolishly to his lips and touch?

And yet even as I felt my cheeks flush at the memory, I remembered Doran's intake of breath, the rapid beating of his heart, the immediacy of his own response as I moved against him. Our encounter had stirred something within him as well, no matter what had been his initial intent.

Or had it?

"Tomorrow I shall see Prescott," Julia said, her eyes shining in the darkness as she lay down and pulled the blankets up over her shoulders. "And you shall, too. Everything will begin to come together at last. The things we have been waiting to see, to find. . . ."

Wearily, I unlooped the laces from my boots and placed them deep in the bottom end of my bedroll to keep them warm for the night. Then I removed my jacket and bunched it up as a pillow and crawled into the bedroll myself. I stared up at the sailcloth ceiling, listening for sounds of Will and Doran returning to camp. Julia's breathing beside me was already regular.

I was tired, too—exhausted and aching and

sore. The ground beneath me was hard and cold, and yet I could not close my eyes.

In a moment I heard what I had been waiting for: the thud of heavy boots. Now I did close my eyes, to feign sleep, listening to the sounds of the two men moving about the campsite and preparing for bed.

Stopping a few feet away from me, Doran was very still for a few moments, and I could fairly feel his eyes boring into me. In another moment he dropped down lightly onto his bedroll beside me, and I let my eyes flutter open for just an instant.

He was sitting with his back to me, only inches away, pulling off his boots. As he shifted, I closed my eyes again. I heard him move again, and then he seemed to settle. Everything was quiet, except for Will's low snores on the other side of Julia.

I opened my eyes again, turning soundlessly on my side. There was Doran Hunt, only inches away from me, his long, lean body encased like a mummy in his bedroll. His back rose and fell in rhythm with his even, steady breathing.

He was asleep—asleep beside me.

I quietly turned to the other side, my back facing Doran's. Even so, I could feel him there beside me, like a pulsating force reaching out in the darkness. I listened to the lonely howl of the coyotes, wondering again about Doran Hunt: who he was, what he wanted of me, what *I* wanted of *him*.

I closed my eyes again and tried to sleep, but it was a very long time before I finally drifted off.

* * *

A great clattering din awoke me the next morning. Starting at the sound, I sat up and hastily rubbed my eyes, only to be met with the sight of Will Kendall, his shirt haphazardly buttoned and halfway tucked into his denim trousers, hopping about on one booted foot near a scattered heap of overturned pots and pans. His other foot dangled in the air, covered loosely in its gray wool sock.

"Durn skunks!" he cried. "Got all our bacon! Just let me lay a hand on one a them . . ."

"Don't you dare." Doran, fully dressed, walked calmly into the campsite's circle holding the speckled coffeepot in one hand. "If you go and get skunked now, we're leaving you behind."

"Well, durn it! I thought we had that bacon strung up high enough last night! And all these pots and pans stacked up . . . I was sure they'd all clatter down just like an alarm and wake us up good if any skunks came around." Will shook his head, bewildered. "Instead, our food gets stolen and I get up still half asleep and run into 'em all myself!"

"I guess the skunks were smarter than you." Doran laughed as he set the coffeepot on a bed of coals glowing hotly where our campfire had been.

I sat up straighter and blinked. Julia was no longer beside me, and three bedrolls were stacked neatly in her place. Although the sun had not yet reached our campsite, I saw that its rays had already tinged the mesa tops surrounding us in a crimson glow and were steadily creeping down the slopes of the cliff opposite.

"I didn't realize it was so late," I said, trying to emerge from the bedroll against the excruciating protests of my cramped muscles and joints.

Doran watched my efforts with a smile. "I tried to wake you earlier, but you wouldn't have any of it. I haven't seen anyone sleep so soundly in a long time."

Although Doran's tone was light, I heard a soft intimacy in it that made me blush. Raising a hand to my hair, I felt a quick heat flush my cheeks as I imagined how I must look—my skirt and blouse twisted, my hair tangled, my bleary eyes still trying to focus. I met Doran's eyes, and it seemed something flickered in them as he looked down at me there on the ground.

Then, perfectly poised and immaculately dressed in her gray riding habit—which seemed to show little or no wear from the day before—Julia rustled into the campground.

"Oh, Heather! You're up. Now we can eat breakfast. It is growing so late."

Regally, she gathered her skirts and took a seat on the large flat rock beside the coals. I saw Doran's lips curve in a smile as he watched her, and for an instant, I felt an odd twist in my chest.

"If I could perhaps wash up first," I said.

"No time for that." Doran's words were blunt. "The time you use in sleep you lose somewhere else. Breakfast is ready. If you don't eat now, you won't eat at all. Come sit down."

Embarrassed, I obeyed meekly, taking the tin plate of crude biscuits and what appeared to be runny porridge that Doran offered me. I sat by Julia and ate in silence, warmed by the coals of the fire and the hot cup of coffee in my hand.

The air was cold but fresh, and shafts of sunlight were finally beginning to slant across the canyon floor, tipping the fine wispy hairs of the spiky yucca plants with an almost luminescent white glow.

As I ate, I once again felt the promise of morning. It seemed to affect the others as well, for as we began to break camp and prepare the horses, I sensed a restrained excitement, all of us eager for our own reasons to see what the new day might bring.

"Let's be off then," Doran said, swinging up onto his saddle. "We'll have no time at all to explore if we don't leave now."

I put my foot into Lady's stirrup warily. There was one moment of excruciating pain as I swung my leg up and over and then settled into the saddle, every nerve of my body tingling with the contact, and then Lady fell into line behind Julia's horse and we were off, Doran in the lead and Will taking up the rear.

It was not as bad as I had imagined. After the first quarter of an hour or so, my body seemed to adjust to the saddle, and I found that although sore, I was not entirely uncomfortable. Indeed, as I diverted my mind from the ache in my legs and back, I found myself looking forward rather eagerly to the ride ahead—to the sun on my back, the steady progress on the trail, and to what we would find at the end.

Near the middle of the canyon where we had camped, Doran led us into the mouth of an adjoining branch he called Juniper Canyon. Its sides converged much more closely, rising steeply beside the rocky trail we followed along the base of the gulch. But after what seemed only a short time, Doran turned his horse and led us up a steep, switchbacking trail—one I would never have found had I been alone—right up the slope toward the top of the mesa. The others seemed unaffected by our suddenly precarious path, but I clung to Lady as if my life depended on it—which, I soon found, it did. Twice Lady's hooves slipped on the trail's loose rocks and I felt my heart plunge to my stomach, but then she regained her footing as if nothing had happened, and my heart stopped racing and returned to normal.

Concentrating so hard on guiding Lady up the slope, I barely noticed our surroundings as we climbed. Only when Doran reined in a moment to pause on the trail did I realize what we'd done.

Below us the rock and pine-speckled slope dropped sheerly away, and the path we had just climbed was swallowed up invisibly on its blanketed side. I could not imagine, looking down, how we had ever come up. I think, however, it was the sheer immensity of the terrain that struck me the most: the huge, flat-topped mesas dropping down from their bands of harshly rugged cliffs into slopes that intersected in great vees as far as the eye could see. I could easily understand what both Doran Hunt and Mr. Kendall had been trying to tell me earlier about how Twilight Mesa could swallow up anyone who ventured into it.

"Just around this bend and we're on top," Doran said, spurring his horse up the last short incline. "Follow me, and I'll take you to the spot where Will first saw Twilight City."

We fell in as Doran's horse picked its way through the dense piñon and juniper growth on top of the mesa. All I could see before me was the tangled maze of stunted trees, deeply green against the dark blue of the sky. The scent of hot, oozing pine sap was almost palpable in the air, hitting me in thick waves as Lady made her way over the loose gravel and shelves of broken sandstone at her feet. Birds twittered and darted about in the trees around us; I heard the songs of warblers and nuthatches, and more than once, the raucous screech of a jay as a streak of blue flashed overhead. The round, vibrating body of a hummingbird whizzed by my ear, zig-zagging on its course toward Will's knotted red neckerchief. Pairs of blue and yellow butterflies fluttered tantalizingly by as well, carried on invisible currents of air.

I was glad Doran was leading the way, for had I been alone, I certainly would have been lost in five minutes. Every turn of the forest was so inviting I would have been off investigating until I found myself in the center of the piñon-and-juniper maze with no clue to lead me out.

"Here we are."

We all dismounted and secured the horses, and Doran led the way through the forest. My boots crunched on small pinecones and sank into the loose, thick sand of the ground, and I felt the sudden jab of a sharp rock. A quick gray lizard darted across the ground in front of me just as Doran disappeared into another thick green grove of piñons. I heard Julia's skirts rustle against her boots and Will's heavy tread on the forest floor behind me.

Then, all at once, through the curved, drooping branches of a piñon, I glimpsed a huge chunk of streaked sandstone hanging across the canyon, as if suspended in the air. Doran stopped. We stood on the very edge of the mesa.

It happened so suddenly that I took an abrupt step back. Only a few feet away, a sheer drop below, were the great wild canyons in all their immensity; directly across from me, seemingly only a stone's throw away, was the facing sandstone cliff, its striated hues of yellow, ocher, and black a sharp contrast against the blue sky.

"Come," said Doran, watching me. "You can't see anything from back there. Come up here where there's a real view."

Taking my arm, he led me forward onto a thick yellow slab of rock that jutted out over the canyon.

My heart dropped. Below, the pine-and-rock-covered slopes plunged into a dizzying chasm. I took a breath and closed my eyes.

I would be careful if I were you, Julia had said. *You know how accidents can happen.*

"It's perfectly safe," Doran said, still holding my arm, his voice resonant in the pine-scented air. "Here, take hold of this cedar branch for support."

He let go of my arm and I quickly clutched at the thick, gray limb he indicated. It was surprisingly sturdy, twisted and wrenched by the elements; when I tested it with my weight, I found it did not tremble or budge an inch and I felt a bit more confident with it in my grasp.

I did not see anything unusual at first, just the huge band of sandstone caprock running just below and along the length of the opposite mesa. It was lined with the folds and creases, cracks and crevices that the forces of wind and water had wrought on its grainy surface, molding and sculpting the softened rock as if it were some kind of malleable clay.

I looked, then looked again. And then it happened.

First I saw something in one of the crevices of the rock. It was a cavern, really, a great cave that had been formed in the canyon wall, with a high-vaulted roof that arched in a great semicircle not two hundred feet from the top of the mesa. Deep in its shadowed recesses, I first made out what appeared to be a sandstone wall, barely distinguishable in its surroundings, then a window, black and still in the shadows. Then my eye swept left, and I let out a gasp.

It was all there, just as Will had described it: an entire city, a city of stone, hanging quiet and still in the hushed, recessed shelter of the cliff, pale and peaceful and impregnable above the wilderness of canyon below. As if it had been sleeping there for ages, just waiting for me to come along and see it.

Just waiting. For me.

As my eyes swept the pale walls and terraces, the black windows and rooms nestled one upon the other, the tall, beautifully symmetrical tower rising to its full height in the center, I felt as if the sight had somehow been imprinted on my consciousness long ago and lain dormant until this very moment, when it leapt out at me like a very old, very dear friend. Now, face-to-face, I was greeting it for the first time. I can hardly describe the sight. It was so perfectly right, so *known*.

And yet, as I stood there staring at it, I felt an odd tingling of apprehension as well, as if now, seen and known, something about it was not quite right. Old emotions suddenly stirred and grew within me: a sense of unease, of fear; a sense that something was about to happen and it would not be good at all. This ominous dread was the worst of all, and I did not know where it came from, only that for some reason it went hand in hand with this, my first view of Twilight City.

And from its distance across the canyon, Twilight City stared back at me, sightless and still.

Chapter Nine

✦✦✦✦

"QUITE A SIGHT, isn't it?" Doran leaned toward me. "I still remember the first time I saw Twilight City. It was last summer, and I was standing on this very point." He moved closer to me on the slab of rock, and his hand brushed mine as he grasped the cedar.

The wind's mournful wail howled down the canyon, and all at once it seemed as if Doran and I were standing there suspended in time just like the ruin opposite us. I felt the wind rush against my ears, drying the perspiration and stirring tendrils of hair that clung to the back of my neck. I had unfastened the top button of my dress and rolled up its sleeves while riding up the trail; now the hot sun on my skin, the fragrance of heated pine sap in the air, and the view across the canyon all combined with the morning's exertion made me feel rather languid, almost drugged. As Doran moved behind me, I became aware of his scent, the mingled odors of heat on denim, leather and skin—an earthy, sweaty, and entirely male smell—and I saw the muscles of his forearm flex on the cedar branch. For a moment Doran and I stood motionless, as if we were one with the terrain about us, part of the mesa and the canyon and the day itself.

Just as I started to turn toward him, Julia's voice broke the spell of stillness.

"Well, where is this wonderful ruin we've come so far to see?"

Crackling and tramping through the underbrush, she emerged behind us.

"Oh dear me! Do I have to come all the way out there? I surely cannot . . . oh!"

Glimpsing Twilight City through the trees, Julia stopped abruptly, her gloved hand covering the round, perfectly shaped *O* of her mouth. For a moment the haunting sight of that motionless, lost ruin must have transfixed even her for she remained motionless, and Will, coming up behind her, stopped a short distance to her left, a wide grin on his face.

"Always takes people like that the first time,"

he said, nodding toward the ruin in its protected cave across the canyon. "No other view of the city quite matches this one. Looks kinda like a castle, don't it?"

Julia's eyes gleamed. "Oh yes. And castles are full of treasures, aren't they?"

"Not that one." Doran moved away from me to stand by the peeling gray trunk of a juniper further along the mesa's rim. "Twilight City has been thoroughly excavated. It was one of the first we cleaned out, wasn't it, Will? Now there's nothing of value left—to take, that is. Its value lies simply in what it is and what it can tell us."

"Oh." Julia's disappointment was almost comically evident. "But surely those other ruins . . ."

"We'll see those later. For now, we'll ride back around the mesa until we get to the point where we can get down to the cave. There's just a short drop down a crevice at the beginning, then a set of steps hewn out of the sandstone down to the ruin. It's really quite easy."

"A short drop down a crevice?" Julia's voice was disbelieving. "Surely you can't expect me to attempt such a route! Do you mean we must come down straight off the cliff?"

"Well, it *is* a cliff dwelling," Doran said, the corners of his lips twitching in a smile. "We use the same route the Anasazi used daily—women and children included. As I said, it really is quite simple, and entirely safe."

"Well, I am no . . . no Indian, and I certainly am not dropping down over a cliff or into any crevice!" Julia took a handkerchief from the sleeve of her gray jacket and dabbed delicately at her forehead. "I can see it perfectly well from here. If, as you say, there is nothing of value left, I see no reason to explore it further. I will wait for Prescott right here and save my strength for a ruin that holds more promise."

Doran's smile broadened as he watched Julia, then he turned to me. "Miss Loring? Do you feel the same way?"

I was silent, staring at the mesa top across the canyon and the sheer cliff of sandstone that dropped down to the ruin. I had known all along, of course, that I would somehow have to make the descent into cliff dwellings like Twilight City. But I suppose I had imagined that gathering the courage to slip down the side of a cliff would somehow be easier than it was turning out to be, now that the moment of truth was before me.

"Are there not . . . any ladders?" I asked, turning to Doran.

"Oh, come, Miss Loring! Do you suppose the ancients *needed* such means of assistance?" His voice was chiding, and I felt my face begin to redden. Then Doran relented. "Actually, there are some ladders—good ones—left in a few of the dwellings. But for the most part, the Anasazi came and went from their homes directly over the rock. They must have had a most amazing sense of balance." Doran watched me a moment. "Don't tell me that you are having second thoughts, Miss Loring."

When I did not answer, he went on. "But, of course, you don't *have* to come. You could stay here with Miss Hastings and simply write about your observations from this viewpoint. That would certainly suffice for the articles you plan to write. After all, the staid citizens of Denver don't have to know what it's like to actually be *in* a cliff dwelling. I am sure they would never expect a reporter—especially a *woman* reporter—to take such a risk for a newspaper account they will only scan briefly before throwing into the fire."

Still clutching the cedar for support, I looked over at Twilight City. Although Doran was obviously goading me, his words still rankled. On impulse, I let go of the branch for a moment and let myself stand unsupported on the jutting sandstone rim. It was a dizzying, breathtaking sensation, and for a moment my legs locked and my mouth went dry. I felt an almost magnetic pull toward the edge of the rock, where I would see how steeply the pine-and-rock-covered slopes fell away to the canyon below. I stood there another moment in shaky balance, then stepped back and grabbed the cedar.

"All right," I finally said. "I will ride over with you now."

Doran's mouth curled triumphantly as I brushed past him, but I knew that by agreeing to go with him, I was not responding solely to his goading words. I had my own motivation.

Walking quickly back through the piñons, I was already seated on Lady by the time Doran reached his horse and swung up into the saddle. He led in silence as we rode back through the maze of the mesa top in a roundabout, southwesterly direction. I could not tell then, but I learned later that we were crossing from one mesa to the next, following the curved edge that joined them.

We had only gone a short way, it seemed, when Doran reined in his horse again to dismount. He hobbled both horses and gestured for me to follow him through the trees to the mesa's edge.

We came out of the forest just as abruptly as before. All around the rock-rimmed mesa dropped down abruptly. I stood a moment to gaze across the canyon, and through the thick green growth of the mesa opposite, I saw a flash of red, then blue, then gray. In another moment, Will and Julia emerged from the trees. Stepping onto the sandstone outcropping, Will raised his red neckerchief in salute.

"That didn't take long!" His voice carried as clearly across the chasm dividing us as if he had been standing only yards away. I heard Julia's tinkling laugh, then silence as the two waited to watch our descent.

Doran strode along the protruding lip of the mesa—another great, yellow, and surprisingly stable slab of sandstone—until he reached a gaping cleft in the rock several paces away.

"Here's where we start down," he said. Squatting, he dropped his legs down into the crevice and within an instant only his lean torso was visible above the rock's surface.

"Don't worry," he said, looking at me. "It's very easy. Just follow me. That way I can catch you if you fall."

Doran dropped down further, and his head disappeared into the stone fissure.

I took a deep breath. Then hitching up the hem of my skirt and tucking it firmly into the cloth belt fastened to the waistband of my dress, I, too, sat down on the sandstone slab and let my feet dangle into the crevice. Then, slowly, I turned onto my stomach and lowered myself down.

The sandstone sides of the crevice were close together, and as I felt my arms scrape against the grainy rock, I was overcome by a sudden, claustrophobic sensation. I probed the toe of my boot downward rather frantically. It soon found its footing on several well-placed boulders, however, lodged in the crevice. Taking another deep breath, I paused a moment. There between the sandstone slabs it was cool and rather dim, for only a jagged ray of sunlight pierced through the crack above. Forcing myself to proceed, I felt my stomach drop as my boot continued to probe downward, and I kept my face to the inner portion of the rock so that I could not see the chasm of the canyon gaping behind and below me.

"This is the easiest part," Doran said, his voice rising encouragingly a few feet below me. I felt his hand reach up and firmly grasp my boot about the ankle, placing it at the next lodged rock. In a moment, his hands reached up as well, spanning my waist, to pull me down beside him. Having emerged from the sheltering crevice, we now stood on a bare shelf of rock jutting out over the cliff.

"Just don't look down," Doran said as I began to tremble. "Here. These are the steps I told you about. Just turn around and back down them. They are very simple to negotiate. I'll start down first, and you follow after me. Keep facing the rock. That's it. Do you see how you can use the steps as hand holds, too, as you go down? . . . That's right. Good! Now lower your boot to the next step. I've got it. That's right. . . . Down a few more feet now, and we'll be there. . . . Keep going now, that's it."

Inch by careful inch, my teeth gritted, I descended the rough steps carved out of the cliff. I hardly dared think what I was doing, concentrating only on the pitted, porous surface of the sandstone in front of my eyes. As the wind whistled through the piñons on the mesa above and the canyon below, its persistent, breathy sound seemed like a mocking voice whispering in my ear.

And then, all at once, my boot found a solid, blessedly large surface of rock, and I felt Doran's hands once again about my waist, steadying me. We had reached the flat bottom ledge of Twilight City's great alcove.

"We really need to rig up some kind of ladder for this ruin," Doran said, releasing me as soon as I could stand on my own. "But I wanted you to experience it the way the Anasazi did. They must have used this route several times a day, going up and down from their farmlands on the mesa top. Can you imagine it?"

"No," I replied slowly. "I cannot."

It was quiet. Unbelievably quiet. My eyes swept up, following the chiseled curve of the lofty vault overhead. The cave was immense, its back wall pitted, porous, striated with the black, sooty streaks Doran had told us about. Its roof sloped up and over me in great, powerful impermeability; beneath it I felt small, insubstantial.

"This all used to be solid sandstone," Doran said. "Or so we guess. These great alcoves must have been formed thousands of years ago by water seeping in under the porous sandstone of the cliffs and then freezing in the winter, so that gradually huge chunks would fall off and leave these caverns. When the Anasazi found these cliffs, the caves were already sculpted out."

The sun-warmed sandstone under my hand felt oddly soft and grainy, and it crumbled slightly under my palm as I moved forward. A tumble-down collection of walls and rooms stretched out in a wide arc on the alcove floor before me, built up on terraces from the ledge's outer edge to the dark, shadowy recesses in the rear, where the cave's back wall came down to meet the floor.

"We've counted over one hundred rooms in this one dwelling," Doran said. "Most of those in the front we found in almost total ruin, but some in the rear still stand exactly as they must have centuries ago. That far back they're protected almost completely from the elements. We found some of our most perfect artifacts, including mummies, there."

He gestured again, and I saw, toward the back of the cavern, walls that still rose two and three stories high. Even from where I stood I could tell that they had been built well, made of even blocks of stone and squared off sharply on the edges. Here and there, the walls were punctuated by the black, T-shaped windows and doors I had seen from the other mesa.

I moved forward into the city, feeling as if I were entering the hushed, stately ruins of the Colosseum in Rome or a Greek temple. There was a strong sense of dignity and skill still apparent in the half-ruined buildings. Before me, the tower I had seen across the canyon rose in perfect grace and symmetry nearly three stories high, swelling out at the base to beautifully rounded proportions that attested, vividly, to the skill of its ancient builders.

This had been a real city, I thought with a sense of dawning awe. A city where people had worked and played, ate and slept, lived and died.

Toward the back of the ruin, I found a complete room still intact. Its floor had been cleared of debris, and it was large enough to stand in. On impulse I squeezed through its low, rectangular window and stepped inside.

The room was about eight feet square, made dim and dusty by its shadowed position in the cavern—an atmosphere of perpetual twilight, I thought. I could hardly imagine spending a day or two in such a room, much less living there.

But as I ducked my head and peered out the tiny window, I found that it provided an excellent frame for the view of vivid greens and blues and yellows that spread forth like a painting outside—a skillful juxtaposition of ruin, sky, canyon, and mesa. I was alone; Doran had moved to the other end of the ruin to investigate something in another room.

It was very quiet, standing all alone in that ancient room. A rather eerie, uncanny feeling crept over me gradually, then gained strength, as if gathering power from the lost remnants of lives that still lingered there: so this was what it was like, I thought, to be one of them, peering out, centuries ago.

For I was seeing *their* world. The view then must have been nearly the same—I was seeing it just as they had hundreds of years ago. This sudden realization made me feel as if I were no longer a mere trespasser, but a part of Twilight City. In this silent, almost magically preserved place, we were no longer divided by time, but joined by it.

And then I felt something else still lingering in the isolation of that tiny, sandstone room.

Loneliness. I felt as if I were standing in a long-abandoned home that was once full of life and activity and now, visited once again, yearns to speak aloud and tell the stories of the life that was once played out within its walls. The secrets, the past lives, the inexplicable, irretrievable loss.

For a moment it seemed almost too much to bear. The silence and secrets of centuries. I put my hand on the warm sandstone at the base of the window, feeling as if a dark, heavy weight had settled in my chest, pulling me down with it.

"Not another one of your spells coming on, is it?" Suddenly Doran was beside me. "You look almost as you did in Denver, when you saw the amulet."

"No. No, it's not a spell," I said, taking a step away from him, my hand still resting on the warm sandstone block. "I just . . . I was overcome with a rather vivid impression, standing here."

"Oh?" Doran's tone was sharp. "And what was—?"

Doran's question was cut off by a sudden, resounding shout from across the canyon. Making our way back to the front of the cavern, I saw a tall figure standing on the opposite mesa, waving in our direction.

"Hello there! Are you coming up now? We're ready to ride over."

"Webb," Doran said, muttering under his breath.

Still watching, I saw Julia's trim gray figure emerge from the piñons, gracefully sweeping over to join Prescott on the rim. Prescott wrapped an arm about her waist, pulling her close to him in an intimate embrace.

"Oh yes," Julia called as Doran and I emerged onto the outcropping in front of Twilight City. "Do come up now. Prescott has prepared a most sumptuous lunch for us! We have it all packed on the horses. We'll ride right over and meet you on the mesa."

Before we could reply, both Prescott and Julia vanished into the forest. Doran looked at me and then shrugged.

"It will take some time for them to ride over. But we should start up anyway. The climb up is much easier than coming down," he said, leading me over to the stone steps and standing aside so that I might go up ahead of him. "But again, you might not want to look down."

Taking a deep breath, I squared my shoulders and started up the steps, determined to climb them without hesitation. I felt both reassured and uncomfortable with Doran behind me; the only bad moment occurred when we reached the open ledge between the steps and the crevice and I felt, for an instant, a kind of irresistible pull on my back, as if the very air of the canyon behind me were trying to suck me down into its depths.

But I forced myself to go on into the crevice, and from there it was only the short steep climb to the top. In a moment I felt Doran's hands about my waist again, lifting me up onto the mesa.

"Well!" Julia cried, her sharp, lively face the first that met me as I stood, rather shakily, on the sandstone slab. "Was it all just terribly exciting? Oh, do come over and tell us about it! We have a place all laid for you. I'm afraid Will won't be joining us. After Prescott arrived, he decided to explore a bit. He said he would meet us later and eat his own lunch on the trail. What a pity he will miss what Prescott has brought us!"

Taking my arm quickly, Julia led me over to a nearby clearing. There, spread out over the rock-and-twig-strewn ground, was a red-checked cloth festively laid with tin tableware, linen napkins, and a fully prepared meal. Prescott Webb was beside it, dressed in a tailored suit. He stood when I approached.

"Miss Loring," he said, extending a warm, well-manicured hand in greeting. "How nice to see you again."

"Isn't it wonderful?" As Julia indicated the picnic spread at our feet, her light laugh joined in song with one of the mesa's native chickadees. "You can understand now, Heather, why I consented to marry Mr. Webb. Who else could have provided such a feast for our pleasure? It simply cannot compare to our . . . repast around the campfire last night."

"Oh, come now, Julia," Prescott said. "This is hardly an exceptional meal, although I do admit I went to some trouble packing it. I thought you ladies deserved something special your first day in Twilight Mesa. Come, Miss Loring. Sit down. We have bread, cheese, fruit. The peaches are canned, but really quite a luxury here, don't you think? Let me prepare you a plate."

With one knee up, Prescott crouched gracefully in his high leather boots, forking two peach halves

out of an open tin and slicing several slabs of
yellow cheese and dark bread from their wrap-
pings in the center of the checked cloth. Arranging the food carefully on a tin plate, he handed it,
along with a snowy linen napkin, to me.

"So tell me, Miss Loring," he said, returning to
his own place beside the cloth as Julia and I sat
down beside him. "What did you think of our
own Twilight City?"

"It was . . . inspiring," I finally said. "Unlike
anything I have ever seen. The way I felt . . .
it is difficult to put into words. There is a sense
of majesty there still, and such a feel for the
past."

"Ah. Very well put." Holding one of the napkins, Prescott carefully wiped the edge of his long-
handled silver knife along the fabric's white
creases, then set the knife down and shook out
the napkin with a quick, resounding snap.

For some reason, the gesture caught my attention. It seemed both incongruous in that wilderness setting, and yet perfectly in keeping with
Prescott Webb's smooth manners and suave nature. Again, I wondered about his background
and what might lie beneath his polished veneer.

"Have you been having much success with
your work since you left us, Mr. Webb?" I asked.
"Exploring the canyons, I mean? Didn't you say
you were a kind of independent agent for the
government?"

"How very thorough of you, Miss Loring."
Prescott's tone was smooth and correct. "But
I'm afraid you would find what I do in Twilight
Mesa extremely dull—routine cataloging, sur-
veying, hardly the stuff of exciting journalism."

"That's very modest of you, Mr. Webb." I took a small bite of cheese. "But you see, I am interested in all aspects of work being done in Twilight Mesa. Many readers in Denver might be fascinated by what you do. I had hoped that perhaps I could accompany you and Julia one day as you go about your tasks here."

"Mr. Hunt's work would provide much more interesting material for your articles, I'm sure," Prescott replied, brushing crumbs off his twill trousers. "He is actually doing more excavation in the dwellings than I am. Tell me, Mr. Hunt, have you finished all your work in the mesa, or have you left us a few untouched ruins we could explore nearby this afternoon?"

"Oh, yes!" cried Julia. "That is exactly what we came for!"

Doran—who had taken his own lunch of hard biscuits from his pocket to eat under the piñon instead of joining us at the cloth spread on the ground—paused in his chewing as if in consideration of Prescott's question.

"You know as well as I do that there are a number of undiscovered ruins in Twilight Mesa, Webb," Doran finally said. "But not in this exact vicinity. We have been working on our excavations here for the past six months."

"Well then, I know of at least one ruin we could visit in a branch canyon not far from here," Prescott said, turning to me. "It is relatively unexplored and would take only about two hours to ride there."

"We can't do that," Doran said bluntly. "It's too late in the day. It's after noon now. If we ride two hours and explore the ruin you're talking about, we'll never get back here in time to make camp."

"There's quite an adequate camping spot on the mesa above the ruin I have in mind," Prescott put in smoothly, "as well as a good supply of water in the canyon below. I think we could all spend the night there quite comfortably—that is, if you do not object to my joining your little party for the evening."

Doran did not answer, but his eyes locked with Prescott's. Again I felt the tension between them. What *was* their relationship? I wondered.

"All right, Webb," Doran finally said. "You guide us to your ruin—that is, if you don't mind if *I* come along. I'd like to see it. Perhaps you will even give me permission to excavate."

Doran's last words, although flippant and innocent enough, seemed weighted with a heavier meaning, made evident by the hard edge to his voice.

"Of course," said Prescott, making a slight bow in Doran's direction. "Now, shall we finish our lunch and go exploring?"

"Oh yes!" Julia clapped her hands together. "Let's ride over right now!"

"What about Will?" I asked.

"I told him before he left where we most likely would go this afternoon," Prescott replied, not looking at Doran. "He said he would meet us there before nightfall."

Doran did not comment, and with Julia prompting us excitedly, it took us only a short while to finish our meal, pack up the lunch items, and mount our horses.

As we rode, I was relieved to find that I was

growing much more accustomed to the saddle. Although my legs were still tender and sore I was even beginning to enjoy being on Lady, especially when the sun shone down brightly, filling the air with the piñon's fragrance.

"Here we are," Prescott said, after what seemed much less than two hours. "The ruin is over to the right a bit, and below. My assistant discovered an excellent way to get down to the ruin several weeks ago. There is a set of stone steps, like those at Twilight City only much easier and less steep."

"Your assistant worked in this ruin?" Doran broke in, dismounting from his horse. "Where is he now?"

"At the cabin. He's compiling data." Prescott's answer was smooth, as always, but I thought I heard a slight hesitation before he replied. "Now Julia, let me help you down. You may be the first to descend, if you like."

Julia's movements were eager as she dismounted, and so directly opposed to her behavior across from Twilight City that I had to smile.

"You see, the way is quite easy," Prescott said, gesturing to a long, narrow slab of sandstone that sloped gradually down to a ledge. "Twilight City is situated in a much higher cliff. You will see as you follow me. Here Julia, give me your hand."

Doran and I followed them down the path and set of sandstone steps until, with a surprisingly small amount of effort, we all stood on the solid rock lip of the cliff alcove in which a much smaller dwelling had been built.

"Oh, wasn't that exciting?" Julia cried. "And look, Prescott was right. This hardly looks touched." She turned to Doran, her voice lilting.

"I'm surprised *you* haven't discovered these ruins, Mr. Hunt."

"I've been here before," Doran replied shortly. "I just haven't excavated them yet. Over the last year I have been putting my energies into a thorough search of other ruins." He paused and looked at Prescott. "I don't have time to ride all over the mesa like some kind of pothunter."

Prescott's face showed no change of expression. "Indeed. Very admirable. And now, shall we all proceed into the ruin?"

We followed Prescott into a ramshackle collection of walls, rooms, and half-collapsed buildings nearly buried in sloping heaps of fallen blocks and timber. While this ruin was not nearly as impressive as Twilight City, it had a more personal feeling, perhaps precisely because it was much smaller and had not been excavated.

"Well, what do you think?" Prescott asked from atop a pile of rubble.

Doran spoke up. "This ruin is hardly unexplored," he said, poking about the fallen walls of a room. "It looks like someone has been doing quite a bit of excavating in here—or pothunting. Your assistant, Webb?"

"Yes. I thought I already answered that question for you, Mr. Hunt. Although, of course, our work has hardly been along the lines of pothunting." Prescott's voice was cold and controlled, but as he turned toward Doran, I could not see his face.

"I didn't know that government work involved digging," Doran said. He reached down into the pile of rocks and moved a few blocks with his hands. "Some of these walls have obviously been knocked down and the rubble cleared away. It seems to me that who ever did it was looking for something."

"You and the Kendalls aren't the only ones excavating in this mesa, Hunt. Others have discovered the ruins. And some of them are out to make a decent profit from their labors—not just you."

Doran's voice was controlled as he answered Prescott. "I haven't made a dime on a year's worth of work here, Webb, so don't class me among your greedy profiteers. I'm not digging out relics to sell them. I have other motives."

"Oh, yes, I know. And they are all purely innocent, I am sure."

Turning away from Doran abruptly, Prescott addressed Julia and me. "Well, ladies, are you ready to explore a bit?" he said, rubbing his palms together. "I'm sure we will be able to find a lot of interesting things fairly effortlessly in a ruin like this. In this room, for instance."

He ducked his head through the rectangular window of a nearby room, rummaged a bit, and then turned to us triumphantly with the broken, jagged half of a shallow bowl, its black-and-white painted design still clear and slightly glazed on its inner surface.

"Oh, and here's something!" Julia cried, bending to retrieve a small bone awl from behind a low wall at her feet. "I am not certain what it is, but, oh, isn't this so exciting? Surely, if we look long enough, we will find something of value!"

Prescott smiled again, exposing his yellowed teeth. "Perhaps. Often, I find the search itself reward enough."

Indeed, as I slowly moved about the fallen piles of the dwelling, I understood what Prescott meant. Farther back, in some of the rooms that remained intact, relics fairly lay about for the taking. In one I found several more bone awls, long wooden implements of some kind, and several coils of rope made of tough yucca fiber.

Discovering them myself, I felt an excitement quite unparalleled by anything in my experience. It *was* a treasure hunt, and the items I found connected me with the ancient people who had used them in a much more profound way than simply viewing them. What I had felt in Twilight City came back to me—a sense of past lives yearning to speak.

"Look! I've found something. Come here!"

We all looked up in startled unison at Doran's shout. His voice was strong, excited, as I'd never heard it before, and it came from the far, opposite end of the ruin. Glancing at each other, the three of us started in Doran's direction, climbing over and through several half-collapsed rooms, more piles of rubble, and finally a narrow T-shaped door in a two-story wall built in the back corner of the dwelling. There we found him.

He was standing almost against the back of the cliff, where the overhanging roof of rock met the sandstone floor. With a dust-covered red kerchief tied over his mouth and his wide-brimmed hat pulled low over his eyes, he had unearthed something beyond the pile of fallen blocks at his feet. To his right stood a long-handled shovel propped in the rubble; at his feet were the remains of what once must have been a small wall protecting a hidden back room.

"Come closer," he said, lowering the kerchief. "This is quite a find."

As we stepped over the heaps of debris, the light, fine dust of that enclosed space filled my throat and lungs and I was seized with a fit of coughing.

"Here," Doran said, handing me another kerchief from his back pocket. "Put this on. It may look rather odd, but it will protect you. This is truly the dust of ages."

What I saw then made me gasp and immediately draw back. There at Doran's feet lay three adult skeletons, their mouths gaping, their legs pulled up and bent at the knee and their arms pointing downward. They were lying on some kind of grass or willow mat; alongside one of them was a long bow and two mugs; between the others were several bowls, as well as two long, pointed sticks. The farthest skeleton had some kind of hide moccasins on its feet, and beneath two of the other skulls was partially decomposed feather cloth similar to remnants I had seen at the ranch.

"I found over a dozen arrows above the skeletons," Doran said, dirt caking his face above his lowered kerchief. His eyes were alight with emotion. "And these bowls are the best I've come across in several months. The Anasazi believed in sending the dead off with whatever they would need in the afterworld."

I looked at the three skeletons again, and my stomach gave a quick heave.

"I suspected I would find something back here," Doran went on. "I saw that door and found this shovel nearby, so I went ahead and began to dig. When I turned up this willow matting, I knew I'd stumbled on a burial site. I've found others before, but most of them lie in the refuse heaps in front of the dwellings. Only occasionally do you find them sealed up in back rooms like this. This one is a little different and very well preserved."

Looking at the skeletons, I remembered Mr. Kendall's words about the old Indian Kianeech and his warning about the penalty paid for disturbing the spirits of the dead. The skin along my back prickled. For a moment I felt almost as if someone were standing behind us, watching us. I turned quickly, but there was no one else in the ruin. Prescott and Julia stood behind me and off to the side a bit, seemingly engrossed in Doran's find.

"We can learn so much from burial sites like these," Doran said. "But come over here—I've found something even better. I was saving the best for last."

Doran took us to a far corner of the dwelling, over to the side of a small, round estufa—an open, pitlike room in the ground, formed of stone. Its sides had caved in partially, and at one time it must have been filled almost completely with rubble, for now piles of broken blocks were heaped along its rim as if tossed up from the floor. Obviously efforts had been made quite recently to dig it out.

"This is where I found the shovel," Doran said. "Evidently your assistant has been working on this, Webb. I was quite surprised by what I discovered inside."

Doran pointed downward, and I followed his gesture with my eyes. This time my recoil was more violent. Outstretched haphazardly across the floor were five skeletons. From their sizes and what remnants of clothing still clung to their bony frames, I could make out that the two larger skeletons were men, while next to them lay a woman clutching an infant's remains. The last skeleton was a small child—male or female, I could not distinguish—gripping the bone of one of the larger's arms. All five skeletons were sprawled out across the estufa's bottom. Unlike the neat burial in back of the dwelling, these people were left as they had fallen, in death.

All five of the skulls had been crushed, the infant's so badly it was nearly shattered.

"This is what did it," Doran said, holding up a large stone ax blade, heavy, intact, and still lethal. "I found this on the floor by the skeletons. It's strange, because I've seen no other signs of violence in this dwelling at all. These skeletons are such a contrast to the other burial site. Someone attacked this family. But who—and why?"

Doran's voice was not tinged with the horror I felt but with a burning interest and curiosity. I looked at him in shock. From the moment I had first looked down at this hideous ancient scene of murder, I had been transfixed by a sense of horror so deep that I could barely breathe. I could almost feel the violence that rose from the estufa, as if finally released after hundreds of years—freed, ready to roam and do its damage once again.

Did not anyone else feel it? Glancing at the absorbed, interested faces of Julia and Prescott and Doran, I barely heard their animated discussion of what might have happened in that spot centuries ago.

Again, I felt that chill at my back.

When you intrude on the spirits of the dead, you die, too.

The hairs on my neck lifted as a familiar sense of foreboding began to grow in me, fairly daring me to look over my shoulder again, to see what lay behind us, watching us, listening to us, we intruders who had disturbed the dead.

"Shouldn't we leave this all alone?" I asked, my voice sounding thin in the buzz of excited voices around me. "Shouldn't we just cover this . . . grave back up and leave it the way we found it?"

At first I thought no one had heard me, but then Doran looked up, his brows drawn together in a frown. "Why? This one estufa will give us priceless information. Don't you want to know what kind of people they were? Why this happened?" His eyes were vague yet animated, as if he were eons away from me and the others in another place and time altogether.

I looked down again, and saw Julia touch the shattered skull of the infant in its mother's arms.

I thought I would be sick, so strong were the sensations of terror that washed over me then. Something was wrong; something was horribly wrong. Doran had uncovered something hidden for a purpose, not meant to be discovered. There had been a great violence done here—a murder, a terrible, terrible thing. And it was meant to be concealed.

Then it began: the faint, faraway rushing in my ears.

Yes, before me lay the scene of a murder, a mystery that should remain covered up for-ever. . . .

The rushing became louder, more intense. I knew I had to get away from that place then or succumb completely. No one noticed when I began to stumble away, up and over the broken walls toward the bordering edge of the ruin. My footsteps were barely audible on the soft sandstone—or perhaps it only seemed so because of the sound filling my ears. The sensations engulfing me were worse than any of my spells had ever been; they seemed to emanate from an elemental part of myself that in turn seemed a part of the cruder elements of life.

I could not force myself to go back toward the estufa. Instead, I sought another way up onto the mesa, where I would be far away from those bones, those hidden truths that I did not want to discover.

Just above and to my left I saw a small, narrow ledge, on which several stunted pines grew. It was about five feet above me, and I judged that I could climb to it by lodging my boots, step by step, in the rocks and hauling myself over the edge. From there, I was certain, I could find a further route up to the mesa.

Under normal circumstances, I do not think I would have attempted such a thing alone, but a sense of utter desperation drove me that day—up, over the rock, snatching at the scrubby pine, and finally, shakily, crawling onto the ledge.

And there, standing up, I saw what others who had explored the ruin below might not have discovered, had they not been motivated so strongly to escape.

The ledge did not lead to the mesa top, but it did not end where I stood either. Nearly hidden by its fringe of bordering pines, it continued on around the cliff, turning at a slight bend and coming out onto another small lip of rock also hidden by pines, facing north. Using branches as support, I edged along the ledge there and, to my surprise, found another small cave hidden far back in the cliff. Back in its sheltered niche were the remnants of walls and loose sandstone blocks of another small ruin.

It was small—less than two dozen rooms—but surprisingly well preserved. Most of the walls still stood, their rectangular windows well buttressed and intact.

Drawn forward, I entered its shadowy recesses and felt a curious, immediate sense of relief. There was a safe, protected feeling to the ruin. It was dim and cool inside, completely cut off from the heat of the afternoon summer sun.

Why would the Indians build on this northern exposure? I wondered. Most of the mesa's ruins were built facing southwest, where their inhabitants would have been able to take best advantage of the sun's direct rays in winter and indirect slanting in the hotter months. Here the cave was blessedly cool, but in the winter, it would be quite cold.

I took a few steps inside and saw that the ruin had indeed lain undisturbed for centuries. Beside one of the broken walls lay three bowls, one a perfectly formed example of the kind of coiled ware Doran had shown me, and they were sitting there as if whoever had left them would be coming back any moment.

I looked quickly over my shoulder. No one. Over the high green branches of the pines outside the cave, the sky arched full and clear and blue over the canyon below. And yet for a moment I had felt it again—not that awful sense of terror and foreboding, but a sense that something vivid and vital lingered here in this ruin, a kind of fullness of life, well preserved but interrupted.

Where had these people gone? I wondered. Why had they left these bowls, tools, and simple household implements lying here, as if they had gone away only for a short time and would be back, perhaps that day, to resume their daily lives?

But they had not come back—not that day, not ever.

As I moved throughout the ruin, I found more artifacts, perfectly preserved: jars and baskets of maize; awls of all sizes made of bone; then two objects that, at first, puzzled me. One was a stiff bunch of dried yucca leaves and grass, bound together so that their sharp tips were gathered together tightly and pointed in one direction on one end; the other was a small, hollow animal bone, tapering near one of its open ends and pierced with a small hole.

As I picked them both up, their intended use came to me in a sudden flash. The dried bunch of leaves and grass was a crude kind of hairbrush, I realized, and the pierced, open bone a whistle—a very small whistle, perhaps for a young child.

Holding these objects, I was overcome with the feeling I'd had as I examined the relics in the Kendalls' barn.

And then, as I stood there, imagining, experiencing what these past lives must have been like, something clicked in my mind just as a key, after much fumbling, finally finds its proper fit in a lock. The truth that had evaded me for so long suddenly unveiled itself in perfect crystal clarity.

Just as the life in this ruin had been preserved in time, waiting to be discovered, there was something in my own life—a moment, an hour, a day—the memory of which lay hidden in my mind. That was why I had been so drawn to these ruins and artifacts, I realized: because my mind must have known, instinctively, that they would be the tangible link to release whatever it was that had lain buried so long in my memory.

As I stood there, the voices and images of the lost Anasazi began to fade and were replaced by another scene, another time in another life. A morning, a fresh, cool summer morning . . .

I was outside, in the backyard of our house in St. Louis, beneath the big willow tree in the corner by the fence. The morning was still and full, like a ripe peach. The grass spread out before me, green and glistening with dew; the poplars and oaks were green, too, fat and full, their leafy edges almost translucent in the early morning light. The apple tree next to the willow was heavy with newly forming fruit, and my mother's roses had all bloomed and were surrounded by their feathery fringe of lacy white baby's breath.

Mother had gone to market, as she did every other morning, and Father was upstairs in his room resting.

But that was odd. Father never remained in his room resting on a weekday morning. As long as I could remember, he had always risen before me. Listening from my own bed in my small room upstairs, I could hear him getting dressed, speaking to Mother, his tread heavy on the stairs as he descended to greet Cook, to open the front door, to retrieve the morning paper so he could read it over breakfast. He would greet me, too, when I came downstairs to eat my porridge, and he'd listen soberly as I told him what Mother and I planned to do that day. He was very kind, but I was always a little shy around him, for he was also very tall, solemn, and was away most of the time, off right after breakfast, tossing his napkin on the table and adjusting his frock coat in the front mirror so that he could greet the first customers who came into his bank.

But that morning was different. For some reason, my father had stayed home, something I had never seen him do before. As I sat under the willow out in the yard and looked up at his window, its curtains drawn against the sun, I felt uneasy. Was he home that day because of what had happened the night before? The stranger had come, and I knew that had upset him. . . .

Peter came out in the yard then, after Mother left. Peter, with his shock of unruly hair, his lean face, and adolescent awkwardness. My brother, Peter, whom I adored more than anyone else in the world. He came to me in the yard and asked me to join in a new game. I was thrilled, quite tremulous with delight, for Peter so rarely included me in his activities, keeping to himself much of the time, as, Mother often told me, thirteen-year-old boys were apt to do.

But that morning he had included me for some reason, and whispered to me the rules of his new game. Yet as he spoke, it seemed in my memory that the bright summer morning turned dark somehow, as if a great black cloud had passed overhead and snuffed out the light, and I smelled an odd odor of something burning. . . .

All at once, the images of that summer morning began to fade and I was back in the Anasazi ruin, overcome with that sick, uneasy feeling I had felt when Doran had showed us the skeletons of the murdered family—the feeling that certain secrets should not ever be unearthed.

But it was too late.

For something odd was happening in my mind, something frightening. Triggered by the Anasazi ruin, the lost memory that had been playing itself out in my mind now twisted itself into a kind of living nightmare I could not stop.

The faces in my memory—familiar, beloved faces—faded and reformed themselves into images of skulls, their gaping mouths wrenched and held rigid in horrible screams of pain and agony, knowing that they were dying a most horrible, violent death and they could do nothing, nothing . . .

Her face was the worst. To see it twisted in agony wrenched my heart so fiercely that I thought I might die, too.

But even as the image faded and the rushing sound started again in my ears, I could not let the memory go, let *her* go. I reached toward the image drifting out of my consciousness. . . .

Suddenly, I glimpsed something framed in the drooping fringe of the pine bordering the ruin: a shock of hair, a flash of dark flesh, a sharp, yellow-brown eye peering directly at me, only yards away.

I gasped. It was a face—a *real* face. It had hung as if suspended, just below the rim of the cliff's edge, part of the sky and canyon and mesa behind it. And it had been staring at me.

Or had it?

Was it only part of the horror I felt, part of the pain and violence and death? It was a face at once familiar or unfamiliar, a face long buried in my memory, but different and changed, as if in this timeless place my past had gotten jumbled with the present until I no longer knew what was real and what was imagined.

Perspiration broke out in a beaded line on my lip and I felt the waves of nausea rise inside me. My mind was trying to fight it off, but finally I saw what my mind had been trying to protect my consciousness from all these years.

The horror, the desperation and agony, the deep, wrenching guilt . . .

Darkness began to descend, to protect me again, but I threw my arms out to fend it off, for there was something in what I had seen that I could not let go. I lurched forward, trying to reach it before it disappeared entirely, but it was swallowed up by the hot, choking smoke that rose like an impenetrable cloak, blocking me, preventing me from reaching what I was seeking, who I was seeking. . . .

"No! Wait!" I screamed, my voice sounding faraway to my ears, as if sucked down to the canyon below. "Wait! I have it! I have the key!"

But no matter how I tried, I could not reach the face. It appeared again for an instant, vivid and twisted, and then it was gone.

And I knew, as I had always known, that I

would never reach it. Never. It was gone forever.

With that realization, I came back to the present. I felt my boot slip on loose rubble, and I realized that I was no longer in that hidden moment of my past but in a cliff dwelling at Twilight Mesa. Now, unknowingly, I had gone too far. In my blindness I had stumbled to the very edge of the cliff, to its bordering fringe of trees where I thought I had seen the face.

But even now those ancient, hardy trees could not break my fall as the rubble beneath my boot began to tumble down the cliff, taking me along with it.

I had gone too far. It was happening, and there was nothing I could do to stop it. I felt my foot suspended for one moment in the clear, sharp blue air of the canyon, and then I was slipping down a deep hole, a well. I heard a shrill, terrified screaming, and darkness began to descend in my mind, claiming me, obliterating all else but that horrible, terrified screaming.

Too late, I realized the screaming was my own.

Chapter Ten

✦✦✦✦✦

IT WAS STILL dark, but not the black obliteration of before. The shrill screaming had finally ceased. I could hear the distant call of a coyote and the sound of the wind whistling mournfully through piñon branches. Gradually I became aware of the hiss and pop of a nearby fire.

I was lying down. The ground beneath me was hard and cold and rocky; I felt small pebbles jab at the muscles in my back. My body was sore and stiff, as if I had been beaten, and the skin of my arms and legs and back felt as if it had been scraped raw. Some kind of thick, wooly blanket was tucked about me, pinning my arms. Its rough edges came up around my neck and chin, and scratched the skin of my cheeks.

I heard a rustling movement behind me, and then the thud of heavy boots near my head. I opened my eyes.

The sight of the leaping fire met me first—large, powerful, intense, a blazing red-orange, sending its flames and sparks shooting upward in a searing fountain to the sky. Even as my eyes were drawn to it, my body recoiled.

Then the dark bulk of a man's figure intruded in the fire's circle of light, blocking its flames from my view.

I could not see his face, and I was filled with a sudden wariness. Why was it so vital that I see his face? It seemed that the last image in my mind had been that of a face, twisted horribly. . . .

The man dropped his load of piñon branches

beside the campfire, and then made his way around its opposite side. My mind was moving so sluggishly that it dawned on me only gradually that I had seen him in just that way—framed by the light of the campfire—the very night before: elfin, elusive, the green eyes cast down so that the fire made deep shadows in the soft hollow beneath his lower lashes and highlighted his fine, high cheekbones.

He looked up.

"You're awake." He moved swiftly to my side. "How are you feeling? Are you all right?"

"I . . . I don't know," I said slowly. "I don't know what happened. I can't remember . . ."

"That's understandable." Doran dropped down beside me, his lithe body folding up into a graceful crouch and his heavy clothing smelling strongly of piñon smoke. "You were nearly gone by the time I reached you. I didn't understand what was happening at first. It looked as if you were sleep-walking—your eyes were glazed over and it seemed you were reaching out toward something, like a blind person."

I turned my face away. "I . . . don't know what happened," I repeated. "I . . . why were you there? How did you find me?"

"Will saw you, on the other side of the canyon. Will and his brother Charlie—they were standing on the mesa looking for us. They saw me and Webb and Julia, in the larger ruin, and then they spotted you over in the smaller one. Evidently it worried them that you were exploring alone, because Will gave a whistle to get our attention and gestured in your direction. I didn't quite understand what he was trying to tell us at first, but he was beginning to look upset, so I went round the cliff. Then I saw you, and I lunged and got ahold of you—by the collar of your dress, I'm afraid—just in time. I'm sorry I couldn't have done it a little better; the trees helped break your fall, but you got tangled in them and banged your arms and legs against the cliffside pretty badly as I pulled you up. Otherwise, it was a fairly miraculous rescue, considering what might have happened had not Will and Charlie seen you. You were in a dead faint and I carried you back here. We're in the larger ruin we explored earlier. You've been unconscious for over four hours."

Doran stared at me, frowning. "I wish I knew what happened before I got there. Did you see something? Someone? A pothunter, perhaps? What were you reaching for?"

I thought again of the face and felt a shudder ripple through me. Had I really seen it? Even immediately afterward I had doubted it. Had it simply been an image called up by my own imagination, twisted and warped in my mind and stimulated by my odd reaction to the unearthed grave in the other ruin?

In this ruin.

"The grave," I said, looking at Doran. "Is it . . . did you finish excavating it?"

"Yes." Doran turned away for a moment, but not before I saw the quick expression of self-reproach on his face. "I apologize for not realizing . . . I see now how caught up we all were in it, but at the time, I didn't notice how much you truly were affected . . ."

"Where are the others?"

"Seeing to the horses and bringing down supplies. We're camping here for the night. I didn't know . . . we didn't know when you would wake up or if you would even be able to make it up to the mesa. You gave us all quite a scare, you know."

As Doran stood, his voice was tinged with suppressed emotion. His eyes, looking down at me from above, were nearly black in the darkness.

"She's alive!" Will's hearty voice boomed behind me. In a moment I saw his leathery, friendly face appear beside Doran's, followed by that of Charlie. All three faces seemed to float as if suspended there above me, in the dark.

"We thought you were a goner for sure," Will said, dropping down to peer worriedly into my face. "When we saw you starting to walk right off that cliff . . ." He paused a moment. "Although I have to say, I *have* seen things like that happen before hereabouts. The mesa affects people like that sometimes. There's powerful feelings stored up in them ruins. More'n once I've come across a new one and felt something prickle at my back, like there's something there behind me." Will's worried look changed into a wide grin. "But now I'm scarin' myself! Let's forget about this for now. You just rest up, Miss Loring. We got you all taken care of here, safe and sound, and in the morning—"

"Oh, Heather, you have revived!"

I never would have imagined that I might be glad to hear the piercing sound of Julia Hastings' voice; perhaps it was due to the injured state of my body—and mind.

Julia's skirts rustled and swished behind me,

and then I saw her bright blue eyes peering down at me as well. "Why, we thought you might have died! Whatever were you doing? If you had only called or let us know where you had gone . . ." Gracefully, she dropped down beside me and lowered her voice. "Of course, Mr. Hunt *said* that Will and Charlie Kendall alerted him from across the canyon, but it seems to me that perhaps he noticed you had gone . . ." Julia cast a glance toward Doran, now standing off to the side of Charlie. "In any case, it is so *fortunate* that he reached you in time. I suppose only the two of you know what happened in that ruin, Heather dear. You will have to tell me all about it."

"Julia, darling, you must let Miss Loring rest." Prescott Webb joined the group. "After all, she has been through quite an ordeal. She needs time to recuperate."

"Oh, yes. Especially if we plan to leave for the Snake Dance tomorrow!" Julia stood up quickly, excitement evident in her movement.

As Prescott wrapped an arm about her waist, I saw him shake his head warningly at Julia.

"Snake Dance?" I said, struggling to sit up. "What do you mean?"

"I am afraid my fiancée spoke too soon, Miss Loring. We can discuss this all later."

"Oh, why not now, Prescott? It is *so* exciting! Oh, Heather, Charlie has come with the most wonderful news. There is to be a snake dance held at the Hopi Indian village in only a few days! They live beyond the mesa in Arizona, and for this dance all the warriors gather and prance about, and they actually carry live *snakes* in their mouths. . . ."

"That's enough." Doran stepped forward. "You must leave Heather alone. She needs to rest."

"Yes, Julia dear. Mr. Hunt is quite right. You and Miss Loring can talk in the morning. We mustn't rush things."

"No," I said. "I want to know—what is this snake dance? What did she mean, that we will leave tomorrow?"

I saw Doran shoot a warning glance toward Julia and Prescott. It was Charlie who finally spoke up.

"It's all my fault, Miss Loring," he said, a sheepish expression on his broad face. "You see, when I heard about the snake dance I was so excited, thinkin' that you being a reporter and all, you'd surely want to see it. It's held at a different time every year, and I thought, what luck! Miss Loring'll sure want to see it, because the Hopi are supposed to be kinda like them Anasazi were. So I quick-like packed up a wagon and headed for the mesa, hopin' to head you all off on your way out and talk you into going to the snake dance from here. It's another few days' ride, but I never knew, doin' all this, what was gonna happen to you in here. If I'd known you was going to just up and walk off a cliff, Miss Loring, I'd have never . . ."

Doran cleared his throat and Charlie's words trailed off.

"That's all right," I said. I managed to sit up, the blanket still wrapped around my legs and waist, but the rest of my body free. I was still wearing the mattress ticking dress, but it was quite ripped, and Doran's heavy denim jacket had been thrown about my shoulders. It smelled of him. "I am . . . beginning to feel better now."

"But you should rest anyway." Doran's voice was firm. "We can talk about this in the morning and decide what we want to do then. For now I think we should all prepare for bed. We've had our supper, Heather, but we saved you some bread and some of Webb's cheese, and there's coffee on the fire."

"Thank you, but I don't think I could really get anything down right now. I . . ."

"Then have some of this." Squatting beside me, Doran placed one hand on the back of my head and put a tin cup to my mouth with the other. Obediently, I opened my lips and drank, and then sputtered and choked as I felt the liquid trace a hot, burning trail down my throat and into my stomach, where it seemed to explode. But within seconds it sent a reviving warmth shooting through my veins.

"What was that?" I asked when I could speak, tears springing to my eyes.

Doran grinned. "Whiskey. I thought you might need it. It'll help you sleep. Here, you'll need more if you want it to work right."

I had never tasted whiskey before, and I wasn't sure I wanted to again, but as I choked and sputtered on a few more sips of the amber liquor and felt its warmth spread even more fully throughout me, I found that Doran was right. I had needed it.

As the others moved about the fire, rustling in the packs, conversing in whispers, I felt as if I watched and listened to them from a far, far distance, and that as their images began to fade in my mind so did those more horrible images that were still lingering just below the surface of my memory. Perhaps Doran had know that whatever had frightened me so in the ruin would return to haunt me in sleep, and that was why he had forced me to drink the whiskey. When my eyes inevitably began to close, I was hoping that the twisted daytime horror I had seen would not invade my nighttime dreams.

And I awoke the next morning remembering nothing but a deep, dark hole that had swallowed me up in a kind of formless void, an emptiness for which I was extremely grateful.

But it hurt to move, to sit, to stand. Upon awakening, I had inspected my arms and legs first and saw that, indeed, much of the skin had been scraped raw. But someone had washed and dressed my injuries and protected the open wounds with fresh cotton bandages.

My heart quickened at this. Doran. Had he been the one who had rolled up my sleeves so carefully, lifted my skirts to wash and dress the tender skin on the backs of my calves and thighs?

The thought made a hot flush spread swiftly across my features. He had been the one who found me, who pulled me back and up over the edge. Had he also been the one to care for me, to tuck the scratchy wool Indian blanket so tightly about me? His face, I remembered, had been the first I had seen upon regaining consciousness the night before.

Or had one of the others cared for me? Will and Charlie, after all, had seen me first. Doran had not come after me until they had signaled him. And he had arrived at the ruin just in time, he had said.

But had he really?

I do not know why I mistrusted him so. Perhaps Julia's words had made me wary, or my own suspicions of his activities caused my doubt.

Or perhaps, I thought slowly, my mistrust was a mere defense against the stronger emotions I held for Doran Hunt: the way I felt when he looked at me, touched me, took my arm, the way he caught me about the waist or held me close against his hard, lean body, as he had that night in the canyon by the spring. Perhaps I could not admit to myself how I had felt watching his face in the glow of the campfire, full of life and promise and a deep, pulsating energy that seemed directed straight at me.

Yes. Perhaps I simply could not admit to myself that I had fallen in love with Doran Hunt, with all that he was and would be.

It frightened me. I did not know him, or what he wanted of me, or what he wanted for himself. I did not know what my growing love for him meant or where it might lead. And still I did not trust him.

"I would like to go to the snake dance," I said to Charlie as we gathered around the small cooking fire Doran had built in the ruin. "You were right. I do want to write about it for my concluding article on Twilight Mesa."

"Concluding article?" Doran's eyes were watchful from across the fire.

"Yes," I said, not returning his gaze directly. "I think, with all I have learned on this trip into

Twilight Mesa, I will have enough material for my articles. After we arrive back at the ranch—after the snake dance—I plan to return to Denver."

"But you can't do that! You'll spoil—" Julia's shocked exclamation was quickly checked by Prescott's hand on her arm. But only momentarily.

"Why, we've just *started* exploring the ruins!" she cried, not to be suppressed. "You can't return to Denver so soon. After the snake dance, Prescott had another trip into the mesa all planned, perhaps even on the way back."

"I hardly think that Heather will be ready for another trip that soon," Doran said calmly. "Indeed, I can't imagine why she's even considering the journey to see the snake dance. If we want to arrive in time, we will have to leave this morning." He looked at me.

"I am aware of that." I met his eyes squarely. "Charlie seems to have come very well prepared. I would like to go."

"That is most admirable of you, Miss Loring." Prescott looked down at me with a smile. "Miss Hastings and I will enjoy your company at the dance. I have only seen the ceremony once before, and it is very compelling."

Doran said nothing as we gathered up our packs and supplies and climbed to the mesa, but there he took my arm and pulled me rather roughly aside.

"You are very foolish to try and make this kind of trip," he said, his face very close as he looked at me. "Why are you doing it?"

I tried to shake his hand off my arm. "I told you—for my last article."

"No. I mean the real reason. What did you see in that ruin? Why are you so desperate to leave this place?"

Doran increased his pressure on my arm, and the intensity of his eyes was so riveting that I felt myself go limp.

"I have seen all I came to see here," I answered dully. "There is no reason for me to remain in Twilight Mesa any longer."

"Isn't there? Did you really find what you were looking for here, Heather? Or did what you saw in that ruin frighten you so badly that you have to run away?"

My heart began to thud as I remembered the face, the memory that had opened up so fully and horribly in my mind. . . .

I knew that I could not endure that again. I was not ready to confront the truths that Twilight Mesa held for me. And perhaps I never would be.

For why else, I wondered, had my mind been protecting me all these years? Something within it had always known I was not strong enough to face whatever was buried in its depths. I now realized by how wise a Maker I had been created—one who knew just how much the human spirit could endure before shattering completely.

I knew that now. My instincts had led me thus far, but they were wrong—they had nearly sent me plunging to my death. Now the logical part of my mind had taken over to stop this ridiculous search before any more harm could come to me.

Doran was right. I was desperate to leave Twilight Mesa. It was as the Indians had always claimed—a place of danger, of death. It swallowed its victims whole. Why had I ever imagined myself strong enough to withstand its truths?

Doran's voice was very quiet as he said to me, "Yes, I can see now how afraid you have become." He paused. "And I am sorry." He looked at me in silence for a moment. "I might not have blamed another woman for your decision if she had gone through what you did yesterday, Heather. But you—" Here Doran suddenly reached out and I felt the feather-light touch of his fingers, for just an instant, on my cheek. "I wouldn't have expected it of you, Heather."

He turned then, as if to go, and I felt with his words that he had taken his fist and knocked all the breath from me. What else, though, could he possibly expect me to do? Only a fool would continue on the path I had chosen. Doran did not understand. He had no concept of what I had seen and felt, of what, even now, I held hidden within me.

"Oh, I forgot." Sliding a hand into his pocket, Doran extracted an object and, reaching for my hand, pressed something smooth and cool against my palm. I saw the lanky, loose bones of my amulet.

"You must have dropped it in the ruin," Doran said. "Now I suppose you'll hardly be needing it."

Without looking at me, he strode over to saddle his horse. I curled my fingers over the amulet in my hand and placed it deep in the pocket of my dress, feeling an odd, hollow sensation as I watched his retreating back.

He does not understand, I thought again. But even had I wanted to, I would not have been able to explain this to him. We left soon after, and Doran rode off immediately, far ahead. For the length of our trip, arduous only in the tediousness of the miles ridden across the arid countryside, he did not touch me or come near me or even talk to me beyond the limits of common courtesy. I knew that he watched me, though, his eyes shaded from the sun under the brim of his hat so that I could not see their expression.

And in response, I felt myself yearning for him in that ridiculous, frightening way that grows out of love, a love I could no easier still within myself than I could conquer my fears about it.

It dawned on me our third day on the trail, watching him astride his horse. What was I really running away from? Twilight Mesa? Myself?

Or Doran Hunt?

Julia's attitude toward me was equally odd. That first morning, after I announced my decision to return to Denver, she seemed fairly to seethe with anger. As I was getting ready to mount Lady, she came over to me, her face like a storm cloud about to unleash its fury.

"You haven't let that little spill you took in the ruin scare you off, have you, Heather?" she said. "It was quite a foolish thing to do, but you have learned your lesson, and it won't happen again. You *must* stay a little longer. You must promise to go on one more trip to Twilight Mesa with me and Prescott."

"And why is that, Julia?" I asked. "It's obvious you seem to want something of me. What is it?"

Julia's eyes gleamed as she looked at me, and her lips began to curl in a smile. She opened her mouth to speak, but at that moment Prescott

called to her. He had decided to ride back to his
cabin and speak with his assistant; he would either meet the rest of us on the trail or at the Hopi
villages the day of the snake dance.

"If I am not to see you for several days, my
beloved," he called to Julia, "you must at least
give me a proper good-bye." I knew he had been
watching us; perhaps he had heard my question.
In any case, his distraction was effective, for Julia
never did answer my query. Instead, she went
over to Prescott and they moved away into the
piñons, whispering, and when they emerged
again, Julia was smiling quite brightly. As Prescott rode off, she beamed at me and her anger
seemed to have passed as quickly as a summer
thunderstorm.

"Oh, Heather," she said, squeezing my hand.
"I am so excited about the snake dance! Just think
how wonderful it will be. And afterward . . . perhaps you might just reconsider your decision to
return to Denver."

She left me with that cryptic remark, and I could
only guess that she and Prescott had some new
plan brewing. It almost made me smile. I no
longer cared. I was no longer involved with what
anyone was doing in Twilight Mesa.

I told myself all this, and yet when I noticed
how Julia seemed to be spending much more time
with Doran, I felt something twist painfully in my
breast. Watching her rein in beside him, seeing
her toss back her head and look provocatively at
him, listening to her tinkling laugh ripple out over
the desert and her soft drawl drift back to me like
warm honey . . . And then, witnessing the responsive tilt of Doran's smile and the way he

turned in the saddle, appraising Julia with interest in his eyes . . .

I remembered again Doran's words about expecting more of me. Obviously what I had imagined to be mutual attraction had really been based on no more than the role he thought I might play in Twilight Mesa. Now that I had decided to leave, he was finished with me.

And it was just as well, I told myself. There had been two nights on the trail when I was jerked out of sleep with a scream stifled in my throat, awakening from the nightmare I had lived that day in the cliff dwelling. I had seen them all again, in vivid detail: the horrible, twisted face, the bleached skulls, the haze of choking smoke, my own feeling of helplessness, immobility, desperation.

Nothing could make me go back now. I longed to resume a normal life again, in Denver or even St. Louis, to write my articles and be done with them.

Surprisingly, however, it was in the writing of these articles that I found the most relief. Now devoid of any hidden, deeper meaning for me, the project was engrossing enough to require a large amount of my attention and concentration.

During the long days on the trail, I would think about the project, and at night around the campfire I would try to put my thoughts into words, shaping the articles I would eventually polish at the Kendalls' ranch or in Denver. I would write about the mystery of the Anasazi, not my own, I determined. As I made notes of my impressions of Twilight Mesa's relics and dwellings, it was from a strictly objective viewpoint. This was the most difficult section to write, but as I did so, I found myself slowly being purged of the darker sensations that had haunted me there, and those feelings and experiences faded and then vanished, as if they had never happened.

And I was glad that I had decided to conclude my articles with a description of the snake dance, for the Hopi Indians, so similar in many ways to the Anasazi, would help link all my information together.

"Every year about this time, the Hopi hold the dance so the gods will send them rain for their harvest," Will explained one night around the campfire. "See they believe they all came from Mother Earth at one time, and their gods are still down there in what they call the underworld. So they catch all the snakes they can find, and during the dance they send them back to the underworld with their message for rain. And it usually does rain right after the dance or some time in the next day or so." Will paused with a smile. "Course we all know that it rains most every afternoon this time of year, but nobody lets on."

"Do they really dance with the snakes . . . in their mouths?" I asked.

"You bet! That's the best part of the whole thing!" Charlie's grin stretched from ear to ear. "Them snakes is wrigglin' pretty fierce—and the Indians put them right in their mouths as they're dancin', holding them right in their bare hands!"

"They dance in pairs, though," Will said, "and the Indian behind the one with the snake in his mouth has a kind of eagle-feather whip—snakes *hate* eagle feathers—to keep the snake from striking."

"Surely the snakes aren't harmful," Julia said.

"Oh, yes, most of 'em are rattlers," Charlie answered, poking at the fire. "One bite, and them dancers're dead."

At Julia's gasp, Will went on quickly, "We ain't never seen one get bit or die, Miss Hastings. They're mighty careful."

"It gets kinda excitin' toward the end," put in Charlie, " 'cause after the Indians dance around awhile with one snake, they drop it on the ground and go get another. That's when the other braves jump in and grab the throwed-down snakes right in their hands and stand there holding 'em in bunches. It's quite a sight! And sometimes they don't get to the throwed-down snakes in time, and a rattler gets loose in the crowd."

At Julia's horrified expression, Will interjected, "Now, Charlie, that's enough. Don't worry, Miss Hastings, it's all safe enough. We stand way back from the dancers. We can even sit up on a terrace if you want. And we better stop talking about this now—won't be any surprises left when we get there!"

But, of course, there were. More surprises than I could ever have imagined.

Chapter Eleven

✦ ✦ ✦ ✦ ✦

WE ARRIVED IN the land of the Hopi four days later. Up on top of the mesa, several broad dark women, clothed in woven blankets and carrying large water jars, stopped to stare at us. As we rode toward the Hopi village ahead, I felt the force of dozens of black silent eyes peering at us from every direction. Although at first I tensed under this blatant scrutiny, I soon realized that the villagers' eyes were not hostile but insistently, probingly curious.

Several of the older male Indians, also wrapped in blankets, seemed to know Will and Charlie and greeted them as we reached the village's small plaza. Will smiled at one of the old men and began a rapid conversation of sign language intermixed with a few words of English and what sounded like grunts in the Indian tongue. A moment later, Will turned to us with a grin.

"He has a place we can stay tonight after the ceremony; it's on the rooftop terrace of a villager's home." Will paused. "If you've ever been inside one of the pueblos, you'll understand why most of us prefer sleeping on the roofs. Let's just hope the snake dance makes it rain tomorrow instead of tonight!"

As the men led the horses away to be corralled and fed, I had my first chance to look around the village. It was a sight I will not soon forget. Against the bordering clusters of earth-colored adobe buildings—built one upon the other, wooden ladders leading up to their open terraces and roofs—milled a living, pulsating mélange of color and activity. At least one hundred people had come to witness the snake dance, all thronged tightly together in that tiny plaza: some on foot or on horseback, some sitting on the terraces of the surrounding buildings and standing on the roof-tops.

In one corner of the plaza were grouped a tight-knit cluster of Indians Will told me later were visiting Navajos. They wore the most striking native dress I had ever seen: velveteen shirts in shades of crimson, turquoise, and rich chocolate brown; the men in white cotton pants slit to the knees; tan hide moccasins; and wide, red head-bands. Some had their long black hair pulled back and knotted at the napes of their necks in a curious hourglass shape.

In another corner I saw more Hopi. Most were draped in broad blankets. Some of the women wore knee-length sleeveless tunics and rather thick leggings which looked like oversize moccasins; the tunics were caught about their waists with wide, colorful belts and colorful woolen mantles were knotted at their shoulders. The women wore their hair in shiny black rolls, either combed and fastened right above the ears or in back of the head. Some of the men, I saw, wore calico smocks with trousers as well.

Scattered sparsely here and there about the plaza were a few other whites: all men, dressed in rugged trousers and leggings and battered hats like Charlie and Will and Doran, still dusty and dirty from their ride across the surrounding desert.

Julia and I were the only white women there.

Charlie had brought along the clean suits Mrs. Kendall had insisted on packing for us and we wore them now—Julia in dark blue twill and I in my tan serge—and I must say I've never felt more conspicuous in my life. In our long, draping skirts, starched blouses, and high collars, we stood apart from the dark Indian women like some kind of stiff, unnatural species of plant that would soon wither in the desert setting. In their native dress, it seemed these villagers perfectly matched their surroundings, just as the Anasazi must have once in their yucca sandals and coarsely woven feathercloth.

Glancing over the rooftops of the buildings, I glimpsed the edge of the mesa and was suddenly filled with exhilaration. It seemed that there, on top of that mesa, we were on top of the very world. The sun, dropping in its steady descent across the far arc of the sky, slanted across the desert that stretched beyond the mesa into a hazy, purplish horizon. About me I heard the buzz and murmurs of expectant voices, felt the milling and shifting of the crowd as more spectators arrived in the village, watched the packs of children and dogs darting about, smelled the potent, almost overpowering odors of woodsmoke, cooking meat, and closely gathered humanity in that small packed space.

"I do hope the men hurry," Julia said, smoothing her skirts with quick, tense movements as, jostled by a pair of running boys, she glanced around the village. "I don't want to be left here with these . . . *natives* for long."

We heard a shout and glanced up to see Prescott hailing us from across the square. Julia's face immediately brightened and I heard her sigh in relief. She raised her arm in greeting and Prescott maneuvered his way to her side.

"So the weary travelers have arrived!" As always, he was perfectly composed, poised, and attired. He had removed the jacket of his heavy dark suit and loosened his narrow tie, but despite his apparent calm, I sensed in his stance and the gleam in his black eyes the same kind of contained energy and excitement that swirled all about us. He smiled at me and caught Julia about the waist. As they looked at each other, I saw something pass between them: Prescott's slight nod of the head and then Julia's answering expression of . . . what? Relief? Excitement? Triumph?

Before I could wonder at this, I felt an excited ripple pass through the crowd and looked up to see a half-naked, painted and feathered Indian male dart out from one of the pueblo buildings, carrying a large buckskin bag that seemed to bulge and writhe with inner movement.

"Those are the snakes," Prescott said. "And that is a Hopi priest, taking them to the *kisi* there in the middle. Do you see it? That kind of round, enclosed bower made of cottonwood boughs? The priest will wait inside with the snakes. Ah, there he goes. That is the signal that the dance is about to begin."

There was another little stir of excitement and shifting in the crowd as the brave disappeared inside the kisi. I looked around at the faces thronging the square but did not see Will or Charlie or Doran. Prescott pulled Julia more tightly against him, looking down at her with a smile, and then, suddenly, the crowd's movement about me stilled and the entire plaza grew silent.

I first heard an odd swishing noise, sounding like a distant, oncoming spell of rain or wind, and I spotted a marching train of Hopi braves emerge through the parting crowd. The rhythmic sound of their moccasined feet shuffling on the grainy rock of the square mingled with the hollow clanking and swish of the pebbles inside the white, T-shaped rattles they held in their hands. This, I realized, was the simulated sound of rain.

"Those are the antelope dancers," Prescott whispered. "The snake dancers will follow shortly."

The combined, rhythmic sounds of the dancers and rattles was almost hypnotic, as was the sight they made in the crowded square. The dancers wore only white, embroidered kilts that hung to their knees. A long embroidered sash was fastened about each dancer's waist, accompanied by a fox skin, which nearly swept the ground from the dancers' sashes in the rear. On their bare chests were draped heavy strands of turquoise, shell, and silver beads, and in their black hair, which hung long and loose to their shoulders, eagle feathers were clustered. They wore white armlets on their biceps, embroidered anklets about their legs, and buckskin moccasins on their feet.

What struck me most, however, was not the colorful costumes but the great expanse of bare skin left unclothed and vividly painted on the dancers. Elaborate slashes of black and white zigzagged down their chests and arms, and across their backs and faces, covering every exposed part of their dark, lean bodies. It was a powerful depiction, I realized, of the lightning and subsequent rain they were trying to invoke through the ceremony.

After four consecutive circuits around the kisi, the antelope dancers lined up, and all heads quickly turned toward the far edge of the square. There, I saw with a sudden thump of my heart, came the silent line of snake dancers, approaching in single file.

They were costumed almost identically to the antelope dancers, but their faces were painted almost entirely black, giving them a demonic look. Their black eyes gleamed from their painted faces as their lithe, moccasined feet shuffled forward in another dance. After they, too, had made their four rounds, they lined up, linking arms to face the line of priests.

Now began the rhythmic chanting I shall never forget: low, high, low, high, seeming to rise from deep within the snake dancers' chests as if pulled up from the underworld itself. They kept time with what I recognized as snake whips and rattles, and then the two lines began to sway, eerily snakelike, and their chanting became louder, larger, a part of the very mesa on which they stood and the sky arching above.

I was transfixed, the sound and sight and motion of the dancers taking hold of something deep inside of me until I felt myself almost begin to sway in hypnotic response to their movement. I felt the brush of Julia's skirt against mine and saw that she *was* swaying, Prescott's arm tight about her waist and her face turned up to him. I looked once at their faces and then quickly glanced away, not wanting to intrude on their private moment.

Then the chanting stopped, and the snake dancers regrouped into clusters of three. As two dancers in the first group advanced toward the kisi, I felt the crowd suddenly tense again, everyone holding in their breath.

The first dancer reached the kisi, then stooped low before the buckskin entrance. When he stood up, there was a four-foot rattlesnake writhing and squirming in his mouth.

I gasped, jerking back, and my stomach heaved with a sudden spasm. For a moment I thought I might be sick, but I could not tear my eyes away from the spectacle. He began a slow, shuffling circuit about the kisi and the second dancer was close behind, one hand holding the protective snake whip and the other hand on the first dancer's left shoulder. Together they made their circuit, their moccasined steps short and quick, their movements rhythmic and sure. I saw the head of the rattlesnake struggle and flip only inches from the first dancer's mouth, and again my stomach heaved as I watched the dancer grip the reptile's squirming shape with both his hands.

By now, other pairs had emerged with snakes in their own mouths, starting off the queer, shuffling paired steps of the first dancers. As a pair of dancers made their ritual circuit, the first dancer would drop his snake and return to the kisi for another. Here the third snake dancer in each group sprang into action, bending lightning quick to grab the snake slithering on the ground before it had a chance to coil. Snatching with his right hand, the dancer would quickly transfer the wriggling, dangling snake to his left and then wait again for another snake to be dropped.

By now the square was a swirling, shuffling mass of color and movement and sound, the reptiles slithering, the paint-blackened snake dancers shuffling and stooping, the antelope dancers still shaking their rattles and chanting, the largest rattlesnakes buzzing in anger. It was like a terrible nightmare and an oddly natural phenomenon at the same time. The rhythm, the chanting, the macabre and ghoulish spectacle, the savage bravery of the dancers so confidently and blatantly displayed, all tugged at something deep within me until I felt as if I were all part of it too, absorbed by the movement, the brazenness, the sound.

And then, across the square, through the mass of squirming reptiles and dancers, I saw Doran, staring at me with the same intensity I felt in my breast, as if he were part of it all, too—the energy, the rhythm, the strange unreality and hypnotic rise and fall of the chanting, the rattles, the earth itself.

He stared at me and at that moment I knew. I knew and finally accepted.

I felt oddly weightless as I watched Doran slowly make his way around the outside of the crowd, moving with a grace and sensuality that drew my eyes, as if mesmerized, to his lithe body. It was as if he were keeping time with the dancers, I thought, or with some kind of dance between the two of us that drew me, tugged at something vital and warm within me.

The snake dancers were growing more frenzied. Doran disappeared for a moment on the edge of the crowd, and I strained forward in sudden panic, my breath stopped. I could not see him; the connection between us had been broken.

Frantically I looked around. Julia and Prescott were no longer beside me. I was caught up in a mass of blanketed and jeweled Indians, alone, enveloped by the ceremony, the sound, the movement. . . .

Then Doran was beside me, gripping my arms, pulling me back, away from the crowd, back into a darkened crevice between two adobe buildings. His hands slid up my back, pressing me against his heat, his hardness, the intensity I had seen in his eyes, and I felt my legs go weak, my breath suddenly cut off.

His mouth came down on mine, and my head began to spin. I heard the chanting of the dancers against the rush in my ears, felt their rhythm as Doran's tongue met mine, probing, yearning, like the body that was moving in its own rhythm against mine, sending its needful message coursing through my body, across the nerves of my skin, into the very center of my being.

His lips moved down my neck, and it seemed he became one great flame, igniting my body as well—a liquid flame, its source starting deep and fluid within my center and flowing upward until we were both the fire itself, burning hungrily, evoking in me sensations I never knew had existed.

Doran's lips found the open neck of my parted shirtwaist; his hands came around and across the rounded swelling of my breasts. The sensation of his lips on my hot skin was almost too exquisite to bear; I found my fingers tangled in the curls of his thick, dark hair as his lips moved lower and his smooth fingers slid up under my chemise to the satiny skin of my breasts.

I gasped as Doran's thumb found the stiffened peaks, teasing them so that they grew taut and hard, and my back seemed to arch of itself, offering more of myself to him. Doran moaned low in his throat and his mouth moved up to claim mine again, devouring it with his heat and need.

As his palms flattened to circle my breasts and his tongue teased against mine, I felt myself instinctively responding in a way as old as the mesa around us, as basic as the Indian ritual supplicating the gods for rain. It was as if my very essence flowed outward and into Doran until we melded into one with the ceremony around us. Never before had I given myself up as fully as I did then.

Doran's lips left mine and trailed downward again, and I lifted my head, offering the column of my throat to his mouth.

Across the square, something shimmered.

It was far away, appearing as if through a haze, mingled with the dancers and snakes that were still swarming in their frenzied movement.

A face. The face in my memory. The face in my dream, and the face I had seen outside the ruin in Twilight Mesa.

It was Peter's face. My brother. He was here.

I cried out and pulled away. Doran's hands were like vises clamping down on my wrists as I tried to tear them from his grasp.

"What's wrong? What is it?"

With a great wrench, I tore away from Doran, frantically searching the faces of the crowd. I felt Doran grab at me, try to pull me back as I ran into the crowd, pushing my way through the throng, searching.

The dance went on, its movement and sound

swirling about me, but I could not find Peter. I *had* seen him. His face had not been a delusion, a part of the ceremony's unreality. It had been real. Even now I could see my brother's features: lean, drawn, beloved. He *was* here.

The dancers stopped, suddenly. The square became very still. The snakes, all captured, were now squirming in slimy masses from the hands of the waiting carriers. As if on cue, the Hopi chief emerged ceremoniously from the entrance of the kisi and crossed to the middle of the square with a basketful of cornmeal. There he spread it out in a clear pattern: a large circle with six radiating arms.

The dancers leapt forward in one great rush to fling their bounty into the circle, covering its pattern with the twisting bodies of the snakes. The priest chanted a prayer, and then all the snake dancers flung themselves forward to plunge their hands into the mass of writhing reptiles, emerging with as many as they could grasp in their hands. With a great shout, they were off, running toward the edge of the mesa, over its side and down the winding trail toward the desert, where they could release the snakes in all four directions so they could slither back to the gods and ask for rain.

As the dancers disappeared over the edge of the mesa, the sun dipped and finally sank below the far horizon, and the crowd began to disperse. I stood alone as it parted, still looking for my brother, Peter. He had simply vanished—as he had so many years before.

"Miss Loring?" The image of Will's square, worried face swam up before me. "We got kinda separated from the crowd, but I thought you'd be okay with Julia and Mr. Webb. Where are they? Have you been alone all this time? Hey, are you all right?''

Will moved closer and peered at my face. ''Come on.'' He took my arm firmly. ''We need to get you inside. Looks like you got sunstroke. Or maybe it was the ceremony. I should have never left you alone. Them snakes and all's enough to scare the socks off anybody!'' Shaking his head, Will began to lead me from the square. ''That old Indian's got us some coffee fixed and some stew. Now if I can just find everybody . . . saw Doran a minute ago; he said he was headin' out tonight. Can you believe that? Said he didn't want to stay here no longer. Never have been able to figure him out, always goin' and comin' and leavin' half the time without a word to anybody. . . .''

Doran. Even now I could feel his lips, his hands, his body against mine. I shook my head, as if waking from a dream. Had Doran and I simply been overwhelmed by the pulsating energy around us, swept beyond all reason by the frenzied heat of the ceremony itself? Now Will said Doran was leaving. But why?

I did not know. Just as I could still feel Doran pressing against me, I could see Peter's face vividly across the square. They had been real at the time, but now . . . they were gone. And yet I felt curiously giddy, as if something hard and sharp lodged inside me for a very long time had suddenly broken free. Something had changed in those last few, chaotic moments of the snake dance.

''Hey, look at that!'' Will cried, pointing toward

a rising bank of dark clouds beginning to build beyond the mesa. "I'll be darned! I guess them snakes got their message to the underworld in record time. Come on, let's get inside. If I were a wagerin' man, I'd place a pretty sound bet that it's gonna rain tonight!"

Chapter Twelve

✦ ✦ ✦ ✦

WE ALL LEFT early the next morning for the long trip back to the Kendalls' ranch. Except for Doran. He had gone the night before, but no one was certain where he was headed—or for what reason. Prescott, preparing to ride a different route across the desert to Twilight Mesa, soon took his leave of us after we descended the mesa from the Hopi village.

I watched only a moment as he and Julia made their good-byes. Between them still was a kind of intimacy that I did not want to be reminded existed. The feelings Doran had provoked had been too intense—and far too dangerous. I knew that I had been swept up by something much larger than myself—the dance, the night, Doran himself—and that I'd had little power to stop what had happened between us.

It still frightened me.

I was glad that Julia and Prescott's parting was brief, but it was also intense, punctuated by sharp words from Julia as Prescott mounted his horse.

"Don't worry, my beloved. I will return to the ranch soon," I heard Prescott say. "Only a few more days, and things will progress more rapidly. I promise. In less than a week, we will be there."

I did notice Julia's expression as Prescott rode off—sullenness mixed with lingering anger and, strangely, a kind of narrowed, concentrated calculation—but it didn't dawn on me until later, when we were all silent and riding across the interminable desert, that Prescott had said, "*We* will be there." What had he meant by *we?*

Our trip was uneventful and tedious, and as we rode along, I found myself in an odd interim state, as if I were suspended between two positions in place and time. I knew I was waiting, instinctively, for something to happen.

We were met with much to-do from Mrs. Kendall when we finally returned just in time for supper five days later. She clucked and fussed as we dismounted and unpacked, sending Charlie and Will off to take care of the horses and Julia and me in to have our baths. When she heard about my accident in the ruin, she threw up her hands and insisted on seeing my scrapes, which were nearly all healed, and then took off in a great huff to berate her sons for allowing me to go to the snake dance. But as I sank back into the steaming bath she had prepared for me, I hardly heard her. I was so exhausted that I fell asleep before dinner and slept right through the meal, all night, and onward well past dawn.

I felt quite odd when I awoke, groggy and slightly displaced, but I rose feeling ready, I think, for what I had sensed would happen quite soon.

"Oh, Heather, you're up!" Julia entered the kitchen behind me. "Mrs. Kendall asked me to tell you that she had to take the wagon into Jackson this morning. It's her marketing day, and she hadn't planned on our arrival yesterday. She left your breakfast warming on the stove." Julia paused, wrinkling her nose. "The coffee is too strong, and I am sure the biscuits are quite hard and tasteless by now. Nevertheless, I have told you about them, as I promised, and now I am going out for a ride." Julia paused, her eyes gleaming curiously. We had just finished five long days in the saddle, I thought. Where was she going now, and what did she plan to do?

Perhaps Julia's odd manner prepared me for what happened next, or perhaps it was simply my own, inexorable instinct that morning. Whatever the cause, I was not startled or surprised when, a short time later, I heard the hoofbeats of approaching horses. Nor did it surprise me to look up and see Prescott Webb in the lead, dashing as always on his horse, followed by a more shabby looking companion in a battered felt hat.

No, it did not surprise me, and yet . . . there was something about Prescott's companion, dressed in his dust-covered, colorless clothes, his face bent beneath the brim of the shapeless hat. . . .

I stood very still on the porch, my hand clutching the door frame behind me and my heart beginning to beat in queer little jumps. And then everything fell smoothly into place.

Prescott drew up beside me, his rotten teeth exposed briefly in a grin as he pulled on the reins, his horse's head tossing in protest. Through the dust the horses had stirred up, I looked beyond him to the other rider.

It was just as I had known it would be, yet different; an expected sight, but with a surprise contained within it, making me realize that there were still things I had to learn.

For although the face staring at me from the horse was one I had seen many times before—in the photo, at the ruin, during the climax of the snake dance—there was an almost ghostly quality about it, as if it were not quite real. Indeed, it was an odd comingling of images in my mind, both young and old, strange and familiar.

"I have brought someone along with me today I would like you to meet, Heather," Prescott said, turning slightly in his saddle to indicate the man behind him. "Although, I suspect you two really don't need any introductions. Heather, this is my assistant, Peter Fisk. Peter, this is your sister, Heather."

Time seemed frozen in that instant as Peter and I stared at each other. For the man I stared at was my brother, and yet he was not. Something was wrong about him, different. I could not grasp what it was.

In a flash I saw it. Peter was a man now. He was no longer the thirteen-year-old boy I had idolized as a young girl. His features were the same— sharp, lean, hungry looking—but his face was more lined and tanned, and his lanky brown hair was streaked blond here and there from exposure to the sun.

And in another sudden, swift flash of insight, I saw something else. Peter's adult features were also that of a different face, one I remembered in another way, from another time. From a night long ago, when there had been something stirring in the air, something about to happen, the scent of lilacs, or perhaps only my memory of their scent. . . .

"Well, aren't you two even going to say hello?" Prescott said, his eyes dark and watchful.

Still, neither of us made a move. As Peter sat there on his horse, I saw pass across his face a series of emotions that made him seem even more like that other, lost face in my memory. There was wariness and a kind of fear, a subtle furtiveness and the same sort of desperation that I'd seen on the stranger's face as he'd pressed the amulet and doubloon into my hand and said . . . what?

"I understand," Prescott went on, swinging down smoothly from his saddle. "These things take time. After all, you haven't seen each other for over fifteen years, have you? And until now—or recently, perhaps—neither of you knew the other was alive." Prescott gave a dry laugh. "Why, in some ways, it must be like seeing a ghost."

It was. Peter's tawny eyes stared at me as if I were, indeed, some kind of apparition. It was, I realized suddenly, the same look he—had it really been Peter?—had given me in the cliff dwelling. There was something between us—an invisible barrier made up, I thought, of time, all the years we had passed separately, not knowing if the other was dead or alive.

But no. The barrier had been there all along, I realized, even when we were children. Hadn't Peter always been distant and unapproachable, touchy and guarded? Hadn't I always fought that as a child? I had never been able to break through his reserve, even as I followed him about, hoping he would finally include me in his world.

It had hurt then, and it hurt now. Staring at Peter, feeling the empty, yawning distance between us, it was as if I were suddenly the left out five-year-old I had been sixteen years before, yearning for the love of my older brother. And for just a moment, as Peter stared back at me, I thought I caught far back in his eyes a glimmer of something that had once connected us as brother and sister despite the difference in our ages and the barriers between us. My heart leapt as I saw it, just as it had when Peter would relent, suddenly opening up to me and including me in the life I'd found so fascinating.

I must have smiled, for I saw something shift in Peter's eyes, and then the corners of his thin mouth turned up ever so slightly in response.

"That's a start." Prescott moved to my side and encircled my shoulders with one arm. His grip was firm and surprisingly strong. I realized then how very large Prescott Webb was, how powerfully his contained energy seemed to radiate outward. I felt small beside him.

"Why don't you go in the house and wait for us in Mrs. Kendall's front parlor, Heather?" he said, his voice near my ear. "Or perhaps you could fix us something to drink. We have come a long, hot way, and we have much to discuss."

I felt again Prescott's energy, his persuasive power, before he released me and turned to Peter. "Come, Peter. We'll tend to the horses and then meet your sister inside."

For some reason I did feel a sudden need to be

in the parlor, waiting for them. Perhaps I realized the magnitude of what was about to happen; perhaps I knew I would have to gather my wits about me before I spoke to my brother again.

I heard the heavy clomp of boots in the hallway, and then Prescott and Peter appeared. Prescott had removed his hat and dusted off his clothing somewhat, but Peter kept his hat low over his eyes and was still coated with the reddish dust of travel. As they came into the room, Prescott smoothly took a seat opposite me in an overstuffed, chintz-covered chair .draped with faded lace antimacassars, while Peter perched stiffly on a straight-backed pine chair, appearing extremely uncomfortable and avoiding my eyes. Even as I reminded myself again of Peter's nature and of the years of unfamiliarity between us, I felt a quick pain in my chest at his obvious slight.

Prescott took a slim brown cigar from his jacket pocket. "Now then," he said, lighting it and offering a second cigar to Peter, who shook his head in refusal. "As I said, we have much to discuss. Would you like to begin, Peter?"

Peter flinched slightly, and it seemed a flash of apprehension crossed his face as he shifted again uncomfortably on the pine chair. He did not answer, and in the silence, I heard the slow, measured ticking of Mrs. Kendall's antique clock on the mantel. Finally, Prescott turned to me.

"You see, Heather," he began after drawing deeply on his cigar and tilting his head back to blow the smoke outward in one smooth rush. "What your brother has to tell you is somewhat . . . difficult, I believe. He did not want to come here today, as you must see is obvious. I'm afraid I'm partly to blame for that. I insisted that he come, you see, against his will. What we have to tell you may not be pleasant, but it is time we bring this entire matter out into the open. We must join forces."

Prescott puffed on the cigar again, expelling more smoke into the stuffy room. "You see, Miss Loring—or Heather, if I may—what your brother has to reveal today may be unexpected and perhaps shocking for you to hear. Do you feel you are ready?"

Glancing over at Peter, who met my eyes and then looked away quickly, I nodded slightly at Prescott, my mouth suddenly dry.

"Very well, then," he went on, "Peter, would you like to fill in the details from the beginning?"

Peter stiffened, and I saw him swallow and wipe his grimy hands reflexively on the front of his trousers. He looked trapped, I thought, like a miserable, cornered animal.

And in another of those quick flashes of memory, I realized that I had seen that exact expression—a sullen, truculent look—on Peter's face many times before when he was younger and had been forced by Father into doing something he did not want to do. There had always been a kind of tension between Peter and Father, I remembered, although I could recall only good feelings between he and Mother.

"All right then." Prescott fixed his direct black eyes on me. "Well, Heather, it seems that the man you have always believed to be your father, Samuel Loring, was not your father at all. It seems your real father, you never knew."

Prescott paused with a slight smile, seemingly satisfied with my sudden flinch, my swift intake of breath. After only a moment, he went on. "Your father, Heather, was Brandon Fisk—the man who came to visit you and Peter that night in St. Louis so long ago." Prescott paused again, still watching me carefully. "Yes, Peter has told me of it. But surely you were too young to know all the details. Let me fill them in."

He settled back in his chair. "My dear Heather, perhaps you were never told, but your mother was married once before she became Samuel Loring's wife. It was not unusual, really; when she was quite young—seventeen, to be precise—your mother was swept off her feet by a young, dashing, ambitious fellow named Brandon Fisk. Their courtship was quite brief, but intense; Brandon was nearly ten years older, visiting St. Louis for only a short period of time. They met by accident one day, and she fell immediately in love. Of course, all this was long before you came along, my dear. In any case, Brandon Fisk proceeded to court your mother, but since she came from one of St. Louis's more prominent families at the time, her parents of course had long since made plans for her marriage and were horrified at the thought of a wedding to this unknown Fisk. So he and your mother ran away and were wed in Kansas, where they set up housekeeping quite happily, although your mother's family cut off all ties with her once they heard of her secret marriage."

Prescott paused, inhaled on his cigar, and looked over at Peter. "Am I relating this all correctly, Peter?" When Peter didn't answer, Prescott turned back to me. "Your brother has told me all this, you see, as told to him by your mother, who had always cared deeply about keeping the memory of your real father alive even after she remarried. To pick up the story again, after Peter was born—and much later, you yourself— Brandon left his family to travel farther west, seeking the means to support his dependents. A year or two later, your mother got word that he had been killed in a mining accident in Colorado and, desperate, she returned to her family in St. Louis. They must have well known the parable of the prodigal son, for they accepted her—and her young children—back. Shortly after that, your mother, still mourning the husband she believed dead, met and eventually married Samuel Loring, an influential and affluent banker who could amply support her and provide her children with the father she knew they needed. Although she had resigned herself to the necessity of her remarriage, your mother kept alive Brandon Fisk's memory for Peter's sake, to carry on the sense of his heritage. You, Heather, were too young for such stories, and evidently your mother decided it best to let you believe, until you were older and could understand, that your real father was Samuel Loring. Perhaps he even adopted you, I do not know. What it is important you realize now is that you have roots elsewhere, and that you must help us carry out the work your real father left for us here in Twilight Mesa."

My hands, gripping the folds of my skirt, were clammy. I could hardly comprehend all that Prescott was telling me. It was difficult enough to imagine that I once had another father. But another home? Unknown roots and an entirely unknown past? Could this be the reason I had always felt such an odd emptiness inside of me? Was this the key to the lost part of myself I had instinctively sensed for years, ever since that night when I was five?

And yet . . . I thought of Samuel Loring, the man I had always believed to be my father: his great, tall lankiness, his gentle smile, his long, sweeping moustache, the slow deliberation of his gestures as he would settle me in his lap at night to read me a story or tell me about something that had happened at the bank that day. Was he really not my father? *Did* I have another father who had died and never come back? But Prescott had said that Brandon Fisk *had* come back, that night. How could that be? My head buzzing with confusion, I turned toward Peter.

"You look so much like her," he blurted, his voice sounding loud and rather hoarse in the small room. "Mother, I mean. You . . . are so much like her."

On my brother's face was an expression I will never forget: an expression of such raw longing and regret and sadness that it wrenched my heart.

I felt a sudden, deep need to reach out and touch his face, to soothe the hurt and pain I saw there. On impulse I started forward in my seat, but something in Peter's expression stopped me. I could still feel it, as if tangible in the air between us—the barrier still dividing us. Peter was not ready yet.

"He came back, you see," Peter said haltingly. "There had been a mining accident, but he wasn't killed. Whoever had told Mother that had not known the truth. So when she married Samuel

Loring, she was still married to Father. Their marriage was wrong, all wrong. I knew that; I felt that, all along."

In Peter's voice I heard the derision that, I remembered, I had often heard in his sullen behavior to Father. Now I began to fully understand the tension and resentment between them.

"Father came back that night for you and me and Mother," Peter went on, finally looking at me across the room, his eyes intense. "He had found a fortune, a great treasure in the West. We could have all been rich. Father hid it, and then came back to St. Louis to get us so we could all go live with him in comfort. He had spent all those years searching for a way to provide for us, to find a way we could all be together. Think of it! And then when he finally came back to get us, he found Mother married to another man. . . ."

Here Peter's words sputtered off, and I could feel his anger. It fairly radiated across the room. "There was a terrible fight the night our father came back. I hid under the stairs and listened to it all. Finally Loring threw Father out, and I ran after him into the yard. That's when Father gave me the treasure map. He told me to keep it, and to follow him as soon as I could. He told me that someone was after him and that he was in some kind of trouble, but he trusted me to keep the map safe. I was planning to show it to Mother, to convince her to come, too, but the next day—"

Peter's words cut off. "The next day was the fire and Mother . . . you . . . I tried to stop you from going in there, tried to stop Mother. I tried to help you, to save you, but the fire was so horrible. . . ."

In Peter's eyes I saw reflected the pain that suddenly began to well within me. This was it, the memory my mind had tried to shield me from all these years. Now it came back in a sudden, swift flash. The fire, the heat, the searing, awful heat. The steady rumbling and roaring, as of a great, greedy monster devouring everything in its path. The strangling smoke; my steps mired, slowed; something huge, heavy, burning, crashing down on me. . . .

I felt myself beginning to slide downward, into an enormous black hole that narrowed at the bottom like a hallway. I clenched my hands in my lap so hard that I felt my fingernails pierce my palm and red marks flared across the white of my knuckles. I willed myself to gain control. I would not, *would not*, slide further into that hole. For I knew that at the bottom I would find a door, and I was not yet ready to open it. Still clenching my hands, I forced myself to concentrate on Peter's next words.

"I must have been injured in the fire or knocked on the head sometime during it," Peter went on, "because I don't remember anything but trying to save you and Mother, staggering outside and then . . . nothing. The next thing I remember is waking up in a strange city miles from St. Louis, alone. All I had were the clothes I was wearing and Father's map in one of my pockets. I remembered the fire, you, Mother; I tried to get back home. I had no money. I didn't even know where I was or how long I had been there. So I stayed in that town for a time, doing odd jobs, trying to earn money to get by. I asked about Father, and the fire, but no one helped me. I think

I was in Kansas at that time. I don't remember. I have forgotten most of what happened in those few months."

Peter paused, and in his eyes it seemed I saw the frightened, adolescent boy he had been then—alone, confused, homeless. My heart went out to him again.

"But there were plenty of us then," Peter continued, his eyes hardening slightly. "Runaways my age, trying to get by, working their way west. Some had left home to help support their families, some to *escape* their families. Some were just homeless like me. We got by. And after a while, with winter coming on, I decided it was best to work my way further west, too."

"But why didn't you come back?" My voice came out thin and plaintive, like a child's voice, like the voice of the child I had been, asking my aunt and uncle again and again when my brother would return. *If* he would return. "I was still alive. Uncle Charles and Aunt Natalie took me in and raised me. They would have raised you, too. We could have been together."

"No." Peter's voice was suddenly hard. "They didn't want me. Mother's family made that plain enough when we lived with them after Father left. They never liked Father, and they didn't like me. They never would have taken me in, and I never would have gone back to them."

I slowly began to understand what had made my brother the way he was. Peter had never had the security I was given growing up, I realized. He had never really known where he belonged. He would have been old enough to remember when Brandon Fisk left him and Mother in Kansas, old enough to feel grief at the news of his "death." How must Peter have felt when he and Mother returned to her old home in St. Louis? And when she remarried? With only good intentions, I am sure, Mother had always kept the memory of his real father alive. But how had Peter felt when life went on in such a changed way, and he, however unwillingly, had to continue on with it?

Yet it was still difficult for me to understand how Uncle Charles and Aunt Natalie could have treated Peter that way, to make him feel so alienated. Why had he thought they would not take him in, when they had been like parents to me, so loving and caring throughout all my life?

Some of my confusion must have shown on my face. "Mother's family knew that I understood about my real father," he said. "They resented that. They did not want to be reminded of him. But you had been made a part of the family from the beginning. It was different with you—you could have gone back any time. I couldn't." He paused a moment and when he spoke again his voice had changed.

"And, in a way, I think I was . . . afraid to go back. Afraid of what I might find there." Peter's words came out slowly, seeming to stick in his throat. "I didn't want to see for myself that you were all . . . dead. So I began to look for Father, to follow him, as he'd said. I knew he had gone back west, but I didn't know exactly where, so I began to head that way myself. I went from town to town earning money to live on, asking about Father, moving on. And finally, about a year later, I found out what had happened."

Peter stopped. I saw his thin, pointed jaw clench and the hardness come into his eyes again, along with a kind of fierceness and fury that made me draw back. "Father was murdered. In Kansas City. An old man there told me about it. They found his body in an alley; he'd been beaten, shot, left to rot. He wasn't even given a proper burial, and they never caught the man who did it. They knew it was Father from the papers in his pockets. But the people who found him didn't know who to notify. A drifter, that's what they called him. A bum. My father. He had no home, no connections. Like me."

The bitterness, the banked fury on Peter's face tore at my heart. What had he gone through over the last fifteen years, this bitter, confused brother of mine? I was beginning to recognize an odd quality in Peter: it was as though, somewhere along the line, his growth had been stunted, as though he had never fully recovered from what happened to him when he was thirteen and during the years immediately afterward, so that he had been unable to mature in a normal way. Even though an adult now sat across from me, it seemed that Peter was, in essence, an adolescent still searching for his place in life.

Seeing this, I ached to help him, to heal the wounds that time and circumstances had wrought, to give him that place in life he lacked. For I knew that I had been the lucky one, growing up. Peter had had nothing but pain.

"I started looking for what he'd left me then,"

Peter went on. "I knew it was there, somewhere, waiting to be claimed, and that I was the one to claim it. I had the map. Father had given it to me. But I was sick awhile, and I didn't have any money. It took me a long time to get anywhere. I don't know how many false starts I made, dead ends I hit. . . . You see, the map was—*is*—incomplete. Something important has been left out. Father must have done it purposely so that no one else could find the treasure. He had expected to take us there himself, you see, and then when he couldn't, he gave the map to me, thinking that I would follow him and find him, and we'd return to claim our fortune together. He was smart. He made sure that no one else would ever find the fortune he'd made for us. It was meant for me, and for Mother—"

"And for Heather," Prescott put in smoothly. "At this point, your brother met me, Miss Loring. What he didn't realize in all his long years of struggle was that he was not alone. I had befriended Brandon Fisk many years before, when he first left his family in Kansas and came west to seek his fortune. We prospected together and tried many other endeavors. We were young then"—here Prescott gave a wry chuckle and, with a wave of his hand, indicated the gray streaks at his temple—"and full of energy and high hopes. We became partners, always searching for that elusive fortune. . . . And in time we found it."

Prescott suddenly leaned forward, his black eyes gleaming. "A fortune in gold, Miss Loring. Spanish gold. A hoard of ornaments and doubloons hidden by the Spanish centuries ago—lost, found again, stolen by outlaws, hidden, and then, finally, found again by Brandon Fisk and me. We were in New Mexico at the time. We had heard the legends about this particular treasure, but no one had ever been able to find it. Then one day, while we were prospecting, we saved an old Mexican's life. He was a sheepherder and had taken a bad fall in the hills, breaking his leg; when we found him, he was nearly gone. But we got him to the next town, and as payment of what he perceived as his debt to us, he gave us something that had been handed down through the generations in his family. It was a set of written directions to the treasure we had heard rumors about. The old Mexican died soon after, but we began our search immediately. After over a year of fruitless effort, we finally found it: an ancient, rotting trunkload of Spanish gold."

Prescott's brows drew together in a frown, as if he were trying to concentrate. "Yes, we found the gold and then . . . something happened.

"Fisk was in some kind of trouble," Prescott went on slowly. "Something he hadn't told me about. We were in the mountains, where we'd found the treasure. We kept it with us there in camp, and at the beginning of the week, I went into a small, nearby town for supplies. When I came back he was gone. The treasure was gone— along with the wagon and our other two horses." Prescott paused again. "I knew something must have happened in my absence. Fisk must have been threatened somehow, or maybe someone else had found out about the treasure. I realized that Fisk must have had to leave on the spot, to get out of the area and stash the treasure in a new place. I knew he would contact me sooner or later and let me know what had happened. So I went back to our campsite and waited for word."

Prescott's voice had taken on an intensity I had not heard before, and his grammar roughened somewhat; he seemed to have momentarily relapsed into the man he had been then. I was not surprised at his revelation of this younger, cruder self. Although I had never known the details of his background, this was, I realized, what I had always sensed about Prescott Webb, hovering below the surface.

"When I didn't hear from Fisk, I realized something had happened," Prescott went on. "We were partners, and I knew if he couldn't get word to me, he was in trouble, and it was too dangerous to contact me. He'd mentioned the family he'd left behind only vaguely—Fisk wasn't one given to talk—but I figured that he might go there first. I made inquiries, but got nowhere. By then, you see, your mother had returned with you and Peter to St. Louis, and I was unable to trace them. I had run up against a dead end, as Peter did later. Only I had nothing to go on. And part of that treasure was still mine." Prescott's last word was proprietary, final. "So, like Peter, I began searching with barely any clues. I made inquiries about the area, trying to trace where Fisk had gone when he'd left the mountains. I knew he wouldn't have taken the treasure with him if he'd fled east; he must have hidden it somewhere. At the same time I was hired by a large mercantile firm in San Francisco to seek out rare items for them to buy and sell, which facilitated my own searching. My work for the firm took me all over the country, where I continued my inquiries. But after many years, I still had had little luck and was about to give up entirely when my company sent me to Twilight Mesa to collect artifacts. I went under the guise of a government surveyor to stifle any local protest of my work, and when I arrived, everything at last fell into place. As I explored, I finally realized that this was where Brandon Fisk had gone to hide our treasure. It made perfect sense: the mesa was not far from where we had found the gold in New Mexico, yet far enough, and deserted. Isolated. And Fisk had once mentioned Twilight Mesa to me, I remembered. He'd been there once, he said in passing; he'd commented on how immense and wild it was, how easy it would be to get lost in. Few had ventured into the mesa, and even fewer had reason to. Don't you see? Don't you see how it all made sense? I began to search myself, but soon saw what a hopeless, lifelong pursuit it could be without any kind of direction or assistance. Fisk could have hidden the treasure anywhere, in any one of those canyons.''

Prescott paused, pulling on his mustache and looking sharply over at Peter. "And that is when I met your brother. He, too, had traced the treasure to Twilight Mesa, not purely from trial and error as I had but with help from the one resource I was without—the map. Fisk's map contained no names—no towns, states, rivers, or mountains. It simply looked like a large hand, with fingers radiating outward. But when your brother stumbled into this area, suddenly the map took shape, and people were able to tell him what each feature was. He arrived here shortly after I did, and someone in Jackson told him that I might be hiring day laborers to help me with my work. He came to me, not telling me who he was, but as I became acquainted with him, his identity became quite obvious. He was Brandon Fisk's son in every way: looks, manner, personality. Peter tried to hide the map from me at first, just as he had tried to hide his true purpose in coming to Twilight Mesa, but it wasn't long before I guessed the truth. I told him who I was, and I found myself a new partner that day."

As Prescott glanced over at Peter again, I saw a strange mixture of emotions cross my brother's face. There was guardedness, and still some of the bitterness I had noticed earlier. But as Peter returned Prescott's look, I also saw a kind of tentative trust in my brother's expression; it was very brief and barely discernible, as if Peter were not at all used to the emotion and, indeed, did not like it. I began to realize then the bond that must have formed between the two when Peter, after years of connection to no one, had finally discovered someone who had not only known Brandon Fisk but who had even been his partner.

"Since then," Prescott went on, "for the last year, we have been methodically searching Twilight Mesa. It has been a difficult task, and we have come to believe that we are in need of some missing piece of information. We both agree that Brandon Fisk was too smart to leave Peter with the only incomplete map, yet smart enough to realize that he could not leave Peter with all the information, for his own safety's sake. That, Miss Loring is where *you* come in. We believe you have the missing information we seek."

My heart began to pound. So this was what it had all meant. Why the strange man—my father—had come, why he had taken me aside, given me the doubloon, the amulet. It had all been to lead me to this place, this moment. Prescott and Peter stared at me, their eyes sharp, both leaning forward in their seats as they watched my reaction.

"How . . . how do you know that?" I blurted. Seeing their expressions, I stopped abruptly. "I mean . . . why would you think that?"

"Ah!" Prescott's exclamation was triumphant. "I knew it had to be you! For you, my dear Heather, have been the missing key all along, our key to Twilight Mesa! I knew it as soon as Peter told me that Fisk had taken you aside that night. Peter did not remember at first. It was only after I had forced him to go over and over in his mind those few moments in the yard with his father that he finally remembered you had been there, too. After Fisk gave him the map, Peter remembered that your father saw you, hiding in the bushes. He drew you aside and gave you something, told you something, Peter remembers. . . ."

Prescott leaned toward me, in his eyes a sharp gleaming light. "What was it, Heather? What did Fisk give you? What did he tell you?"

The pounding of my heart was almost painful. My mouth had gone dry, and I ran my tongue quickly over my lips. "I . . . he just gave me an amulet, you see, from one of the dwellings, and a doubloon."

"A doubloon?" Peter's tone was sharp and edged with anger. "Why did he give you that?"

"I don't know," I said, confused by Prescott's demanding eyes and the sudden hostility Peter seemed to be directing at me. "The man . . . my father . . . he just gave them to me; I don't know why. And then he told me something. . . ."

"What?" Prescott was nearly out of his seat now, his face intense.

"I . . . I don't know." Stupidly, hating myself for it, I felt tears welling in my eyes. I was suddenly five years old again: afraid, unsure, aware of a sense of extreme urgency and desperation as the stranger placed the two objects in my palm and whispered some jumbled words to me. Then he told me to remember; he expected so much of me. He wanted me to remember it all; he said it was very, very important. I was so afraid, so stiff with fear that I wouldn't remember and be able to do what he had told me. And I was afraid of the man himself. He was a stranger, someone I didn't know. I felt only the power of his fear and his desperation, and this became imprinted on my consciousness.

"What did he say?" Peter spoke this time, his tone as sharp as a knife.

"I . . . it was just words . . . some kind of rhyme, perhaps. I couldn't understand him, what he was trying to tell me. . . ." To my horror, I felt the tears begin to spill down my cheeks and a sob rise up and break in my breast.

There was a silence in the room as the two men stared at me. Then, seeming to regain his composure, Prescott reached over to touch my hands, still clenched tightly in my lap.

"Dear Heather, do forgive us," he said. His words were tinged with surprising gentleness. "I can see that we moved entirely too rapidly. We have told you too much. Our story has been too much of a shock. Am I right?"

I nodded, my throat too tight to speak.

"Yes, I see." Prescott paused, looking so intently at the coiled circles radiating outward from the center of the large rag rug on the floor that it seemed as if he were searching for an answer in their pattern. After a moment he regarded me again. "Perhaps we should start over. What you need to understand, Heather, is that we are not asking these things of you, but *for* you. You hold the key to a treasure that belongs to all of us. It is yours as well. It is part of the heritage that your father left for you. We ask you these questions only so that we may all find and share the fortune together."

As I glanced over at Peter, I saw him stiffen slightly, in anticipation of my reply.

I think it was then I began to see that I was not only the key to the treasure Peter was seeking, but to the only thing of real importance left to him in his life: his heritage. And I was the key that would enable him to him possess it now. Looking away from Peter, I swallowed hard.

Prescott went on. "Now," he said gently. "When Brandon Fisk came that night, he gave you an amulet and a doubloon. Is that right?"

I nodded.

"And what did he tell you about them?"

"He just . . . told me to keep them. To keep them safe. He said I'd know what to do with them when the time came."

"And then what did he say? You mentioned some words, a rhyme, perhaps? . . ."

"That's all I remember. It *was* some kind of a rhyme, I am sure of that, for it sounded like the nursery rhymes Mother would recite to me at bedtime. But this one was different from anything I had heard. It made no sense to me. I tried to concentrate on it, because the man told me to, but I couldn't make sense of it. I was so afraid . . ."

"I see." Prescott's tone was precise, like my doctor in St. Louis, questioning me about one of my spells. "But as you must know, Heather, the memory is quite an adept and amazing thing. At the time, perhaps, you thought you would never remember it, thought, indeed, that you *didn't* remember it. But perhaps the fear of the situation simply blocked your father's words from your mind, as your entire memory was later blocked about the fire the next day."

I glanced up in surprise and noticed Peter do the same. "Yes, Julia told me about that, Heather. Remember you explained it to her on the journey here. But the point I was trying to get across—"

"You don't remember anything about the fire?" Peter interrupted suddenly, staring at me.

"Well, no, I don't. Only that morning, when we were playing. . . ."

"You remember that?" Peter's tone was sharp again, as sharp as his eyes on me.

"Peter—" Prescott began.

"I only remember that we were playing something, together, and feeling a sense that something wasn't quite right. And then my memory just stops. Sometimes it comes back in bits and pieces, but evidently the events were too traumatic. I have spells sometimes, that prevent me from remembering."

"Let's not get into all that now," Prescott interjected with a frown directed toward Peter. "The point I was trying to make earlier, Heather, was that, with the proper prompting, perhaps you can remember what your father told you that night. The words are obviously there, we just need to find the resources to bring them back up into your conscious mind. The facts about the fire, perhaps, are meant to stay buried in your mind."

"But you don't understand. Those memories are all mingled together. If I remember the rhyme, I'm afraid that—"

"That you will remember everything?" Peter finished.

"Yes. And as I said before, if something has stopped me from remembering it all these years . . . I began to remember that day in the cliff dwelling—it was you, wasn't it? I saw your face, and all at once it came back in a rush: that night, the next morning, the fire. . . . I lost control."

"And what a frightening incident that was!" Prescott's voice was smooth. "We certainly wouldn't want that to happen again. No, Heather, we must go about this very slowly and carefully. We want to help you, to protect you from the buried memories. We have come here today to ask you to travel with us into Twilight Mesa again, before the summer is out. We have narrowed down our options somewhat but have several canyons yet to explore, and we think that perhaps if you come with us, you will see something or hear something . . . And perhaps your father's words will come back of their own volition without endangering you in any way."

"You want me to come with you into Twilight

Mesa to look for the gold?" I repeated rather dumbly.

"Precisely. And of course Peter and I—and Julia—will be there all the time to make certain nothing happens to you. Remember, it is your fortune, too, Heather, your heritage. Don't forget that it was all that was left to you by your real father."

My real father. The words had an odd ring. For I could not yet reconcile the thought that the stranger who'd come that night had been my father.

It was all too much. I simply could not take it all in so quickly. "I will have to think about it," I said softly.

"Of course. We understand." Prescott stood up and smoothed his wool pants in one graceful gesture, then picked up his hat from Mrs. Kendall's small walnut table. "That is why we came only to discuss the subject itself today. We will return again in three days to hear your answer." Prescott paused, his eyes intent on me. "But I think I already know what that answer will be, Heather. How could you refuse your own inheritance? Your own brother?"

Peter turned his eyes away quickly, but in them, for just an instant, I had glimpsed the same odd, mingled expression I had seen earlier when he looked at Prescott, seeming to want a bond, a connection with someone, but unused to the idea and afraid of it.

Yes. How could I deny my brother, and withhold whatever key I held from Peter, who, possessing nothing else, had been searching in vain all these years?

And, I was beginning to realize, how could I deny myself what was left to me by the father I had never known?

Seeing my face, Prescott smiled. "We will be back in three days. After that, if you agree, we will arrange another trip to Twilight Mesa."

With that, Prescott started toward the door, Peter after him.

"Wait!" I called suddenly. "There is so much that I do not understand. You have not explained how you knew I was Peter's sister."

"It's very simple, really," Prescott said. "After Peter told me about you, I made inquiries and discovered you were still alive. Evidently it had never dawned on Peter to do so, so certain was he of your death in the fire. But, as you may have guessed, I am not one to leave any clue uninvestigated. After I discovered you were still alive, I traced you to Denver, saw your byline in the *Crier*, and then it was a simple matter of sending Doran Hunt up to check on you."

"Doran?"

"Yes, didn't you know?" Prescott's voice was as smooth as butter. "He's a private investigator. Or at least he was. That was his line of work before he became involved in Twilight Mesa. When I learned he had an investigative background, I came here and made him the proposition of traveling to Denver to see if you were, indeed, Peter's sister. He agreed, of course."

Prescott paused, watching me closely. "If you have not already discovered this for yourself, Heather, Doran Hunt is a man who will do anything for the right price. Really, in a way it is quite admirable. For everything he undertakes there is a specific reason—usually one that suits his own purposes."

Prescott was quiet a moment, and then he went on in a low voice, "That is why I feel I must issue you a word of caution now, Heather. You see, I have begun to suspect that Mr. Hunt might know about the gold we are seeking, and may even be searching for it himself. I did not realize when I hired him what an astute man he is—or what an opportunist. And since you have arrived, Heather, I have noticed how much more intent his interest in my work has become. And I am afraid that by investigating your background, he may have learned just what an important role you play in the discovery of our fortune. He may realize that you are the key *he* needs as well. Perhaps that is why Mr. Hunt has been paying such close attention to you. I could not help but notice his, ah, attentions at the snake dance, as well as in Twilight Mesa. And Julia tells me he has been quite attentive here at the ranch, as well, asking you numerous questions and so on. And wasn't Mr. Hunt the one who persuaded you to come down to Twilight Mesa? I did not ask him to; that little matter he took into his own hands."

I listened, stunned, thinking of Doran watching and following me in Denver, speaking to me at the exhibition. I remembered all his careful questions, the way he had probed persistently about my background and my past, the uncanny way he seemed able, at times, to see right into my mind. Had it all been for his own benefit? Was that why he had accompanied me into Twilight

Mesa and seemed to watch my reactions so carefully?

And then, at the snake dance—when I had decided to leave and return to Denver—had Doran's passion during the ceremony been a ploy, a way to ensnare me, to prevent me from leaving? Had he planned to wrap me in a false sense of love and trust only to betray me for a hidden treasure?

My mind whirled with questions and uncertainty. In less than two hours, Prescott Webb had turned my world upside down.

I watched the men leave. Peter had not spoken since Prescott mentioned Doran Hunt, and now he sat somewhat slumped on his saddle. Although Prescott smiled and tipped his hat, Peter made no gesture of farewell; he did not even look at me as the two spurred their horses and rode out of the yard at a gallop.

But instead of the twinge of loss I had expected to feel at Peter's disregard, I was struck with a quick, fierce sense of determination to bridge the gap between us, to somehow give Peter whatever he had not received that made him act the way he did now. I did not know him, really. But he was my brother. And we were bound by something that went deeper even than blood: the heritage left to us to find together.

I had just started to go back inside the house when I saw someone emerge from around the far end of the porch.

He stopped when he saw me, and for a moment we stood there, staring at each other. I felt a sudden wave of shock ripple through me at the sight of him—lean, lithe, magnetic. In the shade of the porch's wooden awning, his shadowed eyes looked, again, like dark bruises in his face. He was wearing denims still covered with the dirt and dust of the trail, and his thick hair was matted with it. In his left hand he held a dirt-caked wide-brimmed hat; his other hand went slack at his side when he saw me.

My eyes were drawn to that hand, remembering how easily it had glided over my body, stoking the unfamiliar fires of desire, drugging me with the need for his touch.

My mouth went dry, and for a moment I could not breathe. Although Doran stood yards away, the distance between us seemed full of him; so overpowering was his presence that it seemed to take up all the space around me.

"Why were they here?" he asked, after staring at me in silence for several moments. "Webb and his assistant. What did they want?"

I could feel Doran's anger like a tangible object in the space between us. As his abrupt words lashed out, I took a step back toward the house. I remembered what Prescott had told me. Was Doran using me now, exerting the power of his physical presence to draw and attract me despite my misgivings? I felt that power; I could not help myself. My body yearned for his even as I asked myself if his actions at the snake dance were but a careful strategy to manipulate me.

Suddenly I too was filled with anger.

"Surely *you* know why they were here, Mr. Hunt," I said, feeling behind me for the cool chinked wall of the house. "You *are* on Mr.

Webb's payroll, are you not? That is your job, isn't it, to spy on people for him?"

Doran stiffened at my words. "No. Webb has no hold on me. My work for him consisted of a single job, one contract only, completed and terminated weeks ago."

"To investigate something for him. To spy on me."

"I can see that Webb has been talking to you, evidently for some time," Doran said. "Yes, he hired me to investigate your background—to spy on you, if you will. And he paid me well. But I took it for my own reasons, not for any benefit he might have derived from it."

"Oh? And what might those reasons have been, if not for the money?" My heart had begun to thud in my chest. *My own reasons*, Doran said. Prescott's words echoed again in my mind: *For everything he undertakes there is a specific reason—usually one that suits his own purposes.*

"The job intrigued me," Doran said.

He did not go on.

"I see." My heart beat harder. "Tell me then, Mr. Hunt, did Mr. Webb pay you more for persuading me to come down to Twilight Mesa? As I understand it, that was not part of the original bargain between the two of you."

Doran's eyes swept me. I pulled myself up straighter, vowing that he would not gain control of me or of this moment between us.

"No," Doran said, his eyes probing. "That was my idea."

"And was it your idea to take me into Twilight Mesa as well? Is that why you taught me to ride, and took me down into the dwellings yourself—to watch my reactions? To continue to spy on me? Is that why you made me feel as if I were failing somehow, by leaving? Is that why you came to the snake dance, and why you . . ."

My voice faltered. My anger had suddenly dissipated at the memory of that night, at what had bound us so powerfully, so vitally. I looked at Doran mutely, hating myself but unable to hide the question I knew he must see plainly, unguarded in my eyes.

Did you feel as I did, that night? Were you affected as strongly by what passed between us?

Something in Doran's face changed, and I thought I saw that unguarded and vulnerable part of himself shift far back in his eyes as well, that peculiar look I had seen only a few precious times before. For a moment it seemed his softened gaze answered my silent questions and bridged the distance between us.

Doran hesitated a moment before he said, "I don't trust them, and I don't like what they've been doing. Webb is not who he seems. And neither is his assistant. There's something about him I don't quite trust. . . ."

"You don't even know him," I said, suddenly defensive.

Doran's gaze sharpened on me, at once alert. "Oh? And you do?"

I shifted my eyes away, uncomfortable under Doran's scrutiny. "Prescott's assistant is my brother, Peter Fisk."

There was a short, charged silence between us. "So it is true," Doran finally said. "It *was* his face in the photograph. I suspected as much, but I had no proof."

Hearing about Peter, Doran's mood shifted abruptly from the intimacy I had felt from him only a moment before to a kind of cold, calculated musing.

Or perhaps, I thought, I had only *imagined* the intimacy between us. Doran frowned, turning his eyes away from me as if I were not even there.

What a fool I had been!

"Really, Mr. Hunt," I said, my voice cold and steely hard. "I am quite amazed that you were not able to identify my brother sooner. It seems like such sloppy work. Any good investigator would surely have turned up that information early on."

Doran's face hardened. "You didn't answer my question," he said roughly. "Why were your brother and Prescott Webb here?"

"To ask me to help them in their work at Twilight Mesa."

"And what exactly is that?" Doran's tone was still rough.

"Surely you know: Mr. Webb works for the government, and my brother helps him. They came to tell me that they are planning to take Julia on a trip to the mesa again, and they invited me to go along, to observe and assist them."

"I thought you had planned on returning to Denver."

"That was before Peter came here. Things have changed now."

Doran's eyes were so dark and piercing they felt like hot coals burning into mine. "Yes," he said slowly. "I can see that they have." He paused, and for an instant his expression changed. "Don't go, Heather," he went on, his voice very low. "Don't go with them."

"Why?" I said, staring at him. "Why shouldn't I go?"

"I . . ." Doran paused and swallowed. Exposed above the open collar of his denim shirt, the thick tanned column of his neck looked suddenly defenseless. "Stay here, Heather. If you should go . . . I don't know what will happen this time. You might be hurt again. Or something else might happen . . . something worse. The mesa is full of dangers you don't know anything about." He paused again. "Stay here, Heather. Please. Don't go with them. I . . . don't trust them," he finished lamely.

Listening to him, I thought of all the time we had spent together, from the moment he approached me at the exhibition to the snake dance and how I had responded in unison with him. And then I thought about what both Julia and Prescott had told me, and what I had just learned about Doran.

What did he really want? Who was I to believe?

"*You* don't trust them?" I said, my voice beginning to rise with all the conflicting emotions building inside me. "And tell me, Mr. Hunt, what reason on God's good earth do I have for trusting *you*?"

My last word came out with the force of an arrow thrust, and for a moment it appeared to have hit its mark. Doran flinched suddenly, and whatever openness I had seen in his eyes before disappeared completely.

"Very well, Heather—Miss Loring," he said, his voice as hard as mine had been a few moments before. "If that's how you feel, I won't try to stop you." He looked at me from the end of the porch and what seemed a long, unbridgeable distance. Whatever had been between us when we first saw each other was gone now, and the air was filled only with a cold kind of emptiness.

Doran stared at me another moment, the muscles of his jaw clenched and the skin pulled so tightly across his cheekbones that it looked almost opaque. Then he turned to go. But before he reached the corner of the porch, he turned back to look at me.

"Just don't forget that I tried to warn you," he said, his voice harsh and cold. "I told you what might happen. I told you that you might be hurt."

His words fell on me with a chill, a snaking draft of cold air on that sultry day. As I watched him walk away, his back straight and unyielding, I felt very, very alone; had I just lost something terribly important?

Or had it ever existed?

Just remember that I tried to warn you. I told you what might happen. I told you that you might be hurt.

Although Doran was out of sight, his words replayed themselves in my mind with all their initial force. Shivering, I looked down to see that gooseflesh had broken out on my arms.

I stared out at nothing for a long moment. If I were to ride into Twilight Mesa in three days, I thought, I would have to begin preparing immediately. I would tell Mrs. Kendall my plans as soon as she came home.

Chapter Thirteen

✦ ✦ ✦ ✦ ✦

IT WAS ODD, this time, riding away from the ranch with none of the Kendall family as company. It was just past dawn; behind us, the sun had barely tinged the rim of the far mountains with its pearl-like translucent first light. Prescott was in the lead on his horse, followed by Julia on her gelding and me on a mare named Chestnut. Peter brought up the rear, keeping some distance behind the rest of us.

We planned to camp in Jackson Canyon that night, but to ride much further into Twilight Mesa the following day, penetrating into far branch canyons that Peter and Prescott had only partially explored. Julia seemed quite excited, even by the prospect of such an arduous trip, although now she seemed lost in thought, as I was.

It was still so difficult to readjust my thoughts to the truth about my parents, to imagine that Samuel Loring was really not my father at all, but just a man Mother had wed after my birth. And yet he had always been a father to me; he had cared for me, provided for me, loved me. In many ways, he was much more of a father than Brandon Fisk had ever been.

I still could not think of Brandon Fisk as my real father. I had never known him and never would. But I knew that I had to go to Twilight Mesa and finish what he had started in my life so long ago. For Peter's sake.

Mrs. Kendall had been flabbergasted when I told her the news. "Your brother!" she cried.

"Why, land, child! Why . . . why, how wonderful! It's just like one of them books, ain't it? Reunited after all these years! Why, my gracious goodness sakes!"

Her four sons were equally surprised but seemed a bit confused, not quite able to reconcile Prescott Webb's assistant and my brother being the same person.

"Well there! You were right after all, Miss Loring," Charlie said. "You *did* recognize that face in the photograph! If I ever would've thought you were talkin' about your own brother, why, maybe I would have thumped this old brain a little harder to remember somethin', though I never would've guessed such a thing as this!"

For a reason I did not quite understand myself, I postponed telling Mr. Kendall about Peter and my return visit to Twilight Mesa as long as possible. I had not visited his room since our arrival back from the snake dance, and as Mrs. Kendall told us he had a touch of stiffness in his old bones, he had not appeared in the dining room for any meals. But on the day before we were to leave for the mesa, I came in from my morning ride and slipped down the hall to his open doorway.

The room was just as it had been before, as if not a minute had passed since I had left it last. The fire was blazing in the hearth, and Mr. Kendall was huddled in his Indian blanket in the chair beside it.

"So," he said, turning his wizened face to me as I sat down across from him. "You're leaving us, eh?" He paused. "Well, I saw Prescott and that assistant of his ride up the other morning and then leave later on, all right. But it surprised me some when Mrs. Kendall told me that Webb's

friend was your brother. I hadn't guessed that."
Mr. Kendall's topaz eyes sharpened. "But you
did, didn't you, girlie? You knew, and that's why
you came down, why you were askin' all those
questions, goin' off on that trip to the mesa. So
you could look for him—your brother."

"I didn't really know that Peter would be down
here working with Mr. Webb," I began.

"You didn't? That's kinda strange then, ain't it,
the way you just found him? Specially that it
turned out he was with Webb, and you comin'
down here with that fiancée of his and all. Seems
like an awful lot of coincidences to me. Why was
that you said you were goin' into the mesa again?
To do what?"

"To help Mr. Webb and my brother with their
work before the summer is through."

"What kind of work? Webb ain't never been too
clear on that."

"Well, it's government work—exploring the
canyons, surveying, writing reports and the like."

"Well then, what's he need you for?"

"He doesn't really need me, I suppose. He just
asked me to come along thinking I would want to
be close to my brother while he worked. And
then, there are my articles. I'm hoping that I'll
find more material for them on this trip as well."

"Oh, sure, them articles." Mr. Kendall looked
at me with his head cocked to the side. "And
where does Hunt fit into all this? Is he going,
too?"

I could feel my face begin to redden. "Not that
I am aware of. I am not sure what Mr. Hunt's
plans are."

"Hmmm. Mrs. Kendall tells me he hasn't been

around much over the last few days. I saw you and him on the porch t'other mornin', though, after Webb and your brother rode off. You looked kinda mad at each other. You two have a disagreement?''

When I did not answer, Mr. Kendall smiled. ''Thought so. That means Hunt probably ain't goin' with you. But I'll bet he'll be there all the same, watchin' like he always does.''

Now, as we made our way across Jackson Valley and started up the steep, narrow ascent of Twilight Mesa's northern abutment, I glanced back over my shoulder. Was Doran Hunt following us? Or was he already in one of Twilight Mesa's far canyons, waiting for our arrival?

Although I had not seen or heard from him since our charged encounter on the porch, like Mr. Kendall I suspected that Doran Hunt would indeed be watching us in Twilight Mesa—watching us all very carefully. For I could not forget his parting words.

Just remember that I tried to warn you. I told you that you might be hurt.

Oh, why could I not trust him?

I reached down into the pocket of my heavy skirt and touched the cool, smooth shape of my amulet. I had placed it there before we left that morning—a foolish gesture, perhaps, but one that comforted me in an odd way and somehow made me feel more secure.

Ever since Doran had walked away from me, I had not been able to overcome the empty sense that I was now quite alone. Being at the Kendalls' ranch had helped, but now, steadily approaching Twilight Mesa, I felt almost abandoned.

This was ridiculous, of course. I knew that I had made the right decision. And I was in the company of my closest living relative. Why should I feel so alone?

Perhaps because Peter was still acting so remote. He had hardly spoken to me since we had left the ranch, despite my efforts to draw him into some kind of conversation. I had hoped, when I had agreed to come, that Peter would see how much I wanted to help and begin to drop the barrier between us.

But I saw that it would take time. Too much had happened since we had last been together. As I felt his presence, silent and guarded, on the trail behind me, I willed myself to be patient, to give Peter the distance he needed until we grew used to each other again.

For although Peter did not speak with me, I caught him watching me several times, that curious look—the one he'd had when he'd told me I reminded him of Mother—on his face, and I knew that whatever separated us was only temporary. What joined us—our parents, our heritage, our blood—was lasting and firm, a binding foundation that could never be taken away.

The trip passed without incident until we stopped to camp for the night. Prescott chose a different spot, closer to the twisting branch canyons and further from the spring. I was grateful for this; even as we paused at the spring for water, I felt a painful tugging on my heart and memory, thinking of the time I had stood there in the dark with Doran's arms twined about me. . . .

Until I remembered the sudden flash of his smile. I shivered as I saw the sun dipping down below the steep, surrounding cliffs. Where was Doran? I wondered.

"Well, now," Prescott said, rubbing his hands together over the campfire of piñon and juniper logs he and Peter had collected. "Let's get to work!"

His uneven teeth glowed yellow in the firelight. Julia sat next to him, her features also caught by the fire's glow, and I sat opposite, on a juniper trunk split and set by the fire. Peter sat off to the side, his face cast in shadow.

"Tomorrow we will be riding into some canyons you've never seen before, Heather," Prescott went on. "Between the two of us, your brother and I have explored almost every canyon in the mesa. Even so, we have not even come close to finding what we are looking for. You have seen the condition of many of the ruins; it takes months to dig out even one. We need some kind of specific indication of where to look now and where to dig once we find the right dwelling. You must remember, Heather. What did your father tell you on that night sixteen years ago?"

I felt three pairs of eyes turn to me, probe my face, burn, it seemed, into my very mind. I swallowed, feeling a sudden chill at my back.

"You mentioned a rhyme," Prescott continued. His voice was smooth and controlled, as always, but now I sensed an underlying, steely quality about it. "A nursery rhyme, perhaps. It seems rather unusual, knowing the nature and character of Brandon Fisk, that he would recite such a rhyme to you, but you *were* only five years old."

"I didn't say that it *was* a nursery rhyme, only that it sounded like the kind Mother would recite

to me at bedtime." My words came out rather
thick and hoarse, as if I had not spoken for some
time.

"Yes? And what was it? What did he say?" Julia
leaned toward me eagerly, her eyes almost indigo
colored in the black stillness of the canyon.

"I . . . I cannot remember." Squeezing my eyes
shut, I clenched my hands in my lap and forced
myself to think back to that night when the
stranger had come.

I could feel the heavy, cold weight of the gold
doubloon in my palm, hear the slight rattle and
click of the smooth bones of the amulet as the
man placed them in my outstretched hand. Then
he had curled my fingers around the objects, closing my hand into a fist, and had laughed.

"Now I'm going to tell you something very important, dearie," the man had said, his face dark
and very close. "Remember this. You will need it
when the time comes. Now listen closely . . ."

I strained, lost in my memories, but the words
would not come clear. Then all at once in my
mind I saw images: the sky, arching overhead
and, within it, a star or a gem. . . . For some
reason I thought of my parents' mementos stored
in their gold jewel case: my father's medals, my
mother's watch and breast pin and diamond ring.
Her ring. A star. A gem.

"A diamond!" I cried, my eyes flying open.
"He spoke of a diamond in the rhyme, I am sure
of it! A diamond, he said, high in the sky."

I looked over at Prescott in triumph, but his
expression was confused, his brows pulled together in a frown. "A diamond? But the trunk

we found contained only gold and some silver. Perhaps he was referring to something else."

"No! I think there was also mention of silver in the rhyme, or at least a word like silver." I closed my eyes again, willing the words to surface into my consciousness. "He said something like silver, something *shimmered* like silver. And there was a tree he told me about, too, I think—"

"Oh, for heaven's sake!" Julia's exclamation surprised me, jolting me out of that charged, past moment I had been concentrating on so fiercely, back into the present again. "What a silly rhyme. Diamonds, trees, skies! Why, what does that have to do with anything at all? I think you must be terribly mixed up, Heather. Are you certain that man told you a rhyme at all, or have you just jumbled this all up in your mind with something your mother told you at bedtime?"

"Well, I . . . I . . ."

"Now Julia, my dear, look what you have done!" Prescott's tone and expression were angry as he turned toward his fiancée. "You have confused Heather and made her upset, just as she was beginning to remember something that might help us."

"Help us? How could those silly words possibly help us? Why, there is sky everywhere! And trees! And almost anything shimmers like silver in the right light! As for diamonds—it is gold we are looking for. *Gold!*"

Standing abruptly, Julia flounced over to where our packs lay and began rummaging through them with a vehemence that startled me.

Prescott leaned toward me and said confidentially, "As you have probably realized, Heather, my dear, Julia is quite a sensitive creature, and this trip has not been easy for her." He paused. "Perhaps it has been too much of a strain, including her in this matter. Indeed, perhaps it has been a mistake altogether. . . ."

Prescott's voice trailed off as he gazed past me toward Julia, and in the waning firelight, I could not see his expression clearly. Was he already thinking of returning to the ranch?

Peter moved closer to us around the fire. He seemed agitated, uneasy as he shifted his position. In his bearing I sensed a kind of apprehension, as if he were afraid I would not remember the words we needed to lead us to the gold. "Oh, I am sure I will remember all the words soon!" I cried to Prescott. "My memory . . . it is so elusive. At times, things are so clear, and then . . ."

Peter peered at me intently.

"Don't worry, Heather dear." Prescott said, his dark eyes returning to my face. "We all have plenty of time. We must not try to force your memory until it is ready to come forth with what we need of its own volition. I will speak to Julia. Tomorrow we will ride further into Twilight Mesa, and perhaps you will see something that will spark your memory again. I am quite encouraged by what you have remembered even tonight. It is only a matter of time now."

Prescott went to Julia, then drew her off into the shadows of a small clump of pines. I heard her voice rise in shrill exasperation and then Prescott's smooth tones soothing her. In a moment there was no sound at all, and I saw their figures merge into one, drawing back further into the darkness of the sheltering trees.

I glanced around the campsite. After Prescott had gone to see to Julia, Peter moved from his position near the fire. Now my eyes searched for him in the surrounding darkness. I had hoped, riding ahead of Peter on the trail today, that once we made camp I would be able to finally talk with him, to ask him about the years of our separation and what he might do at the end of the summer. And I had hoped that at that point, after we had found what our father had left here in Twilight Mesa, perhaps together we could even—

A coyote called in the black stillness of the canyon. I was alone. Peter was gone.

Most likely attending to the horses hobbled further up the trail, I thought, or down at the spring drawing more water. And some instinct told me that Peter would stay away until I was in my bedroll and already asleep. With a sinking sensation, I realized what I think I had already known, even that morning: Peter was not ready to talk with me yet. He was not ready to close the distance between us.

Crossing over to the packs, I began to prepare my bedroll for the night. The fire was nearly out, and I shivered as I moved away from its lingering warmth. As I took off my boots and crawled into the woolly warm blankets, I thought of the last time I had camped in this canyon, when Doran Hunt had lain not a foot away, beside me through the night. As I dozed off, I remembered why Doran had been there. *To protect against snakes and critters and such*, Will had said.

Perhaps it was that last waking thought—or perhaps it had been the conversation around the campfire—that induced the dream that followed.

It was a horrible, hideous dream, full of great writhing snakes and creatures that pursued me down steep, twisting canyons and up sandstone cliffs, forcing me finally to fling myself off into an arching blue sky that suddenly turned murky and thick, trapping me in its mire so that the only way I could free myself was to remember something, something so very important. . . .

There were faces in the dream, too, calling to me from a distance: Prescott's face, and Julia's, and Peter's. And Doran Hunt's face was the furthest away, but as I watched, it moved toward me, steadily closer, until he was there beside me, catching me up in his arms, then bearing down so tightly upon me that I wrenched away, turned from him to another face that drew me across a crowded square. I tried to reach the face, but my feet were stuck again, and as I looked down, the mire turned to dust and in front of me was a huge, coiled rattlesnake, about to strike. I heard the ominous shake of its rattle, but I could not move. . . .

The rattle was louder, closer. I jerked awake, and for a moment I thought I was still immersed in my nightmare. There, not three yards from my head, was the coiled, shadowy shape of a rattlesnake, its black eyes and narrow head pointed toward me. I heard its rattle again; time seemed frozen as I stared at it.

And then all at once the ground exploded before me in an enormous, ear-splitting crack, spurting shards of rock and debris into the air. I ducked my head, protecting my face, and when I looked up again, I saw the limp, prone body of the snake.

"It was getting ready to strike," Prescott said. He

stood near me, a rifle, pointed at the snake, still gripped in his hands. "I woke up and heard it, thank God. It would have reached you first, Heather."

Sitting up, I saw Julia, who had settled herself in the bedroll beside me, now clutching its blankets about her where she stood some distance away, beside the extinguished campfire. Peter was on the other side of her, fully clothed. They both stared at me.

"We were all asleep," Prescott said. "It is well past midnight." He was silent a moment, considering the dead snake before us. "I don't understand how this happened. I have never seen a snake come so near a camping spot in this canyon before."

No one answered Prescott, but I heard words echo in my mind: *I told you that you might be hurt. . . . The mesa is full of dangers you don't know anything about.*

I looked out into the darkness beyond our campsite. Anything could be out there, I realized with a sudden shiver. Or *anyone.*

"Maybe it's the curse."

Startled, I glanced over at Peter, who had been mute until then. He was staring at the body of the snake, transfixed.

"The curse on the treasure," he went on. "This means we must be getting close."

"What do you mean?" Julia's voice was high, querulous. "Do you mean the kind of curse Mr. Kendall told us about? He said there were curses on certain treasures. But how would you know about that? You weren't even there that night!"

"Where?" Peter looked up almost absently, it

seemed, at Julia, his face unreadable in the darkness.

"Ah, Peter is not serious, my dear." Prescott moved to Julia's side quickly and put an arm about her shoulders. "I told Peter about what Nate Kendall said that night, and we have spoken—quite facetiously—about the curse ever since. It is such a ridiculous idea. We have often laughed about it."

But no one laughed as Prescott spoke, or in the silence that fell on us as we stared at the dead rattlesnake. Finally Prescott roused himself.

"Come, come," he said, urging Julia along beside him, back to where the bedrolls were spread out. "We must all get some rest now. The danger is passed. We must sleep while we can, for once sun rises we will have much to do."

Rather reluctantly, Julia obeyed, taking her place beside me. Prescott dropped down to his bedroll on the other side of her, and Peter soon followed a short distance away.

I felt a twinge then, an ache that could not be soothed by telling myself to be patient and tolerant with Peter. Why had he not taken his place beside me? Was there still that much between us? If so, how could I ever hope to close the gap?

Julia sat up for a long time before Prescott's soothing voice finally cajoled her to lie down and fall asleep. It was a very long time before I could close my eyes again. I could not stop hearing the rattle of the snake's tail so close to my head, nor eradicate the images of my nightmare, still lurking just beneath the surface of my consciousness. I lay awake trying to remember and not remember the night the stranger had come back into my life; my mind struggled to find its way back through the maze of my memory.

But in the end I remembered nothing, only the final black unconsciousness of sleep.

Early the next afternoon I saw him—Kianeech, the old Indian. We were up in a small cliff dwelling in one of the branch canyons, and he was standing on the rim of the opposite mesa, watching us.

At first I did not notice him, so well, it seemed, did he merge with his surroundings. He was standing halfway behind a thick, twisted cedar, and his hair was streaked as gray as the aged bark of its trunk. He was completely motionless as he stood there. He was not wrapped in the native blankets I had seen at the Hopi villages, but was wearing an old cotton shirt and heavy trousers. Even so, their dull weathered colors seemed to fade into the earthy colors of the mesa itself, as if he was and always had been one with it. A mass of gray thunderclouds was rising above the mesa behind him.

No one else saw him. Julia and Prescott and Peter were all busy rummaging through the ruin; it was filled with debris, like the others we had found earlier in the day, and Prescott and Peter, kerchiefs tied about their mouths, had been working with their shovels and bare hands for over an hour, scooping up huge mounds of the fallen blocks and tumbled walls of that ancient stronghold and flinging them over the edge of the cliff into the canyon below. Julia searched through the broken pottery and shattered artifacts, tossing most away with increasing frustration and impatience. They were all looking for some sign, any sign, that might lead to a clue about where Brandon Fisk had hidden the gold.

I had been standing nearby at first, watching them, in the hope that I might see something that would open the door in my memory once again. But as I heard the men's shovels scrape and grate against the ancient jars and vessels they fractured, saw the dwellings' walls knocked down and their rooms pillaged, witnessed the last relics of a proud race flung like so much trash into the canyon below, I felt something recoil in me, making me withdraw to the edge of the dwelling.

And then I glanced across the mesa and saw the old Indian watching us.

When you intrude on the spirits of the dead, you die too.

. I could not see the expression on his dark face, but I heard the words as if he had spoken them to me directly across the canyon. Suddenly I wondered what he would do. He was old, but he looked as if he had endured thus far through sheer strength and perseverence—certainly he could cause us some difficulty if he chose to. Mr. Kendall had said he had lived here for decades. He knew the mesa better than anyone else. That gave him the advantage. Would he use it?

"Look here!" A sudden shout from Prescott made me turn my head. He stood in a far back room, covered with dirt, holding aloft a small buckskin bag. "It's full of shell and turquoise jewelry," he said.

Holding her skirts to climb over the piles of rocks between them, Julia made her way to Prescott's side, an expectant look on her face. But when she reached him, she frowned.

"Why, those are nothing but worthless trinkets! I have seen better in the Kendalls' barn!"

"Well, at least I am making an attempt, Julia, my darling." Prescott's voice had an irritated quality about it, like a bowstring that had been stretched too taut.

"Like this?" Julia fairly spat the words as she flung her arms out to indicate the four of us. "This will never work! Scrounging about, scrambling up over rocks and God knows what else, risking our lives to reach these miserable hovels that hold nothing. Nothing! We will never locate the treasure searching like this!"

"Julia, my dear, lower your voice! Sound travels quite far across the canyon."

Almost furtively, I thought, Prescott glanced over his shoulder at the opposite mesa. I looked, too, but the old Indian was gone.

"Oh, who is going to hear us? And who cares if they do? I am exhausted from riding and climbing and acting like some kind of . . . of . . . oh, I did not come here for that kind of life. I came to find gold, Prescott, gold! You promised. You said if I came—"

"Now, Julia. You are growing quite hysterical. Come, sit down. Let's all take a rest. We are attempting too much, too soon. You are right. We should collect our thoughts and decide what course of action to take next."

Prescott gestured toward a fallen wall at the edge of the ruin, and finally convinced Julia to take a seat there. Then he sat down, too, and pulled a wrapped bundle of food from his pocket.

"And I cannot endure any more of this food!" she cried, refusing his offer of hard biscuits and greasy bacon left over from breakfast. Mopping her grimy, sunburned face with a dirt-caked handkerchief, she turned her fury on me.

"It's all Heather's fault!" she cried. "If she would only remember, we could have found the gold and been on a train back to Virginia by now. But no, her precious little mind cannot recall the simple facts we need! It was a mistake to include her at all!"

"Julia," Prescott said sternly, "you are exhausted. Come. Let's go up on the mesa now, and we shall make camp there. We need to erect some kind of shelter for the night. Those clouds might mean a storm."

Julia allowed herself to be placated as Prescott wrapped an arm about her shoulders and took her to the far edge of the dwelling, where a short, steep trail led up over the sandstone to the mesa. Peter, who had remained silent throughout their conversation, now dropped his shovel to follow them, and I did as well.

But just as Prescott and Julia reached the first bend in the trail, they suddenly stopped. Doran stood on the sandstone ledge before them, blocking their way.

"What do you think you've been doing down here?"

Prescott drew Julia closer. "Excuse us, Hunt. We are on our way up. If you would please move aside."

"Not until you answer my question. I said, what do you think you've been doing down here—

and in every other ruin you've explored today?
I've been watching you. You've been acting like
pothunters, the worst kind!"

Doran's face was angrier than I had ever seen it,
and he included me in his sweeping gaze. Still
behind Peter, I drew back a bit, then glanced over
at the other mesa.

Had Doran been standing there with Kianeech?
Had they both been watching us all day?

"What we do is our business, Hunt," Prescott
said. "This is not your mesa. It belongs, along
with everything in it, to those who take the time
and effort to search its canyons. Twilight Mesa
belongs to everyone."

"That is just the point. These cliff dwellings
belong to everyone, and you are destroying them,
leaving nothing for others who might learn and
benefit from—"

"Oh, come now, Hunt!" Prescott's laugh was
short and explosive. "You mean *you* might not
benefit! Stop hiding behind this guise of dedicated ethnologist and admit what you are really
searching for!"

Doran did not answer, and the silence between
the two men was so tense, so charged, that I
could feel it crackling in the air like the heat lightning building in the clouds overhead.

Then, surprisingly, Julia spoke up. She looked
at Doran with a smile that suddenly chilled me.
"Why, perhaps you'd like to *join* us, Mr. Hunt,"
she said, tucking her hand more intimately about
Prescott's arm. "As Prescott says, you may drop
your facade now. We all know what a clever man
you are, and that you cannot possibly be serious
about your archaeological endeavors. I recognized

you that first time I met you in Denver, did you know that? I even wrote Mama about it, and I received her reply before we left the Kendalls' ranch. I saw you at a gathering we attended, and so did Mama. In fact, Mama was so impressed with you at the time, she said, that she asked about you discreetly and discovered a bit of your background. What a prestigious family you were raised in, Mr. Hunt. And from New York! Why on earth did you leave? Did you have some kind of secret in your past, some trouble from which you had to flee? Oh, it was *such* a clever idea to pretend to be some kind of scientist here! Who would have ever guessed? But, knowing your background, there would simply be no reason for you to come here, work here, live with a family like the Kendalls unless you had some ulterior motive. Now would there?"

Doran's and Julia's eyes locked fiercely, and I sensed again that vibrant energy leap between them. What did she mean, Doran *pretending* to be a scientist here? Didn't she know about his investigative work, and the fact that Prescott hired Doran to find me? Or was she referring to something else—something else in Doran's past that made him come to Twilight Mesa? After all, he was here before Prescott approached and hired him. Did he indeed have another ulterior motive, as I had suspected all along?

"That's enough, Julia," Prescott said, seeming to sense what was between them as well. "Come. We have no need to discuss our affairs with Mr. Hunt."

Moving forward, Prescott pushed past Doran roughly, shoving him with a sudden, unleashed strength that startled me. For a moment Doran seemed to lose his footing and teeter slightly on the sandstone ledge. But then he regained his balance and faced Prescott again. The expression on his face made my heart begin to pound. It was violent, murderous. At that instant, Doran Hunt looked capable of anything.

When he addressed Prescott, his voice was so low that I could just barely make out the words. "I'm warning you, Webb. Stop your work in these ruins. If you don't, I'll—"

"You'll what, Mr. Hunt?" In contrast, Prescott's voice betrayed no emotion. "I hardly think an 'accident' would be appropriate, do you? In that case, neither of us will find what we are really looking for."

Doran stared at Prescott another moment, his hands clenched at his sides, and then all at once he looked at me. My heart nearly stopped. The expression in his eyes was too complex to define: still smouldering with rage and barely suppressed violence, intense and direct, and also strangely entreating, as if he were asking something of me, appealing to me in some way. But why? And what did he want?

The expression was gone in a moment. Doran's eyes swept over to Peter, and his face darkened once more. I felt a sudden, swift dart of fear.

Then Doran looked at Prescott again. "I warned you, Webb. Don't forget that."

With his last words, Doran turned and in a moment had disappeared up the trail.

I warned you. Doran's words seemed to echo in the air like the sudden, harsh call of the huge crow that dipped into the canyon, wheeling along the sheer rock face of the opposite cliff. Its sound was shattering in the silence, and for a moment we all stood motionless.

Turning to watch the shiny flash of the bird's black wing across the canyon, I thought I glimpsed a figure disappearing back into the thick piñons of the opposite mesa top.

I warned you. This time, I knew, Doran Hunt's words had been a threat. But directed at whom? Just Prescott—or all of us?

"Maybe we should camp here in the ruin for the night." Surprisingly, Peter's voice broke the silence between us. "We won't get rained on in here."

Prescott glanced about the ruin and then up at the sky across the canyon. "No. It will not rain tonight. Do you see, the clouds are beginning to pass over."

I saw that he was right. The mass of thunder-clouds that had been building all day were moving slowly and silently northward, out of Twilight Mesa and away from us.

Only I, standing so close to Peter, heard his low mutter. "That's not good," he said. "If clouds build up like that, they should break. Something's wrong . . . something's going to happen."

And, as it turned out, Peter was quite right.

Chapter Fourteen

✦ ✦ ✦ ✦ ✦

IT DID NOT storm that night. As we lay in our bed-rolls, unsheltered on the mesa top, the sky overhead was clear and black, its velvety surface spangled so beautifully with stars that it seemed they shone for us and us alone.

But there was a strange tension in the air, a sense of waiting and expectation, as if the storm indeed should have built to its peak and broken, unleashing the pent-up energy that now seemed to linger on, restlessly, all around us.

When we had been preparing our camp, Julia had provoked another argument with Prescott and then stomped off into the bordering maze of trees. After an interval, Prescott followed her. It was obvious his patience was beginning to wear thin and that he, too, was affected by the tension in the air.

Peter had gone off in another direction collecting wood, and when he returned to the camp and dropped his armload of gnarled piñon logs on the ground, I decided to break the silence between us.

"Tell me about our father," I said. "You were old enough when he left to remember him. What kind of man was he?"

Peter jumped at my words as if shot. He turned to me with that covert expression I had seen on his thin face too often before.

"Why do you want to know?"

"Why, simply to . . . to know him. I have always thought that someone else was my father.

Now, I would like to know about my real father."

Peter looked at me a moment. "Mother loved him, you know," he finally said. "It wasn't like Webb made it out to be, that she was young and just swept off her feet. She loved him and she married him. And it wasn't wrong that he left. He was doing it for us."

"Well, of course. I understand that. He must have been . . . very fine."

Peter did not reply for a moment. "Yes," he finally said. "He was gone a lot, even before he left that last time . . . for good. But I remember things about him. And Mother would tell me about him when he was gone. When we went back to St. Louis, she told me stories about him at night, before I went to bed. I think she must have known how I felt in that house. . . ."

Here Peter's words drifted off, and I knew from the expression on his face that he would say no more. Oddly, I did not feel disappointed, but encouraged. However brief, our conversation had at least been a start.

I felt something in my heart lift a bit. For, better than anyone I think, I understood the distance Peter put between himself and others, the barriers he had erected within himself as a defense against the disappointments of his life. Hadn't my own mind done the same to protect me from what might harm and hurt me in life? Peter and I did share one thing, I realized: a past hurt, a hidden wound, from which we were still trying to recover.

Prescott must have understood this as well, for that night around the campfire, when he tried to prompt my memory again, he did so slowly and gently.

"Last night you mentioned a tree in the rhyme, Heather," he said. "What kind of a tree was it? Did your father say? There must have been something unusual about it, some distinguishing feature. Can you remember any more?"

Julia was silent and sullen beside him, watching me with little interest. She and Prescott had reconciled earlier, for she came back to the campsite holding on to his arm, but the unresolved tension between them was still quite obvious. Peter was sitting off to the side again, partially hidden by the leaping and shifting illumination of the flames.

I stared at the fire. "The man told me about a tree, I am sure, but I don't remember . . . perhaps he said it was tall. . . . Yes, I think he did say that—a tall *something* tree, a certain kind."

"Yes?" Prescott leaned closer, his eyes fixed on me. "What kind?"

"I . . . don't know. I don't think he called it a piñon tree or a juniper. I would have remembered those, for they would have sounded so different to me, so foreign. No, it must have been a tree with a more familiar name. . . ."

"No doubt a sassafras tree." Julia's voice was scornful. "Why, do you suppose that somewhere in Twilight Mesa there grows a tall sassafras tree that will lead us right to the gold? You are providing us with such *useful* clues, Heather dear!"

Prescott shot her a scathing look. "Go on, Heather. We will remember the kind of tree in time. What else? I don't quite understand the idea of the diamond yet, but the phrase 'high in the sky' obviously indicates a cliff dwelling, and if we can find the distinguishing tree as a landmark, that will be a great help. But surely Fisk told you something else. What else did he say, Heather?"

Out of the corner of my eye, I saw Peter shift and lean closer, as he had done the night before, and I stared into the fire, as if it could somehow open that narrow gap in my memory again.

A diamond, high in the sky . . . a tall tree . . . something shimmering like silver. Liquid silver, water . . .

The image flitted through my mind and then out again, and then I saw it, clear and glimmering with light.

"A pool!" I cried. "It was a silver pool! He said, 'You will find a silver pool.' "

All at once the line came back to me, as if the words had been spoken aloud. I glanced over at Peter, startled. For a moment, I had thought *he* had spoken them. And I realized then that it had been because he looked so much like Brandon Fisk had that night, partially obscured by the darkness, with that intent, furtive look on his face, expecting so much of me, expecting me to remember. . . . And there was that same, odd tension in the air now as there had been that night—as if a storm were building, and something were about to happen.

"A silver pool!" Prescott's cry was triumphant. "That means Fisk must have hidden the gold in a dwelling that contains some kind of spring! We have run across only a few of them in our explorations. Very good, Heather! This will narrow our search considerably! I believe there is one such dwelling with a spring very near here. We may just find what we are looking for tomorrow!"

Prescott's eyes gleamed with excitement, and even Julia seemed to perk up, sitting straighter next to Prescott and leaning toward me.

"Oh, Heather, do go on! Prescott is right. If you can just remember the rest of the rhyme now, we may find the gold tomorrow!"

Peter had jumped up and begun pacing restlessly near the fire. Watching his barely contained excitement, spurred on by Prescott and Julia's encouragement, I riveted my eyes on the fire and willed my mind to go back all the way, to remember everything I had been told that night.

As my memory skimmed once again over the images of the diamond, the sky, and the tree, I realized all at once why Twilight Mesa had seemed so known and familiar to me that first time I saw it in the buggy with Doran. Brandon Fisk must have described it to me—the mesa, the canyons, the cliffs—and then focused more specifically on the few words in the rhyme so that I would be able to understand them in some kind of context. For now, in my mind, I could almost see a cliff dwelling hanging there gemlike, like a diamond, above a steep canyon, marked by some kind of tall tree and hiding a still, silver pool. . . . I tried to remember what kind of tree it was, what else he had told me. The image of a sharp crevice fixed itself suddenly in my mind—a kind of narrow cleft or gap in the rock. But I could not tell what or where it was. Clenching my hands together in my lap so tightly the nails again bit into skin, I leaned closer to the fire, staring, trying to remember.

The image of the narrow gap became a cleft in my mind, through which I could see something I never had before: I saw the faces of Mother and Father—the father I remembered, Samuel Loring—calling to me, and they were horrible, twisted, and desperate and frightened. They were trapped in a circle of flames, a barrier of flames that separated me from them. And yet still they called, their voices muffled as if by fog or smoke, and their faces turned to me, pleading. They knew I had something, something they desperately needed. And it was my fault I had it, my foolish, childish fault. I wanted to give it to them, but I could not reach them, could not cross that barrier of flames. . . .

"Oh, my God! Pull her back!" Julia's shrill scream pierced the air and I felt forceful arms about me, dragging me backward, even as I struggled against them. "The fringe on her shawl! It's on fire! Pull it away! Put it out!"

I felt a wrenching at my shoulders and arms and then I began to feel cold. It seemed I could not see or hear properly; everything was moving very slowly about me. I looked down in a trance and saw that the lace edging on the wrist of my blouse was curled and black, singed.

"Don't just stand there screaming! Get some water, for God's sake!"

This time Prescott's voice pierced through the smoky haze, and in a moment I felt someone gripping my right arm and plunging my hand into a tin pan of tepid water. At that my senses quickly came back sharp and clear. I jerked my arm back, away from the water, and I felt a throbbing, stinging pain all along the skin of my right arm, from wrist to elbow. Looking down, I saw it turning an angry red.

"Whatever happened to you, Heather?" Julia's face was only inches from mine. "You leaned right into the fire! You reached into it with your hand! Your shawl caught within seconds. Whatever could you have been thinking of? It looked as if you would fall right in!"

As my eyes began to focus, I heard Prescott's voice again and in a moment his face joined Julia's beside me.

"What happened, Heather?" he said, his eyes black and intent on mine and filled with an odd, gleaming light. "Was there something you saw in the fire? Something else that happened that night? Think now, while it's all still fresh in your mind."

"No!"

The explosive exclamation came from Peter, standing away from us with my singed shawl still at his feet. "Stop right now, Webb! You've gone far enough! This is enough, I tell you! Don't push her any further!"

I was a bit shocked to see so much emotion displayed so openly on my brother's face: anger and fear and a hard, strong will I had never seen before. Prescott and Julia stepped back a few paces, startled. My body began to tremble and my teeth started to chatter. I clutched my arms about me, unable to stop shaking.

"It's the shock," Prescott said. "Get a blanket for her, quickly."

Obeying without question, Julia moved swiftly over to the packs and in a moment I felt the woolly warmth of a saddle blanket about my shoulders. Julia tried to lead me toward the fire but I balked and pulled away, and Prescott took my arm, seating me away from the campfire, among the bedrolls. He disappeared for a moment, then returned with a hot mug full of coffee.

No one had picked up my shawl or spoken to Peter, and he still stood off to the side, the raw emotion that had been exposed on his face now contained somewhat but still evident in his quick, twitching gestures and the restlessness of his stance. He watched every move Prescott made, but made no move himself to come near me.

Nevertheless, as I sipped the scalding coffee and slowly regained my composure, the skin on my arm throbbing painfully, a feeling of warmth spread through me at the thought of what Peter had said.

He cares, I thought with a thrill. He cares!

Peter had understood the danger of probing my memory any further, and he had forbidden Prescott to proceed, even at the cost of losing another clue to the location of the gold.

I was grateful for my brother's understanding, as well as for his intervention that night. I knew that what I had earlier feared had proven true: the memories of the rhyme and the memories of what had happened the day of the fire were intermixed in my mind. I did not know if I wanted—or could force myself—to proceed further. For I had already gone beyond the limits set by my mind in those few instants before the fire.

Nothing more was said as we broke camp the next morning and mounted our horses, but I felt the unspoken questions hanging silently between the four of us as Prescott led the way along the mesa top and down into the opposite canyon and then into another branch canyon. He was taking us to a cliff dwelling, he said, which he remembered contained a small spring.

It was hot as we rode, and my arm, although dressed and protected by one of the heavy cotton blouses Mrs. Kendall had packed for me, fairly seemed to pulsate with pain. I tried not to think of what had happened around the fire. I only hoped that when we reached the spring, it would not trigger my memory so violently once again.

It took us over three hours to reach the ruin, and when we arrived we found that Prescott had been mistaken. The dwelling held no spring at all, and, after we had scrambled down into it using a rather precipitous route, I knew immediately that it was not the ruin to which Brandon Fisk's words referred. There was no cleft in the rock, no tall tree, and the ruin itself had been ransacked and cleared out long ago. Seeing this, Julia voiced a question that, I think, had begun to occur to all of us by then.

"What if someone else already found it?" she demanded. "And took the gold themselves?"

Julia's face, streaked with perspiration and dust, was as dark as the thunderclouds that once again were rising over the canyon.

"That is something I have already considered," Prescott answered. "It is possible, but not probable. First, no word of such a treasure has ever come to light over the last fifteen years. If anyone had found it, we would surely have heard of it, as would the Kendalls. Second, Brandon Fisk would never have hidden our cache so carelessly that common pothunters—or anyone else—would be able to find it. As his partner, I grew to know his nature quite well." Prescott was silent a moment. "That is why I feel certain that we must look in these far branch canyons. He would have chosen a remote location, yet one distinctive enough that he would be able to remember it himself upon his return."

"That is hardly helping us now!" Julia burst out irritably.

All our moods, it seemed, were deteriorating as rapidly as the day. It was already past noon; I glanced out at the bank of black clouds rising more and more threateningly overhead. For a moment I thought I glimpsed something else as well, across the mesa—a flash of movement and color—but as I looked more closely, I realized it had simply been a jay extending its bright blue wings among the thick green of the piñons.

But the initial impression had caused a quick pounding in my heart, and I realized that I had been watching for Doran, covertly, all day long. I could not help being afraid of him after all he had said and done in the ruin the day before. He had left us all with a threat, just as he had left me with his warning that day at the ranch.

And yet . . . I felt an almost desperate need to see him again. I remembered how, for just that one instant in the ruin, he had seemed to be asking me something with his expression. What, I wondered, had he been entreating me to do?

*   *   *

"Come, Heather. We don't have much time. I know of one more dwelling quite close, and I am certain this one holds a spring. Come now. You are the last one up."

Prescott was extending his hand toward me from the base of the rocky route up to the mesa. As I took his hand, I again felt how strong he was, how powerful his grip. He pulled me up the last few feet and for a moment I just stood on top of the mesa, wondering that I was here with a man I hardly knew, a woman I neither liked nor trusted, and a brother who seemed as detached from me as a stranger.

As we began our slow journey to the next dwelling, it seemed as though the relationships between all of us had become entirely too tense, as if some precarious equilibrium that had been maintained until then had upset itself somehow and become unbalanced. The explosiveness between Prescott and Julia was obvious, but I also noticed a subtle shifting in the relationship between Prescott and Peter. I had earlier sensed in Peter a kind of deference toward Prescott— perhaps, being the old partner of Brandon Fisk, Prescott had become a kind of surrogate father to Peter. But as we journeyed further into the mesa and the uneasiness became more palpable with each successive failed foray, Peter seemed to draw away from Prescott, demonstrating his mistrust in that same sullen way I had often seen Peter direct to Samuel Loring in St. Louis.

I attributed many of these feelings to the August heat that was becoming nearly unbearable during the daylight hours. It took us nearly an hour to reach the second ruin, and by that time we were all short-tempered from the relentless sun and our own prickly, moody silences.

"The ruin is just below," Prescott said, dismounting his horse. "But I am afraid it is a difficult descent. We will have to climb down onto a small ledge, secure a rope to a cedar growing there, and then lower ourselves into the ruin by rope."

"By rope!" Julia's cry was shrill. "Why, you cannot expect me—"

"There is no need for you to go down, Julia," Prescott said, openly impatient. "Peter and I will go, and Heather, too, of course." He turned to me. "I am afraid we will have to submit you to this, Heather. If you do not come, we will hardly know if it is the right dwelling." His eyes remained on me a moment before he abruptly turned to Peter. "You get the rope and we'll descend immediately. From the looks of those clouds, we may not have much time."

Swallowing hard, I swung down carefully from my mare and walked over to the edge of the mesa. As Prescott had said, there was a ledge about six feet below. It was fairly wide, and ran along the edge of the cliff to the east, where I saw the strong, sturdy trunk of a bleached cedar.

I swallowed again. Before I could act on my sudden misgivings, however, Prescott swung gracefully over the edge and landed on the sandstone ledge with a small jump. Then he reached up his hands to me, gesturing for me to do likewise.

"I will just wait for you here," Julia said sweetly, her skirts swishing against my shoulder as I sat down rather gingerly on the mesa's edge. "Do have a nice time, Heather. I think I may just go for a little walk and pick some flowers."

I paid little attention to her, but concentrated all my energy on edging myself over the cliff and down to Prescott. I felt the back of my skirt slide over the sandstone lip, and then I was suspended in the air for just a moment, until Prescott caught me about the waist and my boots touched the firm, grainy surface of the ledge.

"Good girl!" he cried. "Now, that wasn't so bad, was it?"

I did not dare answer or look over the edge. I felt as a cliff swallow must, building its nest on the edge of a precipice. But I did not have the swallow's wings, I thought, to lift and carry me should I fall.

In a moment, Peter was beside us with the rope. "Good," said Prescott. "Now, secure it to the cedar here. That's it. Tightly now."

I felt a sinking sensation in my stomach as I watched the two men knot the rope several times about the cedar and then let it drop over the edge. And, as I watched the rope dangle below, swaying like a huge snake in the breeze, the sensation in my stomach began to churn. I felt perspiration break out, clammy, on my forehead.

"Please," I said, moistening my lips. "I cannot . . ."

I felt Prescott's arms about my shoulders. "Of course you can, Heather. You must. It is not difficult. The ruin is right below, less than twenty feet. I'll go down first, and I will be there to catch you. And your brother will be up here, holding the rope for extra support."

"But—"

Before I could speak further, Prescott sat down on the ledge and swung himself over it in one swooping motion, grasping the rope in his hands. I saw the muscles in his arm flex powerfully as, propping his heavy boots along the cliff, he slowly lowered himself down.

In a moment the rope went slack and we heard him call up from below in an excited voice. "It's here! The spring! In the rear of the cave. You can come down now, Heather. Hurry!"

I felt myself begin to tremble. This was worse, much worse, than any descent we had yet made. My stomach heaved again, and as I clasped my hands tightly together, I found they were slick and clammy with perspiration. The skin on my arm still throbbed with pain.

"No," I said. "I cannot do it. I—"

"Yes you can." This time Peter was beside me, his voice and face gentle. "I'll help you. Just do as I say. Sit down first, like Prescott did. That's right. Now grasp the rope, *tightly*. You can't let it go. Just hold on as tight as you can and turn yourself there on the rock. That's right."

With a gentle but very firm pressure, Peter guided my movements with his hands until I did as he told me. I felt the rope, harsh and thick in my hands, and then all at once, Peter was pushing me off the ledge.

"Now! Prop your boot on the cliff, quickly! Brace yourself! Don't just hang there. Do it, Heather, or you'll fall!" Whether from the urgency of Peter's voice or my own sudden terror, I did what he said, and within an instant I found myself braced, stable, my boot propped against the cliff and the rope cutting into my palms. I must have moved by sheer instinct after that, for somehow I inched my way down the cliff as Prescott had done. Moments later I felt his firm grip about my waist, pulling me down into the dwelling.

"Do you see?" He smiled, still supporting me as, trembling, I let go of the rope. "That wasn't so difficult, was it?"

I did not answer. With shaking legs, I forced myself to move farther back into the dwelling, away from the cave's rim. As I made my way slowly over the fallen heaps of blocks, I heard a faint trickling sound.

"That's the spring," Prescott said, joining me. "Come look."

As we approached the back wall, I saw a narrow trickle of clear water, seeping from the rock and forming a tiny pool.

For a moment my heart gave a sudden leap. The dwelling was small, barely disturbed. About half the walls had fallen, and the debris had not been cleared away. This could be the ruin, I thought, the one where Brandon Fisk had hidden his trunk full of gold. . . .

But something was wrong. Peering outward, I could see neither the tree nor the cleft. And something else . . . what else had he said that night? I strained again to capture the memory, but his other words danced far back in my mind, tantalizingly out of reach.

"What is it?" Prescott said, watching my face. "Is this the right place?"

"I . . . don't know. It could be, but it seems as if something is not quite right."

"What do you mean?"

"I don't know. It's just that . . ."

Under the insistent pressure of Prescott's gaze, his unrelenting expectations, I felt suddenly confused. The strain, the tension, the building urgency and explosive emotions of the last few days finally broke within me.

"Oh, I don't know! I don't! Why *must* I know? Why do you keep prodding me, as if everything we are doing depends only on me? I only remember a few words—a few words that make no sense at all!"

Looking rather surprised at my outburst, Prescott raised his brows. "Well, I . . ."

"Webb! Come quickly!" It was Peter, shouting from above.

"What's that?" Swiftly, Prescott moved to the edge of the ruin and peered upward. The rope dangled down beside his head.

"Come up! Both of you. Someone has been tampering with the horses!"

Prescott turned to me. "We must go up, and quickly." He hesitated, looking at me. "You will have to go first, so that I can help you up. Grab the rope first, and I will boost you until you can prop your boots again on the cliff. You will have to pull yourself up. It will require some strength, but it is only a short way, and we must go up now. No hesitation."

Without waiting for my reply, Prescott grabbed the rope and shoved it into my hands. Then he grasped me about the waist and boosted me until I felt the tip of my boot graze the surface of the cliff. He let go of me, and I was hanging by the support of the rope alone, feeling as if its fibers would cut right through the skin of my palms.

For one moment I felt the rope taut in my grip and I began to pull myself achingly, agonizingly upward, my arm throbbing and weakened with pain.

Suddenly something seemed to snap from above, and I felt the rope jerk downward, going slack in my hand. I jerked down, too, and dropped down the side of the cliff. Clinging to the rope, I dangled there like a rag doll, praying that whatever fine thread still held the rope secured above would not break the next instant under my weight.

Then I heard a shout below me, and Prescott's hands reached up to grasp my boots, then my legs and waist as he pulled me back down into the cliff dwelling.

I collapsed then onto the cool stone floor of the cave, my legs like water.

"What happened?" Prescott's face was very close. My arm throbbed, and I looked down to see that both my palms were bleeding. A sharp pain shot through me at the hip, where I must have hit when I bounced against the side of the cliff.

Prescott stared at me, and then jumped up and crossed to the cave's rim. "What happened?" he called upward in a fierce voice. "The rope broke! Peter!"

There was no answer for a moment, and then I heard Peter's voice sounding rather faint from its distance above us, over the edge of the cliff. "It's been cut. The rope has been cut."

"What in God's name. . . ?" Prescott muttered under his breath. "I'm coming up! Secure the rope again. I am coming up now, and bringing Heather with me." Prescott turned to me. "You will have to go up with me, Heather. You cannot make it on your own. Hold onto my shoulders, and we'll go up together." He paused. "When Peter throws the rope down, I will grab it, and you will have to take hold of me, tightly."

Still dazed, I did as Prescott said. Within a few moments the rope dangled down again, and Prescott grasped it, testing it with his weight, before motioning for me to grab his shoulders. I did so without thinking, without feeling. When he, muscles flexing and body going taut, began slowly to pull us both up the rope, I grit my teeth and turned my face into his shoulder, trying to ignore the canyon's tunnel of open air pulling on my back, tugging at me again, as if intent that this time it would suck me down into its depths.

When we finally reached the ledge, and Peter helped pull me off Prescott's back, I saw that his face had gone ashen gray.

"It was cut when I got here," he said, his words coming out all in a rush. "I had only been gone a minute, and when I came back . . ."

"What do you mean?" His breath coming hard, Prescott pulled himself up onto the ledge beside us. His face was red and blotched from the effort of pulling us up over the cliff as well as the fury he now directed at Peter. "Where did you go?"

Peter took a step back. "After you . . . after you went down into the ruin, I heard a noise up on the mesa," he said. "Coming from the direction of the horses. So I made sure the rope was secured fast and then went up to see what had happened. Someone had been there and unhobbled the horses; they had already begun to wander away. I gathered the animals again, and then called to you to come up. I didn't know then, didn't realize . . . You must have started up immediately because I barely had time to jump down on the ledge when I saw the rope break. You shouted then, and I saw what had happened: someone had cut the rope." Peter paused, looking at us, his face still drawn and white. "Don't you see, first they unhobbled the horses to distract me, and then whoever it was came down on the ledge and cut the rope because they knew you were below, in the ruin—both of you."

I felt a sudden, deathly chill at Peter's words.

"Where's Julia?" Prescott said sharply.

"She said she was going for a walk."

"Here I am. Whatever happened?" Julia's face peered at us from over the mesa's edge.

"Julia! What have you been doing? Did you see anyone near the horses while you were walking?"

Julia flinched slightly at Prescott's tone. "Yes, I did," she said in an offended tone. "I saw Peter. Peter was with the horses."

"No, no. I mean earlier. Someone unhobbled the horses to distract Peter and then came down here to cut the rope. Heather started up and was nearly killed."

Julia's face was an instant mask of concern. "Oh, my gracious! How horrible! How terrible! Come right up here, Heather, and let me take care of you! You poor child!"

Prescott's tone was impatient. "Julia, my dear, you must think. Did you see anyone with the horses earlier?"

Julia's brows furrowed. "Why, no, I don't believe I did. But there was that old Indian . . ."

"Indian? What Indian?"

"Why that scary old Indian who has been watching us all along. Haven't you seen him? I'm sure Heather has." Julia cast a meaningful look at me.

Prescott looked at her and then over at me.

"But did you see this . . . Indian today, with the horses?"

"Well, no, I cannot say that I did—"

"Let's get up to the top." Peter spoke, his voice flat and abrupt. "It's not good for Heather to be out on this ledge. She's too weak. It's not safe."

I heard in Peter's voice the concerned tone he had used as he'd helped me over the ledge before, and I glanced up quickly. But as I turned to him, he looked away.

"Yes. We will camp there on the mesa for the night." Prescott began to take charge in his accustomed way, his voice once again authoritative and assured. "Here, Julia. Take Heather's hand and help her up."

I winced as Julia did so, the raw skin on my palm sending shafts of pain up my arm and into my shoulders. But as I climbed rather clumsily back over the edge of the mesa and my boots finally touched solid ground again, I felt a relief quite unrivaled in my experience. Shakily, I walked back, away from the edge, and sank down on a large flat rock.

Following, Julia fluttered over me. "Oh, Heather, dear! Are you quite all right? What can I do? What can I get you?"

Prescott hurried over as well. "Get her a blanket, Julia, and some dressing for her hands. Thank God she had not pulled herself any further up the cliff. Any higher, and I would not have been able to catch her when the rope broke."

I shuddered at the thought, at the memory of myself dangling alongside the cliff like some kind of marionette whose strings had been severed.

Who had done it? Julia? I could hardly imagine her unhobbling the horses, jumping down over the edge of the cliff, and slicing the thick rope with a heavy knife. But she said she had seen the Indian. Had he been trying to stop us from doing any further explorations in the ruins? He would know horses; he would know his way around the mesa.

And so, I thought, would Doran. My heart stilled at the idea. He had warned us to stop. He had threatened us. He was the logical choice, the most obvious suspect.

"Julia, dear, come with me. We need to talk. You must tell me about what you remember." Taking Julia's arm, Prescott pulled her away, over into the shade of the piñons. I heard their murmuring voices and saw, now and then, one of them turn to peer at me.

Peter stood a few yards away, also looking at me, hesitantly. All at once he crossed the distance between us and sat down beside me. His face was very close; my own face was reflected in his tawny eyes.

"You shouldn't be here," he said, his voice very low. His thin face was drawn and pinched, his features angular. "It's not safe. Don't you understand? Whoever cut the rope knew that *you* would be going up first, Heather. Whoever did it knows—about the gold we're looking for, and that you're leading us to it. They want you out of the way, Heather. Can't you see that? They want to stop you." Peter stared at me another moment, then sprang up from the rock and walked rapidly away.

I sat there motionless, chilled again by my brother's words, by the intensity I had seen in his eyes. I had not yet seen Peter this agitated and upset.

And Peter was right.

For even then, still in shock from the impact of his words and my accident on the rope, I knew. I knew what I had to do.

If someone was trying to stop me, to hurt me, then all the others were in danger, too. I thought of the rattlesnake. Had someone captured it and turned it loose in our campsite deliberately? And the rope—what if Prescott had gone up first? Or what if Julia or Peter had decided to come down into the ruin?

I swallowed. If we were ever to find the gold, if Peter was to leave Twilight Mesa with what he had come here to find, I knew there was only one thing I could do.

I would have to try to find the gold myself. I would have to ride further into Twilight Mesa alone, the next day.

At the time, it seemed my only choice.

Chapter Fifteen

✦ ✦ ✦ ✦ ✦

By NOON THE next day, I knew the decision I had made was not only wrong, but foolhardy and potentially dangerous. I had been riding for over five hours, and I had found nothing, seen nothing. Before me, the canyon stretched out narrow and rugged, seemingly without end, and above me rose a new mass of black thunderclouds.

For the dozenth time that day, I reined in my mare to shade my eyes from the blistering sun overhead, trying to get my bearings. I knew where I was; I knew how far into the canyon I had come and how to get back out, but the clouds were already sending invisible sparks of tension shooting through the air: sure signs of a coming storm.

The storm could easily break that day, I realized, and in my eagerness and anxiety to be away that morning, I had hardly come prepared.

I had slipped away before dawn, moving swiftly and silently so as not to wake the others. I had learned by then how to saddle and pack my own horse, and I did it as quietly as possible, quite a distance from the campsite. Even so, I thought surely someone would hear me. But when I rode away in the gray half-light of dawn, leaving a note for the others near the packs, no one stirred.

I rode back along the mesa for several miles, and then cut across a flat, broad canyon to another mesa. From there I found a branch canyon that we had passed the day before. I entered it, sure I would find something.

But the only cliff dwellings I had spotted in this canyon were fairly low in the cliffs, easily reached from the canyon bottom and quite thoroughly ransacked. But I had been picking my way for several hours, hoping that just up around the next bend, from behind the next tumbled boulder, I would spot a ruin and know, instinctively, it was right.

I was so certain that the day's ride would be successful—so determined to make it so—that I had brought with me only the barest essentials: a blanket rolled up with a bit of food inside, a canteen of water, my hat, and a warm jacket. Perversely, the more I realized I would find nothing in the canyon—that riding in so far had been a mistake—the further I continued down into it, lured onward well past the time I should have turned back.

I had found a small spring, and stopped there to eat. Shading my eyes to scan the opposite slope, I spotted a small alcove about halfway up, in which I could distinguish the few broken sandstone walls of a dwelling.

I was hardly heartened; I had found too many other fruitless ruins that day. But I also saw that I could reach the ruin fairly easily by climbing up from the canyon bottom.

So I hobbled the mare and went off exploring on foot. My cotton skirt brushed against gray-green sagebrush and caught on the spiky tips of bushy yuccas as I crossed to the opposite slope and, under the glare of the noonday sun, I soon found myself rolling up the sleeves of my shirt-waist and wiping at the perspiration gathered along the line of my collar. When I reached the lower slope, I found the going more difficult, and began to realize just how much of a strain the last few days had taken on me. I was becoming increasingly exhausted.

I nearly turned back then, almost decided to give up on the ruin, mount my horse, and return to the others in defeat. But something spurred me on; perhaps it was the thought of the disappointment I would feel after returning to Peter with nothing . . . or it was perhaps my own stubbornness.

It was not until I was halfway up the slope, tucking the hem of my skirt into my waistband so that I could climb over the huge boulders, that I began to sense the change in the air. At first there was a deliciously cool breeze, which dried the perspiration on my neck, and then the canyon slope fell into sudden shade. I looked up to see the sun blotted out by thunderclouds rising to my left.

I gave this little thought at the time, having witnessed over the last few days how such clouds could build and threaten and then move on without releasing even a spattering of rain. Instead, I continued up the slope, moving rather warily as I remembered how, on our earlier trip, Will Kendall had told me that rattlesnakes liked to sun in and among large heaps of rocks. As I climbed, I felt my skirt catch more than once, throwing me slightly off balance, and I heard thread and fabric give way along the shoulder and arm seams of my shirtwaist. The sun came out again, briefly, hot on my face, but I continued upward, determined in my stubbornness to explore one last ruin before turning back.

I had almost reached the top when I heard the rumbling from above. I glanced up, stiffening, afraid that some rocks had dislodged themselves from the cliff and were now tumbling down toward me. But then the canyon fell into shadow again and I felt a sudden, quick wind whip along my back. The thunderclouds had moved directly overhead—black, swirling, and ominous, emitting more of their low, menacing rumbles.

And then I felt it. The hair on my arm stood on end. The air was static, full of a tingling, palpable tension. Electricity.

All at once, there was a sharp flash to my right, and then a sound that seemed to split the air around me.

Fear shot through me. There, on the top of the slope, I was openly exposed to the coming storm. And I was only halfway to the ruin; I would have to climb over the last of the boulders and through the thick, clinging maze of scrub oak before I could reach the dwelling's shelter.

As I hesitated, the sky vibrated about me and I felt my skin prickle. There was another great flash of light and then a gigantic crack that made me stiffen and flinch. The black clouds roiled directly overhead. This time they were ready to unleash the pent-up fury they had been hoarding for the last several days.

Without further thought, I hurried up the slope, stumbling over the broken rocks in my haste to retreat into the relative shelter of the brush above.

But when I reached it, I found my way slowed considerably by the thick mass of growth that clutched and snagged at my blouse and skirt. I felt more fabric rip, heard another threatening rumble, then jumped again as a bright streak of lightning flashed immediately to my right. Urging my weary, aching body upward, I felt the air grow suddenly more chill and the wind rise sharply down the canyon. The sun was gone completely, obliterated by the clouds, and the world, it seemed, was a great mass of pulsating darkness and tension. I was in the very center of the storm.

The breath was fairly sobbing from my breast, when, fighting my way through a last grove of scrub oak, I came out directly, blessedly, upon a narrow stone staircase. It led to the ruin, winding its steep, twisting way through a tumble-down collection of large sandstone slabs to the alcove's floor.

It took me only a few minutes to climb it, scurrying faster up the rocks. This high, I was a sitting target for the powerful flashes of lightning.

I saw that I only had a short way to go. Within minutes, I was pulling myself up between the last of the rocks and stepping onto the smooth floor of the dwelling.

It was very small. In the sudden dimness, the cave's furthest recesses were shadowy. Taking a step forward, I felt a sudden coolness—almost a chill—as well. I shivered and rolled the sleeves of my blouse back down to my wrists. With very poor foresight, I realized, I had left my jacket on the mare.

I remembered her with a sudden, guilty start. Where was she now? Had she, like I, found shelter from the storm?

I shivered again, and clutched my arms about me. Outside the lightning still flashed and the thunder cracked, but I was safe. The dwelling held only a few crumbling rooms, but toward the back stood one complete wall. I knew that behind it I would find at least one room in which I could retreat should the storm become more violent.

And for once I would not mind the confinement, I thought with a touch of irony. The closer and tighter my surroundings now, the better I would feel.

I think I understood then—better than at any other moment in my time at Twilight Mesa—why the ancient ones had chosen to build in the cliffs. Here, in this one dwelling, they would have been protected not only from human enemies but also from the forces of nature itself, a quite formidable enemy, indeed, from the appearance of the storm breaking over the canyon below.

And now, in one of their rooms built centuries ago for their own protection, I would be protected as well.

But as I moved toward the back of the dwelling, toward the standing wall, I heard a sound.

I froze. My heart seemed to stop all at once, then resume its pace with slow, heavy pulses.

I was not alone in the dwelling. Someone—or something—was behind that back wall.

I thought of animals seeking shelter from the

storm. Small ones, perhaps, or . . . larger. Or a snake, perhaps a nest of snakes.

Suddenly the confining walls of the cave I had found so protective just a moment before closed about me like the walls of a prison. I heard another sound, this one closer, and I knew that whatever it was in the back of the cave had sensed my presence and was moving forward.

Trapped, I stood poised in my spot, half-turned toward the cave's edge and ready to flee back down over the rocks at a moment's notice. I listened, holding my breath . . . waiting.

"Why, Heather, you are as white as a sheet." The voice was strangely familiar. "Who did you think I was? The ghost of an Anasazi, come back to haunt his dwelling?"

The words were spoken lightly, but the man's eyes bored into me with such intensity that I felt myself begin to tremble. Slowly he approached until he stood only a few inches away, almost but not quite touching me, and I looked up into the gleam of his green eyes.

"We do meet in such strange circumstances."

He stared at me, and in that moment I do not know whether I was more afraid of or in love with Doran Hunt. A dozen thoughts flashed through my mind at once: his threatening words at the ranch and in the ruin; the cut rope the day before; the way I had imagined him watching us, laughing at us in Jackson Canyon; the rattlesnake by my head. . . .

The rattlesnake. The snake dance.

I remembered the way I had felt in Doran's arms, against him; his mouth on mine, my body melding with his; his hardness, his heat, igniting me into a flame, a liquid flame.

Doran took a step forward. I saw him swallow as he looked at me, saw the line of perspiration on his neck where it dipped down into the mass of dark hair exposed by his open shirt.

"Fate seems intent on throwing us together."

Doran's eyes were as dark as emeralds. He reached out and drew me to him. I felt the warm pressure of his hand on my back, pulling me up against him; I saw the sky dark and whirling outside; I felt the sudden heat and tension throbbing, pulsating in the ruin.

And then Doran's mouth came down on mine and I felt the same mingled sensations I had experienced with him at the snake dance. My legs went weak even as my body strained against his, with a sense of arousal that sent a tingle rippling down into the very center of my being. As his tongue parted my lips, I felt myself give into him, as if melting—into his body, his mouth, his heat against me.

The pressure of Doran's lips on mine was gentle at first, then more insistent. As his tongue deftly explored the inner, sensitive recesses of my mouth, his palms flattened against my back, pressing me even closer into the hard need of his body. His hands spanned my waist, then came up around the swelling curves of my breasts, and I found myself responding in a way that startled me in its own sudden need and intensity.

Breaking away, Doran took my hand and led me back toward the rear of the cave, where an Indian blanket lay spread on the smooth sandstone floor. He knelt upon it, drawing me down so that I, too, knelt beside him. I felt my heart begin to pound, but I did not move. Slowly, possessively, Doran's eyes swept over my body, and then he reached out to unfasten the button of my shirtwaist. I shivered, a chill racing down my spine, my skin prickling in uncertain anticipation. I was afraid, and yet I knew that what was about to happen was inevitable, a culmination of all I had known and sensed between us over the last few weeks.

My breath came in gasps as Doran's fingers touched the sensitive skin of my throat, my shoulders, my breasts; he slowly released the garment from about me and let it drop to the blanket, then slipped the straps of my chemise down my arms and freed the soft, clinging fabric from my breasts. He stared at my nakedness for a long moment, his eyes very dark. I felt my skin flush with heat. Then Doran touched the pulse throbbing at the nape of my neck and slowly trailed his finger down the crevice between my breasts.

I could not move. His hand flattened against my waist, came up around one breast, lightly cupping it, moving along its curve, his thumb finding its rosy peak and teasing it until I heard myself moan and arched my back toward him.

Quickly, Doran removed his own shirt, and I saw the thick curls of black hair that formed a line from his throat to the waist of his trousers. I began to tremble—more with fear or need, I do not know—and he drew me to him again. The feel of skin against skin, lips and tongue intermingling, was exquisite, but as Doran pressed me down on the blanket and his fingers dropped to the buttons of my skirt, I began to tremble again. I did not want to stop what was happening between us, but it still frightened me, and Doran must have sensed some of what I was feeling, for his fingers moved up from my skirt to caress my back and arms with reassuring silky strokes. His fingers dropped to my breasts, lingering there, and then slowly, he lowered his head and his mouth came down upon one rosy peak. As his tongue tasted and teased, a sensation of such deep need, such sweet intense power throbbed through me that I buried my fingers in his thick hair.

His mouth explored lower, his tongue tracing a trail to my waist, his fingers now moving swiftly to unfasten my skirt and petticoat. In an instant I felt the warm skin of his palm along the length of my bare leg and up my inner thigh, seeking the secret place that now burned, undeniably, for his touch.

And when he touched me there, at the very center of my being, I opened myself to him, to the explosive sensations of pleasure that rippled through me, making me shudder with need and desire.

Clutching his back, I turned my mouth hungrily toward his, pulling him toward me. But his hand stayed where it was, stroking and caressing with such sensitive skill that I arched and writhed against him. Hesitantly, my hand dropped down to the waistband of his trousers, fumbling with their buttons. I wanted to touch Doran, to awaken in him the sensations he was awakening in me. But still I wasn't sure.

Doran groaned in answer to my silent question and rolled over to shed the rough denim of his trousers. Then he was beside me again, the length of him lean and strong and fine. Naked now as I, he took me in his arms once more, lifting me up against him as his mouth came down on mine. I felt his hardness pulse against me and then I was pulling him against me, into me.

There was a moment of stillness, and then Doran began to move within me and we were one—with each other, with the storm, with everything about us. We moved together in a rhythm as ancient as the dwelling in which we lay, as natural as the pulsating storm outside, as basic as time itself, caught up in a force, a power much larger than ourselves.

We moved with one another until it seemed I might burst, and then, at the peak of the storm, at the peak of our union, I did, shattering into a multitude of pieces, stars falling through a black, spangled sky.

After that we were still, and as I felt Doran's weight heavy upon me, I at last gave in—to the blackness of that sky, sinking further and further, until it reached up to envelope me in a soft dark mantle of sleep.

When I awoke, he was gone. I lay on the blanket alone, the sandstone cold and hard beneath me, another blanket thrown up over me to fend off the gathering chill.

I saw that I was dressed, and with a hot flush remembered what had happened—and what must have happened afterward. My shirtwaist was buttoned but torn; my skirt was twisted about me.

Rising rather shakily, I peered out over the sandstone wall at my side. The sky across the canyon was blue, skimmed by long, low, white clouds.

The storm had passed. Doran was gone. Somehow those two ideas interconnected in my mind, but I could not make sense of them. I was left with the same sense I had experienced after our embrace at the snake dance. I had been swept up; I had plunged over a cliff; I had lost myself to him.

Still unsteady, I moved away from the blanket spread out in the cave's shadowy recesses. The sensations I had felt there—how long ago?—had been so strong, so forceful; I could still feel Doran against me, in me, above me. But where was he now? In his absence, what I had felt with him began to take on the outlines of a dream—and the cold, hard sandstone at my feet was, in truth, the reality.

Where had he gone? Why, after all that had passed between us, would he leave?

For everything Doran Hunt undertakes he has a specific reason—usually one that suits his own purposes.

I thought of my mare down in the canyon. Had Doran gone searching for her, so that we could ride out of the canyon together?

Or had Doran left for good, gone to turn my mare loose so that I would be trapped here alone?

And then I thought of Julia and Prescott and Peter. Where were they now? I had only told them in the note I left that I would be gone for a day or so, and they would not know where to find me, even if they knew that they should look.

I peered out over the canyon floor below. My mare was nowhere in sight, and I felt a sudden, tight band of panic clamp down on my chest. How would I get out of the canyon?

Something inside told me to wait, to be patient, that Doran had surely gone searching for the mare and would return soon so we could both ride out. But a stronger, insistent voice taunted me.

"He's gone—you know that. He took what he wanted from you; he used you. And now he's gone."

But what had Doran wanted? I remembered how I had felt at the touch of his fingers, at the pressure of his mouth on mine, the indescribable sensations as he had moved within me. I thought of the passion I'd seen in Doran's own eyes, of the connection that vibrated between us.

If Doran had wanted to harm me, why hadn't he done so? Why had he covered me with a blanket to fend off the cave's chill before he left?

The sun was low over the canyon; I judged it to be late afternoon. I hesitated, wondering whether I should stay in the cave's shelter or climb back down to search for my mare. I thought of the spring. No matter what I did, I would soon need water. Perhaps if I went there to the spring, I would find my horse nearby—or Doran.

I started down to the stone staircase, squeezing between the first few boulders, and then I saw it: a faint, barely discernible trail, over to my right, leading along the cliff's edge. I had not noticed it before in my haste to outrun the storm.

I hesitated a moment, and then, guided by some impulse I did not understand, started along it.

The path skirted the cliff's edge, bending above and around, so that soon I could no longer see my sheltering alcove. It was also steep and rocky, and my foot slipped more than once, sending a spray of pebbles tumbling down the canyonside.

I was just about to turn back when my hand, which I had lifted to rest upon the surface of the cliff, dipped into a large fissure in the rock. I turned to look and then my heart stopped—stopped, and then began to throb.

It was not just a fissure or a crack. It was a long, narrow crevice—a diamond-shaped crevice.

Like a diamond in the sky. The words came back to me clearly, just as they had been spoken to me when I was five years old.

My heart now drumming in my breast, I stepped carefully up to the crevice and peered within. A tumble of rocks led up the cliff from its base, farther than my eye could see.

Holding my breath, I squeezed through the crevice at its widest point, where the narrow diamond-shaped points angled outward. Inside, it was dark and cool; I felt loose sand and rocks at my feet as I braced my hands against the narrow sandstone walls and began climbing upward.

My heard had hardly slowed. After a few dozen paces, I reached another crack in the rock. By then my breath was coming fairly hard, both from exertion and excitement. The fissure before me was both smaller and higher than the previous one, and I had to jump a bit and boost myself to it, then pull and squeeze my way through.

On the other side, I found myself on the ledge of an extremely narrow cave, containing the broken walls of a cliff dwelling.

The ruin was smaller than any I had seen, but as I stepped into it, I stopped and grew very still. Just ahead of me, only a few paces away, was a huge ancient spruce tree, rising with tenacity from the chasm that dropped off almost vertically below. And from the rear of the cave, I heard the faint, trickling sound of water.

Look outside and you will see, a cliff, the sky, a tall spruce tree. And back inside where it's dark and cool, you will find a silver pool. This is where, if you are wise, you will find the treasure lies.

The key fit neatly into its lock; the pieces of the puzzle all fell into place; the words of the rhyme came back to me in their entirety, sparked by the elements I saw around me.

"Remember this," he had said that night, his hand tightening on my arm with a hurtful pressure. "Remember that first you go through a big crack in the rock. It's shaped like a diamond, and it's way up high in the cliff, against the sky." He had paused then and smiled, as if suddenly struck by an idea. "That's it! 'Like a diamond in the sky.' It sounds like a rhyme. That's how I can make you remember. Now wait. Yes. This is how it can go. Now remember these words, dearie, remember them. They're important. They sound just like a rhyme, one of your nursery rhymes: 'Look outside and you will see, a cliff, the sky, a tall spruce tree. . . .' "

My heart thrummed in my chest. I spoke the next words aloud. "And back inside where it's dark and cool, you will find a silver pool. This is where, if you are wise, you will find the treasure lies."

The treasure. The gold that Brandon Fisk had hidden. It was here, in this ruin. By the pool.

Trembling, I turned to start toward the rear of the cave . . . and then heard a sound behind me.

Someone was coming up through the crevice at my back.

As I froze, I knew. I knew why Doran had been in the other cliff dwelling. And I knew why he had left.

He had been hiding, watching, waiting for me to lead him here, to the gold.

My hands grew clammy. Or had Doran discovered this dwelling before I had? Had he discovered the gold, and then heard me in the canyon, or coming up the slope? Had he gone to the other dwelling to wait for me, to divert my attention so that I would not see the trail and follow it? And then, once he had me there with him . . .

But where had he been until now? And what would he do when he found me here?

I turned around to confront whoever was climbing up through the crevice.

I saw the shock of streaked brown hair first, then the long, angular face and tawny brown eyes.

"Peter!" I cried in relief. "It's you!"

Pulling himself up and onto the floor of the cave, Peter stopped, out of breath. He looked at me.

"I've been searching all day for you," he said. "Your mare was at the mouth of the canyon."

"But how did you find me here?" My heart

began to slow and my tension drain at the sight of my brother.

"Hunt told me."

"Hunt?" My heart quickened again.

"Yes. He was in the canyon. He told me I'd find you in that other dwelling, back along the cliff. But when I climbed up there, it was empty, and when I started down again I saw the trail to the right. I thought you might have taken it, and so I started along it. Then I heard someone talking, back behind the rocks. I saw the crevice then." Peter paused, looking at me. "It was you, wasn't it? You were reciting a rhyme, a nursery rhyme."

It took me a moment to shift my thoughts from what Peter had told me about Doran to his final question. But when I realized what Peter had said, I saw how perfect his timing had been, how lucky that he had found me in the cave, at just that moment.

"Oh, yes, Peter, it *was* a rhyme! The rhyme he told me—our father. I remembered it and then I knew. This is it, Peter—where he hid the gold. I am sure of it!"

As I spoke, Peter became very still. Then I saw the excitement, the joy, the triumph, spring to his face, and I felt it, too. On impulse I moved quickly forward, reaching toward my brother to embrace him at last.

Peter recoiled immediately, jerking back from me as if I were a viper.

It was then I saw the other emotions on his face—the fear, the desperation, the hatred.

Something shifted and fell into place in my mind, as the words of the rhyme had before: another memory, from another time. Not the night before the fire, when Brandon Fisk had come, but the day *of* the fire.

For I had seen those same emotions play across my brother's face that morning as we sat out in the yard, just after Mother had left for market.

It all came back at once—all of it.

I had been out in the yard, alone, looking up at Father's closed and curtained window, feeling uneasy. I still did not understand why the strange man had come, but I knew that was why Father had not gone to the bank that day.

The stranger had come at twilight the night before. I had been up in my room preparing for bed and Mother had promised to follow soon to read me my bedtime story. I had just taken the book I wanted her to read from the shelf when, below, I heard voices raised, someone shouting. Creeping down the stairs, I saw a dark man in rough clothing shouting at Father in the hallway. He was saying terrible things. Then the dark man had grabbed Mother's arm and pulled her as if to drag her out the front door, and Father had sprung forward and wrenched his arm away, hitting the man in the face. Then Father had pushed the man out the door, thrown him out of the house.

Through the open door I could see the man shouting at Father, waving his fist in the air. Then he had turned and fallen down the front steps. Father had slammed the door and locked it; then he and Mother had gone into the parlor and shut the door, and I could only hear their low murmuring.

I sat on the stairs in shock for a few moments, and then I saw a shadow slip out from under the niche built into the staircase on the ground floor and start down the rear hall toward the back door. It was Peter. Silently, fearfully, my eyes never leaving the closed parlor door, I slipped out after him, into the near darkness of the backyard.

I could see no one at first, and, trembling in my nightgown and full of a fear I could not define, I ran over to the sheltering line of lilac bushes that bordered the yard—my special hiding place. I climbed behind them and hid, and that is when I saw the two shadows—one large and one small—emerge from around the edge of the house and whisper together in the shade of the large willow.

I could see that it was Peter talking to the dark man, the stranger. He leaned very close to Peter and told him something, gave him something. I could not see what it was, for Peter turned his back to me. And then the stranger glanced up toward the lilacs and saw me.

He called to me softly, and, as bidden, I came out from my hiding place. It seemed he stood and looked at me for a very long time, and then, drawing me away from Peter, pressed the amulet and the doubloon into my hand and told me the words, the rhyme, told me to remember—*ordered* me to remember.

Then he was gone, and Peter was gone, and I went back into the house, chilled, and slipped back up to my room before Mother and Father came out from behind the parlor door.

That was why the next morning felt so odd to me, for I had not slept well and still did not understand anything about the night before.

And then, while I sat in the yard under the

willow, Peter had come over to me with a smile on his face and asked me if I wanted to play a game. I longed to ask him about the stranger, but I was afraid I would anger him, for Peter had not known I was out there in the yard, watching them both.

And so I had listened to my brother telling me about the new game.

"It will be great fun, Heather," he had said. "This is how we will play: I will run up and lock Father in his room, and then come back out here and we'll both sit and wait. When Father wakes up, we'll listen for him. Won't it be funny when he wakes up and tries to open the door and can't? He'll rattle the doorknob and bang on the door and call for Mother, and we'll have the key! Then, after a few minutes, we'll go in and let him out. Just think how we'll all laugh together then."

Thrilled to be included, I nodded eagerly, my five-year-old's thoughts about the night before fading in this exciting new twist to the day. And so Peter did just as he had said; he locked Father in his room, and after a few moments came outside, laughing. He gave me the key and told me to slip it into my pocket—"for safekeeping," he said—and then we sat together and waited. The morning seemed suddenly brighter with Peter there beside me, and I knew whatever had happened the night before, my brother would soon explain—and make it right.

But then a strange thing happened. I looked up at Father's window, still closed tightly, and then at the window beside it. Smoke, first in wisps and then in great clouds, began pouring from that window, and for a moment I was confused.

And then I saw the flames.

Things happened very quickly after that. Now, standing in the ruin, I remembered it all in a blur: Mother returning down the street, seeing the flames, rushing inside the house even though Peter jumped up and tried to hold her back; me jumping up and running after Mother into the house; Father banging on his bedroom door upstairs and shouting for help. It was awful, frightening. Father sounded like some kind of animal caught in a trap.

Then Mother had run up the stairs and I heard her banging on the bedroom door, rattling the doorknob, screaming, "Where's the key? My God, where's the key?"

Now, remembering, I could not stop it—any more than I could stop all the memories rushing back, claiming me: the pain, the searing, wrenching pain of guilt, of agony, of knowing that I had caused my parents' death.

For I had the key. The key was in my pocket, where Peter had told me to put it. When I tried to follow Mother up the stairs, when I saw her in the upstairs hallway through the thickening haze of smoke, when I saw flames begin to lick the hem of my mother's skirt and Mother had turned, looking at me with that horrible, horrible expression on her face—I still could not reach her on time. I could not give her the key. Something had come crashing down on me then, between me and Mother, crashing down onto my head and sent me into a spinning blackness—a blackness that, all these years, had obscured from me that fact that I, and I alone, had been responsible for my parents' death.

Remembering, I turned to Peter. Suddenly, I remembered something else. His face changed.

"So now you remember it all, don't you?" he said, his voice twisted in a way I had never heard before. "I tried to keep you from remembering; I tried to keep Webb from forcing you to remember. I tried to warn you, to stop you. But now you remember, don't you, and there's nothing I can do about it. You know now, like you knew then, that day of the fire."

Peter paused, and the expression on his face made me take a step back. "I thought I had fooled you, making you think it was all just a silly game. You played your part so well, too, putting the key in your pocket like I told you. That way they would never have known I had done it, if *you* had the key. But there was a moment, when Mother came running down the street and smoke was pouring out that window, when you turned and looked at me and you knew. I could see it in your eyes, just like I do now. You knew I had set that fire. You knew I wanted to kill my father—my *step*father."

I took another step back, feeling behind me for the sandstone wall of the cave. Peter laughed.

"Yes, he was *my* stepfather, but not yours. Samuel Loring was your *real* father, just as you've always believed. Webb was the one who thought of telling you that my father, Brandon Fisk, was yours, too. He thought it would make you want to help us, to make you feel you *had* to help us. But I knew the truth all along. I knew my real father had gone off and left Mother and me, and that Mother's family hated me because of it. I didn't belong there, with them, and I didn't belong in that other house, after Mother married . . . him. I hated him. You can't imagine how I hated him."

I swallowed. I had never seen a person's face so twisted before, so awfully, horribly twisted.

"I had to do it, don't you see? I had to get him out of the way. If I did, we could have all come out here and been with Father. We could have been rich. Mother would have been so happy—we could all have been so happy—if *he* hadn't been there." Peter's expression changed again. "I never meant for Mother to die. I tried to stop her, and then you went running in there, too. I couldn't get to you or to Mother, couldn't get to either of you in time. . . ."

Peter laughed, and I felt an icy chill snake down my spine.

"But what did it matter? From what Webb told me this morning, you were never my sister after all. And Mother—or can I even call her that now?—was never really my mother either."

At my shocked expression, Peter laughed again. "Oh yes, my real mother died when I was born, and Father married again twice before he found a wife who would raise me. *Your* mother, Heather. Of course, you weren't born yet; you wouldn't be born for a long, long time. She married Father and took me in and raised me and never told me the truth even after Father left. But the way her family treated me, as if I were dirt or filth . . . I knew I never belonged there."

Peter stopped, and when he went on his voice

was very, very low. "I've never belonged anywhere."

"Prescott . . ." I began, trying to distract Peter's
attention, to make the terrible, murderous look
leave his eyes. "You said he . . ."

Peter smiled bitterly. "Yes, he told me. Your
friend Julia told me some things, too. They got
into a big fight after you left, you see. Julia was
worried that Webb would never find the gold for
her; she told him he was worthless, and they
shouted at each other, and then he insulted her
family. That did it. She left him to ride out of the
mesa alone. But first she came to me, and she
talked."

Peter's sudden stillness sent a knife of fear
twisting in my chest. Again I felt behind me.
There was nowhere to flee. Peter blocked the only
way out of the dwelling.

"Oh yes, Julia was very informative. She told
me what she and Webb had been planning all this
time. They were going to let us find the gold,
Heather, and then they were going to trick us and
run off with it themselves. Did you know that?
They were planning to doublecross us—just like
my father did to Webb sixteen years ago."

Peter let his words fall with their desired effect
in the silence of the cave before he went on. "Because that's what my father did to Webb. I never
knew that. My father and Webb found the gold,
and then after Webb left to buy more supplies, my
father took off with it and hid it so that he and
Mother and I could have it all. He did it for a good
reason. He hid it here in Twilight Mesa, and then
came for us in St. Louis. It all would have worked
out, if we had come, and if—"

Here Peter's words broke off, and his face flushed red with suppressed rage.

"If Webb hadn't murdered my father," he finished.

Peter became very quiet. I heard the sound of water trickling steadily down the back wall of the cave, and the cry of a crow in the canyon below.

"Webb followed my father after he discovered the missing gold. He found him in Kansas City and killed him. And then when Webb didn't find the gold or any indication where it might be, he started searching for it—and for me. Webb knew about me; my father had told him everything. And so when we finally met, Webb lied to me. He didn't want to help me. He wanted the gold. He had killed my father for it.

"Do you know what Webb said after Julia told me that and rode out of the canyon? He said yes, he had killed my father and that he would do it again. He said that my father was scum, that he had never cared about me. Webb told me about Mother—that she wasn't my *real* mother. That my father had married her only so that he could dump me and come out here to be free. That she was *your* mother. That's why I killed him."

Peter stared at me. "I did it just after Julia left. I might have killed her, too, but she wasn't important. Then I came looking for you. I met Hunt down in the canyon. He knew something had happened. He fought with me. I shot him, too. I left him for dead down in the canyon."

Peter laughed at my expression. "Oh yes, I know about you two. I've seen the way he looks at you. That's why I did it. Hunt deserved to die. He was using you, Heather, to get to the truth, to get to the gold. I knew that; I saw it. So I took care of him, too. Now there's nobody to get in my way. The gold is here, in this cave. Now you won't get in my way either."

He took a step toward me. "It's my gold, Heather. You have no right to it. You're not my sister. You never were. Did you know I cut the rope that day? And you were so grateful when I helped you over the ledge! I knew you would come up first. And I put the rattlesnake by your head, too. I wanted to scare you, to make you leave. I didn't want you to remember, and I didn't want you to find what was mine. I knew I would find it if I just kept looking long enough. You and Webb had no right to interfere. The gold was meant for me. It's mine, Heather. *Mine.*"

I turned in panic, knowing that Peter was beyond reason. Nothing I could say would stop him now. I had led him to the gold, and now I was not only in his way, but I knew everything: about the fire, about Prescott, about . . . Doran.

Peter lunged at me and grabbed me about the wrists. Twisting my arms viciously, he began to drag me over to the edge of the cave where the cliff dropped into the gorge below.

I struggled against him, wrenched my arms, and kicked out, lashed at him with my boots. I was filled with a sudden, desperate energy. But Peter only laughed maniacally, gripping me tighter and pushing me closer to the edge of the cliff.

I knew then that it had been Peter in my dream that first night at the ranch. It was his figure behind me, imprisoning my arms, laughing and pushing me into the fire. Deep down, I knew. For even then my subconscious had stored within it the knowledge I could never admit to myself: that Peter had started the fire that day, had killed my parents. That at thirteen, my brother was a murderer.

I gave one last wrenching twist to my body, but Peter was too strong, too fueled by his obsessed, warped anger. His grip was like an iron vise; I struggled fruitlessly against it. I felt my boot slip on the sandstone lip of the cave as it had done once before, and I heard Peter laugh again. He was about to shove me forward, as he had pushed me off the ledge that day before he had cut the rope. . . .

I remember thinking: This time I will go over. This time there is nothing to stop me, nothing to pull me back, and no one will ever know what really happened. . . .

And then a great echoing sound cracked the air behind me. I felt a rush of air at my back and then shards of sharp rock ricocheting past my head, grazing my skin. Peter was no longer behind me. I teetered on the sandstone and felt my boot slip again.

A large, rough hand pulled me back, wrenched me away from the cliff's edge.

I turned and saw Peter's bloodied, prone body on the floor of the cave, the old Indian Kianeech crouching beside it.

Doran was beside me. His left hand still gripped me tightly about the arm; in his right hand he held a gun, now pointing down.

Had I been prone to faint, I think I would have at that moment. But I was only prone to spells, and my spells were now finished.

As it was, I simply turned to Doran and let him wrap his arms about me.

Chapter Sixteen

✦ ✦ ✦ ✦

THEY HAD FOUND my amulet on the trail—Doran and Kianeech. It had fallen out of my skirt pocket before I had climbed through the crevice to the ruin. It had led them to me—and to Peter.

Peter's bullet had only grazed Doran, but its force had been enough to make him fall and strike his head, knocking him out for some time; when he regained consciousness, Kianeech was bending over him, urging him to follow him up the slope he had seen Peter climb only moments before.

Kianeech *had* been watching all of us, but not with the hostility I had imagined. Surprisingly, Mr. Kendall had played a part in the old Indian's vigilance. After speaking with me that last time in his room, Mr. Kendall had suspected something was very wrong. He had never trusted Prescott Webb or Julia Hastings, and sensed a strangeness about the story that they had told me. Worried that I would endanger myself in Twilight Mesa, he had asked the old Indian's nephew to alert Kianeech to our arrival—not only to protect the ruins, but primarily to watch over me.

And he had done so, in his own silent, detached way. Kianeech had observed everything: the rattlesnake and who had captured it; who had cut the rope. He had watched the tension growing between Julia and Prescott, between Peter and Prescott, and he had witnessed the last explosive arguments between them, including Peter's murder of Prescott Webb.

Only then did the Indian step forward. He knew where I had gone that day, and when he saw Peter ride into the canyon, he followed him. He saw Peter shoot Doran and start up the cliff. That was when Kianeech told Doran everything he knew.

Doran had been watching me, too, it turned out. He had also seen me ride into the canyon that day, and had paralleled my movements along the canyon floor from his own position on the mesa top. That is why he had been in the ruin waiting for me—to ensure my own safety.

Among other reasons.

For what I had seen in Doran's eyes, felt in the passion between us that day in the dwelling, had been true and strong and real. When he awoke, before me, he had gone back into the canyon to find my mare, thinking I would be safe in the cave. He had not counted on meeting Peter—or on the crazed, violent state my so-called brother would be in. Doran had not told Peter of my whereabouts, but Peter had seen him descending from the dwelling and assumed the rest.

"I suspected Webb from the beginning," Doran told me that night as we sat around the fire in our camp on the mesa. "I knew he didn't work for the government, and I knew he was up to no good. And then when Webb joined forces with that assistant . . . I didn't know who the man was or where he'd come from. He kept out of sight most of the time. But I could see what they were doing, what kind of damage they were inflicting on the ruins. I knew they were looking for something, but I didn't know what, and so when Webb approached me and asked me to check up on you in Denver, I jumped at the job, realizing that it just might lead me to the answers I wanted. But when I got there . . ." Doran's eyes deepened as he looked at me, and I remembered again our moments together. "Well, you were a little more than I expected."

He paused. "I found out that you were the person Webb seemed to be looking for—that you were Heather Loring from St. Louis, and you worked on the paper in Denver. But I found out other things about you, too. It surprised me to find how . . . intelligent you were. Interesting. Curious. You intrigued me. And when I saw your reaction to the amulet and the photograph at the exhibition, I knew you were involved in some way with what Webb was doing in Twilight Mesa, and that intrigued me, too. I didn't know how you were involved, or why, or how deeply. I had not planned to encounter you at the exhibition, but I used our meeting to my advantage, as you well know. Because by then I wanted you to come down to the ranch; I wanted to learn more about your connection with Webb. And I wanted to learn . . . other things about you as well.

"That is why I asked you to come down, why I even provided the train ticket. I thought you might be the key I needed to find out what was happening in the mesa. I was a professional investigator once, you know; it was one of the ways I made my living before I arrived in the Southwest. I was quite good at it, too. I searched your room in the hotel that day, hoping to find something that would give me some answers. But I found that someone had been there before me and done quite a sloppy job. We may need to discuss that little matter with Julia Hastings. In any case, as I said, I knew you were involved with Webb and Fisk, but I was not certain for a long time whether or not you were involved with them willingly or because of something that had happened in your past. When you told me of the fire, things began to fall into place. I had suspected Webb's assistant for a long time, but as I said, I had very little to go on and no time to seek out the information I needed to identify him. By then events were moving too quickly. I could see how dangerous the situation was becoming, and that is why I kept questioning you, kept trying to make you remember what had happened. I knew that if you did, I would not only have the answers I needed, but you would have the answers you needed as well."

Doran looked at me in the way I longed for, his eyes deeply green in the shadows thrown on his face by the flames. "I could see how troubled you were, and I knew that you had to confront whatever it was that had happened to you. But I did not know how strong this inner conflict might be, or how much it might take precedence in your life. I realized in time why you pulled away from me so suddenly at the snake dance, and why you felt you had to go with Fisk into the mesa. But I knew they were using you, and that you would be in danger. I tried to tell you that day, to warn you—"

Here Doran's words broke off, and I saw from the way he turned away, the sudden clench of his jaw, and the muscle that jumped in his cheek, just how much I had hurt him with my own doubts and mistrust. At the snake dance, I soon learned, Doran's feelings had been as real, as vital, as mine. The intimacy I felt between us had not been in my imagination. If I had trusted my instincts I would have known that—I would have seen that Doran was just as vulnerable as I at that point, just as fearful of what might take precedence in *my* life.

Later, when the fire had died and we were alone under the stars, he revealed to me quite eloquently what his feelings toward me had been all along.

As it turned out, his sudden shifts of mood with me had been due to his own sense of responsibility, and, in a way, his emotions as well.

"I couldn't let what I was beginning to . . . feel for you stop me from finding out what Webb was doing in the dwellings," Doran explained as we lay together among the blankets he had spread out from his bedroll. "And at the beginning, I did not know what your position with Webb and Julia was, what threat you yourself might pose to the ruins and my work there. I had to find out first, before I allowed myself to . . . it was difficult. There were so many times. . . . Down by the spring that night I might have given in if I hadn't heard Will behind us on the trail. And then at the snake dance—"

Doran stopped, his arm tightening about me before he went on. "I followed you and the others into Twilight Mesa this last time, but I was too late to see what happened in Jackson Canyon. Kianeech told me about the snake. I tried to warn you all the next day and then, when you didn't stop, I followed you, still keeping my distance. I had just emerged on the opposite mesa to watch you and Webb in that ruin with the spring when I saw you start to go up and the rope . . . break. I didn't know exactly what had happened, but I vowed to find out. When I saw you leave the next morning, I followed you into the canyon. I knew you would come up to the dwelling in the storm; I waited for you there. And I thought you would be safe there later, while I went to look for your horse. But then I met Fisk . . ."

Here Doran's face darkened in fury and passion. "If I had known, if I had even suspected what Fisk had done . . . I only thank God that we were in time today, that Kianeech showed me where to find you. But when I got there and saw what your so-called brother was about to do . . . I tell you, I thanked the devil then. I thanked the devil that I had a gun in my hand."

The authorities did not charge Doran for Peter's death. When the full story came out, they held him only shortly for questioning and then let him go. They held Julia Hastings a bit longer.

We found her the next day in Jackson Canyon, her horse lame and her supplies depleted, her clothing dirty and torn and her skin burned red from the sun. It was the first time I had ever seen

her look really defeated. She did not appear glad
to see us as we rode up, and showed but little
remorse when we told her about Prescott Webb.

"He was nothing. A nobody." Julia's voice was
hard with bitterness. "He was a liar. He misrep-
resented himself to me and Mama, making us
think he was a cultured, refined gentleman of
means when all along he was nothing—a nobody
from God knows where who was fool enough to
let someone else trick him and run off with a
whole trunkload of gold! Oh, he fooled us all at
first. He attracted me. I thought he would provide
for me in the way I wanted—and he might have,
if only . . . we had such a good plan! Prescott
wrote me to come out and spy on you, Heather. I
thought it would be exciting, and it was. I listened
outside doors, I watched you. I asked you questions. I pretended we were great friends so that
you would tell me everything I wanted to know.
I was so clever on the train, don't you think? And
I searched your room that day in the hotel. I found
the doubloon. And I took it. I knew you would
never know who had done it, and I wanted it. We
needed the gold, Mama and me; we deserved it
just as much as anyone else. And we would have
found it, too, if Prescott had not been so inept. I
should never have given the doubloon to Prescott
that first night at the ranch, never told him all you
told me. I should have handled everything myself. He was a fool, a bumbling, inept fool. I told
him so that morning after you ran off—that he
was a fool for letting you go, for letting the gold
slip out of our hands just as he had done with
Brandon Fisk sixteen years before. I told him just

how worthless I considered him to be, and then he . . . well, I will not repeat what he said about my family, and my own motivations to restore the family fortune. But when he lowered himself so far as this, I went to Peter and told him about our plan—Prescott's and my plan. I did not know he would *murder* him, although by then I would hardly have cared. I rode away. Now I am going back to Virginia, back to Mama, back to a life of real culture, real *civilization* again."

In the end the authorities did let Julia go back to Virginia, but not before she had explained everything and been quite humiliated by the whole procedure. Prescott Webb's body was buried in an unmarked plot near Jackson. He had no relations or next of kin, nothing left at all to show for the life he had lived.

And Peter Fisk . . . we eventually learned, through the questioning of the authorities and Doran's later investigation, the full set of circumstances that had warped his life and, finally, his emotions and mind.

Peter *had* been born of a different mother long ago, a poor and rather sickly woman with no family or connections, who had died from complications in childbirth. Left with the burden of raising Peter alone, Brandon Fisk had married again quickly, to a woman he believed had more resources and money. When, too late, he discovered his mistake, Brandon had simply left the woman to search for another wife—without taking any steps to legally end the marriage. He had come to St. Louis, where he met the woman who was to become my mother—whether by design or

by accident we will never know—and wooed her
for the money and connections he was certain,
this time, she had.

But Brandon Fisk had not bargained on my
mother's family severing these connections when
she agreed to marry and run off with him. When
this happened, Fisk once again picked up and
left, abandoning his third wife and young son to
travel west and make his fortune.

When I learned of this, I ached for my mother,
for the desperate, deserted wife she must have
been. I am sure, as Peter said, she must have loved
Brandon Fisk at one time, or at least thought she
loved him. To think of how she must have felt:
raising a son who was not even her own, returning
to her home in St. Louis in disgrace, trying to instill
in Peter a sense of identity and pride by relating
tales of a father, a husband she must have, by then,
grown to despise.

My aunt and uncle finally told us the whole
story, after Doran wired them about the news.
We learned how, after my mother had returned to
St. Louis with Peter, Brandon Fisk's second wife
had shown up one day on their doorstep, demanding money. It must have been a nasty scene,
with the woman shouting that she was still married to Brandon Fisk by law and that she was
entitled to anything he had acquired since he had
deserted her—including, bizarre as it seems, his
new wife's assets.

Mother was able to annul her marriage to Fisk
quite easily then, but she never told Peter the
truth. In time, she was given a second chance, an
opportunity to make up for some of the bad cards
life had dealt her and to correct some of her own

mistakes. She met Samuel Loring—a kind, gentle man who truly loved her, who took in the son that had never been hers or his, and who helped produce a tribute to their love—myself.

So their love and marriage had always been real, as I had known instinctively. As the full story was revealed, it saddened me immeasurably to think what Mother had gone through. And it tore deep at my heart to think of how tragically their lives had ended.

It was only then that I was finally able to begin to release the agony and guilt my five-year-old mind had produced and then suppressed. For it had not been my fault, I now saw clearly. Peter had been the one to start the fire, lock Father in his room, give me the key. And even though I held that key, I could not reach my parents to give it to them; I knew I was not to blame. I wondered if Peter was not to blame, either. Perhaps the real blame lay in the circumstances of his birth, his father, and the life that had so twisted his mind and heart.

Although my mind had accepted this conclusion from the moment I learned the full truth about Peter and my parents, it took many months for my heart and emotions to release all the pain that my memory had hoarded over the years.

Together, Doran and I finally surmised why Brandon Fisk had involved me in his plot years ago. It was almost as Prescott Webb had said: knowing that someone could trace the gold to Peter, Fisk had used me as a kind of safety measure or last resort. For even if Webb traced down Peter, Fisk thought, Webb would never guess that I—not even Brandon Fisk's own daughter—held the key to the treasure at Twilight. In this way, Peter would have access to the information he needed to find the gold, but Webb would not.

Or so Brandon Fisk thought. As it turned out, he could never have foreseen what he had started that night, when he returned to St. Louis and placed the amulet and gold doubloon in my hand.

We buried Peter's body in the canyon below the ruin where he had died—the ruin where we finally found the trunkful of gold. Protected in a sealed room at the back of the cave, it was just as Prescott had said: an old, rotting trunk full of Spanish gold doubloons and church ornaments. We did not bring it in on our first trip back to the ranch—we had far too many other considerations with which to deal then—but returned to it the following week. It was there, just as we had left it, as if it had been waiting for us all those years.

And when we brought back all that the trunk had contained—half packed in canvas sacks carried out on burros, and half loaded into the ranch's rickety old spring wagon—Mr. Kendall emerged from the house to meet us.

"Well, I guess you found what you were lookin' for, girl," he said, approaching the wagon slowly with the help of his cane, his topaz eyes as sharp and crafty as ever. "I knew you were up to somethin' else in that mesa 'sides writin' all them darn articles!" He smiled when he saw the gold. "Yep, I guess you're the one this treasure was fated for, girl. You saw what happened to the rest. But you found it, and you'll keep it. I have a feelin' this is where it'll all end—with you. This is where that old curse stops."

I did not know whether I agreed with Mr. Kendall or not, but I had to admit that, in finding the gold, Doran and I were able to put it to a use that others might not have. Although the Kendalls would take none of it, I found that I could quite happily repay them, in other ways, for all the hospitality they had shown me. They could hardly return the new stock delivered on their ranch one day, for example, or the lumber for the new barn that was delivered the following week. And Mrs. Kendall could hardly refuse her new cookstove and other supplies; the order was far too large.

I was glad to see the Kendall brothers finally able to fund their excavations in the manner they wanted, with Doran supervising the proceedings. For, as Prescott and Julia had found so hard to believe, he truly was a dedicated ethnologist, a skilled archaeologist who had finally found the best use of his talents and abilities in his work at Twilight Mesa. I eventually learned that Doran Hunt *had* come from a wealthy, prestigious family in New York, just as Julia's Mama had discovered. But Doran had had no secret in his past, nothing from which to flee except the stifling kind of life he had seen his parents live there. At an early age, he had decided he wanted more freedom, and at eighteen left home altogether, working at a variety of trades—including investigations—before coming to Twilight Mesa. I had been right about what I had sensed that night at Mrs. Compton's dinner party. Doran Hunt belonged with the older men—the empire builders, the seekers, the frontier makers. He thrived on challenge, on puzzles, on risk, and he found no better way to fuel all three than with his excavations in Twilight Mesa.

Just as *I* found no better use of my abilities and inclinations than in writing. After all that had happened, I found that the initial series of articles I had planned would be quite inadequate. I wired Mr. McNeeley with our news, and he arrived promptly three days later at the ranch to help me write the story of our find in Twilight Mesa, a story that scooped every newspaper in the state.

In fact, Mr. McNeeley ended up liking the area so well that he sold the *Crier* in Denver and bought a small press in Jackson. He did it, I think, with the express purpose of prodding and harassing its two fledgling reporters.

"Got to show these boys how to find real news," he grumbled when I visited him in his office late that fall, after he had moved in. "Here the gold was sitting under everybody's noses for sixteen years—the biggest story in the state—and it took a *girl*, a sweet young thing like you, Heather, who was more interested in the past than what's going on right now, to break the whole damn thing!"

I smiled at that—it was nice to have Mr. McNeeley nearby, irascible temper and all—and took the assignment he gave me to cover the city council meeting that night in Jackson.

I was still writing my articles, even after all that had happened, and I was working with a publisher in New York on a manuscript about the ruins. A group of concerned citizens, alerted by our newspaper stories about the ruins, had begun to lobby in Washington to protect the mesa's dwellings for future generations.

Doran was involved in this as well, although he was quite busy with his excavations. He was trying to assemble an exhibition worthy enough to take to the Chicago World's Fair, scheduled to open the following year.

We were married that September, beneath the golden, shimmering leaves of the cottonwoods at the Kendalls' ranch. Uncle Charles and Aunt Natalie traveled out to be with me, riding down on the train from Denver with Mrs. Gresham. Doran's family did not come from New York, for he had refused the wedding they offered to give us there, but at the last minute his paternal grandfather clattered into the yard in a wagon rented from the livery in Jackson. When he alighted, spry even then at nearly eighty, I saw where Doran had gotten his fine features—as well as his independent spirit.

Doran's grandfather ended up staying at the ranch for some time, he and Mr. Kendall talking far into the night, each trying to tell better tales than the other. Mrs. Kendall seemed to enjoy all the activity and company, although as usual she grumbled as she worked night and day preparing meals. Perhaps she didn't mind so much; she kept her new cookstove so shiny it gleamed.

As Doran was so busy trying to excavate the ruins before winter, Charlie and Will and Ben and Owen took some time off from their chores to build us a tidy little cottage not far from their land, in the valley just below the mesa.

It was here, sitting at my desk in the small front parlor, where I could look out the window and see the majestic, massive bulk of Twilight Mesa rising to the west, that I wrote my stories—all that had happened before, all that was happening now, and all that was to happen in the months to come, both in Twilight Mesa and there in the wide Jackson Valley where Doran and I would make our home, forever.

The End?

The end of a book is never really *the end* for a person who reads. He or she can always open another. And another.

Every page holds possibilities.

But millions of kids don't see them. Don't know they're there. Millions of kids can't read, or won't.

That's why there's RIF. Reading is Fundamental (RIF) is a national nonprofit program that works with thousands of community organizations to help young people discover the fun—and the importance—of reading.

RIF motivates kids so that they *want* to read. And RIF works directly with parents to help them encourage their children's reading. RIF gets books to children and children into books, so they grow up reading and become adults who can read. Adults like you.

For more information on how to start a RIF program in your neighborhood, or help your own child grow up reading, write to:

RIF
Dept. BK-1
Box 23444
Washington, D.C.
20026

Founded in 1966, RIF is a national non-profit organization with local projects run by volunteers in every state of the union.

A HISTORICAL ROMANCE
TO CAPTURE YOUR HEART!

KAT MARTIN
MAGNIFICENT PASSAGE

Mandy Ashton is fleeing her stifling existence at Fort Laramie and is heading toward California. Travis Langley, a white man raised by the Cheyenne, is hired to escort her, although he mistakenly believes she is the rebellious daughter of the governor. This dangerous deception becomes even more perilous when the two discover they've become captives of a passion as untamed as the wilderness of the American West! Will they be able to overcome their contest of wills and let true love reign?

ISBN: 0-517-00620-0 Price: $3.95

AVAILABLE AT BOOKSTORES NOW